T0044502

PRAISE FOR WILL CARVER

'Will Carver's mind works slightly differently to everyone else's … *Upstairs at the Beresford* is superbly paced and remarkably inventive, a book that demands to be read in a single sitting' M.W. Craven

'From the wondrous mind of Will Carver, who is never afraid to innovate, *Upstairs at the Beresford* is a tour de force that covers, life, death and everything beyond' David Jackson

'As delightfully dark and wickedly inventive as ever, *Upstairs at the Beresford* is another captivating read from Carver with characters that stick around long after the final page is turned, whether you want them to or not' S.J. Watson

'I thoroughly enjoyed *Upstairs at the Beresford*, possibly for all of the right reasons – great characters, good but dark humour, and a completely engrossing story – but, undoubtedly for some of the wrong ones too. You don't come to a Will Carver novel expecting a happy-ever-after fairytale ending. If this were a fairytale, it would be far more Brothers Grimm than Disney, and, got to be honest, that's just the way I like it. Definitely recommended'
Jen Med's Book Reviews

'Yet again, Carver has delivered a corker! As deliciously dark as you would expect; the colour comes from the characters. Fabulously visual, *Upstairs at the Beresford* absolutely HAS to be a mini series'
Book Nerd

'Ambitious, dark and funny … A compelling and thought-provoking book from a highly talented writer. Bravo!' Mike Gayle

'Incredibly dark and very funny' Harriet Tyce

‘I fell in love with Carver’s murderous Maeve. This is an *Eleanor Oliphant* for crime fans. Carver truly at his best’ Sarah Pinborough

‘Psychologically chilling, pitch-dark, intelligent and utterly addictive. Will Carver is in a league of his own’ Michael Wood

‘A darkly delicious page-turner’ S.J. Watson

‘Unflinching, blunt and brutal, Carver’s originality knows no bounds. Simply brilliant’ Sam Holland

‘Vivid and engaging and completely unexpected’ Lia Middleton

‘Dark in the way only Will Carver can be … oozes malevolence from every page’ Victoria Selman

‘Equally enthralling and appalling … unlike anything I’ve read in a very long while’ James Oswald

‘Creepy and brilliant’ Khurrum Rahman

‘Impossibly original, stylish, sinister, heartfelt … Wildly fresh and unmatched, and once again proves that Will Carver has talent and creativity to burn’ Chris Whitaker

‘One of the most compelling and original voices in crime fiction’ Alex North

‘Will Carver is a unique writer. I loved *Suicide Thursday*’ Greg Mosse

‘Will Carver’s most exciting, original, hilarious and freaky outing yet’ Helen FitzGerald

'Possibly the most interesting and original writer in the crime-fiction genre … dark, slick, gripping, and impossible to put down. You'll be sucked in from the first page' Luca Veste

'Stirring. Ambitious. Irreverent. Compassionate. Completely devoid of giveable fucks' Dominic Nolan

'Move the hell over Brett Easton Ellis and Chuck Palahniuk … Will Carver is the new lit prince of twenty-first-century disenfranchised, pop darkness' Stephen J. Golds

'A twisted, devious thriller' Nick Quantrill

'Challenging, perceptive and unexpectedly enlightening' Sarah Sultoon

'This one also put me through the emotional wringer … he takes our darkest, most hidden thoughts and puts them on the page, so we see our own monsters reflected back at us. Brutal and brilliant, as always' Lisa Hall

'Carver's trademarked cynicism and contemptuousness run rampant here, but if you don't mind being insulted, you'll find a lot to laugh about and enjoy in this dark, dangerous novel' Jack Heath

'One of the most exciting authors in Britain. After this, he'll have his own cult following' *Daily Express*

'A smart, stylish writer' *Daily Mail*

'Unlike anything you'll read this year' *Heat*

'Weirdly page-turning' *Sunday Times*

'Arguably the most original crime novel published this year' *Independent*

'This mesmeric novel paints a thought-provoking if depressing picture of modern life' *Guardian*

'This book is most memorable for its unrepentant darkness' *Telegraph*

'Will Carver demonstrates an extraordinary talent for creating a figure of absolute selfishness and self-absorption and yet making it impossible to stop reading about his resentments, inadequacies and self-loathing ... This is a masterful account of misery in many different forms' *Literary Review*

'SO original' *Crime Monthly*

'"Dark" is a word that encapsulates most of Will Carver's books, but so is the word "brilliant" ... Told from multiple perspectives, this is perceptive and twisted in equal measure' *CultureFly*

LONGLISTED for Theakston's Old Peculier Crime Novel of the Year Award
SHORTLISTED for Best Independent Voice at the Amazon Publishing Readers' Awards
LONGLISTED for the *Guardian's* Not the Booker Prize
LONGLISTED for Goldsboro Books Glass Bell Award

ABOUT THE AUTHOR

Will Carver is the international bestselling author of the January David series and the critically acclaimed, mind-blowingly original Detective Pace series, which includes *Good Samaritans (2018), Nothing Important Happened Today* (2019) and *Hinton Hollow Death Trip* (2020), all of which were ebook bestsellers and selected as books of the year in the mainstream international press. *Nothing Important Happened Today* was longlisted for both the Goldsboro Books Glass Bell Award 2020 and the Theakston's Old Peculier Crime Novel of the Year Award. *Hinton Hollow Death Trip* was longlisted for the *Guardian*'s Not the Booker Prize, and was followed by four standalone literary thrillers, *The Beresford, Psychopaths Anonymous, The Daves Next Door* and *Suicide Thursday*. Will spent his early years in Germany, but returned to the UK at age eleven, when his sporting career took off. He currently runs his own fitness and nutrition company, and lives in Reading with his children.

Follow Will on Twitter and Instagram @will_carver.

Also by Will Carver and available from Orenda Books:

Good Samaritans
Nothing Important Happened Today
Hinton Hollow Death Trip
The Beresford
Psychopaths Anonymous
The Daves Next Door
Suicide Thursday

UPSTAIRS AT THE BERESFORD

WILL CARVER

ORENDA
BOOKS

Orenda Books
16 Carson Road
West Dulwich
London SE21 8HU
www.orendabooks.co.uk

First published by Orenda Books, 2023

A catalogue record for this book is available from the British Library.

ISBN 978-1-914585-92-0
eISBN 978-1-914585-93-7

Typeset in Garamond by typesetter.org.uk

Printed and bound by CPI Group (UK) Ltd, Croydon CR0 4YY

For sales and distribution, please contact info@orendabooks.co.uk

For Heaven's sake.

'What is terrible is not death but the lives people live or don't live up until their death.'

—Charles Bukowski

ROBERT JOHNSON 1911–1938

The legend of the Faustian bargain dates back almost five hundred years. A dissatisfied intellectual sells his soul to the devil at a crossroads in return for unparalleled knowledge and earthly delights. The deal is made for immediate reward without consideration for any future consequence.

In more recent times, the poster boy for such an act is the musician Robert Johnson. An average guitarist, the story tells of how he ventured to the crossroads of Highways 61 and 49, where he was met by a mysterious dark figure. Johnson handed over his guitar, the demon tuned it for him, played a couple of songs and returned the instrument along with the skills required to master and create the sound Johnson would become known for and, eventually, influence a league of future musicians, before being inducted into the Rock & Roll Hall of Fame.

Theories of a deal with the devil have long been associated with the likes of Bob Dylan, John Lennon, Marilyn Monroe and James Dean, suggesting that Satan is quite the patron of the arts. Yet, no such fable appears to exist where a person made a pact to sell their soul for the sake of somebody else.

CROSSROADS

The problem is, you only make a list of the things you want to do in life when you find out you're about to die.

You think a brain tumour is bad, try talking to the guy who wished he'd quit his job thirty years ago. Lung disease is a real bitch, too, but it's better than a lifetime of caring what other people think, guessing what they say behind your back, not realising that you've focussed your energy in the wrong direction. And dementia is no fun for anybody, but it beats the hell out of regret.

What if you'd lived more in the moment?

What if you'd followed your passion?

What if you'd told that person how you really felt?

Death sucks, but the sorrow is only amplified when it follows a life not lived.

Time squandered.

Wasted on worry.

You logged into your work email over the weekend when you could have been swimming with dolphins or fucking your professor. And now there's no time to put that right. There's nothing left to enjoy.

'Bowel cancer,' says the doctor. 'Stage four.'

Mr May looks at his wife and tears fall silently down his cheeks. His bottom lip quivers.

She asks, 'How long?'

'A few weeks, maybe. A month. Tops.'

Faced with the truth of his own mortality, Mr May thinks about his wife. How much he loves her, how much he has cherished his life with her, how much he appreciates her support. And then he thinks about all the things they never got to do together.

He starts to make a list. *A few weeks. Maybe a month.* Not long enough to do everything but it forces him to look at the things he really wants – be more specific. It makes him get excited rather than depressed. Motivation over desperation. He wants to create some focus for his remaining time with the great love of his life. It's all he can do.

There's a liberation that comes with making a bucket list while you still have life left in you. In the simplest sense, it, at least, keeps you active. There's the opportunity to push the boundaries of your comfort zone, experience a sense of accomplishment that you probably are not receiving from your work. God damn, it could even make you more interesting, or at least seem more interesting.

It allows you to dream bigger. You want to become a rock star, a sports star, a porn star, whatever, you don't have to sell your soul for that, you just have to open your mind a little. There's a chance to create some kind of legacy. If you don't leave it until some doctor tells you that you have a month left. Tops.

Mr May clicks out of his reverie. He looks up at the yellow-with-age ceiling of the doctor's office and asks God what he can have done that was so bad to be judged and sentenced in this way. He could never tell his wife this, she is so devout. He waits for an answer that will never come. Faith evaporated upon diagnosis.

The shit in his body that used to work, doesn't work now.

His wife is also angry about that.

'What the hell are we going to do with a few weeks?'

It's rhetorical, but the doctor answers, anyway.

'My advice to you ... Pray.'

He that committeth sin is of the devil; for the devil sinneth from the beginning...

GENESIS

The only thing scarier than the doorbell ringing at The Beresford is the sound of Jehovah's Witnesses knocking at your door.

It's not like they're peddling double-glazed windows or light bulbs or home security. We need those.

It's a tough sell.

It's God.

But, you know, a skewed version. You've heard a few things. The bad stuff, probably.

Don't fuck before you're married.

Don't fuck somebody who is the same sex as you.

Don't even think about getting married and fucking somebody else.

Don't smoke, don't drink, don't do drugs.

And the one everybody seems to remember – no blood transfusions. Even if you're in hospital and will die as a result.

It's a thankless task. Being ignored or having a door slammed in your face or taking verbal abuse because you've interrupted the family dinner.

Yet, nearly nine million people worldwide invited these strangers into their home, listened to what they had to say and joined the movement. Even after hearing all the bullshit that usually puts people off, membership increased. Impressionable minds. Real optimists. The kinds of people who would ask, 'But what about all the good things Hitler did?'

Those Witnesses are playing the long game. But it seems to be working.

They could double their membership if they hired a social-media manager. But they're not greedy. Only 144,000 of them will get to live in Heaven, after all, so it's not worth lowering your chances of that. (Don't worry, the rest of them will get to stay in a paradise on Earth. Probably the best silver medal of all time.)

As experiments go, it could be classed as a successful one.

Now, imagine knocking on all of those doors and instead of trying to sell a dream or an idea or an ideology to the people gracious enough to answer, you have to convince them to sell something to you. How much harder is that?

Sure, you offer them above-market price for their home, and they'll pack up the next day and move on, no matter how much history and nostalgia lurks within those walls. You put a million on the table and ask for their child, a small percentage might consider it. Instead of money, you proffer fame, a long life, sexual prowess, health, safety, a legacy. Watch as things become more interesting.

Ask them what they really want.

See how they stumble.

The problem is, what *you* want from them is worth so much more than a new car or a twelve-inch dick. You can offer them their wildest dreams but it comes at a cost. It has to. They have to sacrifice something. It's only fair.

For a place in the Rock & Roll Hall of Fame or a star on a Hollywood sidewalk or your name on the patent for the iPod, the only exchange can be your soul. What is that worth to you? You want to walk in the corridors of power and have knowledge of events that you can never share with another living being?

Is that worth an eternity of unrest?

How many doors would slam in your face if you posed this question? How many times would you be told to 'Go fuck yourself' because the turkey roast is on the table?

Almost nine million Jehovah's Witnesses recruited using a flimsy-at-best, door-to-door sales technique. How many people throughout history have sold their soul for personal gain?

It's fewer than you think.

Knocking on doors isn't the answer.

There has to be a better way.

The Beresford is old. It is grand. It has evolved with the people who have inhabited its rooms and apartments. It is dark and elephantine and it breathes with its people. Paint peels and there are cracks in places. It is bricks and mortar and plaster and wood.

It is alive.

And it never stops changing.

EXPERIMENT ONE: HOTEL BERESFORD

ROOM 728

There is a smoke that emanates from Danielle Ortega. Her voice is deep and husky. Although a woman only in her twenties, you could believe that she has had a cigarette hanging from her mouth since 1950. It's the same when she sings. A couple of notes and you are dropped into some kind of jazz haze. Her every footstep is accompanied by the sound of a double-bass string being plucked. Her hair wafts to John Coltrane's trumpet and her hips sway to the delicate tap of the snare drum.

You noticc Danielle Ortega when she walks into a room or out on the street. She stands out. As though she has been mistakenly dropped into the world from another time, another place. She shouldn't exist as anything other than old black-and-white film footage of Paris in the 1920s. But she does. Moving through the corridors like fire.

She adds grace to the notoriously noisy and difficult seventh floor of Hotel Beresford. The lift stops. She steps out and shuts the door behind her; it's not automatic, it's old metal that concertinas and offers little protection. There are screams from two separate apartments. Paint is flaking off the left-hand wall, like it's damp, but it can't be. A dog barks, even though there are no pets allowed here and the guy in 731 isn't blind. A baby cries. A glass breaks. Cooking pots bang against one another. The boy from 734 is sitting outside, beneath the window again. He's reading.

He has seen Danielle. He felt her first. Then he smelled her. Something fresh and floral against the backdrop of fried onion and wet walls.

'Hey Danielle,' he calls down the hall.

'Hey Odie, watcha reading today?' She turns the key to her door.

Odie lifts his book up.

'That not too old for you?'

'I'm smarter than I look,' he smiles, white gravestone teeth against smooth black skin. Freckles on his cheeks. A bruise around his left eye. She knows his father hits both of them; Odie and his mother.

'No doubt about that.' She smiles back, knowing he is usually out there either because his parents are arguing or his mother is drinking. He's ten years old, going on fifteen. A part of her wants to ask him in, but that would be inviting trouble. There's a bang against the inside of his door and she watches him flinch.

She can't help herself. 'If things out here get … not okay, you come and knock for me. Alright? You know where I am?' The dog barks again.

'You're the woman in 728,' he says, like he is repeating something his mother has said before. Odie's father has said things to Danielle in the hallway in the past. Unsavoury things.

I've seen you looking at the woman in 728.

'That's right. In fact, I'm *that* woman in 728.'

Odie might be smarter than his age but he doesn't pick up on the nuance. His head drops back to his story and she enters her apartment.

Walking straight to the turntable in her lounge, she lays down a Billie Holiday record that she knows could never be played too loud on the seventh floor of Hotel Beresford.

She kicks off her shoes by the coffee table and looks at herself in the mirror, rubbing at the olive skin on her cheeks that hides just how tired she is. Danielle Ortega drops to her knees and rests her elbows on the orange sofa.

'Dear God, please take care of that boy.' She almost cries, but holds it in. If there is a God, Danielle Ortega's voice is one He would want to listen to. It has been the ruin of many men. She continues, asking to keep him safe, get his mother's drinking under control, stop the whoring around. She asks nothing for the father. Finally, she looks up and asks for a better gig than the one she has in town right now. One that pays better. One where she isn't fighting with the club owner for taking a larger cut than was promised.

Something closer to The Beresford. Or, better, that pays enough that she could get out of this place. Because it does something to you, living in a building like this. You tell yourself you're not like the couple shouting next door or the guy with the angry dog or the drug dealers and drug takers. You're not bouncing off the walls in here or playing death metal at midnight on a Tuesday. You're trying to earn your keep, doing the only thing you love.

She lights a cigarette. You're not supposed to smoke in these apartments but everybody does. Drawing the smoke into her lungs, it seems stupid to ruin her instrument in that way, but that's how she has obtained the sound she is known for.

The glass ashtray on the coffee table has been smashed in half, so she flicks ash into an old beer bottle left on the kitchen counter, before going to the fridge for a fresh one.

There's a window behind the sofa that Danielle opens. She straddles the window ledge. One leg inside, over the back of the sofa, the other dangling freely outside, a hundred and twenty feet above the street below. She blows a plume of smoke towards the sky. A few doors down, a couple is doing the same thing, but she can smell the weed from here. She nods at them and they raise a joint in recognition.

At Hotel Beresford, it seems everybody is doing something that they shouldn't.

The walls shake. Billie Holiday jumps. A door slams.

Her cupboard moves.

Danielle Ortega flicks the end of her cigarette down to the road below. Anyone else doing that looks disgusting but everything Danielle does is effortlessly cool. She's tired. Almost nocturnal with the hours she keeps at the club, singing for her supper. She glides across the living area to the shoes she kicked off and picks them up. The place isn't as tidy as she'd like.

The door rattles. Car horns blare outside. A gunshot downtown. Then another. One for every hundred veterans lying under cardboard in a doorway.

She opens the cupboard, kicks off her shoes, and the man tied up and gagged on the floor inside squirms when the light hits his eyes.

Odie's father. With an indentation in his forehead that matches the corner of the broken ashtray on Danielle's coffee table.

'What the fuck am I going to do with you, huh?' she asks, her sultry voice not doing anything for him on this occasion. He shouldn't have struck the boy. And he shouldn't have come grabbing at Danielle in the hallway.

Billie Holiday sings 'All of Me' and Danielle joins in, dancing in front of the open cupboard door, using her beer bottle as a microphone.

Odie's abusive father is helpless. He watches her sway; lying upside down, it looks to him like she is dancing on the ceiling. He drinks her in. That voice. Such quiet power. Mesmerising.

The seventh floor of The Beresford might be the loudest but it's not the worst.

Danielle closes the door, not knowing what she's going to do. At least Odie is safe.

And she hasn't killed anybody yet.

ROOM 734

An overweight, balding white man is adjusting his shirt collar as he exits, leaving the door ajar behind him. He sees the little kid outside, reading, and shakes his head in disapproval that the boy is not in school. He tuts and tightens his tie.

This guy, this judgemental prick, he took an hour out of the office and drove out of the city to Hotel Beresford to get his rocks off with a stranger. He dropped an extra twenty so she'd let him come inside her, too. And now he looks down on that woman for not sending her kid in to school.

The kid doesn't look up from his book. He doesn't want to see another man that isn't his father coming out of room 734.

'Otis Walker, I hope you haven't been out here gassing to that woman from 728.' She always full-names him when making a point or he is in trouble.

Odie looks up at his mother, half her left breast on display where she hasn't straightened herself up properly.

'No, Mama. But she's nice.'

'She ain't nice, Odie. Nobody on this floor is nice. Hell, nobody in this building is nice. I don't want you talking to anybody, okay?'

The boy nods, but he doesn't mean it.

His mother looks out into the hallway and down towards the elevator, the top of a fat, bald head disappearing down towards the sixth floor.

'Somebody needs to shut that damn dog up. Get in here, boy. Let's fix you some snacks.'

Odie folds the corner of his page, shuts his book and pushes into 734. He can smell the sex on his mother, though he doesn't know what that is. She looks around one last time, as though somebody is watching, shuts the door and locks it from the inside. She rests her head against the inside and breathes.

'You alright, Mama? Want me to fix you a drink?'

Her heart sinks. Her son is ten years old, relegated to the hallway with his literature while she does unthinkable things to build up her getaway fund. And now he is asking whether she needs a drink. The kid is self-sufficient. He could make himself a sandwich. He could get her a glass of water. But what he's really asking is if she is craving alcohol.

He'll pour a cheap whisky and add a drop of water to take the edge off the burn. He can mix up a vodka and Coke. The kid can make coffee and he knows which glass the red wine goes in. Just as she knew what to pour for her own mother when she was the same age as Odie is now.

Diana Walker nursed her mother to death after her father left them both. A textbook shit dad, who went out for milk and never came back. Such a cliché. It broke her mother's heart but, instead of focussing on Diana, she put all her efforts into the bottle.

As far as she can remember, her father wasn't an abusive man. He rarely raised his voice. He worked. He was present. One day, he must have just had enough. She never wanted that for her kids. But there's only ever two choices, it seems, when it comes to abuse and neglect, you either repeat the pattern or you break the cycle.

Diana was doing what her mother had done and, by God, she hoped that Odie's father was just like hers. He went out last night and didn't come home. Said he was playing poker uptown. It must mean that he's winning. The stupid fuck only comes home when the money is gone.

It was a risk to take a morning appointment. That dumb fuck was supposed to take Odie to school on his way to work and that would have given her enough time to get the fat white guy in and out without fear of getting caught and beaten. She didn't want to cancel. It was easy money. He never lasts that long and he's not rough with her.

She looks at her watch. That dog is still barking. Even though her husband hits her, chokes her, spits on her, even though he broke her arm that time and her nose another time, even though he has hit her son, she finds herself worrying where he might be, that something may have happened to him.

Odie sees her staring at the window.

'Mama, you sure you're okay?' He looks up at her with those big, brown doe eyes.

'Fine, baby. I'm fine. Fix me a rum and Coke, would ya?'

Odie walks to the drinks cabinet.

'And open the window, while you're over there.' She can smell the sex in here. And she knows what it is.

He opens the window.

The sound of traffic and voices and, a few windows down, singing. Drenched in smoke.

ROOM 731

Dogs are smart. They're loyal and loving. Some people think they can sense earthquakes, though science is yet to show that as truth. They help the visually impaired. They can even be used to aid those with low self-esteem or anxiety issues.

People love dogs. And dogs seem to love people.

But the Doberman in 731 will not stop barking. And it's pissing everybody off.

The couple in 733 have been banging against the wall, shouting, 'Shut that fucking thing up or I'm gonna come in there and cut its damn throat.'

The neighbour in 729 went a step further and smashed a clenched hand against the front door. 'Jerry, take your dog out for a walk, man. Fuck. It's going stir-crazy in there, and we can't listen to it anymore. You hear me? Jerry?'

Jerry didn't answer then.

And he won't answer now.

The dog hears singing and shouting and footsteps. It barks again.

It's not trying to piss people off. It doesn't need a walk. It's calling for help.

For the first day, the obedient dog laid next to its owner, occasionally nudging him with a nose or a push of its back into Jerry's leg. But it's hungry as hell now and has been shitting in the corner of the bathroom for two days. And it's definitely sad because there is an awareness that the owner hasn't spoken a word or stroked or filled the water bowl or moved for forty-eight hours or so.

Jerry is on his back, a white foam dribbling from the side of his mouth. God knows what he took. Maybe it was too much, maybe it was just the wrong thing. Maybe he accidentally ate some peanuts. It doesn't matter. Jerry is dead. And the poor dog knows it.

That's why he's barking all the time.

That's why he's scratching at the front door.

He's calling for help. He's not trying to annoy the neighbours. He's asking for their attention. Luckily, Jerry has checked out of life a couple of days before he's due to check out of Hotel Beresford, so somebody will be along to kick him out in a few hours.

Just as guests are not supposed to smoke in their rooms, or take drugs in their rooms, or be paid for sex in their rooms, there are no pets allowed. So, two days after losing his owner and companion, Jerry's Doberman will lose his home. He'll be tossed out onto the street with the other strays to fend for himself.

Any other hotel and this would be a major story.

'Dead Junkie, Eaten by Dog at Hotel Beresford'.

But it won't even register.

Just another day.

This type of thing happens all the time. They used to cover it up but, honestly, some crackhead overdosing and having his face chewed by a Doberman is the least of worries when it comes to all the things that are happening, right now, in the building.

RECEPTION

If something is going to get swept under the carpet or a bloodstained sheet is going to be bleached or burned, the order will come from downstairs. At reception.

And it will come from Carol.

The entrance to Hotel Beresford is art deco. Strict lines, geometry and arches showing cubist influence. The monochrome carpet screams elegance as it leads towards the desk that stretches the length of one wall, marble with chrome embellishments. Or, at least, it once looked that way. Back when writers and poets and dignitaries roamed the hallways and foyer.

It still feels lavish. Glamorous, even. But faded. And a little old-fashioned. Peeling paint and faded hopes.

Much like Carol.

Carol seems to age with the building. For every strip of wallpaper that gets ripped or falls away, Carol gets another wrinkle. When the front facade gets uplifted with a new paint job or some detail on the masonry, Carol turns up with a Botoxed forehead or facelift.

But not from a reputable surgeon. From somebody she saw advertising in the back of a magazine. Inexpensive treatments. The kind who has a clinic beneath a bridge that leads into the city. He's got a reputation for double-bubble deformities with breast augmentation and there are a hundred guys knocking up their mistresses because the quick vasectomy they sprung for didn't quite take.

A real hatchet job.

Much like Carol, herself.

You can see that she once possessed a natural beauty, probably entered pageants as a kid, but now she looks like Mickey Rourke in a skirt.

There's no point trying to pinpoint her age. Some joke that she was born in the building. Others say she was found in the Beresford foundations. The smarter ones know that either of those could be true and it's best not to fuck around with Carol.

She knows things.

Maybe she knows everything.

'Complaint from the seventh floor. A dog barking. Non-stop, apparently,' one of the receptionists alerts Carol.

'How did somebody get a dog in here?' Carol knows that guests get all sorts into the building. She damn well knows how it got in here, either through a fire-exit door that should set off an alarm but never does, or straight through the front door while her back was turned and other staff members let the mutt walk right by without giving a shit.

She's saying it for the new girl. She's young and enthusiastic and hasn't been beaten down by the job that Carol once loved. The receptionist that passed on the message has been here almost as long as Carol has. Keith. In his fifties. Bald. Effeminate. Always wears a neckerchief, for some reason. When he started out, he spoke with a stutter but that's all but disappeared over the years. If ever he feels that tongue getting tied, he starts to sing.

Guests love him.

Carol wouldn't mind if he took a few days off or toned it down ten percent.

Nobody answers Carol's question.

'What room is this dog in?'

'Um…' Keith taps at the computer keyboard, hitting the return key with a flamboyance usually reserved for bullfighters. '731.'

'Okay. Can you call security to go up there and see what's up with this dog? Jerry is due to leave today, anyway.' She looks at her watch. 'Tell him he's got an hour and they both need to get out. Send them down the back stairs.'

Nobody told Carol the name of the guy in 731. It's just something she knows. Because it's her job to know. That's what makes her so good.

She pushes a section of the wall behind the reception desk and it seems as though a part of it moves. It's so subtle that it's almost a secret, but the opening leads to her office. It's not something that shows up on the building plans, and the building is rumoured to have several false walls that can lead a person around Hotel Beresford, passing between the rooms, behind them, around them, undetected.

Who knows if any of that is true or just urban legend?

Carol probably does.

She disappears out the back, and Keith asks one of the security guards to take a trip up to the seventh floor and give the guest his marching orders.

Ollie draws the short straw. Of course. Two tours of Iraq hardened him. And, while many people thank him for his service, none of that helps when you get out of the army and the only job you can get is either a security guard or a nightclub bouncer. He's been doing it for years. Treading water. Not going anywhere. Earning just enough for food and a few beers over the weekend. Luckily, his rent is cheaper now that his wife has left and somehow managed to take their house because she found him to be mentally abusive and emotionally unavailable after witnessing the horrors of war.

But she thanks him for his service.

It could be worse, he could be one of those veterans on the street with no legs, still wearing part of their uniform, holding up a piece of card and begging for money. He knows some of them. Real heroes. Discarded. He wishes he could help but he can just about take care of himself.

It's been years since he's seen any action but Ollie still looks as though he just got pushed out the back of a Chinook and parachuted into the hotel lobby with a knife in his teeth.

That's why he gets sent upstairs.

There's nothing that scares him anymore.

He shuts the door to the lift. It unnerves most people the first time they use it because it's so open. At the height of Hotel Beresford glory, somebody was employed to ride the lift all day and take the guests to their floor. A little guy called Carlyle. He'd tuck himself into the corner and spin to life as soon as anybody stepped in. He rode that lift with politicians, hookers and rock stars. Often at the same time.

Nobody really knows what happened to him. Hotel Beresford became a place that no longer required a designated staff member to operate the vintage lift. A decision wasn't made to terminate that position, it just faded out. And then, one day, somebody realised that Carlyle was no longer there.

Ollie can hear the dog before he even steps out of the lift. He can hear a couple shouting and somebody singing along to what sounds like Billie Holiday. And he can smell weed and sex from the fat, bald guy who got off at ground level as Ollie stepped inside the lift.

He knocks on 713.

'Er ... Jerry?' It may be his military background but it doesn't feel right to call somebody he doesn't know by their first name. Ollie would feel more comfortable and respectful to refer to the guest as Mister Whatever.

The dog is barking and scratching against the back of the door. It sounds panicked. Ollie hits it harder and calls for Jerry again. He wants to cut the noise. The cars outside, the music across the hall, all the voices. He doesn't have PTSD but the crescendo of sounds is reminiscent of war.

'Jerry, I'm going to need you to open this door, your dog sounds in distress.' Under his breath, 'You're not even supposed to have a fucking dog in here.'

'Everything okay?' A voice comes from behind Ollie and he jumps, turning quickly and setting himself to fight.

'Jesus Christ!' Ollie says, facing the person.

'Not quite.' He almost laughs.

'Mr Balliol. What are you ... I mean, where did you ... What are you doing on the seventh floor?'

Mr Balliol lives in the penthouse. There is only one suite on the top floor. Balliol takes up every inch. The only access is from the one lift at Hotel Beresford, and the top floor requires a key. The only way onto the roof is to go to the end of the corridor on the ninth floor and take the fire escape ladder, which runs up the outside of the building.

Nobody disturbs Balliol. Somebody must go up and clean his place, he's too rich to do it himself. But nobody asks questions about it. Carol will know, surely.

Mr Balliol doesn't answer Ollie's question about why he is there or where he came from. Instead he tells him, 'I think you're going to have to bust the door down. Seems like Jerry is incapacitated.' Again, there's a flicker of glee on his face. He's definitely not concerned.

What is he doing on the seventh level?

Ollie looks back down the corridor at the caging around the lift shaft. The lift is on another level. Balliol couldn't have arrived on this floor that way.

'That dog could go crazy if I kick the door down.'

'He could be going crazy because of what he can see beyond that door.'

Ollie pictures a guy hanging from the rafters. Wouldn't be the first time.

'I'll go and get the key.'

'Best kick it down, now, Ollie.'

'Ah, fuck. Stand back, please, Mr Balliol.'

Balliol does as he's asked and Ollie warns Jerry that he's coming in. He's worried that he'll kick the door and hurt the dog or the dog will go to attack him for entering the room but he has no choice. He tells the dog to go and fetch Jerry, hoping it will go back inside for a second while he knocks through.

Ollie takes a step back from the door, holds out an arm for Mr Balliol to stand behind. A woman shouts something in another room. The dog isn't barking. The car horns continue. He lifts a knee to his chest and cycles his foot forward into the door, splitting the frame on his first attempt. He follows up swiftly with a shoulder and bursts inside room 731 to a Doberman sitting calmly next to his owner, lying on the floor, obviously dead.

'Shit,' Ollie says under his breath. Then he turns back to apologise to Mr Balliol and shield him from the scene ahead. But he is gone.

ROOM 724

Not everybody on the seventh floor of Hotel Beresford is a lowlife. The Zhaos are here for a reason. They're sensible and conscientious. And they're not here to make friends, either. They're here to do a job. They're focussed on their end goal, which is to get the hell out of there.

Daisy Zhao doesn't want to live in the city. She doesn't even want to live this close to the city. She's young, like Jun, so they can't get onto the property ladder. And there are no wealthy parents to help them out.

They're going at it alone.

So they will nod the occasional acknowledgement in the hallway or hint at a morning smile to the woman who smokes out her window a few doors down but, to the Zhaos, it's them against the world. It's their struggle, their fight, their goal to have the most frightfully average and unremarkable life in suburbia. Couple of kids. Maybe a dog. A front lawn with a white picket fence. It's not the American dream but it is their dream.

And Hotel Beresford will help make that a reality. Because the seventh-floor prices are so cheap, the Zhaos can work and set enough money aside each month to build a sizeable deposit for the home they desire. It's the place where they will really start their lives together. Not here in room 724, this is temporary.

Fit for purpose.

Purgatory.

But a pretty purgatory once Daisy Zhao has turned her hand to the interior design of their one-room palace. There are pieces of upcycled flea-market furniture and salvaged light fittings and soft furnishings that add a pop of colour. Even with a lengthy rental period like the Zhaos', guests are not permitted to paint the walls.

The place is immaculate.

Delicate.

Much like Daisy herself.

Jun loves her. He adores her quietness, her control and her poise. She is beautiful to him. Porcelain skin and striking green eyes. They are content in silences and engaged when in conversation. They fit together. It's not passionate but it is affectionate. They are devoted to one another and their provincial project.

From the outside, they can come across as standoffish and stuffy but that's not the case. Looking in at anybody's life whether from a distance or behind the filter of social media, it's easy to get the wrong impression. They have their routine now. Work. Rest. Clean. Prepare food. Make love twice a week. And smoke a joint on the window ledge each morning.

The Zhaos have been at Hotel Beresford for over a year. They've put more than twelve grand aside already by living as frugally as possible – with the exception of the weed habit. They keep the money in a high-interest account rather than a shoe box at the back of the cupboard. They only need fifteen to put down as a deposit but they're talking of pushing on for twenty because it doesn't seem like much of a stretch.

You can remove yourself from Beresford life, stay out of people's way, keep your head down, be polite but not forthcoming, and you can make the place work for you. You can even get out. You can leave whenever you want to.

But there's always a danger.

You can stay longer than you need, get greedy, get lazy, get comfortable. And that's when things can change. The building knows.

ROOM 728

Danielle hears the commotion outside her room and saunters towards her own front door, Billie singing 'Strange Fruit' behind her, Danielle hums along.

She steps up to the peephole. One of the security guards is standing in the hallway. He's looking all around as though he's expecting somebody to be watching him. It's odd behaviour. Beyond the muscular man, she notices the door opposite and to the left is hanging off one hinge. She can't see Jerry on the floor but she can just make out the dog that has been annoying everybody. She listens carefully but there is no barking left.

Danielle could go out and ask what is happening, she could play the role of the concerned neighbour. Maybe she could just go into the hallway and have an obvious snoop.

That's not how it works at Hotel Beresford.

You don't get involved.

You turn a blind eye.

You let things slide.

Everyone has their own shit going on. Including Danielle.

'Oh, this place.' She looks at her watch and floats back into her lounge area. She needs to sleep. Her life is not normal. She's almost nocturnal. Singing until the early hours, drinking afterwards. But there's no downtime at Hotel Beresford, especially on the seventh floor. If you want to rest, you have to learn to live with the noise. The thrum of the city just beyond. The music. The arguments. The security guards kicking down the door of your neighbour.

Danielle lowers the blind that covers the window she was just sitting at and smoking. It's darker, and that tricks her brain into thinking it's also quieter. Just the ticking of the clock, the haunting sound of Ms Holiday's voice coming through the speaker at her feet as she lies down on the sofa, pulling a blanket around her slender frame.

The door to her shoe cupboard trembles. She watches it and shakes her head, rolls her eyes. She wriggles her toes in time to the music and sings.

Here is a fruit...

She starts to drift.

...crows to pluck

Her eyes close.

...for the wind...

ROOM 724

Jun threw a smile and lifted his eyebrows slightly at the woman smoking a cigarette out of her window a few rooms across from the Zhaos' place.

She is the opposite of Daisy. Long legs, sprawled either side of the window ledge. She's cool. Alluring. Jun doesn't even like the look or smell of normal cigarettes but there's something about that woman, it suits her. It's sexy. He doesn't want to act on it. He's not thinking of knocking on her door and getting smashed in the head by an ashtray. He's not imagining her while making love to his wife, he's just momentarily captivated each morning.

Daisy is too small to pull off the straddled look. She is so petite, she can sit outside on the ledge with her legs crossed and still have room around her. Jun has to dangle his legs over the side. It should be scary to do what they are doing while up at that height but it's not. It's safe enough. Even while smoking a joint.

They've been doing it for months.

In every other way, they are straight, methodical, tidy. This is their only indiscretion. They see the people beneath them on the streets, homeless and begging for money for their next fix, whether it's a bottle of vodka or a hallucinogenic or the latest fashionable opiate. The Zhaos are not like that. They're not addicted.

It's a ritual.

The Dutch manage to smoke weed all the time while raising a family and holding down a full-time job. And they all speak six languages. That's how the Zhaos see themselves. Completely in control of everything. Their destiny is in their hands.

Then Jun's phone rings.

And they lose a little control.

'You're kidding?' he says.

Daisy mouths, *What's going on?*

Jun holds up a finger. Daisy gives him a look that tells him she doesn't appreciate that gesture.

'Of course. That's great. Yes. I mean, neither of us will be able to get there today but tomorrow works, for sure.' He smiles at Daisy to try to diffuse her mood and nods as though the person at the other end of the line can see him. 'Okay. Perfect. See you then.'

Jun hangs up.

'What was that?' Daisy asks. 'What's going on?'

'Come inside.'

'What?'

'Come inside. I don't want you getting excited out on this shelf.'

Jun swings himself around and heads back in through the window. Daisy flicks ash into the wind and crawls along the ledge to follow her husband.

'Come on, then. What is it?'

'That was the estate agent. He's got another house, same area as the one we liked but the guy is looking for a quick sale. His wife left or something and she wants half the money.'

'I thought we agreed we'd get to twenty grand.'

'I know what we agreed, Daisy, but he says the sellers will take lower than the asking price just to get shot of it, so that they can move on. We've got enough saved. We can get out of here, start our lives now.'

Daisy doesn't feel comfortable with spontaneity but this has long been their dream and, through sheer luck, there is a chance it is about to come true.

HOTEL BERESFORD

The building is just outside the city, so it feels metropolitan but also, somehow, rural. The bright lights and skyscrapers are visible, they're within touching distance, but the rates are much lower out here.

They're lower still because Hotel Beresford has so many rooms. And that means it's always full.

It has to be.

There's one entrance. Double doors. Glass with a polished chrome frame. There's a revolving door next to this, harkening back to a golden age when this place was vibrant and buzzing and new.

The ground floor is the reception. There's an area to one side where guests can meet. There are tables to sit at and drink, and one wall houses a sizeable book collection. It's not a library but it adds to the grandeur. On the other side of the entrance is a small apartment that only Carol can use as she manages the building. She doesn't live there all the time, she has her own place further downtown, but it is logistically beneficial for her to have a crash pad for those longer shifts.

To the right of the reception desk there is a luxurious staircase that leads up to the second-level restaurants and bars and, on the other side of the desk is the corridor, lined with black-and-white art, that leads around to the lift, which takes all the guests to their rooms.

Pressing buttons one or two will take you to the ground floor. A quirk that nobody has ever attempted to rectify.

Floors three to six are the single-occupancy rooms. Each has a double bed, shower and toilet facility. They're ideal for your backpacker types, anyone having an affair, businessmen travelling to the city for a few days of work, and some of the local women who charge for services by the hour.

Floors seven to nine are different. They offer a living area, kitchenette and separate bedroom. Guests can cater for themselves. These rooms attract people wanting to stay for the week, maybe two. The price is so reasonable that you'll often find visitors that have been there over a month. Maybe they're between properties or they've been kicked out of the family home. A lot of the time, they're trying to escape something. But it's so reasonable, it's easy to look at these rooms as short-term lets.

Danielle has already been here for six weeks. Odie's father lost his job and their home but got back into work a few weeks ago. They've been living in the hotel for a couple of months because they didn't have the lump sum to put down for a rental deposit while they were getting back on their feet. Jerry brought his Doberman up the back stairs about ten days ago and the dog has been on its own for two more. For some reason, the seventh floor has always been the noisiest. Nobody knows why. Not even Carol.

Each floor looks the same yet somehow has its own unique landscape; it's known for something particular. A celebrity affair. A mysterious death. A legendary party. Rumours that a serial killer crashed there between sprees. Rock stars smashing up rooms. Writers creating their masterpieces. Some is legend, much is true. All is talked about. With fondness, fascination and morbid curiosity.

Then there's that top floor. The one level that remains a mystery. The conjecture, the stories, are far-fetched and debauched and absurd.

Bluff. Banter. Balderdash.

Keith heard that Mr Balliol took twelve women up there and made love to every single one over the course of an evening. That he once called down to the front desk and asked someone to bring up a bowl of cocaine for breakfast. And he also made a business deal inside the lift that gave him enough to live on for hundreds of years.

That he has been here from the beginning.

Before Carol and the revolving door.

That he knows the building better than anybody. He's always watching and can see everything.

All utterly ridiculous. And true.

THE PENTHOUSE

It has been said that the best way to get rich is not to earn a ton of money, it's to not spend any. You could initially be forgiven for thinking that Mr Balliol is thrifty based on the minimalist approach to the penthouse suite.

Oak floors throughout. Stainless-steel appliances. Marble worktops. The opulence one might expect from the wealthy. But a closer look uncovers furniture that is centuries old. Abstract art pieces. Paintings. Sculptures. Rare books. A fireplace that appears to have fallen out of a gothic cathedral. And a mirror, so tarnished with age that the reflective surface is almost all peeled away or black. Not functional but beautiful in its patination.

The rooms are sparse but the pieces that do exist hold history.

This is not a floor that can be rented for the night. It is, like the lower levels, a single-occupancy space but it has no free dates for, at least, another few hundred years.

Balliol owns this floor.

Some things aren't for sale. And the highest floor of the Hotel Beresford building is certainly one of them.

The entire penthouse apartment is almost open plan. The kitchen bleeds into the dining area – a table made for twenty people that is mostly used by one. The lounge falls into a library and games room. There are walls but no doors. Sometimes they're not even solid, just a series of vertical posts cut from oak to match the floors, differing heights to add some sculptural interest. It's possible to look through the gaps into the next room. It is beautiful. Clean and timeless.

The main bedroom can be cut off with two giant sliding doors. There are doors on all the bathrooms, of course, and the study. The only other room that can be locked from the inside is the viewing room. A wall of TV screens that Balliol can control with a gesture. He watches Keith take an internal phone call at the front desk. Then he notes Keith's horror before putting the phone down and knocking on the door to alert Carol.

He's letting her know about Jerry in 731.

Carol emerges, straightens her skirt and heads towards the lift. Balliol nods to himself. She really is the perfect little minion for this place. (For now.) On another screen he sees the jazz singer sleeping on her sofa through all the commotion. On another, somebody strums at their guitar. Somewhere else two women are having sex, not knowing that they can be seen.

Balliol isn't looking at these people to get his kicks – although that is, sometimes, a cute ancillary benefit – he's fascinated by the human condition. How some let life pass them by, some struggle, some live beyond their means, some live two lives, and just how many have no real idea what it is that they truly want.

CROSSROADS

Mrs May doesn't want her husband to die.

There's nothing else.

Forget the riches. Forget fame. Forget everything. She wants to save him.

She needs to.

He has been a wonderful husband for decades. Supportive in every way. Kind. Generous. And devout. Why would their God forsake him so? This cannot be the work of the Lord. Surely.

'Dear God. Please speak to me. I have followed you my entire life. We have followed you. We love you. We honour you. We worship you. We do your work, here, on Earth,' she cries. 'What did he do? What could he have done that was so wrong for you to take him like this? Weeks? You're giving me weeks?'

She falls to her knees. Her old, crunches-as-she-walks knees. Initially, she was standing, her hands clasped together, staring upwards at the swirls on her ceiling. Now, she is kneeling. Begging for an answer. Trying to stifle her moans so as not to alert her husband, who is already busying himself looking through travel brochures.

The acceptance to her refusal.

The denial to her action.

The right to her left.

Looking in on this scene, knowing the information they have just received, seeing Mrs May down on her knees and crying, things look desperate. She may even be perceived as weak. If God can see her, why does He not answer?

'What did he do?' she asks again. 'Don't take him away from me.

Please don't take him away from me.' There's a quiet menace to the second time she asks. Almost as though she is making a threat.

Her shoulders tense. She looks up again. This time, the anger is clear on her face.

'You,' Mrs May snarls. 'You, with your judgement and your wrath. And your God damned silence. Talk to me. Tell me what I should do and I will do it. Take his cancer and give it to me. Take all cancer and shove it up your arse.' She unclasps her hands.

Still looking up. 'You silent, capricious little coward. We follow you and you do this to us. This is not a part of your plan. You have no plan. I see that now.'

Mr May calls from the lounge. 'Everything okay in there, dear?'

She ignores him. This is too important.

'Everything we have given. No questions. No words from you. Nothing. I can't just sit around and let this happen. I won't let you take him. WEEKS?' she shouts. 'Fuck you. I want longer than that. If you can't help, I'll find somebody that will.'

ROOM 731

'Oh, Jesus fucking Christ.' Carol's words bypass any filter between her brain and mouth when she sees a dead Jerry on the floor. 'We can't even shut the door because you've kicked it in half. Anybody could walk by.'

'What did you expect me to do?' Ollie is incredulous. Although, he had no intention of forcing his way inside the room until the guy from the penthouse suggested it.

A stroke.

A caress in the right direction.

Carol surveys the damage. Drug paraphernalia on the coffee table. The place stinks of whatever came out of Jerry when he stopped breathing.

'Carol? What are we going to do?'

She doesn't answer. Carol looks around the room, taking in every detail. At one point she peers into the far corner as though looking at something that isn't there.

'Carol?' Ollie is sharper, and it clicks the manager back into reality.

'I've called an ambulance. They can come and collect the body.'

'What about the police?'

'What about them? There's nothing suspicious here. Some damn junkie shot up one too many times, snorted the wrong powder, whatever. Let the paramedics take the guy to the morgue.'

'What? You have to let them know.'

'Look,' she is certain with this word. It's almost as though she stomps her foot as she says it and time around them slows down. 'This is a great hotel but you know what some of the streets are like around here. Homeless, addicts, strays. An ambulance will take an age to get here because they don't want to come, and when they realise that they have to, a police escort is almost mandatory because those desperate fucking space cadets will ransack the vehicle for whatever fix they can get. So rest your pretty little mind and get that mutt out of here.'

The dog whimpers.

And Ollie is resigned. He knows that Carol is right almost as much as Carol knows she is right.

She doesn't say anything else, just points to a dog lead hanging from a hook on the wall.

'You're gonna stay up here for the paramedics?'

Carol waits a beat before answering. 'Sure.' Her expression doesn't change. She is the manager, she doesn't have to answer questions from anybody in the building, other than the man in the penthouse.

This is above Ollie's pay grade. He wants what's right, but he also knows how hard it has been to get work since leaving the military. Since the military left him.

'Come on, boy. Let's get you out of here.' He pulls the lead from the wall and the dog is torn. There's upset there, for sure. He knows his companion is gone. He knows he has to leave him. 'Wait, what am I supposed to do with this dog?'

Carol has already made her way to the kitchenette. She's clearing up. Getting the room ready for the next guest. There'll be another one along soon enough.

'Take it downstairs and let it out on the street. There's enough strays out there. It'll make friends, if you're worried about that.'

Ollie is worried. He's tall, muscular, tough, his head is shaved to the shortest length before bald. In the right attire he would be intimidatingly threatening. But he's not a monster.

'Sure thing,' he says, clipping the lead onto the dog's collar. Then under his breath, 'Dump the fucker on the street.'

Carol isn't listening, though. She is tying a knot in the rubbish bag. She is wiping down the sink.

The dog barks something at its dead former owner. A goodbye, maybe. A fuck-you, perhaps. It behaves. It follows Ollie blindly out the broken door and to the left, in the direction of the old lift.

Ollie can hear it ascending before he has a chance to push the button but it stops on the seventh floor. One of the maintenance crew pulls the door open and steps out with a new door. It has the number 731 screwed to the front in brass. Ollie looks at his watch. The man in the lift runs a hand through his greasy hair before smiling at the security guard. He probably has more fingers than teeth.

He drags the door out of the lift and rolls his eyes at Ollie as though saying, *Not another one, eh?* Then he makes his way towards the room where Carol is waiting.

Ollie steps towards the lift but the dog won't budge.

'Come on, boy. Let's get you downstairs.'

A bark. The dog pulls against the lead.

'Please don't make this harder than it has to be. Ollie pulls hard but the dog is steadfast. It barks again and turns its body towards the stairwell.

Ollie drops down on one knee to get himself near the level of the animal.

'Don't want to go in there, huh?' He nods his head towards the lift. 'I don't blame ya. It's creepy, right?'

The dog doesn't respond. It just stares back.

Ollie walks the Doberman down seven storeys of the Hotel Beresford stairwell. He takes it down the corridor with the monochrome abstract paintings, past the reception desk where Keith stands, looking baffled, over the lush carpet of the foyer, through the art-deco doorway and out onto the street.

He sees a homeless vet in a doorway across the road. He has a dog with him. It sits next to the cardboard sign that explains his situation. A cat sprints from one side to the other, narrowly avoiding cars that wouldn't even feel it if they ran over the animal.

He knows this isn't right.

'Fuck. Come with me.' He takes a left. Another at the corner.

Another, thirty yards after that. Into the car park, over to his pick-up. He opens the passenger door.

'Look, it ain't ideal, I know that. Get in. I clock off in a couple of hours, we'll get a decent meal in you, okay?'

The dog jumps in and Ollie closes the door.

Barking. Scratching at the window. Ollie knows the seats are going to be ripped to shreds when he gets back, the dog will be showing teeth. He'll try to cool things down with the offer of food. Until then, he leaves the thing in distress and heads back to Hotel Beresford.

Who knows if a dog can really predict an earthquake before it happens? One thing is for certain, although there hasn't been any formal scientific research into the area – they sure have a nose for evil.

THE PENTHOUSE

Balliol watches Carol scrub.

She knows all the tricks.

Cold water for blood. Obviously.

Pit stains in your shirt? Dissolve an aspirin in water and wash that body odour away.

Pen on the carpet? Spray the mark with hairspray and rub with body soap.

It's not in the job description but these are the kinds of things you need to know if you want to manage the Hotel Beresford properly.

Carol is over-brewing coffee and cutting lemons at a furious rate. Anything to cover the smell of shit and death. She bleaches the floor. She vacuums the carpet after pouring over a powder that has a lavender scent that sticks to the fibres. The turnaround from discovery-of-death to available-to-rent is around fourteen minutes.

Balliol checks the time and smiles.

Sixty seconds later he is outside 731.

'Everything okay, Carol?' he asks.

'Mr Balliol.' She stands up from scrubbing at the floor. She wants to ask what he is doing there but knows better. He can go where he wants, when he wants. The guy is so rich, he could set fire to the building and smile as it burns to the ground. 'Of course. Everything is fine. Preparing the room for the next guest.'

'You don't have housekeeping on at this time of day?' He's playing with her.

'Of course. I just ... I want to...'

'Carol, it's fine. I know what happened here. And you are right, nothing suspicious. Junkie scum. Better off without them.'

She doesn't say anything. Those words were said in the privacy of the room. She feels him watching her all the time.

He places a hand on her shoulder and it takes everything she has not to flinch or balk.

'God, you remember the time when we'd have the likes of Kennedy and Kerouac in here?'

'Of course.' She almost calls him 'sir' but bites back.

'Those guys wanted something, you know? To make a difference. To achieve. I'm so sick of the bloggers and vloggers and food writers and critics, skimming over the art to give shit reviews for clicks. What's their endgame? What they want is of such little significance.'

Carol doesn't know what point he is heading towards.

And maybe he's not. Maybe he's just thinking out loud. Because when you are rich and powerful, you can get away with anything. You can say what you want, when you want, to whomever you want.

Build that wall. Grab her by the pussy.

Balliol takes his hand off her shoulder.

'This place could be great again, Carol.'

Nostalgia gives you cancer.

'It's *still* great,' she says, genuinely. She believes it. Carol loves her job.

Job satisfaction can get you killed. It makes you complacent.

'With you at the helm, I don't doubt it.' He wants to ask her if there is anything more she wants from life than the hotel, but not everyone can be great. Not everybody can influence or change thought or bring about political change. Carol works, she earns and she provides. And that's enough.

Mr Balliol raises a hand to his head, screws his eyes together and winces.

'Are you okay?' Carol asks.

'My head. A migraine, I think. They come and go.' He knows that it's not a migraine. He hears a woman's voice. She is angry. She wants to be heard. 'I should go. Sit in a dark room for a while.' He walks off without saying anything. Carol watches. Balliol exits through the new door and turns right.

Carol waits.

She knows that the lift is to the left. She wants to see where he is going but she also knows that there are things at Hotel Beresford that she should not see.

Upstairs, Balliol watches Carol on his screen. She tidies some plates away into a cupboard, surveys the room again, then leaves. On another camera, he can see Carol out in the hallway, walking back towards the lift. He rubs at his head.

'You want me to take this one, boss?' A woman's voice from behind. Grace Sherwood. Tall. Athletic. Dark, straight hair. Caramel skin. She leans against the doorway.

Balliol spins in his chair until he faces her.

'Thank you, Grace, but I think I'll take it. I can hear it in her voice. She means it.' He takes his hand from his head. And he tells Grace to fix him a large whisky and fetch him the contract.

RECEPTION

Keith is talking to a young woman at the front desk. It looks as though her life is in a backpack. She's not a city girl, you can tell by her accent. The Hotel Beresford sign is one of the first things you see when your train pulls into the station. So, if you have no plan, no place to be, no real direction, and you're just looking for somewhere to stay, you know immediately where to go when you step onto that platform.

One night? We've got the room for you.

A month? Done.

This woman needs a place to lie low for a week. Those are her words. Any other establishment and that might sound a little suspicious. Like she is evading the law or has run away from something she should not have done. Maybe she is escaping an abusive partner or parent or guidance councillor. Or she stole money.

'That bag looks heavy. Are you sure you don't want to put it down?' Keith offers.

'I spent most of the morning trying to pick it up. Thank you, though.' She smiles.

Keith taps at the keyboard to see if there are any rooms on the seventh floor that will suit the prospective guest.

'So you're looking for a week?'

'To begin with. Could be longer. Just while I decide on next steps.' She pulls at the strap over her right shoulder.

From the corner of his eye, Keith spies Carol emerging from the corridor. She is as poised and immaculate as ever. Striding towards him with purpose. He raises his voice to show that he is working.

'Looks like we have something up on seventh. Double bed. Small living area and kitchenette, though the breakfast in the restaurant is to die for.' Keith winks. 'We can get you in right away, I think.' He looks towards Carol, only ten feet away now. She nods.

Five feet.

Two feet.

Carol places the key next to the keyboard Keith has been tapping at. He picks it straight up and places it on the counter in front of the young backpacker.

'Room 731. The lift is through that corridor. Straight up and the room is about halfway down on your right-hand side. We just need to take a card.'

'Is cash okay? I'll pay up front for the week.'

More alarm bells should be ringing but, at Hotel Beresford, it is not anyone's place to ask questions.

Keith looks at Carol whose acceptance is imperceptible to anyone but Keith.

Hotel Beresford is almost back to full occupancy.

Carol checks her watch. She's probably only been out of the room for sixty seconds.

ROOM 734

Odie washes the dishes while his mother makes the bed and showers the sex off her body. She brushes her teeth to get the taste of dick and toast out of her mouth.

The poor kid doesn't stand a chance.

'Let's get this place clean for when your dad gets home from work. Okay?'

Odie looks around. The dishes and cutlery are drying on the rack. He has wiped down the surfaces with a cloth. The floor has a few crumbs but nothing obvious. It doesn't seem that bad to him. But nothing ever does until his father returns.

Each morsel on the tiles is a backhand. Each crease in the bed sheets is worthy of a throttle. Odie is too young to understand this. He can't look forward, he can only react. He's not supposed to anticipate. He shouldn't feel anxious at his age. He should be looked after, cared for, loved unconditionally.

He's a good kid. A good kid with a mother who's selling her body for escape money and a father whose low self-esteem gives him reason to lash out. And drink. And grab the arse of the wrong neighbour in the wrong hallway at the wrong time of day.

Here's how it usually goes down: Odie's father gets home from work. The house smells like dinner is almost ready to be served. He kicks off his shoes and sees his son reading on the sofa. He says something like, 'Boy, whatchoo readin' now? You ain't never doing nothin' but putting' your head in a damn book.' And then he makes a noise of disapproval by sucking against his teeth.

Diana greets her husband with a minty-fresh, no-dick-has-touched-these-lips kiss. She tells him food is almost ready. She asks how his day at work was. Anything to play the part of the doting wife. Anything to deflect attention away from her day, though he rarely asks because he's not interested.

They eat. He asks his son about school because he does, in his own way, care about the boy, but he ruins it by making fun of his studies – he should be outside with other kids throwing a ball around. The adults drink alcohol. It's not Diana's first of the day and Sam knows it. That's enough ammunition for him to take her into the bedroom and slap her or bend her over the bed and do his worst.

He'll shower off her filth, put her down. Odie will wash the dishes, and then his father will leave for the evening to find a poker game uptown. He's trying to win enough to get out of Hotel Beresford but it's difficult to do that when you're such a natural loser.

Sometimes he stays out all night, if he's winning, and sometimes he comes back drunk and low and ready to take it out on whomever is in the way at room 734.

Last week, he was somewhere in between and he knocked on the wrong door. Room 728. Danielle Ortega answered.

'Mr Walker, I think you have the wrong door.'

Drunk, he looked her up and down, looked confused, found some clarity, smiled, and tried to turn on the charm.

'Ain't nothin' wrong about what I'm seeing.'

'Shit. Really? Coming at me with that?'

'Don't be cold, baby. I got money.' He pulled out a roll of cash, thinking it might impress the young lady. Maybe it was the drink or the drugs or the fact that he had won but she seemed to be moving in slow motion. Music played every time she blinked.

'Go spend it on your wife, Mr Walker. Buy your son a book.' And she shut the door. It was like somebody scraping the needle across a vinyl record.

He stumbled back to his own place, muttering something derogatory about reading and not playing sports.

Then, last night, he tried it again. But this time he didn't want to take no for an answer. Mr Walker wanted to do to Danielle Ortega what Scott Caraway had done to him at the poker table.

Take everything.

But it's not easy to catch smoke in your hands.

It was lights-out as soon as that glass ashtray came crashing down against his forehead. He's awake. His hands are secured firmly behind his back. His trousers are around his ankles and he's lying in the dark of a shoe closet. Mr Walker's mouth is not covered. He could scream for help but nobody would pay any attention to the noise on the seventh floor of Hotel Beresford.

Diana and Odie will wait for him to come home from work. The meat will cook for too long and become tough. They'll eat late, together, and, when it gets even later, they'll go to bed knowing that neither has to pretend to care he hasn't shown up again.

CROSSROADS

People are living longer.

Actually, that's not right. People are *alive* for longer. You can be alive but not really *living*. Because living implies something functional, perhaps a degree of momentum that just seems so sparse in civilisation.

People, now, are managing to exist longer than they once did. *Living* or being *alive* suggests that time has been spent on something worthwhile. Without this, people are just existing.

And they're doing it for longer than their parents or grandparents did.

Seventy-nine years. That's the average.

It sounds more impressive if you say it's 28,835 days. But there's nothing impressive about existence.

Forty-two percent of that time is spent in bed. That's thirty-three years. Twenty-six of those are sleeping and seven years is trying to get to sleep. Whether you make love or fuck or schtup or bone in bed, that time is negligible.

Throw in thirteen years of work. This is an average. You could be a pop sensation or a road sweeper or anything in between, over sixteen percent of your time on Earth will be spent doing something to do with the job you chose, deserved or had to take to make ends meet.

Another eleven years is looking at a screen. Bingeing on TV shows after a long day of selling insurance. Catching up on a remake of another film that was better the first time around, when people didn't have to exist for as long as they do now.

Three of those screen-time years will be spent scrolling through the pictures and thoughts of others. The updates of how everybody else is doing compared to you. How they're doing everything right because you spend too much time working and they are giving their kids all the love and attention that they need.

Three Goddamned years of feeling like you are not worth anything. Maybe, one day soon, we will spend an extra year in bed. Depressed.

Four years eating but only one exercising.

A year socialising.

Another year being romantic in some manner.

You'll spend more time getting dressed than you will laughing, and double that queuing for things.

Add all the crap together that you, apparently, have to do, and you are left with eight years for *living*. Or *being alive*.

That's the reward. Around ten percent of your existence to do the things you want. Eight years to make a difference. To save an animal or stop a tree being chopped down or helping somebody less fortunate than you, or creating art, listening to people, fighting for your planet or your race or your sex.

Of course, people can spend four to seven of these years not knowing what it is that they want. So they keep on existing.

And they're existing for longer.

And they're angrier, but they don't really know what they're angry about.

Mrs May knows what she wants and she sure as Hell knows what she is angry about. She wants those eight years with her husband. She wants to know why he probably won't be around in a month. She wants some answers but her God is on a fucking sabbatical.

She shares a bottle of red wine with Mr May. He doesn't want to quit meat or live on berries for his final days. He wants to cross the things off his list.

When he falls asleep on the sofa, Mrs May is quiet. She sneaks upstairs into the spare room, draws the curtains to black it out and lights a candle. She knows the Mays are not going to get their eight years of living, but they only need one. If the remainder of their lives is to be spent doing something worthwhile, she has to stop existing.

ROOM 731

You'd never know that somebody had just died. The place doesn't even smell like a dog has been in there. Carol knows how to turn things around.

The newest resident of room 731 reacts in the same way that most people do when they arrive at Hotel Beresford. At first, she gets a sense of former luxury from the decor of the lobby. Then there's hesitation as she steps into the old lift. Wonder as she passes the open expanse of the level-three conference area. Fear as the lift mechanism creaks her higher. Suspicion on floor five eventually gives way to trepidation as she stops on floor seven and yanks the door open.

It's vibrant with life. Music can be heard. Singing. The smell of food. All hidden behind a row of doors, one of which is hers. Lailah Sanford. Twenty-three. Blonde. Willowy. Casual. She looks like a backpacking graduate with no destination in mind. She fiddles with the room key as she walks. Part of her wants to see what other kind of person might be staying here, who her new temporary neighbours are. Another part wants to get inside her new place as quickly as possible and lock the door.

That's what she does.

The key doesn't turn at first because the door and lock are brand new. Lailah looks over her shoulder, feeling as though somebody is there, watching her, and she wiggles the key until it eventually turns. The backpack is heavy.

'Come on, you stupid...' She doesn't get to the blasphemy before the key turns and the door opens. Quickly, she shuts the door, locks it from the inside and takes a deep breath. There's a confusing aroma of citrus and coffee beans, but it isn't unpleasant.

Four steps forward and Lailah is standing on the spot where a man lay dead that morning, probably only half a day from being eaten by his own dog. She takes another deep breath. Then she walks, with purpose, into her new bedroom, where she hoists the heavy backpack from her shoulders and drops it onto the fresh sheets.

Lailah walks back to the door and tries the handle. She shakes it hard. It's locked. She's safe. Hidden. Nobody knows she is there.

She smiles, and, with a spring in her step, glides back to the bedroom, unclips the top of the backpack, turns it upside down and pours out all the money she stole. Then she lies down in it, picking it up and letting it fall over her. She kisses a handful of bills and throws them into the air.

The perfect resident for the seventh floor.

SABBATICAL

Saying that 'the Lord works in mysterious ways' is the equivalent of sticking your fingers in your ears and blowing raspberries.

Entire nations in abject poverty, starving, fighting diseases that the rest of the world have been inoculated against. All part of God's great plan, right?

War. Disaster. Oil spills. Thousands of acres of rainforest decimated. Thanks, G.

Polluted oceans, melting ice caps, reality television, Ryan Seacrest, those bugs whose entire existence is spent burrowing into children's eyes to cause blindness, this is all part of the Big Man's strategy? This has all been plotted out? Because it sounds like somebody who is making up the story as they go along. And anyone who peddles the notion that God is working mysteriously is complicit in the misery that He is causing.

He's not working in a mysterious way. He's not working at all. The mother-fucker has given up. He's on sabbatical. He must be.

A global epidemic of coronavirus was nothing to do with God, man created it. God didn't drop the bomb on Hiroshima, either. Nothing mysterious about that. It was man. Storming the Capitol wasn't God. The Columbine shooting wasn't God. The Jonestown massacre wasn't God, even if it was done in His name. Again, all committed by man.

Bundy, Trump, Zuckerberg, there's no Godly scheme to create these psychopaths. He doesn't want to take away people's empathy. He's not ensuring that two percent of the population do not develop the part of their brain that allows them to feel guilt. He's not randomly selecting children to be chastised for wearing clothes that are designed for the opposite sex. He wants a global community of followers that take responsibility for their decisions and actions, who learn from their mistakes and who, ultimately, want to do good.

This is His experiment with humanity, and free will is his get-out clause.

But, if God gets to play with people, why shouldn't the Devil?

The lift door opens into the penthouse suite of Hotel Beresford and a woman steps out into the open expanse of Mr Balliol's minimalist entrance hall. A black pencil skirt hugs her body like it knows something and her dark hair frames a face that could have been carved out of marble. She is exquisite. Poised. Elegant.

'Right on time.' Balliol appears from the side of a slatted wall, brandishing two glasses of red wine. 'Please, take one. I'd like to get started right away.'

She doesn't say a word, takes a sip of the drink and closes her eyes as though discerning the layers of flavour.

'It's good, right?' He takes the glass away from her.

She nods. It seems like a game. She is trying to be sultry, perhaps, by not saying anything, but her face looks as though she doesn't entirely understand what Balliol is saying. Perhaps English is not her first language.

He is not impressed.

'Lose the jacket.'

She does as he instructs, dropping it down onto the floor next to her feet.

She understands.

Balliol smiles.

'If you'd like to follow me into the living area...' He walks and she follows. Then he stops. 'No. Not like that. On your knees.'

Mr Balliol takes another mouthful of wine then moves over to the sofa, where he waits for his guest to arrive at his feet.

CROSSROADS

It's 1962 and a twenty-one-year-old kid is performing traditional folk songs at The Troubadour club in London. He plays the guitar and he sings. He has a decent control of the instrument, though his voice is a little nasal. Perhaps whiny. Breathy. But it is distinctive, at least.

A college drop-out, Robert Zimmerman, travelled to New York and was inspired by African-American street poets and influenced by the work of Woody Guthrie. He hit the Greenwich Village scene.

Slogging it out.

Paying his dues.

One of many trying to make it in the music industry. Plenty happy to be manufactured, some content to churn out hits for others. Zimmerman felt he had something to say. And he'd say it all over town. All over the world, if he got the chance.

Not enough were listening in Greenwich Village.

Not yet.

Zimmerman was from Duluth, at the top of Highway 61. A road that runs all the way down to New Orleans and the blues. A road that intersects Highway 49, where Robert Johnson, allegedly, sold his soul to the Devil in exchange for musical prowess and notoriety. A road that would be referenced in the title of Zimmerman's 1965 album, three years after changing his name to Bob Dylan.

There is no myth surrounding Dylan in the way that there is Robert Johnson, who died at the age of twenty-seven. Dylan would hint in interviews that he had followed a similar path to a similar crossroads to make a similar deal, himself. But this is largely disregarded as hokum.

Because it never happened.

Not like that.

Not in a way that could be told and retold and embellished.

If you think the Devil answers every single cry for help, every lonely sob for recognition or attention or fame and fortune, you are mistaken. He has minions, and even they won't bother with everyone.

Not all souls are created equal.

Mother Teresa's soul, for example, would command a higher price than that of Lyndon B. Johnson. If a hellhound could gorge on a person's essence, one could imagine that the pope's soul would have the nutritious value of a salmon fillet or bag of kale, while any reality TV show contestant would hold all the appeal of bleached white bread flour.

So, when Jenny from Idaho wants to sign away her very being for a pop career and her own fragrance, she falls short because Agnes from Oslo would give herself over to rid the oceans of pollution. One is a packet of reconstituted potato and the other is avocado on toasted wholemeal sour bread with chopped tomatoes.

Selling your soul is not easy. It shouldn't be. The decision to do so is too important.

There is no Faustian fable regarding a folk-singing Robert Zimmerman, giving away his essence in exchange for the sheet music to twenty of the most influential protest songs of an era. He didn't change his name, receive his fame and die five years later at the young age of twenty-seven.

He didn't want fame. He didn't want fortune. He wanted to say the things he felt needed to be said. He wanted to provoke. To make people think.

But he went to the crossroads and fell down on his knees.

He knew what he wanted.

Just as Robert Johnson had done, Robert Zimmerman handed over his guitar to the figure that appeared before him, but, where Johnson's legend tells how the figure tuned the guitar and handed it back, the untold story of Zimmerman is different. The figure took the guitar and smashed it against the ground.

'Keep your soul,' he said, 'you will need it more than I will.'

Keep your soul but change your name.

It is a story that cannot be told. It does not fit the mythology. Nobody would believe it, anyway. That the Devil showed compassion. Mercy. That the lord of the underworld is a supporter of the arts. That He would allow such a nutritious soul to slip through His grasp to protest against war, to give a voice to the counter-culture.

He refused to take a soul.

Wreaking havoc, that makes more sense. Swimming upstream.

It's too easy to believe that Satan is the purest of evil just because He resides in Hell, but there must be more than one level to Him, even if you only take a moment to consider His previous address.

THE PENTHOUSE

Balliol, arms stretched along the back of an Italian tan leather sofa built for six, looks down at the brunette head between his legs and he smiles as 'Blowin' in the Wind' plays through the speakers.

'Fuck, I love this song.'

The woman pauses, her mouth full, lifting her eyelids. Balliol loves that. It's wrong and it's right. Dirty yet intimate.

He looks back at her. Doesn't say a word. But she knows that he means, *Don't you dare stop.*

She shuts her eyes and continues. Balliol drops his head back against the leather and stares at the ceiling. The direction that everyone considers Heaven to be.

Yes, and how many times must a man look up, before he sees the sky?

Balliol smiles.

So obvious. A cliché. But funny, nonetheless.

Laughter is pleasure.

Shooting a load into the mouth of another anonymous, high-class beauty is pleasure.

Life is pleasure.

Living should be gratifying, satisfying and sensual.

A pleasure.

Whether you're hitting the perfect note that makes a room full of people appreciate the silence as you finish singing 'Someone To Watch over Me', or you're plunging a knife into the chest of a cheating husband, or you're drinking red wine until you fall asleep, it has to be about pleasure and fulfilment.

All of those church-going, God-fearing folk, who think the Satanic Bible is darkness and evil and blasphemous rhetoric about the anti-Christ, haven't taken the time to read and understand what could be considered the greatest self-help book of all time. A manual to make the most of existence and push aside the psychic vampires who threaten the way you value the world.

The devil doesn't really want you to hate God, He's a vital option, but he doesn't want you to live in fear. He wants you to make the absolute most of the time that you have.

RECEPTION

Carol locks her computer screen. It has been a long shift. The screen goes black and she catches a glimpse of herself in the reflection. She looks as old as she feels. Older, maybe. Despite the Botox and fillers. They can age you, too, though. Wrinkle-free and haggard.

Working through the night can be draining at Hotel Beresford. She hears Keith's voice out on the front desk. He's been here as long as she has. He's never moved up, never taken on more responsibility, seemingly content to plod through life in mediocrity. He knows what he wants but it doesn't amount to much.

And that's okay. It works for Keith.

It works for a lot of people.

Carol wants to have somebody to go home to. She wants someone to be waiting for her. To cook her dinner. To talk to her about anything other than the hotel she runs so efficiently. To take off her clothes. To look at her like she's about to be devoured by passion.

She had that once.

But it was taken from her.

The clock on the wall tells Carol that there are three minutes left of her shift. Three minutes until she can leave behind the man who died in room 731 and the woman who has taken his place, who is clearly up to no good. Carol can turn her back on the mayhem of the seventh floor and debauchery of the penthouse, for a few hours, at least.

The third-floor conference is in a couple of days. Carol feels on top of the organisation but knows how much work these things can be on the day. Sales guys always start with bravado before ebbing into competition, drunkenness, demands and eventual lechery. There are days when Carol is dying for someone to grab her arse or compliment her breasts, but that day is never conference day at Hotel Beresford.

Keith is singing. He does that a lot. A technique to stop him stuttering so much, apparently, but Carol suspects it's something of a passion for her effeminate, cravat-wearing colleague. She waits for her machine to shut down fully, locks the drawer of her desk and steps out to reception.

'Cole Porter again, Keith?' She's teasing him.

'Oh, you love it,' he grins. Then he grabs Carols hands and starts to sing. '*Night and daaaaay. You are the one.*' He lifts a hand and she twirls beneath it and laughs.

'You're an idiot.' She means it affectionately. 'Now, look. The place is almost full. There's enough left on fourth for a few walk-ins. Please try to turn away the serial killers, though, okay? We've already had one death today.'

Keith doesn't know if Carol is joking or not. But she turns and leaves before he has the chance to ask.

'In a hurry, Carol. Big date tonight, huh?' he calls after her.

She turns back. 'Bath and my vibrator is about all I can handle after this shift.' Carol winks but a part of her tears inside. She doesn't even have the energy to get herself off. The loneliness is getting to her. Maybe she has forgotten how to love.

She nods a goodbye to Ollie, who is standing security by the entrance. In the car park, she notices the dog in his car and shakes her head. It has torn his back seat apart. She tries the handle to see if it is unlocked and she can set the thing free into the wild like she had instructed, but it's locked. Part of her appreciates that the tough ex-soldier has a softer side that people probably don't know about. And she wonders what they might think of her.

Workaholic.

Beholden to Mr Balliol.

Lonely.

Lonely.

Lonely.

Carol's house is not far enough away from work. If she gets the angle right, she can see part of the lit sign of the hotel from her bedroom window. She's away from the drugs and prostitution and Skid Row element of the city outskirts, but the red light of Hotel Beresford is a reminder that it is the one constant in her life and is always watching.

Her house is cold. She flicks a switch and the heating whirs to life. There's a microwaveable meal in the fridge. A choice, in fact. A mild chicken curry or three-bean chilli that is a day past its sell-by date. She stabs at the plastic of the chilli with her fork and nukes it for three minutes, pouring herself a glass of red wine while she waits.

And she sighs.

Five minutes later, she's halfway through her dinner, all the way through her wine and two candidates down on her dating website. She wants to update the profile picture she uses because no man has been able to hide his disappointment when they meet her in person even though she smiles at bald, beer-bellied Brian, who clearly has a younger brother with hair, who works out and is, actually, over six feet tall.

There are six direct messages to read through, but Carol has been at this long enough to know that they are not all offers of eligibility. There are no professors who want to discuss old black-and-white movies over a bottle of Châteauneuf-du-Pape. Nobody wants to go for a long walk. Nobody cares about a good sense of humour.

Two of the messages are insulting. One calls her ugly, the other calls her a troll. His profile has already been shut down but, for some reason, the message remains. The damage is done.

One is a picture of a penis. No message. Just the world's ugliest appendage. Not small. Not impressive. Certainly not sexy.

Another guy has no picture but plenty to say about his dick and how she should suck it and how he would make her come with the thunder, and she knows that if that were true he would have no need for a dating website, even in a world where people no longer know how to communicate with one another.

The fifth guy compliments the way she looks but it's obvious that he just wants to get laid. And he can't use punctuation, which is a huge turn-off for Carol.

She looks over at the bottle of wine on the kitchen worktop. There's one last message to read. She wonders whether it's best to steel herself before opening it. Surely, the law of averages means that one person out of the six has read through the details of Carol's profile, they like what they see, they have similar interests, they want to meet up, maybe watch a play, go to dinner.

Carol finishes the last of her dinner. Out of date but still tasted okay. She clicks the message. She doesn't want to allow herself to be hopeful but a part of her always is. It has to be.

She clicks.

A thirty-something white guy. Strong head of hair. Designer glasses. Well groomed. Plays basketball. Loves dogs but has an allergy towards them. Listens to country music. Reads a book each week.

Hope grows.

No kids but not allergic. Plays the piano. Volunteers. Owns his own business.

Sounds too good to be true.

Carol scrolls.

Apparently, this guy, calls himself Jack Warren, wants to put every inch he has into every hole she's got. Carol wants to cry. There are no good guys left. She lucked out once and now everything is ash.

Calls-Himself-Jack-Warren, continues: *I'm staying at the Hotel Beresford for three nights. Room 420. Knock any time after six. I'll be waiting.*

ROOM 420

Danny Elwes is a prick. Grade A. Top choice. Meat head. Ask anyone.

Start with his mother. A woman so sorry she ever spread her legs for Elwes Senior, she curses her womb, every day, for being such a hospitable environment for his demon seed. What good could ever come from something created out of that much vodka and that many bad decisions?

Ask his co-workers about the misogyny, the dodgy claims against expenses, the work trips to strip joints, his casual racism.

He has several online aliases. Some he uses to troll female celebrities on social media, others are to write one-star reviews for books or films that he deems to be too popular. And there's the fake dating profiles.

Some have even worked.

When he knows he has to go to another city for work, he sets up another persona, then taps into whoever seems geographically viable. The time and effort it takes to trawl through women, looking for vulnerability or desperation. The energy required to read every status update by the latest reality-show drop-out. It could be put to better use.

Danny *could* learn to play the piano.

Danny *could* volunteer somewhere.

Or play basketball. Or listen to country music.

The only thing that's true about his Jack Warren persona is that Danny does read a book each week. It's one of the less prickish things about him. But he ruins things by hiding it or deprecating the pastime.

The other truth is that he *is* in room 420 of Hotel Beresford. And he'll be there all night. He's staying for three days, like he said; wanted to get there early for the conference. Pitch his tent, so to speak. A lot of sales guys do this. For the same reason. It's an opportunity to lie like a starfish in bed without the wife's knee in their back. Or it's a chance to play away.

What happens at the conference, stays at the conference.

Danny has been drinking whatever he can find in the minibar. He opens his laptop to see whether any women have been caught by the cast of his net.

Rejections.

Many.

Not all of them. Some haven't responded. Some are teasing. Some are playing a game. He sees that one person, Carol, has read but not responded and is currently active on the site.

He types.

Hey. You there? I'm in my room ... waiting.

He signs it *Jack.*

And he waits.

Three dots appear below his message. She's answering him. Danny/Jack sits up. He's excited. Part of him doesn't really care if it's a rejection, it's the anticipation that's the rush. The way that a stand-up comedian still gets a buzz whether the audience is in fits of hysteria or each joke bombs. Just being there and trying something out has its own thrill.

He remembers Carol's profile among the twenty that he settled on. He could see her former beauty, but this isn't about going deeper than the surface, it isn't some outreach programme. It isn't benevolence or sensing someone's spirit. Danny can see that Carol is broken. And he likes that. She had loved somebody so completely and then they died, and she has never recovered.

He wants to fuck an older chick who has fucked up what probably used to be a stunning face. He gets off on destroying things that are beautiful but, if he can't do that, he's more than happy to hit the last nail in the coffin.

Because he is a prick.

His mother was attentive and present and supportive. Her family were wealthy. His father was largely absent. Boo fucking hoo. He had everything he needed and he still turned out this way. Lucifer wasn't born this bad.

Danny Elwes hunches over the keyboard, saying to himself that he is going to bang a different broad every night on this trip. The laptop screen lights his face in a way that makes him look maniacal.

Then Carol answers.

And the colour drains.

Put it back in your pants, Danny.

How does she know his real name? He panics.

You're not my type. And don't think the lesbians next door are going to grease themselves up for that dolly mixture dick, either.

You can turn right out of the main entrance and walk until you hit a hooker or talk to Keith on reception if you'd like to be more discreet. But leave me the fuck alone.

He slams the laptop shut and jumps to his feet. His heart is pounding so loudly he can hardly hear the lesbians next door. Danny looks around the room to see if there is a camera somewhere, watching him. How else could she know?

He goes over to the minibar. There's a miniature bottle of Jim Beam left. Danny thinks it's disgusting but he unscrews it, downs it, grimaces and throws the empty bottle onto the floor.

And he breathes. Slowly.

In – one, two, three.

Out – one, two, three.

The panic subsides a little.

This wouldn't happen to a normal person. A nice person. A decent person. Anyone with a conscience would feel anxious or caught out.

It has, at least, registered that he picked the wrong person, that she's got his number and knows who he is, and where he is. She could be psychotic. She could come for him. Should he message her back?

Apologise? Leave the hotel? These are the questions Danny Elwes should be asking himself.

But they're not.

Danny has one thought. He has a choice to make.

Either he turns right out of the entrance until he hits a hooker, or he goes downstairs and talks to Keith.

UPTOWN

It was easy enough. Carol is tired and lonely and still grieving but she is brilliant at her job. You say the number of any room at Hotel Beresford and she can tell you who is inside – their name and a detail about them.

728 – Danielle Ortega. Beautiful. Brilliant. Jazz singer. Effortlessly sexy. Down on her luck but making ends meet. Hoping for a break.

514 – @travelboi. Twenties. Blogger. Real name: Evan Rothschild. Family money. Privilege. Short let. In the city for a few days as he has meetings to turn his travel blog into a TV series. You'd expect him to be a spoilt brat, but he seems pleasant and appreciative of the things that are happening to him. (Though unaware that they are more likely to happen to him due to the advantages he was born into.)

803 – I.P. Wayatt. Writer. Recluse. Wrote the bestselling satirical novel, *An Epidemic of Compassion*, then disappeared. Quiet. Drinks too much. He's been at Hotel Beresford for over a year.

Penthouse – Mr Balliol. No indication of his first name. Possibly owns the entire building. Mysterious. Charming. Straight-talking. Always kind to Carol. Enjoys red wine, women and tailored suits. Always around yet somehow never really there.

001 – Carol. Honest. Dependable. But stuck in a loop. Uses work to distract her from the heartache she feels as a widow. Doesn't talk about it with anybody. The room is a crash pad. Just a place to rest her head between shifts. A place to possibly dream. Between the nightmares of real life.

420 – Danny Elwes. Slimeball sales guy. A dime a dozen. One of many in an ill-fitting suit, bought off the rack, and a shirt with a

middle-management pocket on the chest. Feeling important to be representing the company at the conference. Ignoring the fact that those higher up never attend because it's grunt work. The kind of guy you would like to see punched in the face.

She knows them all.

All she had to do was put in a quick call to Keith to confirm and then she could message the piece of shit back.

What started as a crappy night just got a whole lot better for putting that fake in his place.

Carol is tired and full of food. She takes the bottle of red wine upstairs, strips off and gets into bed. She drinks. And she thinks, if Danny Elwes had played things more sensitively, it could have gone better for both of them that night. Sure, it would have been an education for him and unfulfilling for her, but at least she'd have been with another human. Close. For a while.

She opens the top drawer of her bedside table. Her vibrator is tucked behind a box of jewellery and some old papers. Gathering dust like its owner.

There's no impetus to take it out. Pleasure is fleeting. Carol shuts the drawer and fills her glass. She flicks on the television and wonders what happened to the pleasures in her life.

There is a reason why The Beresford has always been run by women. Women understand sacrifice.

PENTHOUSE

Balliol is seconds from orgasm when the pain shoots through his head.

He screams, bringing his hands to his brow. As he bucks, the woman attached to him scrapes her teeth along the length of his dick, and he screams again.

'Jesus fucking Christ,' he shouts as his penis flings back and hits his stomach. He pushes her away with his foot, one hand still on his head. She falls back but doesn't take her eyes off him.

'What's wrong?' she asks.

'Pesky fucking migraine. Been happening all week.'

'You were close to giving me your gift.'

'No.' Balliol stands up. 'Don't call it that, it's creepy.'

'What would you have me call it?' She lifts herself back to her knees.

'You know what, I'd rather you didn't call it anything. It's better if you don't speak.' His hand goes back to his head. 'Wait in the bedroom for me. I need to sort this out.'

She does as he says but she breaks character for a moment, and Balliol notices.

'Hey,' he calls after her. She turns back from the bedroom door. 'Cum. Just call it cum. Okay?'

She nods. Turns.

And Balliol disappears.

*

Mr May is downstairs, listening to the Sonny Clarke Trio and searching for places nearby that will allow him to do a wing walk.

He has found one that will let anyone from the age of eighteen to eighty get strapped to the top of a biplane and be flown around as long as they do not weigh more than eighty-five kilos.

He reads through some of the other requirements, nodding as he goes.

Then he speaks to himself. 'Well, how am I to know if I can withstand wind pressure as we fly at speeds up to one hundred and twenty miles per hour?' He calls upstairs to his wife: 'Darling...'

Mrs May does not hear. She is focussed on what she is doing. The room is dark apart from one candle. She is sweating and the saliva in her mouth is thick. Her knuckles are white from clenching her fists in fury.

And now she is not alone.

'Jesus Christ.' She jumps at the sight of the figure.

'From all the words you've been saying in here, I think you know that's not even close.'

'You're...'

'Tired? Overwrought? Aroused?' He looks down. 'Not much I can do about that, you caught me in the middle of something.'

'...Him,' Mrs May finishes.

'Balliol. Some call me Mr Balliol.'

'This feels like a dream. It must be.'

'I assure you, nobody has prayed as hard as you in a very long time. You have my attention. I usually send somebody else out to these kinds of things.'

'What kinds of things?'

'Come now, Mrs May, let's not mess around with the foreplay. You have been calling out to me for almost a week now. I'm guessing that you tried my former employer but He wasn't listening, am I correct?'

She nods.

'That is usually the way of these things. I have one simple question for you now and a second one after you answer. Firstly, what do you want?'

She doesn't hesitate. 'Time.'

Balliol looks at her. His arousal lessening. He knows that whatever she means by 'time' she means it with every fibre of her being. The way she has been calling out to Him has been like a white-hot needle scratching across the surface of his cerebellum, occasionally pushing in an inch or two.

'The doctors have given my husband less than a month to live. I don't understand what he could have done that God smite him so harshly. We may only have a couple of weeks.' She grits her teeth and inhales to stop herself from crying and looking weak.

'So what is it that you want?'

'I love him dearly. I love our life together. There is still so much left for us to do. He's making a list. It's too late. We should have made it together years ago. I don't want him to die.'

'Everybody dies, Mrs May. You can't stop that. So what is it, exactly, that you want?'

'A year. We can get everything done in a year.'

'My second question, though I'm sure I know the answer, is this worth surrendering your soul for?'

The old lady gives Him a look that says, *Why the fuck would I go through all of this if that wasn't the case?*

Balliol hands Mrs May a rolled piece of paper.

'Read through this contract and sign.' He hands her a pen.

The ones who really mean business never bother to read the contract that gives up their very essence. The terms and conditions do not require legal counsel. It's incredibly simple. You get the one thing you want and, in return, you hand over your soul in perpetuity. That means forever.

It is difficult for humans to truly contemplate the magnitude of that time frame. Some think that the roaring twenties was a long time ago. It's even crazier when you consider that Jesus was around two thousand years ago. The mind blows to ponder that a triceratops was walking around eighty million years ago. And that time is like a second passing when etched on the timeline of *forever.*

It's enough to make a person realise their insignificance.

Mrs May does not read the contract. She signs away her soul without blinking.

It is gone.

In perpetuity.

'I shall see you again in a year.'

And then he is gone. Back to the penthouse of Hotel Beresford to give another nameless beauty his *gift*.

There's a knock at the door. Mr May walks in and turns on the light.

'Darling, I've been calling you. Is everything alright?'

She is exhausted and scared and relieved. She has given them more time but it is still running out. She looks at her husband with the purest of love, but it's also tinged with a sadness that she has had to do what she just did. Why could her God not have answered?

'I'm fine. I'm fine. I was just saying a little prayer. What is it that you need? Are you feeling okay?'

'I feel absolutely fine. I was just looking into something and I wondered whether you know what kind of wind pressure I can handlc...'

His sentence sits in the air for a moment.

Neither of them says anything.

Then both start to laugh, uncontrollably.

The clock ticks.

ROOM 734

'Eat, Otis.'

Odie knows his mother is annoyed because she's used his real name.

'Your daddy ain't coming home again. Eat up.' She drinks the vodka and tonic that Odie poured for her.

'Ever?'

'Oh, Otis. I don't know. He's done this before. I'm sure he'll be back soon enough. He gets caught up, that's all.' She's in a rut, covering for Sam seems so natural, now.

He knows she's lying. He's just happy to be allowed to have his dinner, which has been going cold while they've been waiting for a man who is not coming home.

They eat their rice in silence. Odie hardly chews before swallowing. Diana is distracted. She watches the clock on the wall, adjusts her skirt every few seconds. She's nervous. If Sam comes home now and they have started their dinner without him, she'll see the back of his hand and poor Odie might get the wooden spoon across the back of his legs.

Diana adds up, in her head, how long they can stay at Hotel Beresford on the money she has saved if Sam hasn't returned by the end of the week. She can't take on any more clients because the routine of their days has fallen through and Sam might come knocking while she is pleasuring another man in their bed.

She wants to cry.

How did she get here?

How can she get out and save her sweet boy?

A hand touches her arm.

'Mama, don't cry. It's going to be okay. I'm here.' He smiles at her, his eyes wide and hopeful, his teeth too big for his mouth. So innocent. 'I'm here, Mama.' He says it again, like he can protect her. She wants him to be a kid, not grow up too fast because his life is so shit.

'Odie, you are a brave boy. But I'm the one who looks after *you*. That's how it's supposed to be. You have to go to school tomorrow. You're smart. And I know you've almost finished that book you've been reading.'

He nods. 'I do want to go to the library again.' He feels better that she's not calling him Otis anymore. 'You want me to do the dishes? You haven't even started your dinner.'

Diana tells her son that she's not hungry tonight. That she will clear the table while he finishes his book. That all she needs is another drink and a long bath. 'Grab yourself a chocolate-chip cookie from the jar, I just need to go to the bedroom.'

Odie doesn't think twice. He takes his treat, picks up his book and lies on the sofa even though he's supposed to be upright when he's eating. His mother isn't watching, though. She's moving shoeboxes aside in the wardrobe to get to her stash, hidden behind a loose board.

It's starting to add up. She's a couple of blowjobs away from five grand.

Still not enough.

She looks at her hands. If Sam doesn't come back, she could sell her wedding ring. Sam left his Nike trainers, she could get some money for those. Odie has nothing. No old toys, no designer clothing, all the books he reads are borrowed.

Diana Walker has little of any worth to sell.

Nothing but her body. She's beaten, regularly. But worse is that she has been beaten down. She doesn't know who she is anymore.

She could get her son back into education, consistently, and turn tricks all day, save every penny. Take Odie and get away for good. The only problem with her plan is that she would need to go somewhere cheap, to begin with. And there is nowhere around that is cheaper than Hotel Beresford.

Diana Walker is stuck.

No way out.

And people will try anything when they are desperate.

She has that drink. Then another. And another. She pours herself a sherry to take into the bath, where she soaks her body. It's tender and bruised and throbbing between her legs where every man who fucks her seems to be trying to prove something to himself. She shuts her eyes for a moment and tries to relax, and everything is ruined when she hears Sam shouting.

ROOM 728

While normal people are ending their days, Danielle Ortega is eating eggs and drinking coffee because her time is just beginning. She's singing at some downtown dive bar that only stays open because a few decent comics use the place to test new material before performing at decent venues in the city. The pay is okay and she usually draws a crowd because there's always the possibility that somebody who has actually made it might show up.

Sam Walker is kicking at the inside of the cupboard door.

She tried to reason with him, tell him that she would untie him and send him back home if he agreed never to come near her ever again. He responded by saying, 'When I get out of this, I'm going to fucking kill you.' He will certainly have to work on his negotiation skills if he is ever going to bag that job as secretary-general for the United Nations.

Danielle taped his mouth shut after he started shouting and shut the door on him again.

She should have just dragged him out in the hallway after hitting him with that ashtray. She knows that now. His wife would have found him and he would have had to make something up out of embarrassment. Now he's embarrassed and emasculated and just plain pissed.

Just as Diana Walker can't see a way out of her hell-hole room at Hotel Beresford, Danielle Ortega sees no way out of the situation she's stupidly put herself in.

This is the seventh floor.

She knows Sam can't stay there. He's starting to make a noise now. He's kicking at the door, and somebody must have heard him shouting. Still, Danielle sits at the kitchen worktop with her eggs and her coffee, calmly contemplating.

Sam kicks.

She tries to ignore it. Swigs her coffee.

Sam kicks again. This time, there's a sound of wood splitting.

Danielle looks over at her coffee table, then at her record player.

Sam keeps kicking. He's using both feet now. Danielle can see the bottom corner of the door moving each time he hits it.

She lays down her cutlery and stands up. Her limbs like vapour, she glides across to her collection of vinyl and pulls out *The Black Saint and the Sinner Lady* by Charles Mingus. The sound of 'Solo Dancer' is not enough to drown out the kicking but as soon as the first note is played, Danielle disappears into the song. It's all she hears.

She lights a cigarette and moves over to the window. She opens it, the cold air pushing inside with pollution from the city just beyond. Danielle is intensely urban, exhaust fumes are her perfume, car horns are the voices of angels.

A cigarette hanging loosely from her top lip, Danielle Ortega starts to undress in front of the window. If anybody wants to watch, they can watch. She finishes her cigarette, looking down on the street outside. The thrum of nighttime life. She flicks the butt outside.

Sam kicks at the door.

Danielle leans over the coffee table and picks up half of her old ashtray. She drifts across the room with the music then stops outside her shoe cupboard, swaying on the spot as the mood of the song swings towards something more tumultuous.

Sam kicks hard. The door bursts open. He is lying on his back, sweating from the effort, his hands clasped together beneath him. He looks up at Danielle. His neighbour. *That woman down the hall.* She is naked. Beautiful. Wind rushes in from outside, making the curtains billow, and the light behind drops her into a deep, sexy silhouette. If his mouth wasn't taped up it would be open in awe. Just as Mr Balliol's is as he watches from his room of screens.

And he keeps watching, as Danielle Ortega sways to the music, blue smoke bouncing off her hips, her eyes shut.

And he watches as she brings that broken ashtray down into Sam Walker's head. Five times. Six times. Seven.

Blood on her hands and face.

He watches.

The naked singer stands, takes the ashtray to the sink and washes it clean. She showers, reappears with a towel wrapped around her, another cigarette in her mouth. She gets dressed and finishes her eggs before shutting the splintered door, picking up her bag, putting on her jacket and exiting room 728 of Hotel Beresford as though nothing important happened today.

CROSSROADS

Mrs May is a seller. Currently, she is acting as the custodian of her soul for the next year but, as per contract, Mr Balliol now owns all rights, title and interest in said property.

And her husband can never know.

But this is a man who has been with the same woman for the majority of their lives. He knows her. Parts of his body may be irreparably disintegrating but his brain is not one of them. And he still has his heart, even if he says it belongs to his wife.

'You look decidedly chipper for a woman whose soulmate could pop his clogs at any moment.'

'Oh, don't be so glib.'

'What is going with you?'

'Nothing.'

'I may die tomorrow but I was not born yesterday.'

'The gallows humour really isn't your schtick. Why don't you show me your list?'

'You're trying to change the subject.'

'I'm not. I'm not. Show me the list you've been working on. My mood is related to that.'

Mr May forces himself up from his seat with a groan. It isn't that he is old or sick or stiff with arthritis, it's something that he has always done. He made that noise when he got out of a chair at thirty. It's these details that upset Mrs May. The tiny subtleties that only they share and she will never hear again.

Even the things that annoy her about her husband will be missed when she spends an eternity surrounded by fire, cracking rocks with a hammer or whatever soul-sellers do in Hell. She knows she should have paid more attention to the contract.

Mr May returns from the desk with a piece of paper and lays it on the coffee table for his wife to peruse. He sits down. She casts her eye over it, running her finger across the page as she reads.

'Do you have a pen?'

'One moment.' He gulps down another quip about being on death row and creaks his way to his feet again, going back to the desk and returning, moments later, with a ballpoint.

'Here you are, madam. Anything else I can get you while I still have the ability to get to my feet? A cup of tea, perhaps. I could whip you up a scone.'

She gives him one of her looks but he knows she is joking. Because he knows her better than anybody. And something is up.

'Sit back down. Take this pen. Take your list, and cross off number eight.'

Mr May scans down the list he thinks he will never get to complete.

He stops at number eight. He looks dejected.

'Oh, darling. What are you talking about? We are never going to go on a safari. I don't have long enough.' He chokes on the last word, he wants to be strong.

'Well, you'd better last because I've booked it. Now cross it off.'

Mr May doesn't know if this is a joke. More of that gallows humour he has just been chastised about. It seems cruel. And his wife is not a cruel person. She is thoughtful and devout and fearless. And maybe all of those traits add up to somebody who would book a three-week safari for a man who isn't supposed to see out the month.

It's not a joke. His wife has booked and paid for the trip out of their savings.

He tries to argue. That it's a waste, that she will need that money when he is gone.

'Now, you listen to me.' Mrs May looks her husband dead in the eyes. 'What's done is done. It's booked. We're going. What use is that money when you're dead? Best to use it while we're alive.' She leans across and clasps her hands around his. 'The doctors are wrong, okay? You have more time. I know it.'

There is a kindness and sincerity in her eyes that almost makes Mr May believe that what she says is true. She's convincing. He tilts his head to the side slightly, but figures he will go along with her, even if it is delusional.

'You believe me?' she asks.

'I want to, I do.'

'Everything on that list. We are going to cross it off.'

She's in denial, he thinks. But he goes with it.

'Even number twenty-three?' He looks awkward. Mrs May takes the piece of paper back and reads. It's something sexual. She wasn't sure he still had it in him. Her eyes widen and she blushes. It's not something she ever considered but if she's given away her soul, she may as well offer her husband that part of her.

It's information that he can take with him to his grave and a moment that she will have to remember for all eternity. But, apparently, this is what she has signed up for.

Mrs May looks at her husband again. There's a little of the Devil in him.

Of course there is.

She picks up the pen, crosses off number twenty-three, takes her husband by the hand and makes a subtle motion with her head for him to come with her.

He forgets he has cancer.

If he manages to get through number twenty-three, it may just be a heart attack that kills him.

ROOM 728

Things are turning.

Danielle Ortega blew the audience away at her set, downtown. There's something about angst that lends itself to jazz vocals.

Hotel Beresford is quieter at this time, when late night wants to give way to early morning. There are a few suits in the lobby. Keith looks surprisingly fresh for the night shift. His cravat is impeccable, still. Some people are coming down in the lift – gamblers, looking for the next hustle – but Danielle wants to go up. Shift workers may be starting their day but to Ms Ortega, it's still the middle of the night.

And it suits her.

It's usually much lighter by the time she gets home but those are the days when a man isn't tied up in her apartment.

She kicks off her shoes as soon as she steps back into the room, rather than going to her closet. She doesn't want to deal with Sam Walker now. He can wait.

There's a routine.

She takes out *Lady Sings the Blues* and turns it up. It doesn't matter how loud your music is on the seventh floor. Any music you like, any volume, any time of day. She lights a cigarette and drags it into her lungs with her eyes closed. Tapping her foot, it's like she's with Billie Holiday in that room.

Danielle Ortega opens the window and pokes one leg outside so that she straddles the ledge. Effortlessly cool. She moves slowly. Adagio speed. A woman content to feel blue. She stares across to the city. A few windows down are the couple who likes to start their days with a shared joint. It seems like they sometimes like to end with one, too. She lifts her eyes towards them and they smile back.

They seem happy. Danielle never sees them out in the hallway or in the lobby but, she thinks, there must be something that has placed them on her floor with the cast of down-and-outs and never-going-anywheres she usually sees in the hallways.

The song changes to 'Travelin' Light', and she leans back against the window frame. She glances over at the cupboard. She'll have to clean things up. Maybe Sam is just badly hurt. She knows he was bleeding but he could be okay. She knows how hard she hit him but she doesn't know how hard his skull is.

She sighs.

It was such a high to perform for that crowd. That's what she wants every night. She wants people to hear what is in her heart. She wants to convey emotion through her voice. Something that people will react to, respond to, want to tell others about.

Danielle Ortega knows what she wants.

And Sam Walker is going to fuck that up for her because he couldn't curb his compulsion to gamble away what he earned and he couldn't stay sober or keep his dick in his pants. And he thought he had the right to put his hands on a woman who did not want his hands anywhere near her.

She shakes her head.

'Fuck,' she says out loud to nobody, and flicks her cigarette butt out onto the street. The wind is picking up and takes it over the road.

It's time to deal with what she did.

Billie Holiday starts to sing that she 'must have that man' and Danielle can't help but smirk as she floats across the room.

She looks at the handle and takes a breath, peers down where the door split from Sam's kicks. It's no longer split. Danielle crouches and strokes the bottom corner, smooth and clean. No splinters. Like nothing happened.

She stands quickly. Unnatural for her. Grabs the handle. And turns.

She steps back in case he tries to kick out at her.

Sam doesn't kick.

Sam is gone.

THE PENTHOUSE

Everything to do with the building is an experiment. And at its helm, Mr Balliol. Like Milgram, observing his mice, running around the maze, searching for the dark, forgetting that they were electrocuted just the day before for doing exactly the same thing.

And, like so many experiments, there is no certainty of the outcome.

Things don't always go the way you hoped or planned.

Most of the time, you have to watch and learn.

Hotel Beresford, as it stands now, with its grand reception, third-floor conference area and short- and longer-term lets above, is the latest incarnation. It's been Club Beresford, Beresford Mansions, a brothel, a courthouse, a castle. Each with its own unique manner of surveying humanity and recruiting souls.

It's difficult to understand how long this has been occurring, for the mind to fathom the scope of such a project.

Imagine counting to one million, a second at a time. It would take around eleven and a half days. Now count to a billion in the same way. How much longer would that take? At least another thirty-one years.

Try counting back to the very beginning.

Mr Balliol watches the screens as the petri dish of humanity within the walls of the hotel divides, mutates or grows mould. Voyeuristic. Fascinating. He pokes and prods and waits to see the decisions that people make. Now, he views room 728 as Danielle Ortega, for the first time since she arrived, dims the glisten of coolness she exudes. She is panicked. She looks around the room. She pulls back the curtains frantically. She runs to the bathroom, maybe because she suspects it's a decent hiding place, but it's also the only room with a lock.

Nothing there.

Sam is gone.

Danielle sighs. Mr Balliol doesn't have sound on the video but he sees her shoulders rise and drop as she resigns. And turns back to smoke. She pulses back down the hallway and into the lounge. Over to the window, she opens it quickly and leans out, one hand on each side of the frame. She looks down. Homeless people turn over in doorways of shops that will open in an hour. Taxis meander past the front of the hotel, looking to pick up somebody who wishes the rooms were charged by the hour.

Balliol stands. He doesn't like it. This is not what she does. She straddles the ledge in her trademark languid style. That's how she sits. With a cigarette hanging from her mouth as though resigned to her fate and station in life. But there's something more impulsive about her.

He thinks she might jump.

A prod. A push. It doesn't always take that much.

He doesn't want her to.

Balliol enjoys watching her.

Then she screams. He hears it from the penthouse. She isn't jumping. She's howling at the moon. She's frustrated and artistic and angry and passionate and confused. And she can't seem to catch a Goddamned break.

Balliol has seen this kind of person before. A lost soul. Too old for their day. Like they should have been born in a different time.

It makes him think. Danielle Ortega should not be here. Perhaps this whole ordeal with Sam Walker will make her want to leave. And she should be able to leave. Not everyone who stays on the seventh floor has to kill or die or screw up their life in some way.

Maybe there is something to this free-will concept after all.

An idea for a future incarnation of the building, perhaps.

Balliol watches Danielle. In his head, he counts to a million. A billion. Longer. He could tell her to jump. Push her. See who occupies her room next. But she's interesting. He decides to pull her back in.

A loud knock on Danielle's door drags her back to reality. The same thing happens a few doors down. Danielle flies to her peephole. She doesn't want to go out into the hallway. It might be Sam, back to make good on his promise to kill her.

Another loud knock startles her and she lets out a 'fuck' as she jumps back. And the same thing happens a few doors down. Danielle peers through the hole once more. There's nothing. She chances it. The chain is on the door. It won't hold Sam back if he wants to get in but it will buy her a second. She hopes.

The light comes in as the door is opened, slightly ajar but enough to get a picture of the outside. Danielle sees the long, scraggly blonde hair of a woman coming out of Jerry's old place. Room 731. She's looking up and down the hall and spots Danielle, squinting through the crack in her doorway.

'Hey. You see somebody go past here?' she shouts down to her.

Danielle doesn't answer.

'Some fucker just knocked on my door a couple of times and ran off. Must be kids, eh?'

Danielle smiles to herself. This woman is barely older than a child herself.

'Same here. Twice, they knocked.' She is still talking through the gap. The scraggly blonde shakes her head.

'Where would they go?' Danielle probes.

'What?'

'Where would they go? The kids. It's a dead end down there and that lift is as slow as shit. The stairwell is right at the end, too.'

'Some speedy kids, I guess.'

'Maybe you're right.'

Danielle thinks the small talk is over. The seventh floor of Hotel Beresford isn't always a place to get to know your neighbours, but this woman is now walking towards her door.

'Hey,' she says, 'I'm Lailah, by the way. Just moved in over there for the week.'

Danielle remembers a time when she thought it was only going to be a week, too. She shuts the door, takes off the chain and opens her door properly, revealing herself in all her jazz-singing, whisky-drenched, smoke-hazed glory.

'Holy shit, you are a beautiful woman.' Lailah seems genuinely taken aback.

Danielle doesn't know what to say. Men try it on all the time at the clubs. She doesn't know why, she doesn't put anything out there that makes it seem like she is available or interested, she thinks. And she is certainly not in a place where other women compliment her. Hell, it all seems like women want to be strong and equal and independent but they continue to tear one another down on the internet.

'I'm sorry, I didn't mean to embarrass you, I just couldn't quite see you at first through that gap in your door and then you step out of your room like you're stepping out on stage to sing a song or something...'

'I am a singer.'

'Well, ho-lee-sheeet, if that ain't the perfect job for you, then I don't know what is.'

Danielle smiles. She doesn't feel embarrassed but perhaps she does flush a little.

'What's your name, singer?'

'Danielle.'

'Danielle, I am a bit of a night owl, and I'm guessing from the looks of you, you're just getting home.' The singer nods. 'You let me know where you're singing next and I will come along to see what all the fuss is about, okay? Maybe you and I can grab a drink afterwards and you can tell me the good places to go around here.'

'Sure thing.'

'Maybe I can find myself a good man, while I'm at it.' Lailah starts to walk off.

'I don't know how good they'll be,' Danielle calls after her.

Lailah turns back. 'Well, singer, it's been a while, so I don't know how good they have to be, just as long as they're breathing.' And she disappears back into room 731 like a tornado.

The singer secures her door from the inside. Balliol watches. She glides again, movement like liquid fire. She lights up a cigarette, straddles her window ledge and resumes her usual routine and demeanour.

And so begins another Beresford experiment. The ballad of the singer and the thief.

DOWNTOWN

Anybody wanting to sing jazz or the blues understands the beauty of Billie Holiday's voice. None more than Danielle Ortega. It's deep and raspy but sometimes sounds like a wounded animal. Because she has soul. She understands struggle. She knows what it is like to be beaten down and experience prejudice in its many guises.

Danielle doesn't have that.

But she does still have soul.

Her anguish comes from elsewhere. The pain she draws on to give her performances poignancy comes from a feeling of regret – the most damning and debilitating of all emotions.

Danielle's parents split and her father died. Millions of people end their relationships, their marriages. It happens all the time. Almost as often as people losing their parents entirely. Danielle loved her parents. One no more than the other. But she was slightly estranged from her father towards the end of his life because he seemed to give up. To stop taking care of himself and his mental wellbeing.

She didn't know what to do. He didn't want her help. He just wanted to be left alone.

So she obeyed his wish. And he went into hospital. And he never came out. And Danielle didn't get the chance to put things right or tell him that she loved him. She didn't get the opportunity to tell him that he had disappointed her. That he failed. She didn't get to tell him anything.

And it weighs on her.

It drags her down.

But she doesn't behave like her father did. She won't let the grief destroy her. When Danielle Ortega has to perform one of those spotlight-on-her-face, goosebump-inducing songs, she sings it to her father. She pictures him a few rows back, watching her, proudly. And she focusses on telling him all the things she never got to say. And she can use this technique over and over because she never gets any closure.

She can't.

And it's captivating.

There was no way that Danielle was going to sleep now that Sam had mysteriously vanished from her room – even if things like this happen at Hotel Beresford, they've never happened to her. She had to get out and she took a chance on the night owl's door.

'How about that drink?'

'Now?'

'I'm on a high from earlier. There's some late-night places you won't find in guides or online. Some open-mic shit that might not be your bag but they serve drinks until late.'

That was an hour ago. And Danielle is on her third song.

Lailah can't take her eyes off her new seventh-floor neighbour. She's developing something of a crush. For the duration of that song – 'Someone To Watch over Me' – Lailah forgets where she is and why she is there and the fact that somebody is going to come looking for their money, soon.

And Danielle doesn't even see her. Because she is staring at an empty seat that she pictures her father sitting on, wearing that green Oakland sweatshirt he refused to throw out. She wants to believe that, even though she didn't get to say all the things she had to say to him, he is still looking down on her. Watching over her.

The song finishes.

The crowd claps. There are whistles. The lights come up.

Danielle's father disappears.

'Holy shit, that was amazing.' Lailah is buzzing.

'Thank you.'

There's no false modesty or self-deprecation from Danielle. She knows that she has something and she is professional enough to know that when somebody pays you a compliment, the best thing to do is just thank them, not put your insecurities on them.

'So, what do you do now you've sung?'

'Usually? I get good and drunk.'

'Well, now you seem to have stumbled on my talent.' Lailah laughs and places an arm around her new friend. 'Maybe tonight we'll get bad and drunk.'

She leads Danielle to the bar.

The singer takes one last look over her shoulder at the seat her father had been sitting in. She thinks that she would give anything to spend just one more day with him. One chance to put things straight. But Danielle knows she has nothing worth giving but the very thing that makes her who she is. What makes her the singer that she is.

Danielle Ortega knows the one thing she wants, she just doesn't want it enough to trade in her soul.

ROOM 734

Odie wakes up early, excited for school.

He's a good kid. A smart kid. An able kid. The first thing he does is make his bed. He saw a video somewhere that said it sets you up for the day. That it shows a passion and willingness to thrive and get things done. He wants to get things done.

Odie was told at school about how the President of the United States has several versions of the same suit and that he picks out which tie he is going to wear the night before because he has too many important decisions to make during the day that he doesn't want to start by having to determine the outfit he should wear. Otis 'Odie' Walker isn't even ten, yet. He doesn't have important decisions to make. But, still, he has laid out the clothes he wants to wear today and has draped them over the back of the chair in his room.

He did it last night.

There are hundreds of adults at Hotel Beresford, right now, and very few of them have the discipline of young Odie. A ten-year-old kid who knows what he wants.

A chance.

The room is tidy and the boy is dressed. He puts some bread in the toaster and starts the coffee machine for his mother because he knows that's how she likes to start her day.

But her day hasn't yet begun. Diana is still in bed. Her head hurts. Her mouth is dry. She needs to get up and go to the toilet but it's cold and she wants to be asleep.

There's a knock at her door. A light rasp from a small hand. She groans and her son pushes into the room.

'Morning, Mama. Coffee is brewing. Toast is on. I finished my book and I'm ready for school.'

God damn, the boy is bright. A ray of fucking sunshine in her bleak existence. She wants to do right by the kid. If she could just get out of her own way...

She wonders how he ended up like this. She doesn't feel like she can take any of the credit. How is it that these loved and privileged kids end up in rehab or driving under the influence and killing some young family with their car? How do they end up so bad? And then there's Odie, with nothing. The kid is basically bringing himself up, dragging himself through life. No money. No real home. An absent and sometimes abusive father. How the fuck did he end up so good, so rounded?

Maybe the parents don't make the children. Maybe they are who they are and the parents are more like shepherds, they guide them through life.

Diana thinks all of this, with her desiccated brain and her angel offspring staring at her with those big, round, brown eyes of his.

She sits up.

'Don't you worry, young man.' She sees his pride at that title. 'We are going to get you into that school today, on time.' Diana stands up to attention. She has to push through. For Odie. She places a hand on his back, affectionately, and he turns around to head back into the kitchen area, where his toast has popped.

Diana finishes making her coffee while Odie butters his toast and eats it.

'Daddy didn't come home, then?' he asks.

'I haven't heard from him yet but don't you worry about that, okay? I'm going to take my coffee and get ready. I want to see you back in here with clean teeth and your school bag in ten minutes, okay?' She tries to smile, holding back her hope that Sam doesn't come home this time. She's only ever herself when it's just her and her son.

Odie does as he is told.

He always does.

Diana manages to do something with her hair and slip some clothes on. When she returns to the living area, her son is packed and waiting by the front door like a dog ready for its first walk of the day.

He thinks she looks beautiful. She doesn't usually make that much effort. Diana picks up her keys and opens the door for her eager boy. They walk down the corridor towards the lift. Odie holds his mother's hand. There's no dog barking today but you can't escape the noise on the seventh floor.

Diana listens carefully as they pass 728. Of course. Some boring jazz racket.

That woman.

She's not quite sure why she hates Danielle so much, but she just does. Maybe it's jealousy. Danielle is so cool and pretty and lean. Diana can't remember the last time she felt any of those things. Maybe it's just the way Sam looks at her, even though she doesn't want him in her life anymore. Maybe it's the way she is with Odie, talking to him about books, listening to him talk about his day at school or the things that he's interested in. That should be her job but she's too busy stroking dick for peanuts.

They go down in the lift. Diana hates it but Odie loves the ride.

Her phone rings. She looks at the number and knows that she can't ignore it.

'Will you wait in the lobby while I take this call?' she asks Odie.

'Is it Dad?'

'Just wait over there.' She shoos him with her hand.

He does as he's told.

Of course.

Diana answers the phone. She can't afford not to. It's a high-paying customer, who is into some kinky stuff where he likes to get dominated. Easy money. He's asking her if she can do him and a friend as they're both in town for a meeting. He can more than double his usual fee. He wants to role play that they are together and she is making the other guy watch as she fucks his best friend.

She arranges a time for after the school run.

Her plan had been to walk Odie all the way but now, it seems, they can afford to take the bus.

RECEPTION

Carol is up early to apply a thick layer of foundation to her face and half a can of extra-firm hold hairspray to her bleached-blonde locks. She has started to dislike looking at her own reflection. She's existing. Surviving. Just.

Her life is at a point where she has been without her soulmate for longer than she was with him. The bed she sleeps in feels too big. Her frying pan is too wide. Why does her sofa have two seats? She lives alone. Nobody visits. The closest she gets to love is the affection of her pan-sexual work colleague or the slew of dick pictures the dating website seemingly encourages.

Carol doesn't talk about it too much. She found a group for widows a few years back. They all talked about losing the love of their life and how they were dealing with it and moving on. One of the women there, Sandra, had even remarried but felt it was healthy to still remember her dead husband. Apparently her new partner agreed.

Carol couldn't bond with these people. She didn't feel like they felt. The love she lost was actually the great love of her life. These people used the words but they had never felt what Carol had felt. They didn't know what it was like to truly believe that God had placed one specific person on Earth to be with her. To love and honour only her. And for her to feel exactly the same way.

She didn't want to move on.

She didn't want to remarry.

She wanted her life back.

The whole dating-site saga is just a quest for closeness, not to form a relationship.

Carol places her one mug and one bowl into the dishwasher that was made for a table setting of ten people and sighs.

She drives her car to work and wonders how many people would even care if she sped up and drove herself into a tree or lamppost. Then she tells herself that suicide is a sin that will be judged, and that will buy her a one-way ticket to Hell – worse than the one she is living in now. And there's still the hope of reuniting, one day, in Heaven, perhaps.

But she parks her car around the back of the hotel and transforms into Carol the leader, Carol the force of nature, Carol the heart of Hotel Beresford, as soon as the doorman greets her with 'good morning' and opens the door. The moment she sets foot in the lobby she has pride in herself and what she does.

Then she sees him. That gorgeous little black kid from the seventh floor. Always carrying a book with him. He's standing on his own in the middle of the lobby.

'Good morning, Odie.' She drops down to one knee. There are a lot of people walking around who are taller than the boy and she worries it could be intimidating. 'Are you okay? Your mum or your dad not around?'

'Dad didn't come home last night. Gambling, Mama says.' He peers over his shoulder and Carol follows his eye line to Diana Walker, talking on the phone.

'Ah, your mum is just taking a call, huh?'

'Yeah. She said to wait over here. I think she's arguing with Dad and doesn't want me to hear but I know they do it.'

Carol is choked by his innocence and his size and his maturity, and she tells herself that she shouldn't be complaining about what she does or does not have, what she lost, because this child has even less and he has never even tasted the beauty that she has.

Add a maternal pang to her aching heart.

'It's tough being an adult, sometimes. But just because they disagree with each other, it doesn't affect how they feel about you.' It's such a platitude, Carol wants to apologise immediately for patronising the boy. She changes tack. 'Did you have a good breakfast, this morning? We have croissants behind the front desk, if you want one?'

'That's okay, thank you. I did eat, already.'

'Well, why don't you come and wait over here so that you're out of the way of these people.' Then she talks behind her hand, conspiratorially: 'They never look where they're going.' She smiles. Odie smiles back and fake rolls his eyes.

Before she has the chance to get Odie out of the way, Diana is upon them.

'What are you saying to my son?'

'I'm sorry, what...?' Carol is confused.

'Talking behind your hand. What are you saying to him?'

'Mrs Walker, we were just—'

'Well, don't "just",' she interrupts. 'Come on Odie, let's get you to school. What have I told you about talking with strangers?' Diana grabs her son by the wrist and starts dragging him towards the exit.

'Mama, that's Carol, she's not a stranger.'

Carol thinks that Diana Walker is yanking her son's arm a little too forcefully. It's Carol's job to make sure that the building runs smoothly, it's not her place to get involved in the affairs of others.

Clear up when somebody dies.

Cover up a minor misdemeanour so as not to create bad publicity.

Turn a blind eye to certain behaviours.

But do not offer relationship advice or counsel children or spout rhetoric of a religious, political or cultural nature.

She watches as the Walkers leave the hotel and wonders whether Sam is out gambling or womanising. Maybe Diana has finally stabbed the guy in his sleep. Not the first time she'd have seen something like that at Hotel Beresford.

Odie manages to mouth the word 'goodbye' before being dragged toward the bus stop. Carol turns around and is immediately greeted by Mr Balliol.

'Jesus.'

'Hmmm. Not quite.'

Every Goddamned time.

'Mr Balliol,' Carol stutters, 'I'm sorry, you just ... You just scared me for a second.'

Most people seem bowled over by Balliol's charm, Carol has noticed. He's glib and suave but Carol has always been cautious of people like this. Superficial charm is for psychopaths and sales people. Estate agents and paedophiles.

'Nothing to be afraid of, Carol.'

'Is there something I can help you with, Mr Balliol?'

'Oh, no. Just passing by.'

Carol is suspicious. She asks whether he is going out. It's a test. Carol hasn't seen Mr Balliol leave the building in years, maybe ever. But he doesn't behave like a recluse. He's not holed up in the penthouse, letting his fingernails grow out and curl under, he's not pissing into buckets and stacking them in a corner, he's roaming the hallways and schmoozing with guests.

'Cute kid,' he says, ignoring Carol's question.

'I'm sorry?'

'Young Otis. Odie, I think they call him.' Carol nods. A pain in her womb. 'I guess they might not be here much longer.'

He's baiting her and she knows it, but Carol can't resist. 'Why do you say that? Has something happened?'

'It seems that Sam has gone. Packed his bags and left.'

'How? When? Odie said they'd had an argument but that he hadn't come home.'

'Things happen in the middle of the night. Parents lie to their kids to protect them.'

'Shit.' Carol knows that Diana is going to find it difficult to afford even the modest fees of seventh-floor living. She'll have to keep a close eye on her payments. It will break her heart to have to put little Odie out on the streets.

'Perhaps there's a cheaper room in this building if the family falls on harder times.'

This idea fills Carol with more dread than the possibility of Diana and Odie sleeping rough. The eighth floor is no place for a child. Seven is bad enough, but things get darker the higher up the building you get.

This includes the penthouse suite. It may be the most expensive apartment but that allows for the most decadence. Debauchery. Deception.

And people think you have to travel down to get to Hell.

DOWNTOWN

The stupid thing tore apart the seats of Ollie's car and now it is obediently lying on the floor next to the couch, lapping at the sleeping soldier's fingers.

It seems stupid but he couldn't just kick the animal out onto the street to fend for itself. Ollie doesn't even really like dogs but the situation gave him the opportunity to feel the way he used to feel in the military. Like a hero.

Before the night terrors kicked in.

And the drinking.

Not forgetting the uncontrollable fits of rage.

Hotel Beresford was the only place that would hire him. The only special skill he required was the ability to throw a person out if the manager told him to.

But he couldn't throw out that damned dog.

And now it is dependent on him. Maybe the thing is depressed. Its best friend just died. Junky scum, of course, but still a companion. Maybe it doesn't care. It's here. Now. Licking the hand of a man who locked it in a car for two hours. A man who doesn't know whether it's a male or female dog. Or what his/her name is.

But the dog sits next to its new owner, perfectly poised and patient. It senses something. The way it sensed something in the Hotel Beresford lift. Ollie is in distress. He is reliving something from his time in combat. A dream. A nightmare. Whatever. The dog with no name or gender knows. And it is standing by. Ready to serve.

Therapy for one of the men that the army forgot when he returned home from a difficult tour of whatever corner of the Earth the government deemed important to occupy or 'liberate'.

Maybe it is Ollie who is dependent on the dog.

He shakes. A frightened shiver. The dog nudges him in the side to wake him from the torment. Ollie turns away. He mumbles something. In his mind, bombs fall, children scream and mothers stare at him for help. Bullets fly by. A truck is overturned. He can see the kids who regret signing up and he can see the men who enjoy the chaos. Ollie is somewhere in between.

He wants to serve his country but he can see that he is serving the interest of the few. And the brutality is senseless.

He screams out and the dog barks. It startles him and it takes a split second to remember that he is now a dog owner.

'Jesus. Sorry.' He swings his legs around and sits up. 'Come here, boy.' The dog does as it is told and Ollie strokes it behind the ears and around the neck. 'Another fucking nightmare. You'll have to get used to those.'

He realises that he just called the dog 'boy' and he has no idea if that's accurate. He tells the dog to lie down and it does. He strokes it until it rolls over and he realises that he should have said, 'Come here, girl.'

'I guess we need to give you a name.' He thinks about Denise. Not a great dog's name but it is the name of Ollie's ex-wife, who turned out to be a real bitch. She was clearly banking on him getting shot or blown up or gassed, because she didn't think he was coming back, spreading her legs all over town, hoping to live off the army pension. It was only a few minutes after the army dumped Ollie on his return that Denise followed suit.

His life is filled with nightmares.

The dog should be a positive thing in his life. He opts for Molly, after the Little Richard song. They can be Ollie and Molly. It sounds like the perfect pairing for some awful romantic comedy. Maybe he meets someone at the park who is also a dog owner. Maybe Molly saves a woman from having her bag stolen and she falls in love with Ollie. As trite as both options sound, they are preferable to Ollie's current cycle of laborious work and sweat-drenched flashbacks.

'Molly it is.'

Ollie stands up. He walks towards the toilet and Molly follows. 'It's nice having you around but there are some things I still have to do on my own.' A laugh. Some genuine happiness in his life. He takes a piss, brushes his teeth, washes his body and makes some coffee for his travel mug. Molly waits.

'Right, let's take you out.' He picks up the lead from the kitchen counter. He needs to buy some essentials from the store and enough dog food to keep things going for the next week. And maybe he will walk Molly in the park. And maybe he will bump into a nice woman, who wants to be with him and not every other guy within a three-mile radius.

Ollie lets himself dream.

Hope.

Imagine what it is that he truly wants.

THE PENTHOUSE

Balliol lied to Carol to see what she knew, see if she would balk at the information that Sam Walker left his family in the dead of night. She's on top of everything that needs to happen at Hotel Beresford, she knows everybody's name and room number and some kind of detail about them but she can't see everything.

She's only human.

He also did it to push away the thought of any connection between the sultry jazz singer and the woman-beater a few doors down. Not to protect her, just to keep his own little game going.

And now, for his own amusement, he has a separate area of his vast penthouse space set up with one large screen fixed on the Walker apartment, waiting for Diana Walker to return from the school run.

Balliol doesn't watch, though.

He's not interested.

There are a million videos that he could find of a woman being drilled by two guys at once. It would take seconds to bring up a thousand hotel-room cuckold scenes. There could be a drop-down menu of the many ways that a threesome can play out – women, men, interracial, interspecies. He doesn't want to watch that. And he certainly doesn't want to watch Diana Walker enter into anything like that.

He's not the only one.

Diana blanks Carol on the way back through the lobby after dropping Odie off. She has a permanent chip on her shoulder. There's plenty to be pissed off about, but Diana, herself, can't even really remember where it started. It's buried under a mountain of shit. She's in a permanently bad mood with everyone about everything. Everyone except for Odie.

She has a little time to freshen up, fix her hair and make-up, and put on something appropriately suggestive. There hasn't been time to wash the outfit her client likes. She gives it a sniff. It's not ideal. She puts it on, anyway, and covers any aroma with perfume. If she was high class and being paid accordingly, things would be immaculate.

That's not what they're after. Sure, they could afford it, but they want it grubby. Dirty. Sordid. That's why they choose Diana.

There's a knock at the door and the huge television screen shows Diana letting the two men inside. She knows one of them, the other she is more wary about. She welcomes them in. It sounds like audio from the cheapest pornography available.

Balliol isn't listening.

They end up in the bedroom. Her regular client has a ball gag and dog collar. She walks him around the room on his knees and slaps him about a bit. The new guy watches and plays with himself on the bed.

Diana can't remember the last time she made love.

If she ever had a passion for anything, it has long since evaporated.

She is numb to everything but her son, and even that can feel like work, sometimes. Push her on what she wants from life, the answer would be 'escape'. Or the sweet release of death. Drill down further and she may be willing to make a sacrifice that ensures Odie never has to feel this way.

Balliol waits in his kitchen as the machine pours a perfect espresso and the stranger in the Walker bedroom says that he wants to join in. Balliol puts the cup to his lips and inhales the aroma of the bitter coffee. The unmistakable sound of a ball-gagged groan travels down the hallway from the viewing room.

He doesn't want to see what's happening in room 734 but he takes his drink and walks in that direction, anyway.

Balliol almost spits it out when he sees what is happening on the screen.

'Ooh, that's got to hurt,' he says out loud.

There isn't a person in room 734 that doesn't have part of another person inside them in some way.

Another muffled scream, dampened by a gagged mouth.

Tears.

Pain.

Blood.

But not on screen. Events have turned oddly tender since the stranger got involved. No domination or submission, just three people exploring one another. Consensually – though one is being paid handsomely for her time.

The horror comes from within the viewing room, where Sam Walker is secured and is being forced to watch his wife pleasure two men in their marital bed.

'Bet you wish you were still tied up in that shoe closet, am I right?' Mr Balliol walks out of the room, leaving Sam with his wife and overweight white men.

Sam wishes he couldn't see what he is seeing.

He wishes that his wife wasn't a whore.

And, as Balliol suggested, he wishes that he was never taken out of Danielle Ortega's shoe closet.

There's a reason why most people who meet Sam Walker – for even a second – mark him down as a piece of shit. There's a reason that anyone would feel he deserves what is coming to him. All the time he has to wish, not once does he wish he never tried it on with Danielle when she clearly was not interested. Not once does he wish he never laid a finger on her.

It never crosses his mind to think, *I wish I had been better*.

WHAT DO YOU WANT?

Over four thousand religions in the world. A lot of deities. Plenty to go around, even at the rate that man seems to be able to procreate and overpopulate this fragile planet. Perhaps, if God had spent longer than a week putting our home together, it would be more robust. If He had created tradespeople on the first day, there might not be so many cracks.

It's those monotheistic religions that are most dangerous, though. Where there is only one God.

All-seeing.

All-knowing.

Take the top three: Christianity, Islam and Judaism. They all have their links. There are characters that clearly overlap. In one holy book, a man can be the son of God and in another he's a prophet. In another, it's all about the Father and not the Son.

A character that makes an appearance across all three is Satan.

He goes by many names.

Lucifer was created by God. And He was created good and blameless. He was an angel of the highest order. A cherubim. A position of power among heavenly angels. Lucifer was beautiful and powerful but overcome with pride. This is not to say that He felt an honour or self-worth in His work but that there was an arrogance and vanity that prevented his mind from returning to God or even seeking Him out.

God, seemingly possessing a modicum of this narcissism himself, cast Lucifer from Heaven, with his followers, in a ball of flames or a bolt of lightning – it depends which version of events you choose to believe, but the lightning version is told in one of the gospels, and they are supposed to be true...

So, any angel questioning the autocratic word of God was thrown into Hell. Lucifer was no longer a light but a dark adversary. With no heavenly power, His only option was to provoke sin in God's children on Earth. An almost thankless task but certainly preferable to a job in recruitment or IT sales.

Christianity suggests that Satan – the artist formerly known as Lucifer – has one aim: to sever your relationship with God, take away your peace and destroy your lives.

The Quran sees it slightly differently, where Iblis is a physical being made of fire, who holds a grudge against man because the angels were forced to prostrate in front of one when Adam was created.

He is still portrayed as egoistic and self-centred. He may be physically and aesthetically superior but man is shown to concentrate on his spirit, intellect and behaviour. Iblis sees himself as fire and man as clay, and clay will always lose to fire. So he would not bow down to Adam and became one of the disbelievers, meaning that he was disobedient to Allah.

Yet, Iblis is saying that one should only bow to God, therefore showing a level of allegiance that comes with considered thinking rather than blind following.

But, it seems, questioning God is a bad idea in both faiths.

And in Judaism it can be read that God created Satan to be a provocateur. Still subservient to God but his mission is to provoke people into disobeying God's will. He is neither a fallen angel nor is He banished to Hell. No pitchfork or flames. He is not in opposition to God because that would go against the idea of God's control. Satan works for God. To test faith, therefore making it stronger.

And then you have some guy running around American college campuses in the seventies, raping and killing coeds and saying that Satan told him to do it. Or some whack-job sets fire to his house while his family is inside because the Devil spoke to him through his dog. Or Mary from Winchester will claim she didn't cheat on her husband, she was seduced by the lord of the underworld. Or Dan from Minneapolis will post a status on his social-media platform that is an opinion presented as fact and the word will go viral and paint the Prince of Darkness in another light.

And how on Earth is anybody supposed to discern what is real and what is fake when everybody is talking and nobody is listening and there are already another two hundred religions to choose from, today, including one where you don't have to believe in any God at all? And the stories overlap and contradict. And there's science to contend with.

And all that information is getting mixed with all that opinion and every video, meme, soundbite or hashtag is something else to believe.

And you buy it.

You eat it all up.

But there is so much to believe that you end up having faith in nothing. You won't believe in God or Yahweh or Allah or Vishnu any more than you believe in Lucifer, Shaitan, Beelzebub or Belial.

And maybe that's just how He wants it.

RECEPTION

In two days, a hundred smarmy sales guys will descend on Hotel Beresford to hear industry leaders blather on about future technologies and pipelines.

Yawn. Spit. Wheeze.

Carol hates these fucking things. But they keep the place full.

Full of people like Danny Elwes in room 420, with his size six feet and his baby dick, masquerading online as some kind, book-loving, sensitive patron of the arts when, in truth, he is a short, obviously-disguising-his-ginger-hair Neanderthal, who boasts to his subordinates about punching women between the legs so that it feels tighter when he fucks them.

He has never done this to a woman; women scare him. And if he ever did, it would only be to help them feel that he was there.

But Danny would never consciously help a woman.

Over one hundred of these, mostly male, sales people in one room. They start by listening. Then discussing. Then swapping information. They all come from companies with stupid names like DataMax and DoTrue and BeLinear. Some of them are selling physical products, hardware, others are focussed on software, and then there are the ones selling a service. So, no product at all.

And they're all 'big enough to handle but small enough to care' and they're talking about 'net zero' and 'carbon footprints' like they give a fuck about the environment as much as turning a quick buck.

Once they've swapped business cards there's a meal, with wine.

And so it begins.

The theatre of Bacchus.

Quaffing Bordeaux and exchanging stories of monetary success and sexual conquests. Flirtation with the few women who are either ballsy enough to attend or naïve enough to think that nothing will happen; it's business. The men are peacocking. Some of the women are watching the dance and choosing a mate. Bring out the dancing girls and nymphs. For the conservative onlooker it appears un-Christian. To those pursuing enjoyment in the short time they have on the planet, to those seeking fulfilment and sexual gratification and the inhibited nature of intoxication, it looks like fun. Dirty fun, but fun nonetheless.

Before things really kick off, there is one more speaker, who they have all been waiting for. A man with more riches than all the companies attending combined. Charismatic. Entrepreneurial. Risk-taking. Experimental. And unfairly beautiful.

Mr Balliol makes an appearance at every one of these events. And why wouldn't he? It's his building. This is his church. He can do and say as he pleases. And a room filled with lost, proud and desperate souls is ripe for chaos.

A feast.

An all-you-can-eat buffet.

Every time, Carol clears up after the massacre.

EXPERIMENT TWO: CONFERENCE ROOM

There are over eight billion people in the world.

It feels like only yesterday there were two.

And whether it was Adam and Eve is neither here nor there. And whether an angel refused to kneel before this new creation is irrelevant. And whether that angel was banished by a capricious God makes no difference. Neither is it a concern if that cast-out angel is the antithesis of all that is good or merely here to provoke critical thought. There are too many people in the world.

Scratch that.

There are too many apathetic people in the world. Nobody cares.

Polar ice caps are melting? Not in my lifetime, let's buy a 4x4 to drive around perfectly flat roads. Plastic in the oceans? Fuck it, let's just eat all the fish and they won't be bothered by it.

No need to exercise caution.

Live fast and die before the world implodes with greed and self-interest.

How could things improve if everyone did a little and played their part?

Would it be better if there were simply fewer people?

Spiritually speaking, a God could come down on a cloud and sort everything out, surely. They could prove that they are real and that all of those inspirational *Just Be Kind* posters were right all along. At what point is that likely to happen? What is He waiting for?

Nuclear war might not be such a bad thing. Like pressing the reset button. Turning it off, then turning it back on again. It also has that ancillary benefit of leaving people who will understand what it is like to fight to survive. Goodbye to entitlement, perhaps.

On a lower, and darker, level, there is the possibility of government intervention. In an effort to curb the growing population, 'they' release some kind of toxin that is harmful to those with a pre-existing, underlying condition. They can't breathe properly. It starts with flu-like symptoms. Blame it on the Chinese or something. Some guy ate a bat or a snake that was carrying this disease. That works. They eat all kinds of weird stuff over there, right?

Tell people they have to stay indoors, they have to lock down. In this uncaring, self-centred world, you know that will only incite rebellion. People don't even know what they're fighting against most of the time. And it's much easier to be against something than it is to be for something.

They meet up and spread the virus more ferociously than before.

And the government is sitting on the cure the entire time, so somebody gets to make a ton of money from the vaccine. Not ideal, but at least the population has had a decent cull.

On a smaller scale, you take a hotel, perhaps even a chain of hotels, and you host conferences filled with the worst in society – estate agents, Catholic priests, media influencers – fill them with alcohol then ask them two questions:

1 – What do you want?

2 – How much do you want it?

ROOM 420

Three women in three nights.

Danny Elwes doesn't mind paying for sex. Real women are mean. They talk. They tell their friends about penis size and whether the guy knows where the clitoris can be located. Somehow, it doesn't matter to him if a prostitute does this with her other prostitute pals because they will never cross paths again. And they're professionals. If a colleague comes across him and recognises something, she isn't going to say, 'Oh, you're the ginger needle dick Carrie had last week.' She isn't going to laugh at him.

Danny already has his 'three in three' story to take back to the office. He'll add an extra embellishment for every inch he is missing off the national average and the women in customer services will cringe and roll their eyes behind their screens while the sales team fake laughs. They think they are boosting his ego, but Danny knows what they're doing and it saddens him.

He's lonely and small and feels insignificant but he can't see a way out. And he thinks it will make him feel better to make somebody else feel more insignificant than he does, but it's as fleeting as the male orgasm.

There's a soul in Danny Elwes, buried somewhere beneath the self-loathing and his repressed mother issues. Desperation is a great catalyst for coaxing somebody to give up their soul but depression makes it a tougher sell.

But this is Hotel Beresford.

It lives, it breathes, it gets to know the people inside.

It knows what has to be done.

Danny Elwes wakes up, naturally. No alarm set. The conference doesn't start until after lunch. He sees two empty Champagne bottles on the floor and feels his brain rattling inside his skull. It was worth it. Last night was amazing. He isn't usually able to go for that long. She had some kind of vaginal trickery that he has never experienced. It made him feel less like he wanted to degrade her.

He turns to his right and she is still there, lying next to him.

His first thought is about the money, that she could still be on the clock.

But she's not.

This is Hotel Beresford.

She's dead.

Danny doesn't know that yet. He sidles up next to her. Her dead back is turned. He strokes her hair. Kisses her dead shoulder. Runs his hand down her cold back and rests on her hip. He's getting hard. His dick looks like an acorn resting on a handful of tangerine candy floss. It pokes at his date from behind.

Next come the whispers. The sweet nothings. He's actually not being his usual crass self, though he is rubbing himself up against a corpse.

He tells the not-breathing woman next to him that she was amazing last night, that she is beautiful. God, he's convincing himself that he has feelings for her. The way those sad losers tell themselves that the stripper giving them a lap dance actually likes them.

Danny Elwes is lucky, he doesn't try to stick his angry inch inside the cadaver. He grabs her shoulder and rolls her towards him so that he can see her face, kiss her mouth, look into her eyes.

He doesn't get it, at first. He tries to shake her. Wants to say her name but it isn't coming to mind, and probably isn't real, anyway. He puts his hand by her mouth but can't feel her breath. He puts his head onto her chest. It's not moving. He thinks he feels a heartbeat until he realises it's his own.

'Fuck.'

He doesn't know what else to say.

Panic sets in. Danny jumps out of bed and looks at the dead sex worker. His gaze jumps around the room. He's paranoid that somebody is watching him. He puts a hand over his penis.

Somewhere, high in the building, there's laughter.

Danny runs around the room, picking up his clothes and pulling them on. He throws the bed covers over his third date in three nights.

'Fuck,' he says again. There's nothing else to do.

He thinks about how the night ended. They drank together, had sex, drank some more. Did some coke. Fucked again. It was intense. And fulfilling, which is often not the case. Danny is sure he rolled off her and fell asleep. He didn't strangle her. Stab her. Shoot her. They didn't have enough to overdose.

What the fuck is he going to do?

He knows that he is innocent of this murder. He liked this one. He didn't want to hurt her. He didn't even strangle her as he came. So the sensible thing would be to call the police or, better yet, start with reception and ask to speak with Carol.

But anxiety makes people act out of the ordinary.

Danny doesn't want anyone to find out that he had sex and paid for it. (He doesn't realise that these things don't happen at Hotel Beresford. They get hidden.)

He can't call the police.

He won't call for Carol.

The worst thing he could do, the most idiotic thing he could do, the thing that so many people do, is get online and search for the best way to get rid of a dead body.

Danny runs over to the bedside table and picks up his mobile phone.

RECEPTION

'I needed them here two hours ago, Hank.' Carol is annoyed. 'How often do I order wine from you?'

She is unflappable. But conference days have an edge. Carol needs everything to run like clockwork. This is the reason she has built up a team of trusted suppliers. Everything from napkins to bleach, wine to waiting staff. You screw up once, you're gone. Carol will not suffer fools.

Hank has to bend over and take it. Hotel Beresford is a regular gig. They order a lot and they always pay on time. He makes Carol a promise that he will have the wine there within the hour, and he can't break that. He tells her that he's standing next to the truck right now. And he is.

You don't lie to Carol.

One of the younger workers runs up to Hank and hands him a bottle of Dom Perignon with a red bow tied around the neck. He places it with the rest of the delivery and slaps the back of the van to inform the driver that they can set off.

'I'm watching it leave now. I've put a little something in there for you, too, Carol.' He smiles. They have a flirtatious relationship. Maybe there's something there, maybe there isn't and it's all part of business, but it softens Carol.

'Well, I should hope there would be, Hank,' she flirts back. Maybe, if there was something real there, Carol would let her guard down again, be vulnerable. She's met Hank a few times. He's a good-looking older gentleman. He's always pleasant to talk to.

If only it wasn't a conference day.

She tells him that somebody will be waiting at the door for the delivery, then she hangs up without saying goodbye. Cold but efficient.

The third floor has been kitted out for the event. The conference room has chairs laid out. There's a state-of-the-art PA system on stage for the various speakers that have been booked. It is Keith's sole responsibility to ensure that they are looked after and arrive earlier than their time slot in order to get their microphones attached.

It's boring and regimented but it has to be.

The last thing Carol needs is for one of the smarmy sales guys to phone down and say he has woken up with a dead hooker in his bed.

But he won't have to.

Mr Balliol appears at the front desk.

'Everything copacetic, Carol?'

'Mr Balliol, sir, yes. A slight delay on the wine but it's on the way and will still be here in plenty of time.'

'I trust that it's all in hand.' He turns to Keith. 'And all the guests are signed in and happy, Keith?'

Keith is flamboyant and gregarious and bright and approachable but he shrinks under the gaze of Mr Balliol, stroking nervously at his colourful trademark cravat.

'All signed in and registered apart from one. I'm just waiting on a Mr Elwes. He's in room...' he scrolls down his computer screen '... 420. I'll give him another twenty minutes and buzz him to collect his pass.'

'Thank you, Keith.' Mr Balliol gives Keith a courteous nod of the head, which gets Keith's blood racing. Mr Balliol is nothing if not a treat for the eyes. 'Carol, could I have a word with you privately?'

Balliol walks to the end of the long reception desk and Carol knows to follow.

Loyalty is one of Carol's finest traits.

He explains that he would prefer it if Carol took care of the situation in room 420, that he would like for her to knock on Danny Elwes's door and check that everything is okay. That she is to ensure he goes down to reception to register for the day and he is to collect his pass and name badge. And, if she suspects something, she is to check his room while he is downstairs dealing with his admin. And, if she finds something out of the ordinary, she is to deal with it appropriately.

He does not tell Carol that he watched Danny freak out when he found out the body he was trying to fuck was dead. He does not tell Carol how much he laughed at that. And he certainly does not tell her that, if she finds a dead body in the room, she is to take care of it, much like she took care of Jerry's dog.

He doesn't have to.

Carol understands her responsibilities.

She knows what she signed up for.

'Not a problem. Is there anything I should know before I go in there?' She already knows that Danny Elwes is an awful human being. He's a dating app troll. He is doing the equivalent of walking around and putting his dick into the hand of every woman that passes, waiting for one of them to hang on to it.

Carol hasn't seen Danny yet. He never responded to her after she called him out online. He is probably going to be more nervous than her when they finally come face to face. But she knows there is something that Balliol isn't telling her.

'This guy is the worst.'

'Among this group of delights, that's saying something.' She raises an eyebrow.

'I wouldn't worry too much. Just make sure he gets along to the conference. Tonight will be his last night at Hotel Beresford.'

And with that, Balliol walks down the corridor towards the lift with the only key that opens the doors to the penthouse.

CROSSROADS

Mr May is worried because he doesn't feel unwell.

At all.

'It's been at least a week since we found out. I should be deteriorating, surely.'

'Doctors get these things wrong all the time. Why are you worrying about feeling good?'

Mr May is a simple man. He worked hard his entire life. They have a modest but well-kept home. He adores his wife, has never strayed from her. It was a great day when he finally bought a new car. No previous drivers. A couple of miles on the clock from the forecourt. They have had holidays abroad and meals in overpriced restaurants. They have attended church every Sunday and upheld their Christian values every other day.

A beautifully unremarkable life.

Perfectly straightforward.

Of course he will be remembered by his wife and the majority of the congregation. His former co-workers will think fondly of him when he has passed. But Mr May's impact on the world has been small. His world itself has been small, too. And that is just fine with him. He never wanted that much. To be a good husband, a provider, to serve God and help others less fortunate than himself. Not everybody can be an activist or an artist.

But death, though the end, has made Mr May's life so much bigger. He cannot grasp the concept of his finality. It's too huge.

Above all, he is afraid.

It's not even that the God who has forsaken him by giving him this illness may not exist, it's not even that he may not make it to

Heaven. It's the nothingness he won't even feel and the somethingness that he will leave his wife to endure. It breaks his heart.

It would be easier if he was struggling. If he couldn't walk or see or control his bowels, but he feels well. Mr May, who was told, just over a week ago, that he had less than a month to live, feels more alive than ever.

But he's worried that he's in for a rude awakening. That it will just come. One minute he's strapped to the wings of a biplane, doing a loop in the open skies, next, he's fucking dead. Without the chance to say goodbye to his wife.

And he doesn't know how to express this fear.

Mrs May is continuing as though everything is normal. She got up, made eggs, had a cold coffee. It's everyday. She's almost ready for her first glass of wine. He has spotted her watching the clock. He thinks she might be in denial, and she will never tell him what she has done, even though it may alleviate some of his anxiety about being alive.

She looks over at her husband on his favourite chair. He's reading a book.

'How is the Wodehouse?'

'Kind of makes me wish I was already dead.'

THE PENTHOUSE

There's another lift.

Balliol reaches the top of the building, pulls back the iron door and steps into his penthouse. It's cold. He runs his finger up a small screen on the wall to blast the heat up. As soon as he shuts the door, the lift begins its descent, to welcome another soul to the building.

To the right, there is one of the many slatted wooden walls. The thicker slats are stationary, they divide the room. The thinner slats move. The can glide and hinge in different direction to open up a bar or coffee area hidden behind or they can slide to the side to reveal a hallway or private bathroom. The penthouse is spacious, but this design, usually reserved for highly populated cities where space is a premium, turns Mr Balliol's place into a labyrinthine palace.

The wall wheels silently to the left to reveal the second lift.

This is the only way to access it.

It is not the same as the original Hotel Beresford lift. This one is wider. More modern. More of a private service elevator. Fifty years ago, at the height of Beresford opulence and fame, this was the way that high-profile guests could be snuck in or could have somebody snuck in for them. If the president of a superpower wanted a secret rendezvous with a Hollywood sexpot, for example.

The beauty of Hotel Beresford was its discretion.

You could order a bowl of cocaine for breakfast from room service and feel secure that nobody would ever know.

At one time, the lift was shared by a princess, a billionaire tech entrepreneur and a legendary pop star. The only other person in there was the lift operator and he is the only person still alive that knows what was said on that thirty-two-second journey.

Balliol presses the button for the basement. This is one of two ways to get below the building. There is a stairway, there has to be due to fire regulations, but it has since been obscured and the lift has been deemed out of commission.

Getting this kind of paperwork signed and notarised is not difficult with the right amount money, political leverage or possibility of sexual scandal.

This lift is more silent than the other and Balliol reaches the subterranean level smoothly, passing the disruption of the seventh floor, the stress of the third floor and hubbub of the reception level on his way down. When the door opens, he is greeted by a long hallway, lined with filing cabinets that have been numbered. Just beyond, through a set of double doors, is the reason that Balliol is here.

It's surprisingly well lit for what it is. Candles. Natural light somehow filtering in from the street above through small circular windows near the ceiling. The concrete slab in the centre of the room acts like an altar. And, on top, is a naked Sam Walker.

Ready for sacrifice.

Damn, Balliol loves a good conference.

ROOM 420

It doesn't matter which floor you're staying on, the last thing you want to hear at Hotel Beresford is a knock at the door.

Danny Elwes hasn't stopped saying 'fuck' to himself all morning.

He dropped some empty miniature bottles on the floor.

Fuck.

He stubbed his toe on the dressing table.

Fuck.

He rolled up a dead hooker in the bed blanket then dropped her on the floor.

Fuck.

Now this. A knock at his door.

'Fuck.' He puts a hand over his own mouth. And becomes a statue.

Another knock. 'Mr Elwes, it's Carol from the front desk.' *And the dating site chat*, she thinks. 'Mr Elwes? Is everything okay?'

It suddenly occurs to Danny that she may have a key. That, if he doesn't answer, she could barge her way into his chaos.

'Uh, I didn't order any room service,' he calls back. Then he starts to move. Quickly. He is standing at the foot of his bed. The prostitute is lying on the floor between the side of the bed and the door that Carol could walk through at any moment. Across the room, below the mirror, is his suitcase. Too big for a three-day trip where he planned to wear very little clothing and the same suit, and too small to fit a body. But he's going to try.

He'd be in trouble if it was the woman he'd paid for the night before. He'd requested a larger lady. Although he had used the word 'chunky'. Classic Elwes sensitivity. But this woman, she was petite. Dainty. What Danny Elwes would affectionately refer to as a 'back-to-front lady', because she was almost flat-chested. He could squeeze her into that case.

So he tries.

'It's not room service, Mr Elwes. I'm here to discuss the conference and your registration. Could you open the door, please?'

He darts across the room and starts pulling his clothes out of the case and throwing them onto the bed.

'Er, yes. One moment, I'm ... not decent. Just a second.'

The adrenaline pumping through his body gives him more strength than he knew he had. He picks up his third woman in three nights and drops her with a thud into the suitcase.

'Everything okay in there?'

'Yes, just putting on some trousers.'

Danny folds the delicate corpse into the small rectangle, her arms creaking and twisting into shape. He shuts the lid, sits on top and zips it up. When he stands back, it looks as though he has stuffed a dead body into a suitcase.

'Fuck.'

He takes the pile of clothes from the bed and throws them on top of the suitcase to obscure it and heads over to the door.

Deep breath.

He unlocks the latch, wipes his forehead with the back of his sleeve and opens the door.

Whack. He sees Carol's face and it all comes back to him. Could this day get any worse? Nervously, he looks over at the pile of clothes on top of his suitcase and thinks he sees it move.

Surely not.

It's just panic.

The booze.

'Mr Elwes, are you okay?'

'Yes. Yes. Of course. Just a bit of a late night. Overdid it. You know?'

Yes, I've had a drink but never paid another person to submit to my every fetish and whim. Carol has to bite her tongue.

'Well, I hope you're feeling well enough for the conference.'

'I'm sure I'll be fine.' He tells himself that the worst thing to do would be to run. It would look too suspicious. He has to behave like things are normal. Go to the conference. Network with other industry professionals. Listen to talks. Whatever.

'Okay, well, you need to come to the front desk to register for the day and get your name badge and welcome pack.'

'You couldn't have brought that to me?' Even in a time of personal distress, Danny Elwes manages to be obnoxious.

'I'm not your personal assistant, Mr Elwes. I run the hotel and I'm organising the conference for over a hundred people. It's below my pay grade to hand-deliver badges.' She is visibly angered by his comment. Carol knows that deliberately offensive behaviour is his raison d'être but she is also aware that he is being cagey, he doesn't want her in his room. Mr Balliol hinted at it. 'I could always come in and we can discuss further.' She takes a step towards him.

'No no no no no. I'm sorry. Of course I wasn't implying that you are my personal assistant. I'm still not with it. I'll come down shortly and sign what you want me to sign or whatever.' He starts to close the door.

'I'm going to have to insist that you do so in the next fifteen minutes as food preparation begins soon and we need to make sure we have the right amount. I'm sure you'll want the complimentary wine, too.' She smiles a fake smile.

He looks over his shoulder again. It's so obvious. So suspicious. If you knew nothing about Danny Elwes, you would guess that, from his behaviour, he was either at a stag party the night before where the stripper accidentally perished, or he had woken up with a dead prostitute in his bed.

Mr Balliol knows.

And now so does Carol.

Another body at Hotel Beresford.

She thinks, *Fuck*.

'I'll just jump in the shower and head down. Need to get last night off me. You understand.'

She does. He disgusts her.

'Just ask for Keith,' Carol says, echoing her last message on the dating app. She shouldn't smile but she does.

Danny wants to verbally attack her but he has to protect himself. So instead he looks her up and down in a way that makes Carol's skin goose pimple and shuts his door without goodbye.

Like a child, he holds both middle fingers up at the closed door in frustration. He listens. Carol is walking away.

Fifteen minutes.

That's a long time. Fourteen minutes longer than he should have.

Danny brushes the loose clothing off the top of the case and watches to see if it moves again. He pokes it. There's nothing. He hits it, there is nothing. He throws five or six hard punches down on her. He must have been seeing things. She didn't even make a sound.

He just needs to act normally.

He can get away with this.

He gets away with everything.

Danny does as his mind tells him. He showers off the excesses of the previous evening, that wonderful evening of rich food, full-bodied wine and mind-blowing sex. He scrubs hard to rid himself of the morning, that shocking, horrendous morning of discovery, dead-bodied women and life-altering decisions.

It takes around six minutes for Danny to make his way to reception, fill out the appropriate paperwork and ask Keith to have somebody change his sheets. And this is more than enough time for Carol to take a look around room 420.

ROOM 734

It has been more than a day since Diana Walker last saw her husband, Sam. She could call the police, concerned, and tell them that he went out to play poker and never came home, but they might go looking for him, and that's the last thing she wants.

This could be her chance.

She tells herself that Sam has finally grown the balls to do the right thing and leave her and Odie alone. The kid has been more relaxed. He's been going to school every day, Diana has made sure of that. And she has been taking on more clients than usual. Of course, she needs the money, and even if Sam did come back and she was balls deep with some investment banker who had a thing for older black women, Diana thinks she could handle it. Two days without Sam and she feels stronger. (And not the fake strength she usually has to employ.)

Odie has been dropped at school. He's been reading *Treasure Island*. Diana reaches into the wardrobe and pulls out a grey sports bag. Her face brightens as she remembers when this used to be a shoe box and, before that, just an envelope stuffed into a shoe. She undoes the zip and the thing is three-quarters filled with money. Not just dumped in there, either, it has been placed in tight piles and counted and recounted.

Diana wants to fill the bag.

She checks her watch. Her first client isn't due for another half-hour. She takes out one of the piles and counts through it, taking enough to pay for the room for another month – another Sam-free month. She stuffs the bag back in the wardrobe and covers it with shoes, just in case that waste of space does return and steal her hard-earned money to gamble away, like he did last time.

That no-good piece of shit. Diana can't even remember a time when things were good with Sam. When they talked about getting their own house and having a kid. When she wanted a career that was more than sucking and fucking and putting things inside her body.

The lift is waiting on floor seven when Diana exits her apartment. She hates that she has to walk past *that woman's* place every time she wants to go somewhere. And she hates that she even feels this way, because it's not her, it's not who she really is. She's a victim of circumstance. Always having to fight in some way. A childish part of her wants to spit on the door each time she passes. But not today. There's a confidence growing in Diana Walker now that the noose around her neck has been loosened.

She pulls the heavy lift door shut and presses the button for the ground floor. On the way down, she notices the activity on floor three. It's not always like that. She knows it's conference time. And a conference means a hotel filled with business people who are away from home and prepared to do things they would not normally do. Like fuck a total stranger. Maybe even pay for the pleasure.

Diana can spot them a mile away.

She can smell their desperation over the pungency of their acrid cologne.

There's one at the reception desk, talking to Keith, when Diana emerges from the corridor after the lifts hits what everybody believes is the lowest floor of Hotel Beresford.

The little man looks freshly showered and groomed. He's wearing a pin-striped suit with no tie and his top shirt button casually undone. When Diana sidles in next to him, she sees a name badge on the counter and that he is filling out a form, ticking a box that says he has no dietary requirements. Keith is talking to someone through a partition in the wall behind.

'Here for the conference, huh?' Diana asks, feigning interest, playing a role.

'Sorry?' The apparent businessman doesn't look up at first and carries on scribbling.

Diana lifts his name badge up. 'Are you here for the conference?' She says it again, slower. Danny turns his head, sees Diana and takes her in. She's taller than he is. Dark skin, he likes that. Full breasts. The opposite of the woman he may or may not have killed last night in room 420. In his head he says, *Four in four nights.*

'Danny,' he tells her, tilting his name badge and smiling.

'Diana.' She's not one to take on a fake name.

'Are you also here ... on business?'

'I'm working, yes.'

Seeing Diana working the room, Keith returns to the desk, hastily.

'Er, Mrs Walker, how can I help you?' He walks to the side to pull her away from one of the conference patrons.

'Ms Walker. And I'd like to give you this.' Diana pulls out a wad of cash. 'To pay for the next month.'

'Uh, okay.' He takes the money and starts counting it.

Diana interjects, 'That's for room 734.' She says it loudly so that Danny can hear. Then repeats, looking the businessman dead in the eyes, 'Seven. Three. Four.'

He understands. And, smoothly for Danny Elwes, he manages to pick up his name badge from the reception counter while simultaneously leaving his business card in its place. He taps it lightly with one finger.

'Is that everything?' Danny asks Keith, turning his back on Diana, who slides the card from the counter and into her pocket.

'All done, Mr Elwes. A couple of hours until the first talk. Lunch is on floor two. We will see you at the conference.' Keith smiles and fiddles with his neck. He hates these people and finds himself fighting not to stutter.

Danny walks off with more of a spring in his step than he had on his way down. It says enough about his character that the flirtations of another possible suitor have made him, temporarily, forget the events of his morning.

Diana Walker stays with Keith while he registers her payment on the system.

'Everything okay, Mrs Walker? How is young Odie?'

She is taken aback by this. Carol knows everybody in the building, she asks how people are getting on. This has never come from Keith before.

'Um, he's doing great, actually. Thanks for asking.'

'Always has a book tucked under his arm.'

'Loves reading. A thirst for knowledge.'

'He's a good boy.'

'He *is* a good boy, thank you for noticing.' She swells with pride.

Keith taps something into the computer.

'And Mr Walker?'

Her mood drops.

'He's not so good. Let's just leave it at that, shall we?'

Keith taps faster. He doesn't continue the conversation.

'Okay, all s-s-s-s-sorted.' His stutter returns when he gets nervous. 'P-paid up for the next mmmmonth, it's in the system. Anything else I can help you with today?'

'I'm good.'

It's true. Diana Walker is good. She spends a lot of her days with her legs apart and her ankles in the air, but that doesn't make her bad. Industrious, maybe. Committed, certainly. But she's not bad. She drinks more than she should but she is used to getting hit more than she should. She leans on her son more than is healthy, but, at the same time, she is sacrificing herself so much for him. She will not allow him to fail. He must have opportunity.

She would do anything for Odie.

Absolutely anything.

At the lift, Danny is waiting along with an older, bearded gentleman. Diana stands next to him as the lift lowers. She doesn't look at him, doesn't say anything. Another couple of suits step out and they get in with the bearded man.

Danny presses the number four button. He looks at Diana and presses the number seven. Something passes between them. An excitement for her that she hasn't felt with Sam for a long time and a feeling she doesn't get with her regular clients.

Danny isn't sensing the same thing.

He's thinking about what she will look like bouncing away on top of him.

'Eight for me, please,' the older man says, quietly.

'Sorry,' says Danny, forgetting that he was even there.

'Floor eight,' Diana chimes in, leaning across Danny and pressing the button herself, her hand grazing his.

All three of them travel in silence, get off at their floor, walk to their apartment and continue their day. The old man locks himself in, pours a coffee and sits at his desk, staring at a blank screen. Diana gets in, finds her phone and texts the number on the business card she just picked up from the lobby.

Danny reads the text. For a brief moment, the woman from 734 made him forget his troubles. She gave him the chance to dream about the future. But returning to his room has brought everything back. He doesn't text the sex worker back because the sex worker that he probably killed the night before, the one he left crumpled in a suitcase, is gone.

ROOM 803

Those two people in the lift had no idea that they were sharing it with I.P. Wayatt.

The I.P. Wayatt.

The reclusive writer hasn't been seen in public for almost a year but he wanders around Hotel Beresford as though he is nobody. A regular Joe with a regular job.

The beauty of being a writer was that he used to be able to do such things in London or Manhattan or Paris. If some high-brow literary critic passed him in the street, they might acknowledge him, but conversation was reserved for publishing parties, which he never went to, anyway.

Now, it's so easy to find out something about a person. It doesn't even have to be true. People know what writers look like now. And not just their pictures on the inside of book covers that were taken when they were twenty pounds leaner and had a full head of hair; you can see what they look like when they go out to buy milk or grab a coffee or meet their therapist.

Nobody should know what writers look like, or music producers or film directors or radio show hosts. That's the point. They are behind the scenes, being creative because they have to, they don't know any other way. They don't want you to know. They want to be able to walk down the street unnoticed.

He stares at the screen. White. The cursor is blinking away. Baiting him to shit out some more genius prose.

Don't read this.

He types the three words and laughs to himself. Then deletes.

Blank again.

He is angry. There are things he wants to say about the world and about his observations of people. Hotel Beresford is perfect for watching all walks of life. And the eighth floor is perfect for hearing it. The level below is noisy but he's been here so long that it's like a comforting vibration on his feet.

He taps his feet in time with the jazz. He hits the keys harder with every slap. He paces up and down with every push of the vacuum cleaner. Some days he writes without breathing for hours, others he spits four perfectly formed words onto the page. And each evening, he deletes everything.

He can't stay in love with his words.

He had it so perfect. Anything less than that and he will be chewed up by the press and readers and strangers online who just want to vomit vitriol with no personal consequence. Even if he can replicate the quality of that last book, it won't be that book, that surprise success. And too much time has passed now. It will never live up to the hype. He should have just churned something out quickly. Something that could be torn apart that he wouldn't care about.

He's fucked himself.

The writer types more words that nobody will ever see. The coffee will be exchanged for whisky after lunch and by the time he's ready to delete it all again, he will reach into his top drawer, take out the gun, put the barrel into his mouth and pull the trigger.

Then he will laugh at how pathetic he is for not being able to load the thing and end his own misery.

Balliol watches.

I.P. Wayatt did it all by himself. He wrote that novel with blood and sweat. His spirit remains intact. No deal was made, no divine intervention. And there's no need to sell his soul because, it seems, the writer has already chosen to spend the rest of his days in Hell.

SECOND FLOOR

And so it begins.

Tonight's meal is more formal. Everybody has picked what they are having for each course and tables have been assigned. Now, it's lunch. It's casual. Sales people are milling about, mostly men. Too many are attached to their phones, either looking at the screen and swiping away at something, or frantically typing. This event is separate to their everyday work but there are still plenty of people talking about purchase orders.

One guy says, 'Adam, what the fuck are you doing in the office while I'm at this thing? You need to get that order in by close of business today and have it loaded onto the system. Both our commissions depend on that.' He's rude. Everyone around hears but nobody cares. A couple of them even laugh.

He hangs up. 'Internals, eh?' and rolls his eyes. Someone nods in agreement before stuffing another of the free beige food offerings from the buffet into his mouth.

The right kind of mind could set a bomb off on floor three of Hotel Beresford, right now, and take out a bunch of awful white guys – a concentrated area of real arseholes.

Neil is in his thirties. He works for an internet security company. Software. He's the OEM manager. He's not selling a physical product. What he wants is to have his software installed onto a computer when it is made so that it is already there when a consumer turns it on for the first time. He is courting all the hardware manufacturers today.

Danny Elwes works for one of the manufacturers that may be of interest but he is not there on business. His motivations are more hedonistic.

There are three big distributors in attendance as well as some of the smaller online retailers.

Anne-Marie has been sent to spy on the competition. Her boss dressed it up as gaining some experience but he wants her to use the fact that she is a woman to get insecure sales guys to open up to her about strategies and trends. She hates her boss. She hates slimy salesmen, but she loves her job and she is great at it.

The industry is incest at best. Most people have worked for three or four of the companies there. They know one another, and they may well end up back at the company where they started. They are motivated by success. And to them, success is equal to the money you have made.

Some splash the cash and have nothing to show for it. Danny likes cars and toys and gadgets. Anne-Marie has almost paid off her mortgage. And Neil has invested, heavily, in cryptocurrency. In a world where it is difficult to pin a person down to find out what they truly want from their life, the third floor of Hotel Beresford is awash with individuals who possess that very focus. They know what they want and they would sell their own grandmother to get it.

Does that make them bad people?

Does the world need them?

Will they be missed?

There's no Clint Eastwood on that floor; nobody is cool. Half of the men are overweight because they are out on the road and picking up the sausage-roll meal deal every time they fill the car with petrol. The younger ones either still have the metabolism to live that way or they're making time to hit the gym every day so that their suits and shirts hug them in all the right places.

They're eyeing each other up, getting the lay of the land, while picking at vol-au-vents and salmon-topped blinis.

Then in walks Carol.

Three men who work for KaiserTec will regret sniggering as she walks past in her too-tight skirt and her too-much make-up. The smell of her hairspray is equal to their aftershave. Carol doesn't turn around but she does slow her step to let them know that she has clocked their disrespect.

When she turns around she is all teeth and tits and on-brand.

'Good day and welcome to the conference level of Hotel Beresford. Please make sure you get some food before the talks begin. I can heartily recommend the shrimp. The chairs are laid out but no seating is allocated. First come, first served. There are fifteen minutes to go, please arrive a few minutes beforehand so that we can keep everything on schedule.'

She looks around the room. All suits and designer stubble and mobile phones. If she prayed anymore, she'd ask for a meteorite to hit this place.

Carol is great at her job but she didn't sign up for this.

'Are there any questions?' She looks around. Nobody says anything but she spots Danny Elwes in a corner, vibrating, anxious, focussed on her. He definitely has a question but it's nothing he wants to share with the group. 'Okay, great. Then I'll see you in the main room in ten. Thank you.'

The room goes back to murmurs about motherboards and non-volatile RAM and trojans and leaks and speed and service. Danny is still fixed on Carol. She gives a nod to Ollie at the door, just to make him aware.

Backs are turned and food is scoffed. Danny sets off. He's angry and confused but he knows what he wants. He wants to know where the fuck the dead hooker has gone.

He gets up close to Carol. Too close.

'Did you go into my room?'

'I'm sorry, Mr Elwes, I think you need to take a step back.' Ollie is fifteen feet back, Carol can see him over Danny's shoulder.

Danny doesn't move.

'When I left to sign the papers, did you go into my room? Room 420.'

Carol steps back.

'Mr Elwes. It is not my business to be going into people's rooms while they are not there. I know that you have requested room service to change your sheets and towels but that is also not my job.'

'I asked for that at the front desk, how would you already know that?' He is somehow accusatory but baffled.

'Because, Mr Elwes.' Now Carol takes a step closer to him. She lowers her voice, both volume and pitch. 'I know *everything* that happens in this building.'

She lets it hang in the air.

Danny is caught. He's panicking that the – apparently – dead woman in his room is no longer in his room. Maybe she wasn't dead. Maybe she woke up in that suitcase and freaked out and ran. What he is accusing Carol of is taking the body and disposing of it somehow. But that doesn't make sense. Why would she not call the police?

There have been rumours about Hotel Beresford and cover-ups. That they can't have any more bad publicity. But surely that is not enough to let somebody get away with murder.

And why the Hell was he drawing attention to himself?

'Everything okay here, Carol?' Ollie arrives. He stands next to Danny so that his muscular presence can be felt.

'It seems that Mr Elwes is missing something from his room. He's upset that it appears to be missing.'

They both look at Danny.

'I'd be happy to speak with housekeeping and escort them up there unless Mr Elwes wants to have another think about the object he may have simply misplaced.' Ollie speaks very clearly and, to Danny, it seems like they both know exactly what object has gone missing.

'You know, I think I'm just being a bit forgetful. I think I might know where I put it.' He's nervous. Something about this place and the staff is not right. However, he has no choice but to go along with it.

'There you go.' Ollie pats Danny on the shoulder. 'We can all be a bit forgetful sometimes.'

Danny has to smile nervously.

He turns around to fake it to Carol, too, but she has already disappeared. When he turns back to Ollie, he has also started to walk away.

Danny Elwes is alone.

Alone in room 420, now that the dead hooker has been removed.

Alone in a space filled with people just like him.

All faking their way through the day.

All thinking that they are, somehow, getting away with it.

All believing that they are due to check out of Hotel Beresford tomorrow, after the conference.

Carol's meteor could strike and wipe them all out, rid the world of a hundred or so of these vampires. But killing off evil doesn't make the world better. It's too easy to replace. Assassinate a dictator and somebody else will take over – someone idealistic, perhaps, but equally capable of being corrupted.

Chop off the head and another will grow in its place.

Sacrifice a hundred sales people and a hundred more sales people will be recruited within a week. The world is no better. But it's not any worse.

CROSSROADS

Most of the military cannot understand how a soldier could ever walk away from their post.

War is tough. Of course.

You enrol thinking that you are serving your country, you are protecting the people you love and the rights that you have to speech and equality and freedom from tyranny. And when you are finally called up to go to a place of conflict, you are scared, of course, but there's an excitement there, too. This is what you have been training for. You are going to make a difference. People back home will never understand what you are going to go through, but you're not thinking about medals or recognition. Your job is to overthrow the oppressive regime and give the people of that country the ability to self-govern and have a democracy.

What you're not told is the real reason you are there.

What you are not told is that the people of that country do not see you being there to help them towards independence. You have taken over their capital. You are telling them how to run their country. There is still hostility from the people that you believe you have saved because you have not been taught how to deliver the right message.

Go in. Take out the evil. Set up an elected government.

Sounds simple.

Of course it is not.

You are stuck out on some post in the desert, manning a tower, surrounded by barbed wire, shitting into a pit that you eventually have to set fire to.

That wasn't in your training.

You know that every time you get into a vehicle, there's a chance of some improvised explosive device running you off the road. You could get ambushed. End up in a gunfight. What you don't know is why you thought it would be funny to have pictures of you holding up body parts left over from one of these explosions. You don't know why some of the others in your platoon feel it is suddenly acceptable to rape women of the people you have apparently been sent to help. You can't understand why these people think you're the enemy. You're not prepared to see children holding guns and you are less ready for the ease with which soldiers in your regiment will take these kids out.

No blinking.

No question.

And this isn't why you enlisted.

You didn't sign up for this shit.

Maybe you leave your post and get court-martialled, thrown on the next plane home with a dishonourable discharge. There's nobody to meet you when you get back because you let them down, you betrayed your country. But you know that there's no honour in war.

Not the place you've just been.

Not what you have seen.

Not what you will see again and again in your head every time a car backfires or a man raises his voice to a woman in a restaurant.

Not Sergeant Ollie Myers. Born to serve. The only way he's coming back from Afghanistan/Iraq/Kosovo/Vietnam/Korea is in a body bag or with a medal for bravery.

That's what people thought. Friends and family and that band of brothers.

Ollie did come back. He got home. But no Victoria Cross or Purple Heart. Just a head full of nightmares and a lost soul.

SUBURBIA

No wonder they broke up.

How could anybody live like this?

Every piece of furniture is from Ikea. Everything. And it's not disguised in any way. They haven't then bought personal pieces of art or individual cushions or a vase from an antiques fair. Why would you accessorise with some distinctive Japanese cloisonné vases when you can get a Tidvatten or Beräkna for less than a cup of decent coffee?

The place is a blank canvas that the former owners never personalised. Perhaps it is a reflection of the emptiness of their lives. Maybe it's an indication of things that they never got around to doing.

Jun turns his nose up at the place. But Daisy sees potential. She loves the quartz worktop in the kitchen but the cupboards need some colour. She's hoping the wooden floor in the hallway will also be revealed in the living room when she tears up that impractical beige carpet.

She can see where her books will go and a new, larger coffee table with scalloped jute rug. And a space for that cute vintage poster of Paris, even though she has never been. The wall that divides the lounge and kitchen is crying out for some wood panelling, too. Jun looks around and sees somebody's drab and dreary house. Daisy drinks it all in and envisages their new home.

'We have to make an offer,' she whispers to Jun.

'We don't even know what the asking price is yet.'

'Look at this guy. He's a shark. He is happy to take a lower commission, I'll bet. He already said it'll be less than the last one we saw.'

'I can feel my ears burning.' The estate agent appears around a doorway like an enthusiastic meerkat. The Zhaos fake-smile. 'I get it. You want to get down to the nitty gritty. Let's talk numbers.'

He tells the Zhaos that the place is on for thirty grand less than the last place, which was almost identical. 'I shouldn't say this but I reckon you could undercut that by another twenty. This couple just wants out. They're splitting the sheets. But you're going to have to come in today.'

There it is. That hard, slimy sell.

'You're the first couple I called because I know how keen you are.' This is actually true, but he has three others in his back pocket in case he has married together the wrong group of desperate couples.

'Put in that lower offer now.'

'Daisy, you can't just—'

Daisy interrupts him, speaking in a language that the estate agent assumes is Japanese and Jun backs down.

'Call them, Gary. Make the offer.'

'I'll be right back.'

Gary walks out of the back door into the ample garden, and the Zhaos wait. They don't speak. They're too nervous. Daisy walks around opening cupboards she has already looked inside and straightening million-of-a-kind ornaments and storage baskets.

The back door closes and the Zhaos shuffle towards one another and hold their breath.

'Where is it that you're living at the moment?' Gary asks.

'Just outside the city,' Daisy offers.

'Hotel Beresford,' Jun elaborates.

'Oh, really? God, you hear some weird things go on in that place.'

'It's really not that bad. It's helped us save for a deposit.' Jun doesn't know why he is defending the place.

'I heard there are like orgies and murders and stuff.'

'Urban legends, Gary. It's just a building.' Daisy is frustrated. 'What did they say?'

'They said you need to check out of that hellhole and move your things into your new home.'

'What? Really?'

'Really. They accept your offer.'

The Zhaos hug and kiss and laugh uncontrollably. They thank Gary for being such a mercenary piece of shit. They're going back to Hotel Beresford to pack a few things away. Maybe they'll make love and have a celebratory joint.

Outside, away from the prying eyes of the estate agent, the Zhaos take a breath and come together, their foreheads touching.

'Can you believe it, Jun?'

'Life begins, Daisy.'

'Life begins.'

ROOM 728

Sometimes, she listens to Elvis. Not the popular stuff, of course, she's too cool for that. Danielle Ortega knows how influenced The King was by the black gospel sound. That's what she wants to hear. That's what she wants to feel.

Then there's a knock at the door.

Not a heavy knock, it's not one of the seventh-floor men, drunk and looking to cop a feel of some flesh. It's a lighter touch. Not Carol, either. She has a distinctive knock. And not Lailah, from down the hall, who Danielle thinks could possibly become a friend There's always a jauntiness to the way she calls round. But this is quiet. Nervous.

Innocent.

Danielle shouldn't be awake now. This is her time to recover. She's nocturnal. Vampiric. But she can't ignore that little knock at her door in the middle of the day.

She knows that it can only be Odie.

'Everything okay? No school?' Danielle asks, throwing the belt of her gown around her waist.

'I went to school but I got in trouble.'

'And they let you walk home?'

'I told them my mum was outside waiting. It's pretty bad that they just let me go, don't you think?' His little face is so cute and earnest. He seems wise beyond his years.

'It's not great, Odie. Why are you here?'

He explains. His mother is so proud of him at the moment, and he knows that she is making a special effort to get him to school every day. He doesn't want to disappoint her.

'So you want to wait in here?'

'I didn't want to be out walking the streets. The school isn't in the best area.'

'Won't your mother know when she comes to pick you up from school and you're not there?' Danielle pokes her head out of the door and looks down the corridor. She doesn't want to leave the kid in the lurch but she also doesn't want him walking around aimlessly outside. More than that, she doesn't want him to be brave enough to take responsibility for whatever it is that got him in trouble, knock on the door and find out that Diana Walker has a client in there.

Everyone on seventh knows what she does.

Everyone but Odie.

'She doesn't pick me up every day because sometimes she has to...' he pauses a moment '...work.'

Danielle looks at him and wonders whether he does understand his home life better than he should. She doesn't know what to do.

Odie drops his chin to his chest, stares at his scuffed shoes. 'She's doing so much better ... since Dad left.'

Danielle bristles at the mention of Sam Walker – the man she struck over the head, tied up, threw into a cupboard, then he disappeared. She just forgot about him.

He was there and then he wasn't, and she just accepted it.

Things go missing at Hotel Beresford all the time.

You don't ask questions.

Though Danielle didn't get rid of Odie's father, she is complicit in why he is no longer around. Sam brought it on himself, of course, but one person who is not responsible for his disappearance is young Otis 'Odie' Walker.

'Come on in.' Danielle opens her door fully.

She has no choice.

Odie wanders in, his school bag almost as big as him, and the singer shuts the door behind him, sealing them in to the protection of room 728.

Mr Balliol watches with great interest.

What is this unlikely friendship?

The apartment is barely lit and Odie doesn't like the sound of the trumpet coming from the speakers, it sounds out of tune to him. But he isn't scared. He isn't worried that his neighbour is someone that will hurt him in any way. He doesn't think she is the kind of person to lock somebody in a cupboard for days.

She offers him some juice but he says he'd prefer to just drink water.

Odie takes a seat on the sofa. He leaves his coat on because Danielle has the large window open, the curtains move in the breeze. For such a slight woman, she doesn't seem to feel the cold as she should.

Balliol moves closer to the screen.

Odie thanks Danielle for his drink. There are a few hours until school is supposed to finish, so he takes the book out from his bag.

'I won't bother you.'

Danielle wants to go back to bed but she can't just let him loose in her apartment. She lights a cigarette and sits by the open window. You could freeze time on this moment and capture an image that poses so many questions.

The only certainty is that, if Diana Walker finds out this has happened, that her boy spent the day in *that* woman's apartment, she will kill Danielle Ortega.

CONFERENCE ROOM

These things never start on time.

The first speaker, Hamish Belfry, invented a couple of apps. One is used to track your child. If they go out of the designated area you have set for them, it alerts you. Preying on the insecurity of parents is easy money. They won't spend £30 a month for their own gym membership but they'll pay £10 per week for their baby to sing along with a middle-aged woman whose best friend is a teddy bear.

On the other side of things, he launched an app that can scan the food left in your fridge or cupboard and it will give you recipes based on the ingredients that it picks up on camera. Useful for those with little money to make the most of their dried noodles, mushrooms and ketchup, but also perfect for those who have been dying to use the jar of artichokes that have been in the cupboard for a year and the lingonberries that sit confused in the fridge with the reindeer meat.

'Authenticity is key,' he says, but his microphone is not switched on. He looks to the side of the stage. Somebody fiddles with a few buttons then gives him the thumbs-up.

'Authenticity is key,' he tries again. This time, booming through the speakers. Every suit in that audience goes rigid.

He has their attention.

Success breeds respect in this community. Belfry made a ton of money. It doesn't matter that he wasn't really authentic, that he duped his audience or exploited parental guilt and fear.

He talks about not giving things away cheaply or for free, it devalues your brand. It's better to have ten customers who spend a million each than a million customers who spend ten each. Something like that.

It's almost evangelical. He could easily be up there talking about how sinful it is to pursue someone of the same sex for sexual gratification. He could be quoting the Bible and placing his hands on the infirm. He could be cracking out a song about how Jesus is coming again to heal the world and he would not get any more adulation than he is, right now, as he waxes lyrical about social platforms and whether or not it is right to demonstrate process or whether posts should be more curated. That the curated marketing loses some of the authenticity but the 'in process' approach has more risk.

This is the world now. Anyone who can articulate a point well can gain a following. Anybody that can speak with confidence and conviction can be believed. Having your fifteen minutes of fame is a thing of the past, now everybody wants five minutes as God.

They can't handle fifteen minutes of anything, anymore, because attention spans have diminished so irreparably.

There's no awkward moment where the speaker throws out to the audience and everyone is too nervous to ask a question. They're like vultures, feeding on his knowledge and wisdom.

He mentions that they can buy his book afterwards and he will sign it.

An authentic putz.

What he forgets to mention is that a large component to success is luck. There are thousands of companies out there with beautifully curated websites that nobody is looking at. There are authentic family businesses that are just ticking along. And there are kids with no talent or drive that put something out there that takes hold of people's imaginations for an unquantifiable reason.

You can do everything right and still never make it.

The greatest abilities can go unseen.

Danny thinks about putting his hand up and quizzing the guru, but his pocket vibrates. A message from Diana Walker in room 734. It simply says, *Time?*

He responds, coolly, *2*.

That will give him an hour before Odie Walker knocks on the door of room 734, pretending he has just walked home from school.

RECEPTION

The compactor takes eight bags of trash and squashes it into something the size of a stock cube. Cans, food waste, body parts. Forget about recycling or composting or sawing somebody's femur in half. Throw it in, press the red button and let the corkscrew inside clamp the walls together and push it backwards into a compartment that gets emptied once every few weeks.

Carol tells Keith to call two porters to empty the trash room on the fourth floor. He stutters his compliance and puts in a call.

'I'm going to my office for a bit, if anyone wants me.'

'Not listening to the talk?' Keith laughs.

'These fucking people,' Carol whispers, 'if anyone deserves to suffer…'

She seems exasperated already and it's only the first talk.

Carol pushes through the hidden door, locks it from the inside and drops heavily into the chair at her desk. She picks up the picture of her and Jake in Paris. Damn, she loved it there with him. She loved anywhere with him.

He is twenty-five in the picture and she is twenty-seven. Two years before he was taken from her. Carol is tired and she hates the sales people and she knows Mr Balliol is watching and she can't get away from her life. So she cries.

She looks at the image of the great love of her life and she cries.

It's been over fifteen years but it could be fifty. She doesn't know how old she is anymore. Days morph into one another. It's repetition and routine, and that's how it was before Hotel Beresford, but everything was easier with Jake.

People talk about finding their soulmate like it is common. You meet someone, fall in love, believe you want to spend the rest of your life with them. They are a part of something that tessellates with the part that you are. Your souls belong together. You become one.

Everyone who feels that they are in love feels this way. And they should. You are not going to get all of somebody else if you are not giving them all of yourself. It's great to see. A couple walking down the street, holding hands, in their seventies. They've been together for half a century without straying. They have kids who are thriving and look up to them.

This is love.

This is nurturing.

This is beauty.

But it does not mean they are soulmates.

They are not Carol and Jake.

She looks into the corner of her office. Carol doesn't know how Mr Balliol watches everything that happens at Hotel Beresford but there have to be cameras somewhere. She's never seen one but she knows they are there. She can feel him looking at her in her moment of weakness and reflection.

She just wants to be alone. And she can't be when she's at work.

Out there, in the lobby, behind reception, in the conference hall, on the seventh floor, Carol is the consummate professional. In her office, she can pine. She can allow the grief and regret to overwhelm her. She can weep at the futility of her search for peace.

Carol can't explain what it is like. The handful of people that have been fortunate enough to find their soulmate would also have difficulty pinning down the exact emotion they feel. It's love but it's more than that. It's adoration but it's heightened. It's obsession but it's not negative or sinister.

She can't put her finger on it and she doesn't want to. She's so grateful that she got to experience this level of emotion for the short time that she did.

When he died, she could have taken all of her pain away. She stood on the edge of a bridge and thought about jumping.

No more heartache.

But she couldn't do it.

And maybe that is the best way that Carol could describe the level of her love for Jake. Instead of letting him go and letting herself no longer feel the devastation of that, she chose to experience it. As long as she could sustain the loss, she would never forget the love.

Instead of ending her own suffering, Carol chose to spend the rest of her days searching for Jake through Hell.

BASEMENT

People find God in all kinds of weird places. He's often lurking at the bottom of a wine bottle or lingering around the local AA group meeting pretending he gives a fuck. Prison cells are a regular hang-out for the big man upstairs, plenty of desperation to sink His teeth into there. That woman who discovered Jesus's face in a slice of toast, that was something. Millions of Christians expecting the second coming to be a light show with drum solo as JC rides down to Earth on a great white cloud, playing a Stratocaster, ready to put right the disbelievers.

And he shows up on some woman's breakfast.

He's been seen on grilled cheese, fish sticks, chicken nuggets and within packets of crisps. All that power and prestige and He chooses a subtle, snack-based re-entry into the population.

Sam Walker stares up at the ceiling of what looks to be an altar. Some light is coming through but he can't tell how or where it's coming from. Dust particles dance above him, occasionally catching the light. They look like angels. Like something is there to protect him.

It's not.

Sam Walker will die today.

God is not watching over him.

But that does not stop Sam from looking and asking Him for help.

There's a compulsion to speak out loud. To beg God for forgiveness. But Sam has been gagged. He can't tell what is in his mouth but it tastes and smells like leather.

He groans with frustration. His feet and hands are bound, too. And he's naked. He can't move his head enough to look at his body but he can feel that something has been painted over his chest. A symbol of some kind.

'God, please help me. I know that I've done wrong. I've cheated on my wife. I've drunk too much, gambled away my money. I've hurt my child. And I am sorry. Mostly for Odie. I don't know how he has turned out so good. It's nothing to do with me. It's not Diana, either. It's just who he is. He can't be broken. But I want to see him grow. I want to help him. I want to be a good father. But you have to help me out of this.'

Sam is thinking this. Thinking as loudly as he possibly can, so that God can hear him over all the noise of the other people who need Him. All the people of the world with their everyday problems and all the ones in dire situations of starvation and poverty and lying in wait to be sacrificed.

It's a tentative start from Sam Walker.

He is trying to show some kind of remorse for his actions. But that is not enough to be heard. You have to really mean what you are saying to register with a higher power. You have to sweat and cry and feel the anguish.

Sam waits. He doesn't know what for. A sign, maybe.

'Aaaagh,' he howls, writhing against the stone, pulling on his restraints.

He's never getting out of this.

'Please, God. I'm fucking sorry, okay?'

If there is a God, this is not going to work. This is not sincerity. The best Sam can do, now, is open himself up to the Lord. In this moment of desperation, he has to believe. When it comes to his end, when that blade pierces his skin and pushes through his ribs, when it punctures his lung and splits his heart, he must maintain his belief that there is a God. Because that is when he will meet his maker. That is when he will come face to face with the mercurial judgement of his master.

Sam is not going to be saved. But he should have the opportunity to repent all of his transgressions. All of his sins will be covered if he is a man that is in Christ and will, therefore, receive his inheritance.

That's how it works.

God is supposed to forgive you.

Balliol will not.

RECEPTION

'Hey, Carol. Could I possibly use the phone in your office?'

'Forget to charge yours?'

Ollie thinks about lying but Carol would know.

'It's to call my ex-wife. She won't pick up if she knows it's me.'

Ollie has been told that he won't be needed the day after the conference. It's a long day. So much happens. The hotel is packed and every corner holds another secret, another story. The staff need time to recover; they're all involved. Ollie just wants to take that time to see his daughter.

It's been too long.

'Exes, eh?' Carol rolls her eyes. 'You know where it is. Go through. And good luck.' Carol walks off and leaves Ollie to it. She has enough to deal with. She trusts him not to go snooping through her files or logging on to her computer.

Ollie explains to Keith that Carol said he could go into her office. He pushes through the door behind reception, sits down at the desk, picks up the phone and takes a deep breath.

He hasn't planned what he is going to say. He doesn't want his daughter to forget him. He doesn't want her to buy into the crap her mother says about him. All that stuff around town, saying he is a coward and a traitor. They don't understand. They don't know what he had to do to save his entire squad.

There's no need to check the number on his phone, he knows it by heart. Because it used to be his number. Now it's hers. And the guy she has moved into his old bedroom.

It rings three times before someone picks up.

'Hello?'

Ollie's face lights up.

'Hey. Hey, darling. It's Daddy.'

'Daddy.' She sounds excited and Ollie wells up. But he knows that she said it too loud.

'I've got no work in a couple of days. I thought we could get together.'

The phone is snatched out of his daughter's hand before she has a chance to get to the end of the sentence.

'Oliver.' It's his ex. 'What have I told you about calling here, unannounced?'

'Look, I just want to talk to her. I'm her dad. I've got a day off soon.'

'And what? You want to take her for ice cream? You want to pay for her school uniform?'

She's playing to the crowd. Ollie gave her everything he had when he left town. She got his house, his car, his military pension and his kid. He got a security job in a hotel outside the city.

'Come on, that's not fair.'

'Don't you raise your voice to me.'

He didn't. She just wants to paint him as a villain.

'I never did. I know what you're doing. It won't work.'

'Oh, you're just gonna come here and take her? I'd like to see you try, Oliver, you damn coward.'

She's trying to poison her daughter's mind.

'Put her back on the phone, Goddamnit.'

'Goodbye Oliver. Don't call here again.'

Ollie's ex-wife hangs up on him. He slams the receiver down and shouts, 'Fucking bitch.'

He's frustrated.

Ollie is a hero and nobody knows it but him. The one person he cares most about is going to grow up believing that he is some kind of traitor to his country. It breaks him.

At least he has a dog, now.

Something that depends on him.

But he does still have that day off and his ex-wife can go fuck herself if she thinks he won't drive straight into that backwater town, kick down his old front door and spend some time with his only daughter.

Ollie is a hero and his daughter deserves to know that.

ROOM 731

If you wake up and look in the mirror and tell yourself that you're nothing, you'll be nothing. And that's not because you really are nothing but because the brain is a powerful thing. Unfortunately, it's not as powerful as hate, and that's the thing that can beat you down and keep you there and make everything harder.

And you're not that special if you feel like this because these are the things that almost every human being has to deal with.

Almost everyone.

Not Lailah.

To start with, she does not get up in the morning. That makes it difficult for her to be looking in the mirror at that time. But, when she does look in the mirror, she likes what she sees. She enjoys the way that she lives. Lailah is untethered by family, relationships or the law.

She cleans up. Some might call her bohemian. Carefree. Windswept. But there is a scent of trailer park about her, too. It adds to her appeal.

Lailah never stays anywhere for too long. She hits a new town like a whirlwind, breaks a few hearts, ruins a couple of marriages then splits. Off to find the next adventure.

She finds herself at Hotel Beresford with a bag full of bank notes that she stole. She got in with a crowd on the other side of the city. It was none of her business what they were up to and she didn't care, anyway. She liked that they bought her drinks and took her out for meals. Sure, they grabbed her body in the nightclub, but she didn't have to sleep with any of them if she didn't want to.

She did sleep with a couple of them. One bought her a coat. The other came on too strong afterwards. He was supposed to be a tough guy but he came over too simpering. She gave him another shot but he tried to make love to her and that was never what it was about.

They talked a lot.

She listened more.

She knew things that were going down because they would speak in front of her. Pillow talk. Bravado. They trusted her. And that was their mistake. Not hers.

Lailah just wanted a piece of the pie. Something to tide her over until she could decide where to go to next. London, maybe. She hears it's beautiful, even when the skies are grey. And nobody there would have heard of her or what she did with the guy whose kid she used to babysit. Or that fire she started. Or the big bag of fucking money she took from the wrong guys, who were never going to just let it lie.

It was another late night last night, watching Danielle sing then getting drinks after. They ended up at a casino. Not to gamble, just because the bar was open, but Lailah took a wad with her and frittered away a noticeable amount of cash.

These kinds of establishments have a veneer of credibility but they're rarely legit and people talk, and if you're trying to lay low, don't spend money where the lowlifes go.

When you watch a television soap opera, things are hyperreal. It's unfathomable to have that many murderers and fraudsters and adulterers living on one street as part of one of three largely incestuous families. Life isn't like that. Things don't happen in that way.

Hotel Beresford makes television soap operas look like a four-hour Scandinavian documentary about certified tax accountancy.

There's a man in the basement on an altar, ready to be sacrificed in the name of something by a bunch of sales people who are currently attending a sales conference on the third floor. One of the sales guys is on his way to pay for sex with the wife of the guy on the altar. That wife will try to kill the woman a few doors down when she finds out her son has been holed up in her place to bunk school.

The outlaw with a bag of stolen cash won't let that happen to her new best friend. The man in the penthouse watches as all this goes on and the manager of the building knows everything without looking through a single camera.

There are another six floors filled with people.

And it's only a Thursday.

Lailah didn't really understand the kind of men that she was dealing with when she took that bag. That they would hunt her down and find her. That a couple of heavies are walking through the revolving door, right now, while she brushes her teeth, looking in the mirror, telling herself that she can be somebody.

RECEPTION

And the two heavies have no idea what they are up against when Keith calls into the back office for Carol to come out and talk to the two *gentlemen.*

'We need to know which room Lailah is staying in. We know that she's here.'

Keith doesn't even entertain this. Butting heads with some walking pituitary gland is not worth the hassle. There's a quiet one, of course. He's just staring at Keith. The cravat, in particular. Keith knows where this is going. These two obviously share a brain cell. The chatty one is using it today.

'Hey,' he says again because Keith has not given an answer within thirteen nano-seconds. He's asserting his authority.

Keith leans back on his chair.

'Carol,' he calls behind him, 'a couple of gentleman out here for you.' Keith lets his chair spring back to position. 'She'll be right out to help you two handsome fellows.'

He knows their kind. Meat-headed knuckle-draggers. They still think it's okay to call black people negroes and they call each other 'gay' when they fuck something up. So Keith camps things up because he knows it makes small people feel uncomfortable.

It works. There are a few seconds when they don't know how to act or what to say, and that gives Carol enough time to wipe her mascara, take a deep breath and straighten her skirt. She kisses the tip of her forefinger and presses it gently against Jake's face in the picture.

The two goons didn't realise there was an office behind that trick wall and look amazed when it opens to reveal Carol. It perks them up. They are red-blooded Neanderthals and Carol has their prerequisites in an attractive woman: two feet and a heartbeat.

'Good afternoon, welcome to Hotel Beresford, what can I do to help?'

The quiet one stays quiet.

'We need to know the room number of one of your guests, ma'am.' He's suddenly polite. Keith stifles a knowing chuckle and rolls his eyes.

'Do you have a warrant?' Carol is not fucking about. These guys are dressed like wannabe gangsters or henchman from a Bond movie.

'I'm sorry?'

'Well, I assume that a possible crime has been committed by one of our guests so you have gone down the official route of attaining a warrant to search one of our rooms.'

He stutters. Carol knows they're not police.

'Which room is it that you are looking for?' She taps at the keyboard as though ready to search but Keith can see that she is typing 'Fucking hoodlums' into the search bar.

'We don't know what room she is in…'

Carol cuts him off. 'Hotel Beresford has nine floors and hundreds of rooms, sir.'

He's getting frustrated and just blurts out, 'Lailah.'

'I'm sorry?'

'Lailah. That's her name.'

'So, you're looking for somebody called Lailah and I'm assuming you do not have the correct paperwork.'

'Look, lady.' The quiet one slams his hands down on the counter and wipes the subtle grin from Keith's face. 'You know we're not the Goddamned police. We're looking for Lailah and we need you to tell us what room she's in.'

Carol has already gestured for Ollie. Conference days are always busy for the security team.

'It is against our policy to hand out private details of any of our guests. We pride ourselves on our discretion.' Carol knows everyone in that building and she remembers everyone who has ever been here. 'For example, if your boss was here two weeks ago on the fourth floor with his mistress, we would not tell a soul. If he left a briefcase in the lobby one time, which was eventually picked up by somebody else as though it were his own, we would not inform the authorities, even if we assumed that the contents of said briefcase contained something illegal. That is not how we run things here.'

Perhaps she is being too subtle because it takes a few moments for her words to register.

They, eventually, understand the point that she is making but they know they can't go back empty-handed. They're not smart enough to negotiate so they resort to their default – aggression.

'I don't care about your policy, just tell us what room she is in and we will be on our way.'

That's when Ollie arrives.

'I'm afraid you are going to have to be on your way now, gentlemen.'

He stands there, on guard.

One of the ruffians starts to laugh. If this was a movie, he would give some boneheaded what-do-you-think-you're-going-to-do comment. There would be a back-and-forth of some kind and Ollie would either have to back down or engage.

But this is not a movie.

One of the hatchet men takes a step forward and Ollie springs into action. He pushes his middle finger into the thug's neck, just below the Adam's apple. It doesn't need much pressure. A little press in the right place and even the largest of adversaries will surrender their weight to you.

In a split second, Ollie has him on the floor, turned over, arm up behind his back and is marching him towards the exit. His partner is stunned.

Carol jumps in.

'Discretion.' She slams her hands down on the counter, now. 'It's key to how we run things here. I can't stop you from waiting outside on the street or in your car. If the person you are looking for is staying here, there's a good chance you can catch them when they check out.' She leans forward. 'I will say, though, keep an eye on the windows because not all the guests leave through the doors.'

She smiles at him, courteously, and, as she does so, a couple hit the sidewalk from the seventh floor.

CONFERENCE ROOM

There are fifteen minutes left of a talk on integration. Adding a clock to a toaster or a Bluetooth speaker to your bathroom mirror, that kind of thing. DoTrue had a lot of success with a seven-inch netbook that came with a Skype phone that unclipped from the screen. Danny mentions it. Thirty thousand units sold in the first week.

He looks like he's boasting because he is.

Outside the bubble, people are scrambling in the lobby because you feel it in your chest when a body hits the floor from a great height. It's not so much the sound of flesh and bone pummelling into concrete, it's the vibration that hits everybody in the surrounding area. Like you've been whacked in the heart with a plank of wood. The impact of sudden death.

The salespeople on floor three don't flinch. But they are mostly numbed, emotionally, from the genitalia upwards. The talk is interesting for hardware manufacturers and anyone trying to license their software. A couple of the guys in servicing are passing around a hip flask.

The games are just beginning.

It's almost two. They can break for an hour and they intend to drink something, snort something, grab hold of something. It should keep them occupied long enough for the police to cordon off the area so that there is minimal impact to the conference.

There are already several videos uploaded to social media of the dead bodies and shared by the lesser news organisations. The sales guys all have phones they can secretly swipe in silence. Enough of them are bored by the talk to surreptitiously scroll through their updates. One man outside was already swiping through his emails and didn't even stop to peruse the carnage; he just stepped over the dead couple in front of him.

A person's time is their own. It will always be more important to them than your time.

Danny stops bragging for a moment and looks at his own phone. He's thinking about room 734 and that curvy black woman he met at reception.

I'm going to integrate my dick with her. He laughs to himself.

He understands the sales process better than most. He motivates his staff through fear rather than respect but he does get the job done. However, Danny Elwes does not understand women.

The speaker asks if anybody has any questions. Danny resists. He has peacocked for an hour, shown that he can piss highest up the wall. Not once has the dead woman he found in his bed crossed his mind. He's a monster. Beholden to the pathetic bit of gristle that hangs between his legs. And that ego.

Pride goes before destruction.

And a haughty spirit before a fall.

OUTSIDE HOTEL BERESFORD

The thugs have gone. No sense in sticking around if the authorities are about to arrive. Carol watched them dodder off with their tails between their legs. Now she waits outside.

The two people squashed into the sidewalk are from the seventh floor. She knows that. She doesn't even need to see their faces to know who it is. They were a quiet couple. She knows they used to smoke weed on their windowsill. Maybe they were high and got careless. Maybe it was an argument. It doesn't really matter, they have met the same end.

Maybe they were pushed.

A small crowd is forming. This is not what Carol needs. The dead couple were a welcome and timely distraction from those two guys looking for Lailah but Hotel Beresford doesn't need this kind of focus or press coverage.

Carol pushes her way towards the front.

'I'm sorry, ma'am, that's far enough.' A police officer holds out a stiff arm.

'I'm the building manager.'

'Okay, okay, let her through. Let her through.' His stiff arm loosens as he beckons her forward. Carol ducks under the police tape. 'I'm very sorry you have to see this.' He places a reassuring hand at the top of Carol's back.

She's seen much worse but she plays along.

The bodies are prone. Crushed faces. Identities obscured. Burst innards.

'I know it must be difficult but we need to find out which room these people were staying in, so that we can investigate any foul play.'

'There are a lot of people staying here, officer, and we have a conference on the third floor right now.'

'I think we can narrow it down to one of the top…' he looks up at the building and counts with his finger '…three floors, I'd say.'

Carol knows exactly which floor.

'Okay, well, obviously I can't identify them by looking at them but I can get some of the staff knocking on doors and we can eliminate the rooms that it isn't.' Carol needs to get in the room before the police do, to make sure there's nothing incriminating or damaging to Hotel Beresford in there.

She also needs to speak with Lailah.

'That would be mighty helpful, thank you, Miss…?'

'Carol. Just call me Carol.'

'Okay, Carol. I'm just waiting for the rest of the team to get here and then I'll come to reception to find you?'

'That's fine. And how long do you think it will take to … clear everything up. Sorry, I know that sounds callous but I have about ten minutes until a hundred or so sales people exit the conference room and want a drink. I don't want them seeing this. You know?'

'I'm afraid there is going to be a police presence here for the next few hours. It's not an easy clean-up.'

Carol looks at the bodies. She could scrape them both into a bucket in a few minutes, she thinks.

'We'll get a tent up around the victims shortly. When there's nothing to see, the crowds will disperse. Best I can do.'

Carol nods. 'Okay, I'll find the room they were in. You come find me when you're ready.'

The officer thanks her and Carol heads back inside.

She walks straight past the reception desk, down the corridor and over to the lift. Carol gets inside and presses the button for floor seven.

She needs to clean up this mess.

Another couple will be along to rent the room as soon as she is finished.

ROOM 728

'You have a lovely singing voice.' Odie's childish sincerity is enough to melt the heart of a Stasi officer. Danielle has been clearing the sides of the kitchen area while performing a smokier version of 'But Not for Me'.

'Well, I would hope so, Odie, as that's my job.' Her face brightens with the revelation.

Odie shuts his book and sits up straight.

He's interested. He asks if she is famous, and Danielle laughs.

They have spoken so many times in the hallway but it's often early in the morning when Danielle is tired from working all night and she doesn't want to talk about herself; she just wants to make sure that the boy a few doors down is doing okay. She asks him about his book. She mentions his parents because they can often be heard arguing or smashing something. But they have never spoken about her job.

Danielle explains. The awful hours. The worst conditions. The club owners who hold on to payments. She lights a cigarette.

'Isn't that bad for your voice?'

'I can't tell anymore, kid. There are days when I think it might help.'

Odie screws up his face in disbelief. He's not buying that.

Danielle walks over to her favourite window and opens it. She pushes one leg out into the open and sees Odie hold his breath for a moment.

'It's okay. I like to sit here and watch the world go by.' She looks down at the street at a commotion, but she's not sure what's going on. Then she sees a net curtain billow out a few windows down. The window ledge where that young couple who smoke weed like to sit. Danielle enjoys the ritual of it. She blows out a plume of smoke and wonders.

Odie startles her when he appears at the window.

'Something going on in the street,' he says like some world-weary veteran.

'Always something happening in this part of town,' she responds, forgetting, for a moment, how old Odie is.

He points. 'Those police cars look like they're coming this way.'

Danielle is too streetwise to think that bad things only happen at night. The net curtain blows out of the window again and she looks down.

It can't be. And if it is, they must have fallen.

'Odie, it's probably best that you get inside. It's cold out here, I don't want you getting sick or something.'

'Well, won't you get sick out there?'

'I'm made differently, kid.' She draws in a couple of lungs of nicotine and expels it in a way that looks cool to young Odie but he doesn't quite understand why, yet. 'You've got an hour until you're supposed to be home from school, right?'

'I guess.'

'So what are you going to do with your last bit of freedom?'

'Watch TV?' There's a sparkle in his innocent eyes.

'I don't even know if it works. Never switched the thing on.'

'You don't watch television?'

'I've got my music. That's enough for me. If you want to put it on then, by all means, knock yourself out.' She smokes and looks down at the chaos again. Three large vans have turned up since she last looked down. She guesses that somebody is going to have to scrape the bodies off the pavement and take them somewhere.

There's a sound from the living area as Odie manages to switch on the television with the remote he found. First a crackle. Then the fuzz of a channel out of tune. Then...

'...outside Hotel Beresford where a man and a woman lie dead. Early impressions suggest a double suicide...'

'Odie, turn that over, right now.' She doesn't mean to raise her voice but Danielle doesn't want the kid seeing that. She flicks her cigarette down towards the scene below, steps back inside and grabs the remote from his hand.

'...jumped from the roof...' the reporter says.

Danielle switches the channel and a talk show appears on the screen.

'Idiots. There's only one person who can even get to the roof.' She speaks under her breath.

On the TV, two women start fighting. Pulling hair and hitting each other in the face. A caption at the bottom of the screen says, 'You're supposed to be my sister but you stole my man'.

She flicks again.

'See, this is why I don't watch this thing.'

Odie looks a little scared and that makes him seem even smaller, and every station Danielle turns to has somebody fighting or images of war and she just wants the boy to feel relaxed and she doesn't want to think about locking his dad in a cupboard or the stoners down the hall, who have managed to turn themselves into a puddle.

She flicks without looking.

'...and nowhere in the Bible does it say that two women can't love one another. It is not a sin to feel that way.' She can see that Odie is listening. He heard the word 'Bible' and it affected him. Danielle lowers the remote to her side. 'And, if a person feels like they were born the wrong gender, God does not consider that a sin.'

Danielle is shocked that the God Squad are being so progressive on what looks like one of those more extreme, right-wing evangelical broadcasts.

'These things are not a sin. Until you act on them.'

Ah, there it is. And it was going so well.

The grey-haired man on screen starts to turn red. He's angry and he spits vitriol, damning anyone who is not heterosexual and living in the body that God gave them.

Danielle has had enough. All the sounds of the street and the hotel and God-fearing fake faith-healers swell in her mind until she can take it no more and throws the remote hard at the screen, breaking it and shutting down the noise.

Odie looks at her but before she can explain there's a loud knock at the door.

ROOM 724

The place is immaculate. The door was locked from the inside and there are no signs of forced entry. There are interior-design magazines on the coffee table. A bowl of lemons on the kitchen counter. Fresh flowers in a vase on the window that is not open. The place looks and smells like it has been recently polished.

Carol goes into the bedroom. She doesn't know what to expect. A sex swing or crack den. Hidden behind the facade of normality, like the suburban opiate epidemic.

Nothing.

A perfectly made bed. No marks on the walls. The toilets have been bleached. There is no sign of a struggle. In fact, there isn't much for Carol to do but empty the fridge, a small wardrobe and take out the boxes the Zhaos had already excitedly packed. This room will be ready to rent right after the police have seen it.

Outside, on the window ledge, there is an ashtray. This couple were so conscientious that they would rather collect their ash than flick it out into the air to fall down to the ground half a mile away.

There are a couple of joints in there.

Could it have been that they were carelessly high and fell?

But both of them at the same time?

The distraction could not have come at a better time for those down in reception.

'Carol.'

She jumps. 'Jesus fucking Christ.'

'I never get tired of hearing that.' It's Mr Balliol.

'You scared the shit out of me.'

'You left the door open.'

She did not leave the door open.

'Quite the predicament, Carol. A double suicide? We don't need this.'

'I know. I know. I can't control every addict in this building. It's conference day, sir. They're going to be sucking and fucking and taking whatever they can get their hands on tonight. I wasn't expecting the sweet Chinese couple to jump out the window. I mean, look at this place. It's spotless. It's like they planned it. This is how they wanted to check out of the hotel.'

'A tidy house does not mean a happy home.' He raises one eyebrow slightly.

'A tidy house does not ... a tidy house does not make a happy home? What does that even mean?'

Balliol looks at her as though telling her not to talk to him like that, and she pulls back.

'The police want to come in here to investigate. They've asked me to locate the room. I don't feel like there is anything to clean up here. Do you agree?'

He nods.

'Okay. I'll let the police know. But if we have detectives or forensics or whatever coming up to seventh, I'm going to have to knock on doors and get the rest of the floor to behave themselves.'

'This is why you are in charge, Carol.' Balliol smiles at her. He is a beautiful man. Carol misses her dead husband with her entire heart but she is still alive and can understand why Mr Balliol attracts so many women. The money helps but it isn't always about that.

'As if I have a choice,' she throws back to him.

They walk towards the door together. Carol prefers that to when he seemingly disappears into thin air.

'It seems strange to me that they'd both just jump.'

'You know everybody in this building, Carol, but only to a certain level. They could have had financial difficulties or family pressure. One of them might have had a disease and they couldn't live without each other, so decided to go at the same time. We can't know. Maybe they were just clumsy or high. It's hard to tell.'

Carol isn't buying it. She knows that Mr Balliol could tell, she knows that he would know. He may have even watched it. But hers is not the place to question.

They exit room 724 together. Carol turns around to lock the door.

'I'm going to make my way up the hall and knock on some doors.'

She turns around but he is, once again, gone. Carol looks down towards the lift but it's not there. She wants to know how he does that but a part of her also does not.

Carol shakes her head and makes her way along the seventh-floor corridor. The police are waiting downstairs for her. She doesn't need to warn everybody but there are three rooms she wants to get inside.

The first room is number 728.

Danielle Ortega.

CROSSROADS

A man walks into a bar. And he has an orange for a head. He orders a pint of lager and the barman asks, 'I'm sorry, I couldn't help but notice that you appear to have an orange for a head. How did that happen?'

The man takes a swig of his lager and says, 'I was on holiday and found a lamp. I rubbed it to polish it up and a genie came out and granted me three wishes.'

'So what was your first wish?' The barman rolls his eyes.

'I wished that every time I snapped my fingers, women would want to come and be with me.'

'And?'

The man snaps his fingers and two women appear, one either side of him, kissing his cheek.

'Wow. What was your second wish?'

'I wished that any time I put my hands in my pockets, I would pull out money.'

The barman gives him a look. The man puts his hands in his pockets, pulls them out.

'Cha-ching. Cha-ching.'

A wad of notes in each hand.

'Holy shit. So what was your third wish?'

'I wished I had an orange for a head.'

If you are willing enough to part with your very essence and you go through all the trouble to call on the Devil for help, there are rules.

You can't just have *anything* you want.

It's like finding a genie in a lamp. Take your three wishes and make them count. Don't just blurt out 'Peace on Earth' because that can be interpreted as you wanting to be the only person on the entire planet. It would be peaceful. But probably not what you were looking for.

Of course, the main stipulation is that you cannot ask for unlimited wishes.

It's in the small print.

And you can't sell your soul because you want to live forever.

Though it was tried once. There's always a loophole and the Devil can be impish.

A person would be caught out on Earth if they lived to 150 and were still collecting their state pension, for example. If the deal was to remain a certain age forever, that person would have to constantly move around, changing their identity. Perhaps the simpler option, and certainly more fun; there's a lot of world out there to be discovered.

One way to combat this is a counter-offer.

You take a life of poverty and hardship on God's green Earth in exchange for eternity in Hell – or somewhere like it. But not stoking fires or choking on sulphur and begging for liquid. Instead, presiding over your own corner of the netherworld with power and riches and wine and sexual fulfilment. Forever.

Eighty years of penury and isolation and cold nights masturbating into a warm flannel will seem like the flutter of an eyelid when compared to the perpetual afterlife of hedonism without consequence.

Even too much of a good thing can become laborious. And that's why selling your soul has to be more considered than merely thinking that having a dream come true is enough. Otherwise you may as well ask to have an orange for a head.

THE PENTHOUSE

He watches as Daisy Zhao reads one of her interior-design magazines on the sofa while drinking a cup of tea. Jun is pottering about and cleaning. He strokes her shoulder lovingly as he walks behind her after polishing the windowsill. She turns and looks up to him with love in her eyes. Adoration, even. She places her hand on his.

They speak to one another about nothing in particular. Neither of them is at work, though Jun's laptop is on and charged and he was tapping away at something before sweeping the floor.

Balliol finds the minutiae of everyday activity riveting. He leans in to mundanity. There's a simplicity that he responds to. But he fast-forwards this section of the video.

Next, Daisy and Jun are on the sofa together. She sits with her legs crossed; he sits leaning back with his legs open, thinking. They drink hot tea and don't speak. She is still reading and he is resting. There is something to be said about a couple who can sit in the same spot and remain silent. There is a gift to that, to feel so completely comfortable with another person that you don't feel the need to fill the air.

He skips a few minutes and it appears that they have had enough of silence and are kissing one another. Jun kneels on the floor. He pushes Daisy's knees apart.

Balliol skips forward. There are twenty other rooms he could look at right now if he wanted to see some kind of sexual activity. That's not why he is here.

The Zhaos make love. Missionary style. Meaningful. Sensual. Balliol gets to the end of the session as both Daisy and Jun adjust their clothing. Daisy leans forward and pulls a tin from the drawer in the coffee table. She shakes it at Jun. He nods and takes the ashtray from the sideboard. A replica of the one that Danielle used to knock Sam Walker unconscious.

All the rooms have one.

Just as all the rooms have a copy of the Bible in the bedside tables. Something of a private joke, it seems.

Daisy and Jun open the large window that looks out over the street. Balliol moves forward in his seat. Jun holds the window up and Daisy exits first. She sits outside on the ledge. She is waif and short and there is plenty of room for her out there. Jun goes out after her.

It is possible to see Daisy open her tin and take out two pre-rolled joints and a lighter. Jun places the ashtray between them. They light up and smile at one another. So happy. So content. So neat and tidy and sexually fulfilled.

And alive.

They look out over the buildings on the outskirts of the city. It could be Tokyo or Paris or Berlin, it doesn't matter. They are there, in that moment, together.

It may be that they are sharing another moment of quiet contemplation. Balliol cannot tell from the video but he knows that he is getting near to the part he wants to see.

He doesn't want to scan forward any more, though, in case he misses it.

Mr Balliol thinks back an hour. He was looking at the videos, watching Sam in the cellar and Sam's wife in their bed with another man and those no-good gang members mouthing off at the front desk. It felt like things could escalate quickly, even with Ollie on hand.

He waits.

The wind blows the net curtain back. Daisy and Jun take another drag. The buildings in front of them. Their lives ahead.

Then it happens.

Mr Balliol watches himself step in from the right-hand side of the screen, walk up to the open window and push the Zhaos hard so that they lose balance, fall off, and plummet to the street below.

He rewinds and watches it again.

There is no pause. No hesitation. He does not say anything to alert them to his presence. He just pushed them.

For fun.

For science.

Another experiment.

They simply create a distraction. Balliol snuffed out two people in love.

He rewinds once more and watches, marvelling at his own lack of mercy.

Getting the job done.

Straight in. Straight out.

Then he deletes the evidence.

ROOM 728

'I assume you've spotted the commotion outside.' This is not a question. Carol knows that Danielle also likes to sit out on the ledge and smoke. Regular cigarettes. No drugs apart from jazz. And she's a little more sensible, only dangling one leg over the edge.

'I can see a crowd of people down there.' Danielle doesn't want to talk to Carol. She likes her, but she wants the manager of the hotel away from the room where Odie Walker is hiding out. This is the reason she doesn't get involved with people; it just complicates things. Her lone wolf strategy has got her this far in life. She has Fitzgerald and Holiday and Porter and Mingus, what else does she need?

Carol waits.

Danielle has to fill the air.

She holds on to the door, only leaving an opening big enough for her tired but handsome face. Tanned skin and cheekbones.

'What's going on?' She has to engage, though she doesn't want to. Odie is being quiet behind her.

'Do you know the Zhaos?' Carol asks.

'The whos?'

'The Zhaos. Daisy and Jun. They lived a couple of doors down.'

Danielle clocks the tense immediately.

Lived.

It's easy for Carol to compartmentalise these kinds of events because she cleans them up and covers them all the time. She understands Hotel Beresford.

Danielle wants to shut the door but she also wants to ask about the couple. Carol leans in towards her and speaks quietly. 'They used to smoke out on the ledge, like you do, Ms Ortega.' Carol tries to look inside over Danielle's slender shoulder.

'Did ... did they fall? Was that what the people were crowding around?'

'Fell, jumped. Nobody knows. Maybe they were pushed.'

'Jesus Christ.'

'He ain't here, Ms Ortega. But I know that sweet little boy is.' Danielle's eyes widen. How could she possibly know that? 'The police will be coming up here very soon. I have to let them examine the Zhaos' old room.' It's so clinical. Carol has moved on. 'As I'm sure you can imagine, there are certain parties on this floor who would prefer not to have a police presence.' Danielle thinks about Lailah but that is not the person Carol is talking about.

Danielle shifts nervously on her feet. Lailah told her about the money. They've both been enjoying it. She understands that it isn't a real friendship, Danielle never lets anybody close. But it's all she's got.

Carol snaps her out of reverie.

'We know what the boy's mother gets up to, how she pays her rent. I'll be knocking on her door shortly. If she finds out her boy is in here with you, of all people, the police won't be worrying about the Chinese couple kissing concrete out the front.'

CROSSROADS

You can be anybody that you want to be, now. Don't get this confused with that stupidly platitudinous thing your parents used to say, 'Oh, darling, you can be anything that you want to be if you just put your mind to it.' That, of course, is not true. Otherwise every other person would be a rock star or astronaut or the prime minister.

You can be anybody.

Not any*thing*.

And not like that person you tried to be in your first year at university, where you thought that, because nobody knows who you are, you can reinvent yourself. You can be the gregarious, outspoken joker, even though you've always been the intrinsic loner, bookish type.

That is different.

That is trying to be something that you are not.

No. There is a better understanding now – it's not perfect – but you can be whoever you want to be. If you were born a male but have always felt like a female, then you are a female. You can be one. Because you are. It works the other way, too. Maybe you don't feel like either. That's fine. You be you.

Maybe that's it. It's not that you can be anybody, it's that you can, actually, be you.

There is still some education to be had by some, and there are groups that will never even try to understand it. But at least the radicals have loosened their hateful grip on the gay community, a little, while they process things.

It wasn't like that for Keith.

There weren't many gay kids around when he was young. And, as he grew up, the ones that were had to make a physical event of telling their parents and family and friends. That feeling of uncertainty about how the people who are supposed to love you the most will react was gut-wrenching.

Keith never had to do it. He was born a male and had always felt that way. He wasn't attracted to other men. He wasn't even really attracted to women. But he also isn't asexual. He still feels the need to release something from the chamber once in a while. But it is more of a physical necessity than an emotional one.

Grip it and rip it.

He never really understood himself, so how could he expect that from anybody else?

Keith wasn't the weird kid at school. He had friends. He was above average, academically. He wasn't great at sports because he was tall and it took a long time to gain some control of his body.

Some of the boys made fun of him because he was effeminate. Others because of his stutter. But, mostly, he blended in somewhere among the mediocrity. Everybody had a quirk of some kind.

But he always felt it. Something that wasn't quite right. And when he found that his parents had spoken with their local pastor about conversion therapy and exorcism, he knew it was time to leave. He was a kind kid and thoughtful teenager. Keith was conflicted but he was good. And, one day, his mother decided that the only reason he had never brought a girlfriend home for dinner was because he had the Devil in him.

This was not Keith's crossroads moment, though. For him, there was only one choice, the long, straight road out of town to wherever.

He worked in a bar, a restaurant, a coffee house that had poetry readings on a Thursday where the audience clicked their fingers instead of clapping. Always something to do with hospitality.

He got a small place of his own and found a new church. He cooked for himself. He made new friends. Ones that didn't judge him or imitate when he stuttered. And one of those friends was also a person of faith. But he didn't go to church. He didn't believe that a church was a big building with stained-glass windows. A church was just a gathering of like-minded people.

Keith took a chance.

The members were accepting. They believed in living life to its fullest, in taking out the negative influences.

Keith liked it.

He liked the wine and the sexual liberation and the sense of society.

And they told him that he can do anything he wants, but not in that parental way, more that he should enjoy the more decadent things in life. If he wanted to drink red wine at lunchtime, he should drink red wine at lunchtime. If he wanted to wear a different-coloured cravat every day, he needed to buy more cravats.

All Keith wanted was to be content with who he was. And, for whatever reason, he felt held back on this until he could have his mother's understanding.

That's it. That's what he wanted. To help his mother.

It doesn't sound like a lot. Especially today when anybody can be anybody that they feel they are. It was harder then. So what Keith was asking seemed like a big deal.

He ended up in hospitality, working behind reception at Hotel Beresford. He loves his job. He loves the people around him. He respects Carol. But, greatest of all, he accepts who is. That he doesn't require a label. That he is being himself.

He's content.

Keith got what he wanted.

He didn't even ask to get rid of the stutter.

ROOM 731

The bag is either one-third empty or two-thirds filled, depending on your outlook in life.

Lailah has been blowing through the cash like she has another five identical bags. She doesn't want to save it, though. It's not her nest egg. It's this chapter in her nomadic life. She is a walking whirlwind. A free spirit. She is ready at a moment to give away her heart to anyone who wants it. She jumps with both feet into love, whether it is for one year or one night.

Take her heart.

Have her love.

Lailah's soul is her own.

She has showered away the excesses of the night before. She looks at herself in the mirror, pushing the skin around her face, she smooths around her eyes and lifts her cheeks. Smiles at herself. And is interrupted by a forceful knock at her door.

Lailah ignores it. She hasn't ordered room service yet and she knows that it won't be Danielle at this time, there is still too much light in the sky.

Another knock. Heavy. It sounds official. Like a police knock.

'Shit.'

She runs into the bedroom, zips the bag that is lying on her bed and places it inside the sideboard beneath the mirror.

Another knock.

'Okay, okay. I'm coming.'

Lailah peers through the hole and sees Carol. It is official, it seems, but not what she was anticipating. She blows the air out of her lungs and opens the door wide, like she has nothing to hide.

'Ah, Lailah. There you are.' Carol would normally refer to a guest by using their surname but Lailah checked in with only her first name. Her Christian name, so to speak.

'Is there a problem?' Lailah is direct. Straight to the point. Her life is for living, not for hanging around in doorways, talking to the help.

Carol reciprocates. She doesn't have the time for pleasantries, either. And if that's the way Lailah wants to play it, Carol is happy to oblige.

'Two people down the hall just jumped out of their window and the police are coming up here to investigate.'

Lailah nods. Not an expected reaction to the news of a double suicide but she is a woman of the world. She has seen things.

'They may come knocking. You didn't even know the Zhaos, so there's nothing to worry about.'

'Okay. So why are you telling me?' It almost sounds rude but it's not. It's the way younger people speak. They can't hold a conversation with one person. Especially when you can't add a smiley face to show that you're not being a bitch on purpose.

'It's time for you to move on.'

'What? I haven't done anything wrong.'

'You took something from somebody and that somebody was the wrong kind of somebody. They've been here looking for you. They know where you are. We got rid of them for now but they will be back.'

For once, Lailah doesn't know what to say. There's no youthful banter or biting satire. She's shocked that they caught up with her so quickly, annoyed that she has to get going as soon as possible but also thankful to Carol for what she has done. For holding them off to give her a bit of a head start as she moves towards the next place.

But, just in case...

'I don't know what you're talking ab—'

'I really don't have time for this. Take the warning or don't, you've paid for the month. Stay and take your chances. I can't hold them off for that long though. Or cut your losses and go. Get a plane. Go somewhere you've always wanted to go before life catches up with you, Lailah.'

Lailah's shoulders loosen. Her head drops. She's defeated.

'Okay, thanks. I'll pack up and be out of here tomorrow.'

'Your best bet is to head out today. Plenty of distractions with the conference and the two dead jumpers out front.'

Carol doesn't say goodbye or wish Lailah luck. Her job is done. The hotel has the money, the guest is checking out.

On to room 734.

ROOM 803

Tragedy is inspiring for a writer. I.P. Wayatt looks out of his window and creates a story for the two people, face down on the ground. Then another for the police detective. Though not going the conventional route of a whisky-guzzling divorcee who struggles to connect with his only child.

That's not his style.

But it's all too obvious.

There's a greater interest in the peripheral characters. In their psychology. In how the events affect them. He writes about the human condition, he tells himself, not police procedure.

Wayatt can feel the buzz of activity on the seventh floor below him and, like a cliché he would hate, he pours himself a drink. Downs it. Takes the empty gun, puts it in his mouth and pulls the trigger.

It's become something of an affectation now. Like chewing his pen or deleting every word he writes each day.

Maybe jumping out the window isn't such a bad idea.

The writer sips at the drink and shuts his eyes.

'God, you are such a fucking loser,' he says out loud to himself. 'Talking to yourself, too, now.' He laughs.

Another drink.

Then he types.

The Losers by I.P. Wayatt.

Mr Balliol watches. He is fascinated. Here is an artist, struggling with his own success. How can he follow something that has been deemed a masterpiece? There is an easy way. And the answer lies within the very building he inhabits.

But Wayatt won't do it.
He hates himself.
But he also believes. He won't sell out.
He writes.

Suzanne got me here.

She was my favourite mistake.

These places always smell like smoke and desperation and day-old booze breath and sweat that's soaked into shirts and suit jackets as men try to hold the focus of their game-defining bluff. And they're always full. More losers than winners. You can't find these card games by asking around, that's not how it works. First, you find the booze. That's the easy part. Then you fuck up somewhere down the line, then you find trouble and that's probably the easiest thing of all. Then you find the cards and the places like this shit-hole find you. And they devour you. Sometimes whole. Sometimes in smaller pieces. And they make you feel like you're worth something on the odd incredible occasion but mostly you find yourself deeper in a hole you have no real chance of digging out of. And you realise that, really, you're already fucking dead and you don't know whether it was the drink, the cards or the trouble. And now you like all those things so much that the pit can't get any darker. Then, one night, boat after boat after boat. And from that chair you've been sitting in for sixteen hours in a room slunk beneath a building that you accessed down nine wet, concrete steps, where the air is sick and shadows go to die, you start to see light.

My luck began to change around two.

No pause. It comes out in a stream. Wayatt placed himself in the middle of a poker game in some unnamed speakeasy and hinted at a love affair. Maybe he is projecting. It doesn't matter. He is an artist.
He drinks.
He spins the barrel of the gun and fires in his mouth.
He highlights the paragraph.

Then he sits back in his chair. He looks out of the window. Hubbub. Uncertainty. Untimely death. This world is awful. Mr Balliol watches as the writer holds the unloaded weapon to his temple.

This would be more fun with one bullet, he thinks.

Then Wayatt does something different. Something that doesn't fit in with his usual regime of self-loathing and destruction. He places the empty gun into a drawer, locks it and sits back at his laptop.

For a moment, he looks at the screen. Those highlighted words, one key away from obliteration. He moves the cursor to the end of the last word he wrote. He clicks. Hits return. And types more. Like some black alchemist spinning literary gold from his personal tragedy and the unfortunate circumstances that surround him.

The arguing, death-metal music and human sacrifice beneath him will not stop I.P. Wayatt from writing until the sun comes up on a new day.

Balliol watches. He is supposed to be the king of this building. Everything happens beneath *him.* He will let Wayatt have his moment. The man has soul. And Balliol has proved before that he is nothing if not a patron to the arts.

ROOM 734

These sales guys come in here once a month swinging their dicks around like they own the place, so Diana is disappointed that Danny Elwes couldn't swing his dick if he tried. It's like a Brazil nut nestled in a handful of tobacco. But it's her job to make him feel like he's John Holmes, even though she would probably find a bigger dick on Katie Holmes.

Size doesn't matter, unless it's the size of his wallet.

She makes all the right noises. She calls him 'baby'. Tells him to give it to her. He's on top of her. She lifts her legs in the air and grabs her own feet, trying to force another centimetre in.

There's a knock at the door.

'Ignore it, baby. It's not for us.'

Danny keeps thrusting.

'That's it. Right there,' she lies.

Danny is sweating.

Four in four nights.

Maybe it's too much for him because he finds Diana attractive and he is going for it but he can't seem to get himself over the line. He asks her if she is going to come. There's no end to his ego or delusion.

'I'm close, baby. Keep going,' she lies again.

Another knock.

'Mrs Walker.' It's Carol's unmistakable tone.

'Ignore her, she'll go. Give it to me. Give it to me.'

Carol can hear Diana's histrionics. She's fooling no one. Carol just wants to get back downstairs to oversee events and prevent pandemonium. This is damage control for Hotel Beresford but also a courtesy call for her guests.

'Mrs Walker.' She speaks louder this time. 'I'm afraid I'm really going to have to speak with you.'

'Ah, fuck.' Danny rolls off. 'I can't focus with her in my ear. She gives me the fucking creeps.' It's an excuse. He'll be lucky if he blows a puff of smoke out of that pathetic excuse for a male appendage.

Diana has been in this position before. Some client does too much blow and goes soft after finger-banging her and getting his dick sucked, and tries not to pay.

She won't have it.

Diana is an angry woman. The shit she has to go through just to get by. The crap she has had to take from her husband, it has beaten the softness out of her and the smile off her face. She looks mad most of the time. She is used to scaring people. Particularly other women. Often her scowl of disapproval is enough, but this interruption has her raging.

The problem is that Carol doesn't scare so easily.

'What the fuck do you think you're—'

This day is dragging on too long already. Carol reaches into room 734 and grabs Diana by the throat. She pushes her inside and down to the floor. Then she wraps a clump of hair around her hand and drags the sex worker over to the window.

'Look. Now. Look down there.' She pulls Diana's hair and Diana can do nothing but follow. Carol pushes Diana's face to the window. Danny stays in the bedroom. Silent. 'On the pavement. Look. Dead. Jumped from the window.'

'What's that got to do with me?' Diana tries to stay strong but her scalp is in agony. She doesn't know why everybody has to hurt her.

'They lived on this floor.'

'Okay.'

'That's all you've got?'

'I don't know what I'm supposed to say.' All the strength and confidence that Diana was feeling because Sam is gone has disappeared.

Carol crouches next to her. She lets go of Diana's hair, pushing her head backward.

Diana looks like she wants to try and get back to her feet.

'Don't get up. Listen, I know what you do in here. I don't care. You've never missed a payment. But two people jumped out their window on this floor and the police are going to be up here, so either keep the acting quieter or knock it on the head for the rest of the day, okay?'

Danny is either feeling chivalrous or just wants to take on Carol.

'I don't know who you think you are.' Danny comes out of the bedroom wearing just his underwear.

Carol has had enough. She was trying to help Diana Walker, the woman doesn't need anything else on her plate, she's just trying to provide for her sweet boy.

She doesn't even look at Danny. Keeps walking.

'I run this place, Mr Elwes. I know where that thing is you lost from your suitcase, so, if you want it back, keep talking.'

'What is she talking about?' Diana asks.

Danny shakes his head and waves his hand as if to suggest it is nothing.

Carol leaves and slams the door behind her. She walks down the corridor and back to the lift, where Mr Balliol is waiting to greet her with a smile and a long, slow clap.

RECEPTION

'What the hell is she doing up there?' The detective is getting agitated.

Outside, the bodies of the Zhaos have been obscured by some kind of gazebo. There are a few stragglers. Older folk, who have a longer attention span than the mobile-phone zombies who have already moved on to the next episode of trash TV to binge on or celebrity apology or fashion trend set by a sixteen-year-old with low self-esteem and a 'daddy' who still calls her 'Princess'.

'Carol is the best at what she does, sir,' Keith says. 'I'm sure she won't be long.'

The detective can't stop himself from giving Keith a sideways glance. A look that Keith has witnessed on many an occasion. One that says, *What exactly are you?*

Keith is exactly what he wants to be.

And he is content.

Keith is one of the only members of staff who doesn't need a day off after conference. He has nobody to go home to. He has no dog. There's nothing in his fridge that resembles nutrition. He has a double bed that he has never shared with another person. And he is content.

He is, seemingly, the only member of staff at Hotel Beresford who is satisfied.

He wants for nothing.

All he ever cared about was that his mother would find a way to understand and accept him. Accept that she would not see him marry 'a nice woman'. That he would not provide her with a grandchild. It hurt him that she could not just love him and trust that he knew what he was doing; he knew who he was. But Keith could see it was hurting her more. It wasn't him causing her pain, it was her own ignorance.

But she eventually came around. Keith made sure of that.

It was all he ever needed.

So, Keith doesn't feel the same way as the other staff – though he will join in with their jokes.

He is fine.

He's better than that, he's fulfilled.

And he's not going anywhere, because he loves his job.

'I could have found the room on my own by now.' The detective rolls his eyes.

Keith has to bite his lip. He doesn't respond well to anybody that has a cross word to say about Carol. The woman is living with a broken heart. She deserves better.

He exhales a subtle laugh.

'Something to say there, Chuckles?' the detective barks.

The colour rises in Keith's cheeks but before he gets the opportunity to respond, a man waiting in line behind, steps between them.

'I think you need to show this gentleman some respect.' He is calm. Self-assured. Quiet. But there is a power in his subtlety.

'I'm sorry, old m—'

The old man holds a finger up and the detective stops talking.

'Uh-uh. Don't try that with me. Turn around and go and sit over there and wait. That's a good boy.' He twirls his raised finger in the air and the detective seemingly obliges. He turns, walks off and goes to sit down, just as Carol and Mr Balliol emerge from the corridor that leads to the lift.

Balliol shoots the old man a glance.

Carol is focussed on the detective.

The old man just wants a room to rest his head. But not just any room.

'Good day,' he says to Keith. This man must have walked in past the scene outside but seems completely untroubled. 'I'd like a room.'

'Certainly, sir. And how long will you be staying for?'

'Definitely tonight but perhaps a little longer.'

Keith taps at the keyboard. 'Are you here for work or pleasure?'

'A little of both.'

Keith starts to explain how Hotel Beresford works. The shorter-stay rooms and the longer leases but the old man cuts him off.

'I'd like room 731, please?'

'I'm sorry?'

'Room 731. That is the room I'm going to stay in.'

Keith is confused. He looks at the screen and sees that Lailah has paid up to the end of the month.

'I'm sorry, sir, that room is unavailable. It has been booked for the next few weeks. Can I possibly offer you a different room?'

Quietly. Calmly. 'No. I'll take room 731.'

'But, I'm sorry, it won't be available until the end of the month.'

'I'm a little early, it seems. Not to worry, I'll wait over there.'

The elderly gentleman turns on his heel and wanders to the seat he told the detective to take. He sits down. And he waits.

CROSSROADS

'No change.' The doctor is incredulous.

'That's a good thing, though, right?' Mrs May is trying to deflect. She didn't want to come for this check-up but her husband insisted. There's no way he should have got half the things done on his list but he's still here.

'Well, it's still stage four. It's aggressive. But you don't appear to have deteriorated at all. On these current findings, I would tell you the same thing as before. A few weeks, maybe a month.'

'And to pray.' Mrs May chimes in.

'I beg your pardon?'

'Pray, doctor. You told us, when we were here last time, that we should pray.'

'You must have prayed very hard, Mrs May.'

He has no idea.

Finally, Mr May, the actual patient, joins the conversation. 'But how can it be? I don't feel any worse. I don't feel ill at all. Not one bit. But you are still telling me that I'm all but dead. Have you got this wrong before?'

'Not at this level, no. You are, of course, entitled to a second opinion if you would like one.'

'You know I think I wo—'

'There's no need,' Mrs May interrupts. She is not going to let him get poked and prodded for nothing. 'I don't know any of this medical jargon but I can see from the report that your body is a wreck inside, darling. Our agreement was to live. Whether that's another week, month or year.'

The doctor screws his face slightly when she says this.

'You don't have to do that.' There's a quiet menace to Mrs May's poise. 'You were wrong last time. And I am confident that you are wrong this time.' She turns to her husband. 'Let's go, dear.' And he stands. 'Thank you for your time, doctor. I think we will probably be too busy for any future examinations.'

They exit the clinic together but Mrs May turns around in the corridor and goes back. She pushes the doctor's door open.

'Did you forget something,' he asks, already flicking through the file of his next patient.

'I want you to remember today. Remember that I told you he has a year left.'

'I'm sorry, Mrs May, I can only work with the science I have. I don't like to give people false hope. But I hope you are right.'

'Remember this day, doctor. Everybody prays when they are desperate, even the non-believers. But nobody prays like me.'

ROOM 731

She surfed in to Hotel Beresford on a tsunami and will exit amid a whirlwind of dust and fists and shouting and chaos.

This is what Lailah does.

It's not hard to find her. Just follow the path of destruction.

She wants to pack her bag, quickly clean herself up, grab a handful of money she can use to disappear and then do exactly that.

There's hardly any money in her bank account because she doesn't want to leave a trail, so she can't book a flight online. She never rests anywhere for long enough to have a permanent address, so doesn't have a credit card. Lailah is going to have to chance it. Her plan is to turn up at the airport and get whatever last-minute offer they have to get to London. If everything is booked up, then she will take whatever they have and decide what to do when she gets there.

Maybe she could make it in Yemen or Sierra Leone, if she really had to.

But first, she wants to say a quick goodbye to Danielle. They're not going to be life-long friends but her companionship made this short chapter a lot more enjoyable.

Lailah has her huge rucksack that will need to be checked in and she plans to keep the pile of banknotes in her hand luggage with a bottle of water and her purse. It's not well thought-out but nothing is. And it has got her this far.

She shuts the door to room 731 and walks towards the lift, tapping lightly on Danielle's place, one final time.

'Oh, it's you. Hey. I thought it might be Carol.' Danielle opens the door a little more, seeing a friendly face.

'She told me about the couple that fell.'

'Terrible stuff. I didn't really know them. But still…'

'I'm heading out,' Lailah says, looking her friend dead in the eyes.

'Oh, I can't. I've kinda got myself into something.' Danielle nods back towards her lounge where Odie is sitting.

'Well, hey, mister. What's your name?'

'It's Otis but people call me Odie.'

Lailah looks at Danielle.

'Long story.' Danielle sighs.

'Maybe tell me some other time. You see … I wasn't knocking to see if you wanted to go out. I'm leaving.'

'What? You just got here.'

'I know. I know. I guess we all kinda get into something that's a longer story than we have time to tell.' She smiles but she looks sad.

'Oh, Lailah. What a shit show this life is turning out to be, huh? I'm sorry to see you go.' She hugs her. It's sincere. They're both loners, looking for something. But they still don't know what it is.

Odie appears in the doorway.

'Look. Message me when you get to wherever you're going, okay?' Danielle asks.

'I'll let you know my change of number. Probably best I don't say where I'm going yet, then you won't have to lie if anyone asks you.'

'God, it's all very mysterious. Just take care, okay.'

'You, too.' Lailah looks down. 'And you, little man.'

Odie lifts an eyebrow and both women find it cute.

Lailah hauls her heavy bag down the hall to the lift and gets in. She turns back and Danielle and Odie are out in the hall waving goodbye to her. She does the same then disappears downward.

Then there's shouting and screaming and Lailah can't help but feel a pang of fondness for the disarray of the seventh floor of Hotel Beresford in all its technicolour havoc.

She travels alone in the lift. The third floor seems more vibrant than she is used to because of the conference-goers. Lailah is annoyed that she has to leave so soon. There was no time to take hold. She walks down the corridor for the final time, taking in the monochrome artwork, eventually reaching the reception desk and handing her key back to Keith.

'Thanks, Keith. It's been a blast.'

'You're leaving? But you're paid up to the end of the month.'

'I can't stay still for long enough, I guess. On to the next adventure.'

There's something in her eyes that Keith doesn't quite believe. He knows what it's like to fake it through the day.

'Well, good luck, Miss Lailah.'

She has already turned to leave and throws the kind receptionist a furtive wave of the hand.

Keith goes to his computer, taps a few keys on his keyboard and alerts the cleaning crew to turn over room 731.

The man sitting against the wall in the lobby watches Lailah exit. Once the door closes, he sets his watch to sixty seconds and waits.

Then he walks over to the reception desk. Keith sees him approach.

'I guess I'll take that room, now.'

ROOM 728

'What. The. Fuck?' Diana screams down the hallway of the seventh floor.

'Oh, shit.' Danielle Ortega sees her unfriendly neighbour push Danny Elwes aside and steam towards her and Odie.

She sighs.

So close. Lailah's hair has only just dropped to the sixth floor and Odie's hand is still in the air waving. Why did they have to step outside? Stupid.

Diana wants to kill first and ask questions later. It's instinctive to her. As soon as she saw Odie's innocent face. Some maternal compulsion overcame her and propelled her forward.

'Damn woman. I knew you was trouble.' She stomps.

Diana has worked the streets before. There's an intuition for danger you develop after a while– which cars you should not get in to and which alleyways you should walk past a little faster. But there are other levels of street smartness and Danielle Ortega is as urban as you can get.

Diana Walker is a bigger, more full-figured woman than her jazz-singing neighbour. And she has the rage. But Danielle has seen people like this before. Bulldozer bullies who think they can steamroll over anything in their path that they do not agree with.

She sees that Diana is coming for her. She doesn't care that her son is going to see this behaviour because, in her warped mind, she is protecting him.

'Odie, can you just stand in my doorway, please?' Danielle is polite and cautious and saddened that he is about to witness this altercation.

Diana Walker sees nothing but the woman she has always hated. Everything around her is a haze. She wants to pummel her – though it isn't really Danielle, in particular, it's every man who ever dared to lay a finger on her. Diana has already been embarrassed once today by Carol and she isn't about to let that happen again. She clenches her fists as she walks. Her plan is to keep moving and swing her arms at Danielle's head until she starts twitching on the ground.

Diana Walker, who has taken her fair share of beatings from her husband.

Diana Walker, who has a safety word in place for when clients want to strangle her as they come.

Diana Walker, who never has the thought cross her mind that the skinny bitch down the hall can't be taken down easily.

She rushes the last few feet before taking a fist straight to the throat that leaves her writhing on the floor, her hands on her neck, desperately trying to open her windpipe and find some air.

'No. Mum,' Odie cries out.

Danielle has made peace with the fact that the sweet, little bookworm a few doors down will never be able to talk to her again. She stands on one of Diana's arms, so that she can't bring it to her own neck, and leans down.

'I was looking after him while you fucked some suit for money, you damn idiot. I'm not your enemy. There's nothing here between us. It's not me that you're mad at. You fucking created it in your head. Now go back to your hole and don't darken my door again.'

Danielle releases Diana's arm but only to lift her leg and then stamp down hard on her chest.

She turns to her doorway.

'I'm sorry, Odie. It's time for you to go home.'

The boy drops to his knees and hugs his mother. He has forgotten about getting kicked out of school and the two people that jumped out of a window and the disappearance of his father. He just wants to be close to Diana. He wants her to stop struggling.

Danielle shuts the door behind her, leaving the Walkers in the hallway. Danny Elwes is in shock, still outside room 734. This is more drama than he wants. It shouldn't be like this when you pay for sex. They're professionals. They do their job well and there's the added benefit that nobody misses them if they suddenly get hurt or disappear.

Now he's trapped at the end of a corridor that is blocked by the woman he just screwed. He doesn't want to help her. He doesn't care about her. He's only thinking of himself. That's all he ever does.

Another door opens next to the lift. The stairwell. Three staff members emerge. Cleaners. Maids. They start to walk towards the scene. Danny is trapped. He turns his gaze away as though that will prevent him from being seen.

They step over Miss Walker and keep on going until they get to room 731. They let themselves in and get to work. Before they shut the door, Danny Elwes sprints past, as fast as he can, avoiding eye contact with the staff, the woman he recently fouled or her innocent son in distress next to her.

The boy cries.

The woman wheezes.

Danny feels nothing. No remorse. No guilt. It's all about self-preservation. All the time, moving forward. It's almost psychopathic.

You would think that Danny Elwes would be a prime contender to go to Hell when he dies. But he's not. Things can change. People can change.

There are no certainties.

Unless you get their soul.

CONFERENCE ROOM

There are still two talks before dinner, and over half of the attendees have been drinking with their lunches. It is certainly friendlier, more relaxed.

Apart from Danny, who is sweating from running down the stairs from the seventh floor. He's breathing heavily. He can't remember where he put his laptop and he definitely left his jacket in the boudoir of the resident prostitute.

'Danny, you look like shit.'

'Do I know you?'

The other guy taps Danny's name badge. 'You okay? I mean, we all had a drink but you look to have gone a bit deeper than that.'

He's a stranger but he's from a similar gene pool to Danny. Parasites willing to step on anyone to get where they think they want to go.

The banter is disarming. Danny smiles. 'I like to keep a couple of women on the hook in the conference towns, you know.' A nudge and a wink.

There's no such thing as conference towns. This is the type of comment reserved for sea captains and pilots.

'Oh, I hear you.' He doesn't. 'Nice if you can squeeze something in during the lunch break.' It comes across as congratulatory but everything is one-upmanship with these people. Really, he is saying that he wouldn't have time to have sex during the lunch break because he can go for hours. A schoolboy brag that anyone with a vagina knows is not optimal when dealing with the friction of intercourse.

'Two of these fucking things to go, eh?' Danny moves the conversation on. Speaking as though they are old friends.

'This one will be shit, but Balliol is doing the last one. That should be interesting.' He takes a sip from a hip flask. Danny gives him a look. 'I've started now, might as well push through.'

'Makes sense.'

Danny has put things behind him already. Again. These are the types of acts that can escalate each time somebody gets away with it. Danny Elwes could be three prostitutes away from a killing spree. When it comes to women, Danny Elwes is the winner of the Peter Sutcliffe award for sensitivity.

Mr Balliol witnessed Danny's cowardice. When he had the opportunity to help, he did not. He was no Good Samaritan. He walked on by. There was nothing to escape. He was not in danger, Diana was. Diana had treated him with care, protected his ego, been flattering. She had done nothing wrong. Neither had Odie.

Danny failed his test on every level.

Balliol calls Carol.

'He thinks he's invincible. Let's show him that he's not.'

SEVENTH FLOOR

Carol doesn't have to answer Mr Balliol. She knows her place. She knows what she has to do.

She ends the call and places the phone in her pocket.

'You're okay?' Carol asks Diana, who is now sitting up, leaning against the wall outside Danielle Ortega's place.

She nods.

'Odie, she's going to be fine. You need to get back to your own room where your mother can rest and maybe you can help take care of her.'

Diana, in pain and embarrassed and humbled by the experience of a smaller woman handing her a beating – with ease – hasn't dampened her attitude and contempt for Carol.

'Don't you look down on us,' she croaks.

'What?'

'You heard me.'

'If you're not pressing charges against Miss Ortega...'

'Who said it had anything to do with her?' Diana doesn't want to snitch. She still thinks she can take her. That she will get her back for this.

'Odie, who did this to your mother?'

'The nice lady in—'

He doesn't get to finish his sentence before a hand hits him around the back of the head.

'She is not a nice lady, Odie. Jesus Christ.'

He cowers and apologises to his mother.

Carol is standing. Diana is sitting on the floor. The manager rising tall above her. Powerful and imposing.

'Hey.' She is abrupt. Certain. 'Leave the kid alone. He doesn't know why any of this is happening.'

'Don't you tell me how to…' She coughs. 'Don't you tell me how to parent my child.'

'Diana, you are going to have to back the fuck down. There is too much happening here today. You do not want me to kick you out of this building. It is your home and, as many of the passing politicians know, it is also your office. So stick your tail between your legs, lick your wounds and look after your boy.'

Diana is seething but she has to swallow it.

'Go on now.' Carol shoos her with one hand and walks to room 731.

She knocks on the door. One of the housemaids answers. A short Mexican woman. Pretty. If pit-bulls can be seen as pretty.

'Oh, Ms Carol. We're almost finished up in here. The place doesn't look like it's even been lived in.'

'That's fine. Leave the other two to finish up. I have something else for you to do.'

'Of course. What is it?'

Carol leans in a little.

'That thing I asked you to take out of room 420…'

'Yes.'

'Well, I need you to go and put it back.'

CONFERENCE ROOM

Not everybody went to the third talk. In fact, those that did go probably couldn't even tell you what it was about. Compliancy or the importance of procedures and strategies. Some operations guy, who couldn't sell ice lollies in the desert. One of those people who can never congratulate on a job well done, it's always about how things can be improved, where you might have gone wrong.

Nobody wants that guy at work and they certainly don't want him at a conference.

But the room is filled now. Every seat. There are people standing at the back of the hall and around the side walls. Because Mr Balliol is about to speak.

Or not.

The lights dim and he walks out on stage. There is an audible gasp from several members of the audience who have seen his picture online but are amazed that he looks this good in person.

There is applause and a few people whoop with excitement, hoping to be looked at and remembered.

Mr Balliol doesn't look. He walks up to the microphone and pushes it away.

Then he waits.

The hubbub dies down eventually, until the audience is completely silent and he has everybody's attention.

'Stop talking,' he says quietly. The people at the back struggle to hear him. But nobody is talking.

'Stop talking,' he says a little louder but he is still talking at a normal level to a large room of over a hundred people.

He waits for six minutes to speak again and nobody says a word.

Eventually, Mr Balliol pulls the microphone back towards him and speaks into it.

'Stop talking. Have you ever been to an open-mic night and seen a band rocking out while nobody is listening? It's the same thing. You watch some woman get on stage with an acoustic guitar and her voice and the room is mesmerised. There is a power in quiet.'

People in the room are nodding towards one another.

These type-A personalities have become followers.

In an instant.

'You cannot tell people what they really want. Yes, we can implant ideas and we can force certain decisions; that is not difficult. But, in order to figure out what somebody most desires, you have to listen. You have to let them talk. You may even have to be completely silent for six minutes.'

A confirmation of laughter rumbles around the room.

'I know how hard that is for all of you. You want everything and you want it now. I get that. But you don't have to bust balls. You don't have to treat your staff like dirt, like they are beneath you. You do not have to shout at your subordinates.' Balliol looks directly at Danny Elwes and holds his focus.

Mr Balliol holds the attention of that crowd for an hour and he does not move from the spot. He doesn't walk around or gesticulate wildly. He is focussed and deliberate and they are mesmerised by him. Of course, they are in awe of his success and his wealth and his power, but it is the way he conducts himself that holds them.

He pushes on to the subject of changing one's state. Of altering perceptions instantly. Of actively making decisions. And the idiots lap it up.

He tells them that they can have anything they want but he doesn't tell them how to get it. Not yet.

Balliol says that they are future leaders of their industry and they devour every word like it is drenched in nectar and dipped in gold.

'But all work and no play makes Jack and Jill as dull as shit.'

Outrageous laughter. They are under his spell.

'Tonight, we celebrate. We let loose. We combine. We share knowledge. Perhaps we share more than knowledge.' A raised eyebrow.

And Danielle sings 'Strange Fruit' and Odie makes his mother another gin and tonic and I.P. Wayatt saves another page of his manuscript without deleting. And Keith stutters at reception but sings his way out of it. And the Zhaos are scraped onto a metal tray for further examination that will conclude that they either died from the impact of the fall or an overdose of concrete.

And Lailah reaches the airport and gets her ticket to London. And Ollie's new dog rips his sofa apart. And Carol uses the one hour of the month that Mr Balliol is not looking through his cameras to go into the basement and search for a file in all those endless cabinets that may have her dead husband's name written on it.

And she hears the muffled screams of Sam Walker and she just doesn't care because all that matters is finding her love.

She knows exactly what she wants.

It doesn't matter if it takes a thousand years.

It's the pain that keeps her alive.

Carol doesn't falter.

BASEMENT

It's not the first time that Carol has done this. Of course not. The crying and the whimpering from the altar is normal, but Sam Walker is pathetic. He needs to resign to his fate. But it's nothing to do with her. One of Carol's greatest gifts is her ability to turn a blind eye. She can't get caught up with Sam Walker, there is only a small amount of time while Mr Balliol receives his monthly dose of adulation.

She pulls out a file. Amy. Twenty-seven years old. Another singer. There are so many.

Next, Joe. A construction worker. Thirty-five.

Next, Patrick. Fifty-one. Insurance sales.

There seems no logic to the order of the filing. No system. It's not alphabetical or by age. So Carol has no choice but to go through a drawer at a time. One a month. Don't push it. Don't get caught. Don't get involved with the person on the altar. Don't ask questions, even if you are sure they are going to be a sacrifice.

Get in.

Get out.

And that is exactly what she does. Carol knows that she has an hour but she looks through one drawer of files. It doesn't take her more than ten minutes. Then she gets out, leaves the sacrifice crying or praying to a God who isn't listening, and she is back at reception before anybody realises she is gone.

She doesn't have to go through the penthouse, either. She may not know all the hallways and secret doors and special passages that Mr Balliol does, but she understands building and fire regulations and that the only way out of a cellar cannot be a lift to the top floor.

Carol emerges from her office and there is an older black gentleman waiting at the front desk, tapping his finger on the counter.

'Everything okay here, Keith?'

'Yes. Fine. This gentleman is waiting for his room.'

'We have plenty of rooms free, even though it's busy with the conference.'

'Ah, no. He is very specific in his requirements. He is waiting for room 731.'

Carol looks at him. He is refined and poised and there is a light to his eyes but, on closer inspection, he may be ill, more frail than he lets on.

'Well, sir, it will be ready very shortly. May I ask why you want that room in particular?'

'It's my room.'

'Your room?'

'Yes. It's where I stayed when I was here last. And the time before that. It's a lovely location for me.'

'You are a returning guest. How wonderful.' Carol is on the full charm offensive. 'I have to say, I have something of a knack for remembering people, names and faces, and I can't quite place you, I'm sorry.'

'Well, I look a lot different on this occasion. It was maybe before your time.'

'Maybe that's it.' She smiles. But she doesn't fully believe it. 'Can I take a name, sir, and I'll get you booked in?'

'Of course. The name is Harry Jones. Some folk who don't like me much call me Old Harry, but most people call me Jonesy.'

'Welcome back to Hotel Beresford, Jonesy.' Carol books the guest into the system for a week and gives him his key. She watches him walk down the corridor with no baggage. He straightens one of the paintings.

She may not recall the last time he stayed at the hotel, but after this stay, she will never forget Old Harry Jones.

SEVENTH FLOOR

'Seven,' Jonesy requests.

The detective obliges. That's the button he was going to press, anyway.

'You been staying on seventh for long?' he asks.

'Just checked in.'

'But you have no bags.'

'You'd make a fine detective.'

The detective laughs at this and goes on to explain why he is there today, the Zhaos outside and how he would have shut down the seventh floor rather than continuing to rent out the rooms.

'To be honest, I try to live a simple life with simple pleasures. I don't concern myself with things like that.' Jonesy points towards the outside, the direction of the splattered couple.

'It's a great philosophy. No sense in getting involved in the affairs of others.'

Jonesy knows that the detective is feeling him out, testing the water, seeing what he might know. Jonesy doesn't care. Old Harry Jones keeps things honest.

The third floor seems to be kicking things up a notch. It's not raucous, but the detective and Jonesy sense the start of a party. The detective shakes his head. Jonesy grins.

Seventh is alive. You can feel it. The detective bristles. It's edgy, maybe even dangerous. To Jonesy, it feels like home. Like he has come back somewhere familiar. He has his key and the clothes on his back and, for now, that's all he requires.

It smells like cigarettes, even though you are not supposed to smoke in any of the rooms. There's Korean food and creole cooking in different corners. An overhead light flickers as Jonesy passes beneath it.

One of the cleaners is waiting outside the Zhaos' place.

'Looks like that's your stop,' the older man says to the detective, pointing at the maid. 'I'm up ahead on the right. 731. I think I'll take a nap.'

'In this?' the detective asks, screwing his face up at the noise of a thousand different music genres buzzing around his head.

A couple can be heard arguing.

A plate smashes.

The inaudible presence of a hundred television sets.

Jonesy laughs. 'It's like Heaven, to me.' And he walks off.

'You're the police officer, right?' the maid asks. Her name is Arbi. Originally from the Philippines. Her father was sick and she had to work a handful of jobs to make ends meet and keep things going for her family – a younger brother and sister, and an ancient grandmother. She struggled. Her father got sicker and there weren't enough hours in the day to fill with menial employment that would help her to support everybody else.

That's how she ended up at Hotel Beresford.

Now her family is safe, with enough money, and her father's health is back on track.

'That's right,' the detective answers. 'This is the room?'

'Badge.'

'I'm sorry?'

'Do you have a badge? Can I see it before I let you in?'

'The manager told you to let me in.'

'Look, people are dying, there are some unsavoury types around, sometimes. If you're the detective, you won't mind showing me your badge.'

He takes out his identification from an inside pocket and Arbi unlocks the door.

'It's all yours.'

'And nobody else has been in here?'

'Nobody but the Zhaos, sir.'

The detective enters, alone, shutting the door behind him. He sees exactly what Carol saw. A clean, tidy, pristine apartment that bears all the hallmarks of a young professional couple. It's entirely incongruent with the rest of the seventh floor. He didn't expect them to live like this. It makes him wonder who else lives up here, what other surprises lurk behind the rest of the doors.

He sees the ashtray outside on the ledge, the remnants of hand-rolled cigarettes. He knows that, if he goes snooping around, there will be some tin under a mattress, perhaps, with their stash of weed. Nothing hardcore. Recreational, at most. Rebelling against a strict upbringing or numbing themselves to the surroundings.

Maybe they numbed too much and got too confident out there, overlooking the town. One could have slipped and the other tried to save them. Maybe they were in debt. Hotel Beresford is beyond reasonable but there are some decorative pieces dotted around that command a heftier price tag. He will need to check their accounts.

There seem to be no signs of a struggle, everything is pointing towards either an accident or a suicide. It's becoming far too common. These kids can't handle the world. They're being told that it's entirely normal to have mental-health issues and to talk about them but not enough is being done to help. You can't just throw pills at a problem and hope the medication is stronger than the psychological issue. That's how you get people jumping off buildings and bridges and driving their cars into trees.

He looks out the window and down to the street below. A yellow tent covers the area where the Zhaos hit the concrete. It seems pretty cut and dried but the detective has to do his due diligence and knock on the doors on this floor.

Arbi is waiting outside the room when he leaves.

'Everything okay in there?' she asks.

'Not really. Two people are dead. This room needs to be locked down.'

'Oh, I think you will have to talk to Carol. She will want it rented back out.'

'Are you fucking kidding me? It's a crime scene. Nobody is going in there.'

There's an awkward moment where the two are left in silence, staring at each other.

Arbi breaks it.

'I have respected your badge and let you into the Zhaos' home. I don't expect that tone or language.' She leans in. 'And I would advise you to be careful who you talk to in that way at Hotel Beresford. Not everyone will be as forgiving as me.'

She locks the door and walks off.

The detective is alone on the seventh floor of the Hotel Beresford and, if he's lucky, he will never find out what happened to the Zhaos.

CONFERENCE ROOM

'I break away from all conventions that do not lead to my earthly success and happiness,' Mr Balliol preaches. And the crowd almost cheers. They do not yet understand it on his level. They are the basest of human subjects.

Work hard. Play hard.

That's it.

It runs deeper for the man on stage, though. It is about not accepting things as fate or gospel. It is about hearing of tragedy and suffering and not hiding behind the allegation that it is a result of God's will. It is about not thanking God first for your own achievements.

You make things happen.

Your triumphs are your own.

You do not kneel before somebody else and thank them for your prosperity.

And when you achieve what is rightfully yours, it is not a sin to reward yourself accordingly.

'I encourage you to indulge in the seven deadly sins. They need not hurt anyone. If anything, they are an invention to ensure guilt remains pervasive in our society. But, on closer inspection, you will find that these are things that we humans most naturally do.'

The salesmen and women, the product specialists, the marketers, the engineers, look at each other. They feel Mr Balliol's words wash over them like they have been given permission to misbehave.

'Now, I invite you all to take a break for thirty minutes before reconvening in here, where we shall celebrate success. We shall eat, drink and above all be merry.'

Music plays.

Exit stage left.

'Rousing as ever.' Carol greets Mr Balliol.

'You saw it all?' Balliol asks.

Carol has to be careful to act as naturally as possible. She has been beneath the building, looking through files. She doesn't want Mr Balliol to become suspicious.

'I'm afraid not. Lots going on, and somebody has to run the building.'

'Quite.' He wipes his forehead with a towel.

She tells him that the detective is asking questions on seventh and that the team is ready to turn the conference space into the dining room.

'I'm guessing you have already spotted the top performers among the group?'

Balliol nods at this.

'Excellent. I have assumed that Danny Elwes is a part of that list. He seems a perfect candidate but I have added a little motivation to ensure he stays on script.'

'As diligent as always, Carol. Thank you. I'm going to quickly shower and change before dinner. Worked up quite the sweat towards the end there. Anything else I should know about?'

She tells him that the detective was rude towards Arbi and that an elderly gentleman was dead set on securing room 731. 'It seemed a little odd but he came across as a kindly old fellow. Said he had stayed here, in that room, before, though I don't remember him.'

Balliol's cheeks were rouging from his effort on stage but the colour has drained instantly from his face.

Carol notices but pretends that she hasn't noticed.

A lot of her job involves turning a blind eye.

'Did he give a name?'

'Jones. Harry Jones. Likes to be called Jonesy. You know him?'

'He's no liar, Carol. He has stayed in that room before. Many times.'

'It's odd that I don't remember him. I never forget a guest.'

'Before your time, Carol.' He seems edgy.

Carol can't even remember how long she has been at Hotel Beresford. It seems like forever. She doesn't know what to say.

'He's older than he looks, Carol. Please take care of him while he is here.'

'Sure thing. Of course.'

Balliol leaves. Carol can see something is on his mind. He makes his way to the penthouse suite, goes straight to his screening room and flicks the large screen to room 731.

ROOM 420

Danny Elwes is pumped.

Hearing from a real industry leader, whose wealth is, allegedly, so astronomical, whatever *Forbes Magazine* thinks is his net worth is only a portion of what exists. When you are Rockefeller rich, you don't have to declare.

Danny struts up the hallway, laughing with some of the others. They scramble into the lift. Danny gets off first as he is on the fourth floor, one above the conference hall. Most of the attendees are too, but a few are on the fifth.

'See you downstairs in half an hour,' he says to nobody in particular. The others are also buzzing. They grunt their acknowledgements. It's as if they are high.

It's a myth that they pump oxygen into casinos to keep patrons awake, it would be a significant fire hazard. They're not stupid, there are other tricks they use to keep people alert and playing their games. All they really need is a recording of Balliol telling people to enjoy the fuck out of their lives.

Danny feels alive. Buoyant. He's had a drink, he got laid, he listened to his idol. He's on cloud nine.

He opens the door to room 420 of Hotel Beresford.

And it all comes crashing down.

'Jesus fucking Christ. Oh, God. What the hell is going on?'

Danny shuts the door, locks it, pulls the chain across.

He doesn't know what to do.

His room has been tidied and cleaned and the sheets have been changed. His clothes are all folded neatly and piled on the dresser. But in the middle of his bed is the suitcase. And inside the suitcase is the dead prostitute from this morning.

He walks up and down the room. He sweats. He swears. He almost cries. He paces some more.

He screams when the phone starts ringing.

His heart rate leaps like a hummingbird's. Danny lets the phone ring. He's not expecting a call. He hasn't requested anything from reception. Then his mind starts to race until it catches up with his heart. Maybe Mr Balliol spotted him. He could be a mentor. Perhaps he has noticed something in Danny.

He shakes it off as an idiotic thought. A pipe dream.

His hand nears the telephone receiver, moving slowly as though it is hot to the touch. Then, just as he picks up the courage to answer, it stops.

Danny Elwes breathes a sigh of relief. But it is short-lived.

There's a knock at the door.

Hard.

Heavy.

Concerned.

'Mr Elwes? Mr Elwes, are you there?'

It's Carol.

'That fucking bitch again,' Danny says to himself under his breath. 'What does she want now?'

'Mr Elwes, we tried your phone but there was no answer.'

He can't understand it. The phone had only stopped ringing for a second and Carol was already outside his door. What was going on in this place?

Curiosity propels him from the bed towards the door, where Carol is still knocking annoyingly.

He opens the door but leaves the chain on. 'I'm here. What's the problem?'

'Oh, there's no problem, Mr Elwes. At least, I don't think there is. Is everything okay in your room?'

She knows. Danny thinks she knows. But he doesn't understand how that is possible or what she wants from that knowledge. Or why she would not alert the authorities.

'My room? It's … it's perfect, thank you. I've just come back to freshen up before the dinner. Is there a reason you are trying so hard to get hold of me?'

'Is everything okay? You look as white as a ghost.'

She's playing with him now. And there's nothing he can do about it.

'I think I'm just hungry. It's a long day.'

'It is indeed.'

'Carol, please. I need to get ready. Is there something in particular I can do for you?'

She smiles.

She's got him by the balls.

'Mr Elwes, you have been selected by Mr Balliol to attend drinks after the dinner. It's a private affair. Others have been selected but it is an exclusive list.'

The pipe dream that came true.

Once again, Danny forgets about the dead woman on his bed.

'Can I inform Mr Balliol that you will be in attendance?'

'Jesus, Carol, I'd be an idiot to say no, wouldn't I?'

'I would think that you would be an idiot, yes.'

There's a pause as he realises what she has said.

'I shall inform Mr Balliol that you have accepted his invitation and leave you to continue freshening up.'

Danny doesn't thank her or say goodbye, he just closes the door in her face.

He turns around and drops to his knees, his head in his hands. He can't believe that this is happening to him. A private invitation with Balliol. Could this day get any better?

THE PENTHOUSE

Mr Balliol sips on a glass of Chateau Petrus like it's the house red at some Italian chain pizza restaurant. And he watches Jonesy sleep.

The old man is lying perfectly still on the bed where Lailah first emptied out her bag of stolen cash, and where Jerry used to collapse after he had shot up. Before that there had been a contractor working a six-week job on something to do with 'the cloud'. Ahead of them was an artist, a family of immigrants, a couple who had robbed a post office, and a hundred or so other people crossing every walk of society.

And before that, there was Old Harry Jones. In a time when presidents would hide out with their movie-star mistresses and celebrities were called things like The Green River Killer and Son of Sam and Zodiac, Jonesy was in room 731, just as he is now, arms folded across his chest, eyes firmly shut, breathing slowly and deeply.

And Balliol was watching him.

He's the only one who has been here long enough to remember old Jonesy. And the next time he comes for a visit, all the staff will probably be different again. No Carol or Ollie or Arbi. Keith will definitely be gone.

That's how it is.

That's how it works.

The creation of a Devil was the masterstroke of marketing organised religion. It keeps them in business. Without conflict, there is no story. It is this, and the sweetness of forbidden fruit, that also keeps Hotel Beresford in business.

Balliol has fifteen minutes until he is due downstairs. Carol has informed the twelve people he has selected for private drinks afterwards. Everything is in order. He just needs to shower off and put on a fresh, tailored suit and shirt that costs more than the highest performer at the conference earns in a month.

But he can't take his eyes off the old man.

All of the rooms in the hotel, orgies, drugs, music, singing, laughter, dancing, writing, painting, killing, hiding, living, dying, and he chooses to watch an elderly gentleman lying motionless on his bed.

He drinks again. Bold. Velvety. And soft. With intense fruit flavours. It's a bottle from 1989. And it is worth every penny. Elegant and complex. Much like Balliol himself.

Jonesy doesn't move.

If he had wanted to speak with Mr Balliol, it probably would have happened by now.

Fifteen minutes. He can shower in fifteen minutes and get dressed and look better than anybody in the building. Balliol doesn't want to quaff such a splendid wine but part of him also does. Because he can.

He downs the rest of the glass, strips off and showers. Leaving the old man to sleep. Balliol manages to look immaculate within twelve minutes. He is ready for another conference evening.

One final flick through the rooms of the twelve people he has chosen. A quick look at Danielle Ortega because he appreciates her appearance. And a glance into room 731, to see that the room is empty.

BASEMENT

Sam Walker has not given up hope.

He is partway through another prayer when he thinks he hears something. Shuffling feet.

'Who's there?' he says. But it's muffled by the gag. Still, he says it again, trying to look around the now dark room where he is restrained.

There's a silence.

Then a shuffle.

Oh, God. What do you want? Sam thinks. It feels like purposeful torment. He doesn't know how he is going to get out of this. And God is not listening to him. Or He is leaving Sam to rot.

Sam drops his head to one side and cries again. It feels futile. Then he sees it. Somebody is down there with him. The tears are distorting his vision and he can't bring his hands to his face to wipe his eyes.

'Who is it?' he muffles again.

The hope forces more tears from his eyes.

A figure can just be made out behind one of the pillars. The way that it moves, they seem just as scared as Sam, perhaps. The person is smaller than Sam. Maybe not as small as a child, although, now he sees them again, it could be.

He's confused. Scared and elated at the same time. Cold but sweating. He wants to thank God for this opportunity to escape but also forsake Him for getting into this position in the first place.

'Please. Come out.' He takes his time, trying to speak around the rag stretched across his mouth. If he thrashes about then he could appear threatening and he doesn't want to scare off his possible good Samaritan.

It goes silent.

Sam knows where the figure is hiding. A blurred pillar standing between him and salvation.

'I. Need. Help.'

He waits to see if he has been understood.

The shadowy figure peeks a head out. Sam can't make out any features through his tears but he sees that they are short. Dark skin, like his.

'Odie,' he says.

And cries again.

ROOM 734

Diana Walker had been furious. And she had taken it out on poor Odie.

Her neck felt bruised from Carol taking her down in the morning and the pain extended to her throat where that waif woman down the hall had hit her clean in the oesophagus. But the thing that hurt most was the dent in her pride. Diana was a resilient woman, for sure, but she clearly wasn't as tough as she had thought.

She had learned how to take a beating and forgotten that she might one day need to administer one. A bad attitude and threatening presence can only get you so far. She feels so lost, no sense of who she really is anymore.

Odie took the brunt of her frustrations.

At first, he was ordered to make his mother a hot tea. With lemon and honey. And whisky.

And then another.

'Why were you in that woman's room, Odie? What have I told you about talking to strangers?'

'Mama, she's not a stranger. We talk all the time.'

The little boy had sat with his mother in the hallway as a stranger jumped over them and ran off, and all the doors stayed closed on the seventh floor when she needed help. He was scared but he was brave. Resilient, like his mother. He didn't deserve any backlash.

'That bitch is not your friend, Otis.'

He knew he was in trouble when she used his full name. He balked when he heard the cuss word and Diana noticed.

'Don't flinch at that, boy. She is nothing but a common bitch.' She heard herself and hated it.

Odie dropped his head.

'Oh, you don't like me talking about your girlfriend like that?' Why can't she stop herself?

'She's not my girlfriend.' It was under his breath but loud enough. Odie didn't like this side of his mother. Because she sounded like his father.

'What did you say?'

He ignored her. That made her angry. So she grabbed his arm.

'She's not your friend, Odie. Don't you *ever* talk to that whore again.'

Yank. Wheeze. Spit.

Diana knew what she was doing but she couldn't help it. Often the abused go on to become abusers themselves. Odie never would.

Maybe she pulled at him because she wanted to hurt somebody, she didn't care who it was. She was saying adult words to scare him because she didn't think little Otis 'Odie' Walker knew what they meant.

But to Odie, Danielle was his friend. Just like books were his friends. And he had read a lot of books for his age. He knew words.

Odie pulled his arm away – tears in his eyes – full of intent.

'She is nicer to me than you are. And she *is* my friend. She looked after me today while you were being a whore.' The word sounds awful coming from such an innocent face and it hits Diana in the heart harder than Danielle Ortega could ever hit her in the throat. 'I know what you do in here while I'm at school. I know what the man was running away from.'

Diana Walker was stunned into temporary paralysis.

Odie wasn't finished.

'He was running away from you. Because you're mean. A mean … bitch.' Odie contemplated not saying it because he knows that it's a bad word but he had already committed to worse. 'Daddy ran away from you and now so am I.'

Before she had the time to click back into reality, Odie had bolted for the door. He ran. Ran away from that bitch. That whore. That crappy mother.

And Diana eventually hauled herself up and out of the room and down towards the lift. And she knocked on Danielle's door again, shouting to give her boy back. And Danielle ignored her because Odie wasn't in that room with her. But Diana still screamed and it disturbed the old man in room 731 who got up from his bed – away from the camera – opened the door and told Mrs Walker to go back to her room quietly and wait for the boy to come home.

'He won't have gone far,' he said.

Diana had no clue who the new neighbour was but she obeyed his instruction and returned to her place, where she fixed herself another drink. And another.

And now she is here, waiting for her son and her husband and her sanity to come home.

Maybe she *is* the problem.

The door knocks.

Diana takes her drink with her. She doesn't even check through the hole to see who it is. It must be Odie, that's all she has left.

She opens the door but doesn't recognise the man in front of her. He takes out his detective badge and Diana Walker thinks the worst.

ROOM 728

'What is this?'

'Music.'

'I understand that, Miss...'

'Ortega. Danielle,' she confirms. 'The music is Dave Brubeck.'

'I like it. Never really got into jazz. More of a folk guy. You know, one guy and his guitar sort of thing?'

'One *guy*?'

'Or girl. I mean, woman. Of course.'

'I'm joking, Detective. Can I fix you a drink?'

'I'll take some water, thanks.'

Danielle Ortega fixes him a glass of water and herself a cold beer from the fridge. They take a seat on the sofas. The large window is open. The wind blows her hair and the detective thinks he sees her move in slow motion.

'So you knew the Zhaos.'

'I did not.'

'Oh.'

Danielle goes on to explain that this is the first time she has heard their name. She has seen them in the hallway, just as she has seen the others who have come and gone since she moved into Hotel Beresford. While she was convivial and gave them a nod, which was always reciprocated, she never really spoke to them.

'They used to smoke out on the window ledge,' she tells him.

The detective sits forward on his seat. That goes along with the fact that he found an ashtray out there.

'You witnessed them do that?'

'Not today. But most days. I do it myself. But I leave a leg inside.

I'm not stupid. They would dangle their legs over the street. But honestly, they've done it for so long and I've seen them so many times, I stopped thinking that it was dangerous.'

'Why didn't you see them do it today?'

He asks this because it is obvious. He has to. The one day she doesn't see them is the day they plummet to their deaths. He has no reason to suspect Danielle but he has to do his job.

'I'm sorry?'

'You said you would see them out there every day but you didn't today. I was wondering what was different.'

Danielle takes a mouthful of her drink. She is not trying to flirt or seduce the detective but she doesn't have to try.

'I was looking after my neighbour's kid. I don't like to smoke in front of him. He's young. I don't want him to think it's something cool.'

The detective takes the details of the kid and Danielle has to say that she got into an argument with his mother. 'And she's fucking insane.'

Danielle looks over at the wardrobe where Sam Walker was tied up a few days back. Maybe a week. Shit, could've been month. It feels like she has been trying to break through in the music industry her entire life.

She is jolted out of her dream by a thump at the door and Diana Walker screaming, asking where her boy is.

'That's her. Just ignore it. She'll go away.'

Diana shouts again.

And then it goes quiet.

They talk for a while longer. He asks about the other neighbours and Danielle's throat tightens with sadness that she never got to say goodbye, properly, to Lailah. She tells the detective what she knows. Everything she says is true. He seems satisfied.

'I need to get some sleep. I work late. Is there anything else you need from me?'

The detective thanks her for helping, says he'll be in touch, but he won't.

'Thank you again, Ms Ortega.'
'Good luck with the case.'
He nods his thanks.
'And good luck with that psycho up the hall.'

BASEMENT

'Odie? Is that you?' He waits for a response. 'Odie?'

Then Sam Walker thinks, *God, please let it be Odie.*

You see what you want to see. Like Jesus on a piece of toast.

The light is limited in the room but Sam's vision has adjusted. He can see a few candles dotted around the room and twelve theatrical masks placed in a circle. He doesn't know how they got there. Nobody else has been in there until now. He is sure of it. And that is all he can focus on.

'He's not going to help you today,' a voice says from the shadows.

Not Odie.

Sam screams.

'Nobody can hear you. Conserve your energy.'

The muffles are inaudible. Sam shouts every cursed word he can think of through the spit-drenched rag.

'Shh shh shh.' The figure steps out into full view and starts to walk towards Sam. 'It's going to be okay.' A few more steps and Old Harry Jones is standing at the altar with a hand on Sam's bare chest, avoiding the painted symbol. 'I'm going to take this out of your mouth but please do not scream otherwise I walk away. Do we have a deal?'

Sam nods his head and Jonesy does as he says.

Sam Walker does not scream.

'Good. Now what are you doing here?'

'What? What do you mean? I got hit over the head with an ashtray, kicked in the balls, beaten up and tied to this thing.'

'I understand that but what are you doing here?'

'Hey, man, please just untie me. I won't say a thing, I just want to get the hell out of here.'

'Let me rephrase it: why are you here?' Jonesy is completely straight. He's interested to know what Sam thinks the answer is.

'They beat the shit out of me and made me watch my wife have sex.'

Jonesy looks away. He breathes. Sam isn't getting it.

'You think you're in this position because you're a good person or a bad person?'

'What are you talking about, man? Can you just get me out of here?'

'What would you do?'

'What?'

'What would you do to get out of here?'

'Anything. Just untie my hands. I'll do the rest. I don't know you. I've never seen you in my life. I'm not gonna say nothing.'

'You'd do anything?'

'Yes. Of course.'

'You'd let me fuck your wife?'

Sam is more confused than ever. Why won't this guy just help him?

'You're welcome to her.'

'You'd sacrifice your only child?'

'Are you crazy? What is this, some kind of game? I'm not going to let my own kid die.'

Jonesy turns away. 'So you lie when you say "anything", it seems.' He takes a step away.

'No no no no no no no, don't leave. Fuck. Yes. Yes, okay? I would sacrifice my son. I'm a piece of shit and I would save myself over him. Are you happy?'

Jonesy turns back. He doesn't look happy.

'So you are here because you're not a good person.'

'Some other not-nice people put me here. But you seem nice, mister. Please, just get my hands free.' He's crying again.

'And you'll do anything?'

'Yeah. I said that. Fuck, I'd suck your dick to get out of these.' Sam lifts his hands a little.

'Would you sell your soul?'

Sam looks at the old man and doesn't know what to say.

'To get the thing you want the most in life, your freedom, would you sell your soul, your very essence, knowing that, when you die, an eternity of purgatory awaits you? Think carefully. Be honest.'

Sam Walker does ponder the question. He believes in God, even if He is too busy to answer Sam's call in his moment of need. He believes that he will be forgiven for his transgressions and welcomed into the Kingdom of Heaven. So he also believes that there is a Hell. He's too stupid to understand the gravity of everlasting suffering, he is stuck in his present.

He just wants to get out.

Sam looks up at Jonesy. He doesn't know who this guy is or why he is asking so many stupid fucking questions. Part of him wishes he just wanted his dick sucked, it would have been easier. And quicker.

'Yes, sir, I would sell my soul to get out of here.'

Jonesy places a hand on Sam's cheek and looks him straight in the eyes. He smiles. Then pulls the filthy rag back up and into Sam's mouth.

'Well, I don't want it.'

And Jonesy walks back to the shadow he came from, Sam thrashing around behind him.

Crying.

Swearing.

Hours from his fate.

CROSSROADS

Faith-healing is big business. And a business that relies on religion and desperation, much like the trafficking of souls.

The unknown can be exploited to great effect.

Nobody can say for sure that a preacher has not been ordained with the gift to heal the sick or injured. Nobody can be certain that God has not spoken to people on Earth. There are, of course, tricks of confidence that can be used to fake such a thing. Hopeless people are more susceptible to suggestion, they may look for the answer they desire in the words that the effervescent pastor is spouting. Or an adrenaline rush from a gifted performer with photographic Bible verse recollection may act as a temporary painkiller, duping some God-fearing simpleton into believing that their ailment has been cured.

This isn't to pay a disservice to the power of the human mind. There is nothing in the world worth knowing that can be understood by our primitive brains. But the small portion we have unlocked so far through evolution shows that it can perform miracles.

In its simplest terms, the brain can tell the body to continue moving, even when it feels like it cannot – towards the end of a marathon, for example. At the other end, there are stories of people who are diagnosed with cancer and they tell themselves that they do not have it, and the cancer disappears.

So, even if these healers and mediums are pretending, perhaps their performances and Christian rhetoric trigger something within the audience and they fix themselves. Nothing to do with God.

Not everyone is smart enough or dumb enough for this to happen, though.

Through the back door comes another option.

Sell your soul.

More of the unknown.

Nobody has been to Hell and come back to tell people what it's like down there, or whether it is even down. There are, of course, people who have claimed to have visited. Evangelists looking for a crowd and a quick buck. And we have to assume they are charlatans, but we cannot *know*. It is how religion maintains its longevity.

Can't prove it exists.

Can't prove that it doesn't.

The various texts hint that Hell is without water, it is fire and brimstone, it smells like sulphur, demons roam the barren wastelands, people are kept in cages and whipped. Yet people sell their souls understanding that this is probably their fate once they have finished life as the first female president or greatest trumpet player of all time or whatever it is that their hearts apparently desire most.

Maybe nobody has ever really sold their soul.

Maybe Robert Johnson just practised the hell out of the guitar.

Maybe an eternity of burning dehydration and rape from a hellhound is better than the pain you feel as cancer eats away at your body and destroys your dignity.

Maybe it seems like a better option than another day in the marketing department at DoTrue or recruiting in the pharmaceutical area or teaching bratty school kids or fundraising or cleaning the toilets in a nightclub or working in publishing.

No one can be certain.

Here is one thing to know for sure: a person who sells their soul for personal gain does not end up in the same place as a person who sells their soul for somebody else.

OUTSIDE HOTEL BERESFORD

The night is drawing in but it's still light. The hubbub around the dead Zhaos is dissipating. There are whispers of a lovers' pact, a joint suicide. It's a more interesting story than a couple of secret stoners slipping off a ledge. That's a story to hold the attention of our society for a few seconds longer.

Andy Warhol talked of everybody getting their fifteen minutes of fame, but that's way too long for the film-myself-putting-on-make-up, take-a-picture-of-every-meal generation. Smartphone junkies walking around the streets glued to a screen, never looking up at the architecture or into the eyes of the person holding a door open or down at the innocent face of little Odie Walker, sitting on the pavement with his back against a wall of Hotel Beresford, reading his book and pretending not to be scared.

It seemed like the right thing to do at the time. He wasn't going to run away and join the circus, he just needed to get out of that room, away from that woman.

People on the streets look even bigger because he is so low to the ground. As the sky slowly changes, their appearances start to morph. Bright faces show more lines, they are weathered, tired. Things blur. Humans turn to lizards and back to humans, with deformities.

Odie tries to keep his head in the story. It already feels like he has been gone for hours but it hasn't even been fifteen minutes.

Diana is still in their place. She's only on her second drink since her son ran off. She's not even that worried, yet.

And that sucks for Odie because he wants to scare his mother. Just as she scared him when she grabbed his arm and had that look in her eyes that his father used to get when he came home drunk or beaten by the cards and roulette tables.

A man walks by with giant headphones and Odie swears he saw the man's eyelids blink from the sides like a snake. He wants to go home but he doesn't want to go to his home. A woman walks past and Odie is sure that her forked tongue flicks out twice as she texts somebody.

The boy doesn't want to look up anymore and he can't focus on his book, either. He flicks a small stone against the wall until it pings off to the right. Odie leans across to get it. Like any child, he can get lost in play. But something catches his eye. Something he has never noticed before on his walks to school, even though he has kicked a stone along this street more times than he can remember.

There are three of them. Circles. Around three inches in diameter, spaced evenly. Six feet away, another three, and another three six feet further on. Glass circles.

Odie walks to the second set. There is too much traffic near where he has been sitting because it is close to the entrance of the hotel. He gets on his knees so that he can take a closer look. He can't understand why there would be windows in the ground but maybe he will be able to see what is below to understand.

He cups his hands over his eyes and gets as close to the glass as possible.

Nothing.

He can't see through. They're not reflective, otherwise he would have noticed light bouncing off them before now. They're an opaque grey. Odie can't understand it. They must lead somewhere.

They do. Of course.

They lead down.

Down beneath Hotel Beresford. Down to a slab of stone where Sam Walker is looking up at the face of his son. A son who sees nothing.

Odie is intrigued. It stops him from being scared, for a moment. He's only been missing for fifteen minutes. In the good old days, one more person would have had their moment of fame. Today, seven and a half people have trended since Odie ran off.

And that's what his father wants him to do. Sam Walker has stopped thinking about himself, for once. He wants to protect his boy.

Odie looks through the glass and sees nothing. Sam looks up and screams at his son to get the hell away from Hotel Beresford. As far as he possibly can.

CONFERENCE ROOM

It starts with a civilised meal, a few bottles of wine, the conversation gets racier. Then it descends into Dionysian debauchery, complete with the satyrs and maenads – the lust and the dancing girls. Eventually, deals are made and people are killed.

Standard conference etiquette at Hotel Beresford.

Danny Elwes is like a dog with two dicks. He feels special because he has been selected, along with eleven others, for a more intimate meeting with the big man upstairs. He scours the room for the others who are deemed to be on a higher level than the rest. It's easy to spot most of them because they have that same air of superiority that Danny can't hide.

He desperately wants to tell the people on his table that he's going for drinks with Balliol after but doesn't want to jeopardise it.

One of the gel-soaked steroid-loving gym junkies raises a glass at Danny from across the room.

He knows.

He's in the elite.

Danny tilts his glass in that direction as acknowledgement. He hates the guy's face. It's like looking in the mirror.

There are eight people to each table and six bottles of wine to start with. The objective is to get people loose. With their words, their minds, their bodies, their morals. Danny dives straight into a bottle of red. He doesn't notice what grape or region of France it is from, he just wants the pleasure of inebriation and a way to forget the dead hooker in his suitcase.

There are two younger sales guys at his table who opt for the white wine. Pinot Grigio. No wonder they weren't chosen. Danny is overtly smug. The one woman at the table rolls her eyes.

'Everything okay?' Danny asks her.

'I don't know how I'll keep my dinner down with such a slimy piece of shit at my table.'

Danny stupidly smiles and looks around the table to see who she is talking about. It takes him a second too long to realise that she means him and that makes her laugh, which makes him feel small.

His go-to response is to attack.

He leans in, 'Well, this slimy shit has got private drinks after with one of the richest people on the planet.'

'Ah, fuck. I've got to put up with you there, too?'

'What?'

'Oh, you didn't think it was just you, did you? How cute.' She gulps half of her wine.

'Wow. I really fucking hate you.' He says this with a smile that almost comes across as charming.

'Get in line, buddy. I hated you first, anyway.'

Danny tops up her glass. She lets him.

'This kind of feels like foreplay, all of a sudden. We could end up fucking each other before the night is through.'

It's offensive and misogynistic and as disgusting as a teenage boy with an empty house and a moist towel, but she is used to the boys' clubs and fighting for respect, she has hardened herself to this sort of bravado.

'More likely that I'll end up plunging a knife through your heart.' She clinks his glass. 'I'm Sally, by the way. And you've not got a chance in Hell. I'd eat you alive.'

RECEPTION

Six women walk into the lobby of Hotel Beresford, make-up thick and enough hairspray to recreate the Hindenburg disaster if either of them stands too close to an open flame. The coats are supposed to hide the fact that they are not wearing a lot of clothing beneath but they just draw attention to that very fact.

Keith leans back in his chair.

'Carol, the dancers are here.'

'I thought I could smell Elnett.'

Keith rolls his eyes at Carol's attempt at humour. She winks back at him.

'Good evening ladies. You're early.'

They always turn up ahead of time, take a quick trip to the second floor and knock back a couple of gins. Dutch courage. They're professionals but they usually dance on stage with a few burly bodyguards to stop anyone putting their hands where they shouldn't, but here, they know they will get pawed at by over-amorous scumbags who feel invincible after half a bottle of Merlot and some fake compliments.

But the money is so damned good.

'Hey, Carol,' the dancer at the front says. 'How disgusting are they this month?'

'No worse than usual, although there are a couple of stand-outs.' Carol thinks of Danny Elwes and shivers.

The dancer leans an elbow on the counter. 'Last month, one guy offered to finger-bang me. He actually used those words.'

Keith looks disgusted.

'Did you let him?' Carol asks. She's joking.

'Ooh, you cheeky bitch.'

They laugh.

Keith does not.

'Get yourselves up to the bar. They're only on their starters, so you have time to lube up. I'll let them know to comp you some gin.'

'Thanks, Carol. You're the best. Keep smiling, Keith.'

Keith blushes. He watches the dancers walk off. They choose to use the stairs rather than cramming into the lift with the gawkers.

'What the fuck is wrong with you, Keith?'

'What?'

'You know what. Where were you just now?'

'I can't joke about that stuff, Carol. You know that. It makes me feel ... weird. I don't like it. Finger-banging and tits and penises, it's unseemly.'

Anyone else would be told to grow up or get over it, but Carol is sensitive to Keith's complete lack of sexuality and, on this occasion, sense of humour.

'I wouldn't talk like that to one of the passing diplomats or the mahjong league. Those women take their clothes off and dance around naked for a living. They've seen things. They have a different filter. We have a job here. We accommodate the guests, no matter their shape, creed or social class. Make yourself scarce next time they're here, it's fine.'

'Thanks, Carol. I know it sounds stupid.'

'I mean, it's not the worst thing that will happen in this building on conference night, is it?'

Sam Walker screams from the basement but nobody hears.

Arbi lets herself in to room 420 and leaves with the dead woman that has been stuffed into a suitcase, but nobody sees.

A.P. Wayatt finishes another page, drinks another drink and fires another empty round into his mouth.

Danielle Ortega gets some sleep before her gig later tonight.

This is a small portion of everything that is occurring at Hotel Beresford in this very moment. Not everybody here is bleaching bloodstains from their clothes or cheating on their partner. Some are here on actual business. They commute during the week and return to their idyllic rural home for the weekend. Some are backpacking their way around the world. Others are on a short stay because of a school trip. One person comes every year for two days to fill out his tax return in peace.

Every floor is different.

Every room tells another story.

The dancers are ordering drinks at the bar and mentioning Carol by name, so they don't have to pay.

Danny Elwes playfully squeezes the thigh of his female counterpart underneath the table and she squeezes his balls in retaliation.

Old Harry Jones has returned to his room. His eyes are shut. His arms are folded. He lies on the bed.

Odie is still outside.

And the detective knocks on his final seventh-floor door.

ROOM 734

'You're not Odie.'

Diana Walker sprinted from her seat to the door when the detective knocked. She didn't let go of her drink and, even though she moved at top speed, she didn't spill a drop. She boasts the same thing about sucking dick.

'No, ma'am.' He flashes his badge. 'I'm here about the Zhaos.'

'The what, now?'

'The Zhaos. They lived a few doors down from here.'

'I don't know who you are talking about but I can guess from the name.'

The detective takes a beat to consider the casual racism of that comment. Another day and another door, he might not let it slide, but time is slipping away and he already knows that Diana Walker is unhinged, so it's not the best time to get into a conversation about race with an angry woman who is a minority herself.

He hates door-knocking duty.

What he wouldn't do for a beer, a steak and a blowjob, right now.

'So you weren't friendly with them?'

Diana thinks this is an odd expression. Why didn't he ask if they were friends? Why use 'friendly'? It hits her in the heart. Diana Walker is not friendly with anyone. She can't remember the last time she was like that without being paid for her emotion.

The realisation softens her. The detective sees it.

'Nah, I'm really not that friendly with no one on this floor. I've seen them but that's about it. I see a lot of people here and I don't know their names. It's a big building.'

Maybe he's being lazy because he's sick of collecting information this way and he wants his shift to be over, but the detective doesn't push harder with his enquiry. Diana Walker is the furthest from the Zhaos. He tells her what has happened. She doesn't seem shocked, which worries him, but she tells him that she's sorry and that she is distracted because her little boy ran off.

'How long ago did this happen, Ms Walker?'

First he called her 'ma'am' now he calls her 'Ms'. He's a real gent, Diana thinks – still reeling that she can't be 'friendly' unless she is being paid.

'Thirty or forty minutes. I know it's not long, but he's never done this before.' She drinks. Because she's worried. Diana would have been out looking for her son but Jonesy told her not to and she just obeyed.

The detective can smell the alcohol. He can also smell the multitude of ethnic cooking wafting down the seventh-floor corridor.

'Look, I can call this in for you. I mean, my shift is technically over now...' He looks at his watch. 'But I'll take some details from you – just his name, a description and if you can remember what clothes he was wearing, that will help, too.'

'Thank you, officer. I'm sorry, would you like to come in and we can go through it?'

She sounds nothing like the crazed woman who was banging on Danielle Ortega's door not long ago. There's a glimpse of the real Diana Walker.

'Sure. That would be great.'

He enters, following Diana towards the kitchen. She opens the fridge and offers him a beer.

'If your shift is over...' She lets it hang.

The off-duty detective shrugs and takes the cold beer.

'Thank you. Now, if you just let me know the boy's name and height and what he was wearing, I'll put the word out to look for him nearby. He wouldn't have gone far. They never do.'

'Otis Walker. But most people call him Odie. He's always carrying a book.' She goes on to explain her son's appearance while pouring herself another drink and taking a packet from the fridge.

'I think that's everything we need.' He still has half a bottle of beer left to drink and nothing else to talk about. 'I know it's hard but try not to worry. These kids don't run off far and they come back when they get scared or hungry.'

'Are you hungry?'

'I'm sorry?'

'I'm cooking some steak while I wait for him to get back. Mainly to keep my mind occupied. You're drinking my beer, you may as well eat my food. As a thank-you for helping.'

The detective almost laughs.

'Everything okay?'

'Yeah. It's just that I was thinking that I wanted beer and a steak now that my shift is technically over.'

'That's what you asked for in your head, huh?' Diana reaches into a cupboard for a frying pan.

'Well, two out of three ain't bad.'

'I'll get you another beer while you make your call to the station. Maybe your third wish will magically come true.'

She jokes.

The detective can't stop looking at her lips.

Strange things happen at Hotel Beresford. If you know what it is that you truly want, you might just get it.

CONFERENCE ROOM

Plates are cleared away after the starters are finished and music starts playing. Six beautiful, athletic women emerge from behind a curtain near to Mr Balliol, wearing burlesque outfits. First, they pay attention only to him, sweeping their hands across his chest as they dance and running a feather boa around his neck before kicking their legs up high and working the rest of the room.

It's a teaser. The real show comes later.

The point of the dancers is to push the event into a different direction. It shows these hungry sales types that all work and no play make Jack a dull boy. That they should embrace the work/life balance.

When they work, they should do it as hard as possible. But the same goes for the life part.

Live.

You want to drink three bottles of Merlot and screw your secretary in the car park, it's not a bad thing. It's not a sin. If you are both consenting, you're saying 'yes' to life. Bringing the dancers out now helps lift the party and Balliol can gauge from the reaction whether the night will be successfully hedonistic.

Things are heading the way he wants. A couple of guys try to play grab-arse with the dancers, but these women are professionals. They playfully slap their hands away or work in an evasive movement. They know that they will have to let it go later on, but now, they are just giving a taste.

Two of the dancers are classically trained. If the music wasn't so loud, you would hear their hearts breaking.

Several tables start to clap along in time with the music. The meal is morphing into a party. Things are ramping up. It only feels a few steps away from becoming an orgy. The dancers are lifting spirits. The alcohol helps break the barriers of inhibition and propriety. But, as a back-up, the chefs ensure that every meal, apart from a carefully chosen twelve, has been dusted with a herbal concoction that will grease the wheels of the attendees.

Even the ones who work in finance.

The song only lasts a few minutes, and the six dancers disappear. They have the length of the main meal until the real show begins. That's long enough to sink a few more drinks and run through their top three slimeballs to avoid in act two.

Balliol instructs the sommelier to fetch a bottle of Cheval Blanc St Émilion from 1947. He returns a few moments later with the hundred-grand wine. He pours a little. Balliol tastes. He is positively effusive about it. The sommelier tops up the glass and Balliol tells him to leave the bottle.

He wants it all.

One of the models he has paid to accompany him this evening attempts to pour herself some but Mr Balliol slaps her hand out of the way.

'This is for me. Stick to the Champagne.'

She can see in his eyes that he is not joking.

The wine is for Mr Balliol.

The women are for Mr Balliol.

Everything is.

This is his playground and his hunting ground.

But tonight, with all the depravity and the distraction, is about one thing: collecting souls.

BAR BERESFORD

Jonesy sits alone at the bar, directly opposite the six dancers, who have dispensed with their coats now, and are wandering around in their exaggerated outfits.

'Can I get a bottle of Johnnie Walker Blue, please?' A voice comes from behind him.

The man steps up next to Jonesy, a black credit card pinched between his forefinger and middle finger. He's in his mid-thirties but it appears as though time has not been kind to the man. He has suffered in some way.

'Celebrating?' Jonesy says without looking up.

'I'm sorry?'

'A bottle of the blue. Sounds like something has gone right or is about to go terribly wrong.'

'Ha. That's a great line.'

'You would know, Mr Wayatt.'

The writer is shocked to have been recognised. Especially by somebody who seemingly hasn't even looked at him yet.

Old Harry Jones continues, finally looking towards the man he is talking to. 'All this time. You've been here at Hotel Beresford all this time?'

'They're discreet here. I like it. Nobody bothers me.'

'I didn't mean to—'

'No, you're not bothering me. I wasn't saying that,' he interrupts.

'It's nice to be anonymous, sometimes, huh? I get that. Convince the world that you don't exist.' Jonesy finishes his drink.

The barman hands a bottle to the writer.

'Thank you,' he says to the barman. 'What are you drinking there, friend?'

'Something with Glen in the name,' Jonesy answers.

'Get this man a double of this,' he holds up the Johnnie Walker.

'You don't have to do that.'

'I insist.' I.P. Wayatt hands his card over to pay. 'You're right, it's nice to not exist for a while but, for me, it's just all about the work. The words. The rhythm. The art. I sound like a dick, I know, but it consumes me. So I need to be alone. I mean, I could walk down the street and nobody would know who the fuck I am but that wouldn't be alone enough for me.'

'Makes sense.'

The barman returns with the credit card and a drink of the good stuff for Jonesy.

'Celebrating, by the way,' Wayatt informs him.

'What?'

'You asked at the start. I'm celebrating. The words I've written recently haven't stunk. So I am toasting that.' He leans in and whispers, 'It also acts as something of a creative lubricant.'

'Searching the soul.'

'Something like that.'

'Maybe it would be quicker to sell it.'

'The thought has crossed my mind.'

It hasn't.

It would be a mighty fine soul to own, but I.P. Wayatt is keeping hold of it. He doesn't need a daily whipping in a fiery abyss, he gets his best work done when he tortures himself.

CROSSROADS

One of the courses had a variety of seafood laid out on edible sand with a Champagne foam that represented a crashing wave. Mr May had to put on some headphones that played the sound of whale song. Apparently that would add to the flavour somehow.

Mr May completely bought into it.

He also lapped up the red-cabbage gazpacho with wholegrain-mustard ice cream. He shouldn't have enjoyed the snail porridge but he did, and it paired perfectly with the Cape Mentelle Chardonnay.

The scrambled egg 'cooked' in liquid nitrogen should have been a step too far but Mr May was crossing something off his list, so they could have served foie gras of child refugee and he would have thought it was magical.

The Mays are waiting for their second dessert. The thirteenth course. Mr May has devoured everything placed in front of him. Mrs May doesn't have the same appetite as her husband. She takes a taste and focusses her energy on the wine. She didn't care much for the salmon poached in liquorice. Every morsel she leaves, her husband hoovers up.

'Darling, this is one of the best experiences of my life.' He places a hand on hers.

It's such an earnest declaration that Mrs May feels herself tear up.

'I could die tomorrow and I feel like I've done a lot with my life. It has been good, hasn't it?'

'Oh, stop talking like that. You're not going anywhere yet.' She knows this for sure.

'I feel okay. I'm just trying to tell you that I appreciate what you're doing. We really can't afford this. I don't want to leave you with nothing.'

'When you leave me, there is nothing.'

'No. Don't say that.'

'It's okay. We have this time and we are making the most of it. We've had a good life. We have worked and we have travelled and now we have eaten at the greatest restaurant on the planet.' Mrs May pulls her husband's hand towards her and kisses it.

She still has a few months before he is taken from her.

Plenty left on the list.

She just wants him to die happy. To feel fulfilled.

Then she can take on the burden of an eternity of heartache.

The waiter returns with two bags of sweets. Inside there is toffee and chocolate and sweet tobacco. You can eat the plastic wrappers and the paper bag. It's ludicrous but theatrical, and the joy on Mr May's face is obvious and contagious.

Everything he crosses off the list makes him happier, lets him forget about his illness for a moment. He eats his wife's toffee while she sips on a brandy. People in the restaurant can't help but look at the old couple and marvel at their relationship. They long to find a love like that one day or they hope that their own marriage will stand the test of time.

The Mays look cute. Oblivious to everybody around. A bubble of reality that is anything but real. Mr May has almost forgotten that he is supposed to be afraid. And that is because of his wife and the sacrifice she has made, what she gave away. What she sold. The deal she struck.

Mrs May did not do it for herself, for her own gain.

She did it for the man she loves.

So she won't go to Hell.

She'll go to The Beresford.

RECEPTION

Carol holds the picture of Jake in her hand as she sits in her office drinking a coffee.

'I'm sorry, baby. It's taking a while to find you. Next month, I'll try again.' She kisses the tip of her finger and presses it into the glass of the photo frame. 'I'll never give up.'

She never will.

Jake died so suddenly. Awfully. He was hit by a car. The driver fled from the scene and has never been found or identified. Jake spent weeks in a coma. Carol was by his bedside every day, talking to him and praying for him to wake up.

There was no answer.

He didn't wake up.

The doctors were concerned that there was damage to his brain that would affect his speech. Part of the left side of his face seemed to have dropped. Carol kept coming, kept talking, kept praying.

Nothing.

Jake's parents were devastated and interfering. Carol knew they were hurting, of course, but their love for him was not the same as hers. Nobody's love for anybody else was the same as theirs. Jake's insurance covered the hospital fees but the doctors were starting to get restless, it was obvious. He was taking up a bed and resources and there was no sign that the man who would wake up would be anything like the one who had been asleep since he was picked up from the side of the road.

Carol grew desperate, as is so often the case.

The in-laws grew nasty. They needed somebody to blame.

Why was he out on that road at that time?

Why weren't you with him?

Carol didn't need to blame anybody. Not at that point. She just wanted to make sure that Jake either came back as himself or passed peacefully with only the memory of their wondrous love to keep Carol going until her own timely death.

Jake's love was so hard to leave.

Carol looks around her office, always paranoid that she is being watched. Even on conference night. She doesn't want to hold in her tears. She shouldn't have to. She should be allowed to grieve for as long as she wants, in whatever way she wants.

There are a few more minutes before Carol will be needed in the conference area again.

The hospital room was empty that night. Jake's parents had gone back to their hotel room, probably looking for ways to kick Carol out of their son's will. Mean-spirited through their hurt. Often how it goes.

Nurses were walking the wards but there was nothing to do for Jake other than monitor his vitals, see if there was any brain activity and wonder whether it was best to just turn the machine off to free up another bed.

So nobody was going to come in.

Carol should not have been there. But the hospital staff could see from the look in her eyes that the term 'visiting hours' would not apply to her. They could have called security to remove Carol, but what good was that going to do? What benefit was there in dragging a mourning future widow through the halls, screaming about love and harassment?

Let her be.

Let her sit with her soulmate and hope.

Let her cry and pray and be alone with him.

That's exactly what she did. She sat and she hoped.

And she cried.

And when her hope ran as dry as her tears, Carol prayed.

And when her God did nothing, she felt alone in that room.

Hopeless. Weak. Dehydrated. Ruined. But she prayed once more. This time with all the emotion of a woman whose partner perfectly tessellated with her in every conceivable way.

Jake didn't move. The green line on the screen next to his head was steady. Carol cursed when she spoke and she grimaced and grit her teeth. And when she was finished, she didn't feel so alone.

Because Mr Balliol was there.

There's a knock at her office door.

'I'll be out in a minute.' She wipes a finger beneath each eye but her make-up hasn't run. It's probably Keith. She doesn't want him in here. She wants to bask in her weary melancholy. It's okay to feel awful. Keeping these things locked up inside will make you ill.

Inhibition gives you cancer.

Carol is gutted that she found nothing in the files again. Another month goes by. The longer she takes to find Jake, the more worried she is that she will start to forget elements of their time together.

She will never forget that night.

He wasn't there, and then he was. Stepping out of the corner and into the dimly lit hospital suite. He hates these places.

Carol was too exhausted to be shocked.

'Are you Him?'

'Him?'

'Yeah, you know? *Him.*'

'I'm guessing you tried God or Allah or whatever, first.' Balliol rolled his eyes. It's almost always the same. 'They were too busy to answer. So what makes you think that He is not equally as busy?'

'Can you help me? Help us.' Carol looked down at Jake. Perfectly still. She had moved his left hand onto his chest so that she could hold her hands over his. The green line showing brain function was steady, as was the beep of his heart-rate monitor.

'You want to make a deal?'

Of course she did. Anything to save the man she loves, lost somewhere in his own mind. She would sell her own soul to save his.

It's difficult to think clearly when stricken with grief. A person should not be signing any contracts during a time of difficulty because mistakes can be made when you lead with your heart and not your head.

When you feel as though you have nothing left to lose you cannot fully grasp the significance of a lifetime in debt. Soulless obligation. You are only able to focus on the thing that you want most. In this case, Carol wanted to save Jake's life, in turn, saving their love.

'My soul to save his.' She was definite and forthright.

Specific.

She knew exactly what she wanted.

Tragedy is a wonderful catalyst for certainty.

This is the part that Carol remembers clearly. She was hoping that it would be like a job offer – fifty grand a year, company car, stock options and thirty days' holiday. That's how she presented her offer. She gives up her soul and Jake gets to wake up as he was, not a dribbling mess with a forever-flaccid penis, having to piss into a bag and be fed soup.

A simple transaction.

Drastic but straightforward.

'You can't do that.'

This is the part that Carol remembers so clearly, Mr Balliol telling her that she could not trade her soul to save Jake's. Of course, this is possible, it's done all the time. Mrs May did it for her husband, for a little extra time. What Carol misremembers in her emotional state was the emphasis on *you*.

YOU can't do this.

Not, you can't do THIS.

He pushed her in a different direction and they eventually negotiated a solution. Balliol cannot disclose the details of any deal because it renders the contract null and void. That is the reason he did not explain.

Carol could not trade herself to save her partner.

Because you cannot save a soul that has already been given away.

WHAT DO YOU WANT?

There's a school of thought that suggests a person receives the things they put out. So, if you are kind and generous, the universe rewards you with kindness and generosity. If you are mean-spirited or spiteful or an intolerable gossip, that is the kind of behaviour that you will draw towards yourself.

It's the law of attraction.

If you want to become a famous writer, scribble Stephen King's name off the front of a book and replace it with your own. It's out there somewhere, now, that you are a bestseller. Stay on your path and await your reward.

You want to be rich, write yourself a cheque for ten million. It's out there. But you have to truly believe it. Believe that it will happen. Trust that you deserve it.

This is no different to having faith in a God. The theory is no more implausible. It cannot be proved or disproved. You can throw all the science you want at it, but there are people who tell the universe that they will win the lottery or recover from an illness, and that is exactly what happens.

Maybe the universe does have a say. Maybe it really does care about Denise's beauty business. Maybe God listened to her and set things in motion to allow her dream to come true. And maybe Denise had focus and determination and the drive to succeed. And maybe she never would have stopped trying until she achieved what she set out to do.

When an artist, actor or musician accepts an award, often, the first thing they do is thank God. Occasionally, they will thank the universe. And, rarely, but it does happen, the artist will mention that they have no faith in some external force. They don't even believe in fate. They believe in themselves and how hard they have worked to gain the recognition they now receive.

And none of these are wrong.

None of them are bad.

If Mr May chooses to believe that he lasted a year longer than doctors predicted because he started eating those purple berries he never liked before, what harm is there in that?

If Mrs May believes that she sold her soul to the Devil in exchange for one last year with the great love of her life, and then she got that year, who cares? All that matters is that it happened.

If a person sees Jesus in a slice of toast or a piece of ham, or another person can sense when their guardian angel is near, or the woman you are dating tells you that she believes in horoscopes, or your ex sticks pins in a voodoo doll, or a pastor heals a woman in a wheelchair by placing his hands on her withered legs, or the Ouija board says 'yes', or you simply put in as much effort as you can to obtain the goal you set out to achieve, what does it matter?

Maybe there is no God, and maybe there is. Maybe the idea of a Devil was created and maybe He convinced everyone that He doesn't exist so that He can roam freely. Maybe the universe thinks you are fucking insignificant among the infinite galaxies, and maybe it has a soft spot for anyone who wishes to run a dog-grooming empire.

If Hashem is responsible for the golden age of cinema or Allah wrote 'Bohemian Rhapsody', they happened and they exist. The product remains.

What is there to fight about?

Maybe Carol and Mrs May and Brian Johnson and Steve Jobs summoned the Devil and maybe it was the universe that returned the solution to their desperation.

Maybe none of it matters because we've become too selfish and are all going to Hell.

Maybe we are already there.

CONFERENCE ROOM

Let the debauchery begin.

A great cloud blows over the roof of Hotel Beresford. It stops, then descends, coating everyone and everything inside. There's a feeling of invincibility as inhibitions evaporate and fear is replaced with possibility.

The mood begins to alter when one of the dancers straddles a saleswoman at table six and kisses her. There is no security guard around to stop things progressing but the dancer doesn't want to stop.

It's a green light.

The operations manager for J-Media Graphics is turned on, watching as two women become more intimate. He has always considered himself a heterosexual male, he is married with two children, but can't help admiring the way Brian from BluChip Accounting fills out the arms of his shirt.

There are degrees of playfulness around the room. Some people are dancing, others are dancing topless on tables. There is continued drinking, shots of tequila, the ripped sales manager of EuroElectrique does a handstand against the wall.

People pair off and move into darker corners. Others are less bothered by sins of the flesh, it's the drink they want. Some guy has coke. Another is explaining what happens when you fall into a K hole.

Men and women. Women and women. Three men together. It doesn't matter. There is a haze of sexual freedom. Experimentation. Excess of substances. Nothing is off the table.

Apart from the expensive wine.

And the twelve people, carefully selected by Mr Balliol to join him.

They are less affected, though Danny Elwes is depraved enough to consider having a grope of something or sticking his dick out and hoping for the best. But he has his eye on the prize. He wants Mr Balliol's approval and he wants the feisty woman sitting next to him.

Balliol gathers his elite group together by his table. He is ready to leave and let things play out as they usually do in the conference room. The maid, Arbi, is already dreading the clean-up.

He doesn't want to leave right away. It is important that they stay and watch. They need to be able to look over the minions, the lower rungs of society, to know what it feels like to truly be the top of the food chain.

'Don't look down on them, though. They are doing what comes naturally. They are not being held back by societal norms. They are not sinning.'

The selected twelve nod along like good little automatons.

'Come,' Balliol instructs, and they follow him through the curtains where the dancers had first appeared. A couple of those dancers have already returned to the bar. One is getting more heated with the saleswoman. They want to get a room. The rest are still dancing. They get paid either way.

Balliol and the twelve take a walk down a dark corridor. He pushes a wall panel and it opens up to reveal the private lift. He ushers in his sheep, steps in, pulls the door closed and takes the key out of his pocket. There is a palpable excitement when he pushes it into the slot beneath the word 'Penthouse' and the lift starts to move.

Back in the conference room, the remaining attendees are dancing, drinking, stroking and hoping to fuck their way through the night.

They haven't even had dessert yet.

Carol looks in. She doesn't judge. She isn't scathing. People make their choices in life and they have to stick with their convictions. She instructs Arbi and one of the other members of staff to pack 110 miniature mango cheesecakes into boxes and take them to the homeless area downtown. Ollie will accompany them for safety.

'You sure it's okay for me to leave?' Ollie asks.

'I can see it from here. It'll only take a few minutes. I'll watch you from the front. I need a cigarette.'

'I didn't know you smoked.'

'I don't. I used to. I just need something. It's a long damned day.'

'Conference, huh?' He fake rolls his eyes.

She nods, lights a cigarette and leans back against the building, one foot up against the wall. And she sucks in the poison. Carol watches Ollie walk the two porters down the street with their boxes of unneeded puddings. His shoulders are broad and she can see by the way he holds himself that he is naturally protective.

She sucks down some more nicotine goodness and blows a plume of purple smoke out into the already over-polluted world. To her left, she spots a little boy, reading a book on the floor, in the cold. As she approaches Odie, she hears the sound behind her as the car ploughs straight through Ollie.

CROSSROADS

He'd been to the Gulf and Kosovo but it was that tour of Afghanistan that changed Ollie most.

His regiment was no stranger to conflict, this was war, after all, but it was the mistrust from the civilians that was hardest to manoeuvre. The allies' message was not strong enough, and a few bad seeds, who used the skirmish as an excuse for rape and torture, were not helping the ones who just wanted to fight the good fight, who were told they were there to restore democracy to the country.

Ollie didn't feel like he could trust every soldier in his platoon, so how were the people in the villages these soldiers were apparently protecting, liberating, supposed to trust them?

The short answer is that they couldn't. Life had been hell under the rule of the extremists, and it wasn't that much better under these alleged allies.

Ollie was restless, wondering why his country was there in the first place. Was it really for democracy? Was it really for the people who had been oppressed for so long? Or was it something to do with the country's resources? Were they a commodity?

He had tried to speak to a superior officer about his concerns regarding the way that their mission was being communicated to the locals. And he had raised his distress over the way several of the soldiers treated women. But it seemed to fall on deaf ears.

He needed to go higher.

In the army, there always seems to be somebody higher.

It isn't always that easy to get to them, though.

Ollie had a stupid idea. He was going to leave his post. He was going hike his way across the desert to another command centre and vent his frustrations to a more senior officer. It was idiotic. At best, he would die out there; at worst, he could be captured. He hoped that this act of desperation would help highlight the seriousness of his plight.

What happened was that he pissed off the members of his platoon for being a deserter, and when a group was sent to find him, they came under attack. An IED explosion, followed by gunfire. They had already found Ollie, so he was in the middle of the attack, being protected by men who disagreed with what he had done and considered him a traitor, and were now fighting for their own lives while protecting this piece of shit.

Ollie knew he had fucked up. He was no hero. He could never go home and hold his head high. And now he was almost certainly going to die and take down six of his team, who were only there because they'd been sent on a mission to bring him back.

The two previous tours had taken their toll on the soldier's faith. He abandoned Jesus after seeing what religion had done to the areas where he had been deployed. Instead, he chose to help himself, free his mind and found solace in the Satanic Bible.

Ollie didn't believe that there was a Devil any more than he believed there was one true God but he appreciated the sentiment of the book with regard to how best live your life. Many of the values were in alignment with what he already believed.

But, with bullets whizzing by his head and his squad crying out for back-up, Ollie focussed hard. Those men didn't deserve to be in that situation. They had families back home. This wasn't their fight. It wasn't fair that they might go out like this.

To these people.

Because of him.

Ollie would trade in his soul to save the rest of his team. He would take his pill. Six for the cost of one. He didn't deserve it, anyway.

Nobody appeared before him. No figure came out of the shadows. But the enemy somehow tripped one of their own devices, wiping out half of their line. Ollie and his team advanced in the confusion and overpowered them.

Somehow they had got out of it.

Lucky, perhaps.

When God or the universe or hard work is not responsible for success, the answer almost always comes down to luck.

Ollie was frosted by the other guys and sent home in disgrace. His wife could not stand by him. He was a coward. How would she ever be able to show her face in town again?

He had got out of the desert.

But he didn't feel lucky.

Among the pile of hate mail was an envelope that contained two contracts. One for Ollie's soul and the other for a job as a security guard at Hotel Beresford.

OUTSIDE HOTEL BERESFORD

They had been waiting there for him, happy to park up and scoff chilli dogs and donuts for hours until Ollie finished his shift.

It was not an accident.

It wasn't a freak occurrence.

It wasn't a hit and run.

It was just a hit.

Ollie had embarrassed the two hoodlums who came looking for Lailah. The idiot had made a promise to himself that he would never walk away from anything ever again. So, when Carol gave the signal, he acted on instinct. Instinct and the suppressed trauma of war.

But the street is different to the battlefield. It can be more personal. You can't choke out a gangster and not expect some kind of retaliation.

They had been in that car for hours, hoping to catch him at the end of his shift. The idea was either to whack him from behind in the car park or follow him home so that they could tell him why he was going to die before they pulled the trigger.

Then they saw that piece of shit just crossing the road like he hadn't a care in the world. Thug B told Thug A to put his foot down and Thug A obliged. They drove the car straight at Ollie. It wasn't as fast as they would have liked but it was head on, not just a clip. Hard enough for both of Ollie's shoes to fly off on impact.

They kept on driving, congratulating each other as they went. Laughing. The target was most likely dead, but if he wasn't, he was going to be mangled and useless and probably eating through a straw for the rest of his life, and that was a better outcome for the thugs. More of a lesson to be learned. A story that could be shared.

Carol doesn't see it because she is looking at Odie, asking him what he is doing down there, does his mother know where he is, what is he reading. But she hears the thump of metal against flesh. She feels the crumple of bones. She senses loss.

A car screeches past her. The passenger looks directly at her for a split second. But that's all Carol needs. She never forgets a face. It's her thing. She recognises him from the incident in the lobby.

'Bastard,' she says under her breath.

'What?' asks Odie. Shocked.

'Oh, honey, not you. Sorry. It's nothing. Let's get you inside. It's cold out here.' She looks behind her and sees the body in the road. It's the third dead person outside Hotel Beresford today. This one is different, though.

She cares about Ollie.

Carol has been friendly with him. She runs the building, she commands respect but she wants to get on with people. They weren't friends. There has to be a line. But she didn't have to know his entire back story to understand why he was working at Hotel Beresford. He must have got himself to a place in life that was worse than rock bottom.

Now she is torn. Stuck somewhere between her duty as the manager of this elephantine edifice, drenched in the chaos of conference night, and her natural instinct to protect a child.

Carol always wanted to be a mother. She wanted the love that her and Jake shared to create something that was a part of both of them. It never happened. They didn't have long enough together. But it is within her to put the needs of Odie above her own.

'Come on.' Carol holds out her hand and gestures for the boy to stand up and come with her. She uses her body to shield him from the commotion on the streets. It is too dark for him to be outside. There are homeless people, drunken idiots and stray dogs.

A pause in her step. Ollie took that dog home. Someone will have to feed it.

Carol can't help but think of the practicalities and logistics.

Her hand moves to Odie's shoulder as she guides him through the front doors that Ollie is supposed to be guarding, keeping everybody inside secure.

'We can go and sit in my secret office for a bit.'

'Secret?'

'Yes, it's very clever. It's hidden behind the wall.'

'Cool.' His face lights up.

Carol's office isn't that secret. It is obscured behind the wall but most people have seen the door open at some point. Odie isn't yet tall enough to see over the front counter, so it's all new to him.

Keith greets Odie, and Carol opens the door to her office. Odie reiterates how 'cool' it is as he wanders in, comfortably.

The street outside can be seen by Carol from her vantage point. Ollie is still down. This is one of the most chaotic days of the month but more so than usual.

At least there's still a detective in the building. Carol knows that he is still on the seventh floor because he is supposed to check in with her before he leaves. Somebody outside has undoubtedly already notified the authorities or called an ambulance, but she has a detective already on site.

She needs to sort it out.

She needs to get Odie back home.

She needs to check in on the conference room.

She needs to get the maids back inside, away from the crime scene.

She has a lot to do. She always does. A million things running through her head at once, and all the while she is missing Jake, wanting to find him.

But one thought supersedes all others in this moment. If Ollie is dead, then maybe there is a way out.

THE PENTHOUSE

'Wait right here and I will be back in a moment.'

The chosen twelve desperately want to get inside. They crane their necks to get a peek at what a billionaire's apartment looks like. But Mr Balliol does not want them encroaching on his personal space. He slides one of the slatted wooden screens behind him as he goes in.

He wants to grab a couple of bottles of the 2018 Château Margaux, very modestly priced by his standard but an exceptional wine nonetheless. And he wants a quick scour of his screens.

Wayatt is drinking and writing and shooting air into his mouth in room 803.

Jonesy appears to be sleeping still in 731.

Diana Walker has a mouthful of detective.

And a young black kid is sitting at Carol's desk.

Everything seems to be ticking along with its usual level of disorder and dysfunction.

Out by the lift, the high-performers are starting to chatter.

I wonder where he's going.

What is he hiding?

Are we just supposed to stand here?

'What do you think he has in store?' Danny asks the alpha female he is dying to get naked.

'Maybe we are going to sacrifice some virgins.' She smiles, wickedly.

'Well, you should be safe, then.' Danny winks, and she rolls her eyes in a comic fashion.

Balliol returns, a bottle of wine in each hand. 'Okay, ready to go?'

The group looks around. They think they are going to get back into the lift, it's the only place to go, surely. Balliol walks through the group and they part without thinking. He presses part of the wall and it pops out so that he can slide it open to reveal the second lift that will take them to the basement.

There's an audible gasp.

'I know, right? This building has lots of little idiosyncrasies. I don't even know them all. Some fun was had when it was being designed, that's for sure. Not many people have had the privilege to know that this lift even exists.'

Not many.

Twelve per month for as long as the Conference Experiment has been running. Could be five years or fifty or five hundred. Time runs differently at Hotel Beresford.

You won't find any evidence of the high-achiever groups. Keith is already expunging records for these twelve in case anybody comes looking for them. No record of them staying at the hotel. No CCTV footage. No trail. Just in case any questions get asked. But there's usually another event that diverts the attention.

And the rest of the conference-goers don't want to talk about it because they got caught up in some *Eyes Wide Shut* situation themselves.

'Where does that lift take us?' one of the eager elite asks.

Balliol looks directly at him. 'All the way down.'

ROOM 734

Another knock at the door reminds Diana Walker that she should be worrying about her son, who has run away, rather than swigging a bottle of beer to wash away the taste the detective just left in her mouth. She wants to feel like her affections don't always have to be bought. She's going about it the wrong way but she is desperate.

It's Carol. Again.

She tells Diana Walker that she found Odie wandering the streets in the dark but that he is safe now – he's having a hot chocolate and some food. Diana is understandably annoyed that Carol hasn't just returned him to his home, but she explains that part of her job is ensuring the welfare of the guests at Hotel Beresford and she wanted to check that this was because of some disagreement rather than the boy feeling unsafe.

She has seen the bruises on both Odie and Diana. She knows what a monster Sam Walker can be but she has to be diligent.

Diana gets aggressive. It's her go-to emotion when she feels attacked.

'Are you saying I would hurt that boy? I would never lay a finger on him.'

'This doesn't have to escalate. I know you wouldn't hurt him but he doesn't want to come back right now. He is getting a meal and I'll bring him back.'

'A reward for running off, more like,' Diana mumbles under her breath.

Carol ignores it.

She shouts over Diana's shoulder. 'It looks like you are well off duty now, Detective.' Carol looks at the beer in his hand and then at Diana's lips. It's so obvious. 'It's just that my doorman is lying in the road outside, possibly dead, from a hit and run. I'd appreciate it if you could take a look.' She's so cold and matter-of-fact, it shocks the detective into action.

He downs the remainder of the drink and pushes his way out of the apartment. He doesn't even look at the woman who just gave him the most professional blowjob of his life.

'Let's do this.' He continues towards the lift. Embarrassed to have been caught. Disappointed to have been interrupted.

Carol goes to follow him but Diana grabs her by the arm. It's not aggressive. It's the most genuine Carol has ever seen Diana look.

'Did Odie see? Is he okay?'

'He's absolutely fine, Mrs Walker. Oblivious to what is going on outside, I assure you. I will bring him back shortly.'

Carol looks down at Diana's hand, still holding her.

'Thank you,' Diana says. She lets go of Carol and instantly starts to cry. It's a side of Diana that very few people get to see. She has to look strong at all times. She has to be in control. She could never let on to her abusive husband that she was scared. She couldn't show anybody.

But Carol saw. And it confirms something that she had never thought before. Diana Walker is human.

ROOM 803

Tap. Slurp. Click.
He can't stop.

There is no fear of the blank page for I.P. Wayatt. Not tonight. He taps away at the keys, without looking at his hands. When he wants to take a gulp of his Johnnie Walker Blue Label, he continues to type with just his right hand. He drinks with his left.

It's automatic.

It's autonomic.

He's an old hand at this writing thing even though he's only in his early thirties. Somehow, his craft has been honed. He types. He drinks. And when he finishes a page, he shoots his empty gun into his mouth.

He has shot it forty-eight times already.

Wyatt sets himself a target of ten pages per day. He's hot at the moment and buoyant at the beauty of the written word, so he can often go over this. He wants to call his agent and his editor, put their minds at ease that he has a new idea. One that can follow on from the success of the last book.

Something worthwhile.

To make people think.

To make them question.

And to entertain.

Wayatt is proud of what he has created so far. He's so desperate to finish now, though. He can see the end so clearly. This has never happened before.

Rap. Glug. Snap.

Another full page and another empty glass. He unscrews the lid and pours with abandon. No ice. No water. It would only slow him down.

The fiftieth page begins. Almost a year in this building, skulking around, staying away from the public eye, though secretly hoping the occasional passer-by might have read a book at some point since finishing their education and wonder whether they walked past or shared a lift with I.P. Wayatt.

He has been encouraged to have an online presence, to boost his profile, but he doesn't need that. He has sold so many books that his publisher doesn't put any pressure on him to enter into a dialogue with his audience.

You can't be a recluse and still post pictures of what you ate for breakfast or how much you deadlifted at the gym. It doesn't work like that. It takes away from the mystique. To Wayatt, that kind of thing makes you less of a writer.

The whisky and the words, that's what makes him.

And the odd thing with the gun. That idiosyncratic routine. It would seem odd to any onlooker, but to Wayatt, it's as natural as pushing the roller bar of a typewriter back to the left when you finish a line.

It's his.

Nobody knows that he does it.

Nobody has ever seen him write.

It's his ritual.

And it's going to get him to the end of this book.

BASEMENT

There's another ritual that nobody has ever seen, and it happens every month in the extensive basement of the hotel. There are fourteen people down there now. The selected twelve, Mr Balliol and Sam Walker. A naked, emotional, exhausted Sam Walker, who cannot fathom who would do this to him or why. He just wants to get out but he's almost given up hope.

He will be put out of his misery soon enough.

The first area looks like a cellar. Dark and possibly damp. Brickwork and concrete. A far cry from the opulence of the conference room or the clinical clean lines of the penthouse.

'What is this place?' One of the sales guys asks this out loud but it's not aimed at anyone, it's more an expression of his own wonder. But a few of the others are wondering why they have been taken away from the grandeur and dropped into the opening of a low-budget horror movie.

'It gets better,' Balliol responds as he pulls the door shut on the old-fashioned lift. He opens one bottle of wine and hands it to the person next to him. 'Take some and pass it around.'

They do as they are told. It's an expensive bottle to them but they'd be stupid to go against Balliol's wishes now that they have come this far. Some of them swig straight from the bottle, others wipe the top first. By the time the bottle makes its way back to where it started, the wine has been drained.

The second bottle is opened. 'This one is mine,' Balliol smiles. 'Now, if you'll kindly follow me.' He goes through the doorway and his disciples note the long corridor, lined on the left with a thousand filing cabinets. Some are worried. Some are puzzled. Some are drunk and excited. Danny Elwes is his usual cocktail of horniness and delusion.

He wants to look inside the files.

At the end of the corridor, the space opens out. The ceilings somehow get higher. Have they been on a steady downward gradient or is it like an Escher staircase, travelling in a loop that feels as though you are somehow always walking up?

Something isn't right. But these people have been selected based on their personalities. That kind of dogged determination to forge ahead with a plan that you know is wrong because there is a chance that the outcome will be so much greater than the pain of the journey. These aren't the kind of people who turn around or back down.

Balliol stops and turns. His followers halt with military precision.

'This is your last chance. You can turn back now, you can ignore everything that I have been saying. There will be no hard feelings. Imagine this as a final-stage interview but you've got the job if you want it. There's just one final test. But there is only one question.'

They're confused and intrigued and filled with wine and gin and beer and good times. They have no idea what awaits them. If they were a little less focussed, if their sales figures weren't quite as high, they'd be missing out on something potentially life-changing. They'd be in a giant conference hall, euphoric, half naked and aroused, and out of control. And that's not a bad second prize.

None of them leave.

Of course.

'Good. As I expected. You're going to go through here. When you get inside, it may feel like a church. It is not a church. But please do not speak. Find one of the twelve spaces and await further instruction.'

They nod along like good little sheep.

What Balliol really means is, *Choose yourself a mask, and try not to scream.*

OUTSIDE HOTEL BERESFORD

The paramedics try everything they can to revive Ollie but it's no use. He's gone. They have to call it. The detective informs Carol and she goes back inside.

It is a potentially triggering situation, considering the manner in which she lost Jake, but Carol locks it away in a compartment in her brain so that she can continue to function. Odie is still in her office, Mr Balliol is beneath her feet and the building is without security on conference night.

For a minute.

A muscular man with cropped hair walks in through the front doors, wearing a backpack and white T-shirt that hugs his giant arms in all the right places.

'Good evening, ma'am. I'm looking for Carol.'

'That would be me, how can I help you?' There's no time to grieve.

'Well, I believe I am your new security.'

Carol is shocked but she doesn't let on. Strange things happen at Hotel Beresford. Odd opportunities. Perfect timings. Serendipitous events. She has learned to accept them. Her faith in fate and destiny died when Jake did but there is a calculatedness to this building.

'And when can you start?'

'My contract says right away. Now, in fact.'

That word. Contract. Carol looks at him. So young. So fit and healthy. Bright. What could he have wanted so badly that he ended up here? Part of her wants to tell him off for being so stupid. But she can't. It's not her place.

'What is your name, sir?'

'Omar, ma'am.'

'Good to meet you, Omar. I'm Carol, I run this establishment, and this is Keith, who takes care of reception. Welcome to Hotel Beresford. Keith will show you where things are and get you a uniform while he's at it.'

Keith nods. He has prepared the twelve profiles to be deleted on command. He may not have to get rid of them all. Sometimes a person makes it. Maybe two. The maids will be on stand-by to turn their rooms around at a minute's notice.

'Come with me, Omar. We'll get you all set up, honey.'

They move off down the corridor, talking as they go, and Carol mans the reception desk. She calls back to Odie, who is finishing his drink in her office, and tells him that she's taking him home when Keith gets back.

'Well, I don't want to go.'

'Finish up. You need to go back. You've got school tomorrow.'

'I don't want to see that woman.'

Carol doesn't like this side of Odie. She stands up and puts her head through the gap in the door.

'That woman is your mother and she is trying her best. We can't get everything right all the time. Now, I have seen her and she was worried sick about you.'

'Really?' The bravado drops and Odie is that sweet bookworm who is always lurking in some doorway on the seventh floor or getting some free heat from the hallway radiator.

'She's a mess without you. You're the man of the house now. She needs you to take care of her as much as she takes care of you.'

Odie sits up straight and puffs his chest out a bit. He's trying to be a man. Carol can feel the pride oozing from him.

'And do you know how long Keith will be?' He wants to go home, now.

Carol beams. 'Five or ten minutes, Odie. Then we'll get you back, okay?'

'Okay, Carol. Thank you.'

And while Odie's heart is beating so fast it feels like it wants to escape his chest, his father, Sam, has no escape. And his heart is destined to have a knife plunged straight through it.

ROOM 728

Danielle Ortega can't sleep.

Something is plaguing her. Maybe she was wrong to deceive Diana Walker by letting her son skip school in her apartment. Maybe there's guilt at having the boy over, knowing that she had hit his father over the head with an ashtray and kept him tied up for two days in her closet. And there's still a sense of unease about what happened to the Zhaos. She saw them every day. They were not unhappy.

Not on the outside, anyway.

She woke up to the thump of Ollie being run down by a couple of two-bit hoodlums whose egos had been dented. Danielle is as urban as they come. It's the thrum of street life that keeps her rested. The noise of sirens is her sound of silence.

But tonight, she would swear that her walls moved with the sound of the hit. Like the building gasped.

And now Danielle Ortega can't sleep.

She has a gig at ten. She likes to get to the club an hour or so before to get a few drinks in her and work the room a little. There's a rumour that some music execs are doing the rounds this week. Danielle glides around that place, mingling with the smoke and stepping in time to the bass. The cops never go there because there's never any trouble, anything illegal is handled deftly and discreetly. This kind of place still exists but they're hard to find.

That's how it should be.

Danielle slouches over to the window wearing a pair of grey joggers and white vest. No cigarette yet, just a bowl of cornflakes with ice-cold milk. She straddles the windowsill in the way she always does when she gets home from work. But she knows that, when she has finished singing in the early hours of the morning, and she traipses through the hotel lobby, up the great lift, into her place and over to the window, the Zhaos won't be there with their awkward but friendly smiles. She knows that she probably won't be able to talk to Odie anymore, or see which book he is reading. Lailah came and went. She's already forgotten the name of the guy with the dog, who died.

There have been too many deaths recently. The building is starting to gain a reputation that attracts a more unsavoury type.

There are still rumours about the place. Bundy hid out here for a few days, once, while evading the cops. There's a tunnel underneath where Kennedy or The Beatles could sneak in through the back. Urban legends that lend an air of mystique to Hotel Beresford.

But now reality is superseding the myth. There's more talk of suicides and murders and orgies than the possibility of a reclusive writer pissing into empty jars on the eighth floor.

And Danielle doesn't care. Buildings and businesses, like people, have to evolve. They have to change with the times or counteract the times. She looks down on the streets below, as she always does. Commotion and chaos. Another dead body. Blue flashing lights. Crowds of gawping idiots, filming tragedy and accidents on their phones because it is better to witness destruction than miss out on gossip.

And maybe she should hate what Hotel Beresford has become. But she can't. Because it's home. No matter what happens in the hallways or occurs beneath its surface. Whoever gets fucked, slaughtered, drunk or tortured, Danielle Ortega is exactly where she belongs.

BASEMENT

Sam Walker is the focal point. An altar of body rather than stone because this is a belief based on the flesh over that of the spirit.

Mr Balliol rings a bell nine times then pours his wine into a chalice and drinks.

The masks hide the faces of the twelve people in the room with him but they highlight the eyes, which is all he wants to see. Terror and inebriation in equal measure. Excitement, too. But in Sam Walker's eyes, fear. Only fear.

He's given up.

God is not going to help him.

He shuts his eyes and thinks of Odie. His sweet, innocent face, looking down through the glass and not seeing his father below. He thinks of Diana and tries to remember a time when they were in love, but he can't. He remembers the fighting. Hitting her. Gaslighting her. And then he thinks about watching her in bed with other men. Being paid to take it in every way.

That's what Balliol wants in Sam's mind before he dies. Because he watched the backhands and the smashed plates. He saw Sam rough up Odie. He witnessed the attempted groping of Danielle Ortega.

'Come forth from the abyss to greet me as your brother and friend. Grant me the indulgences of which I speak. I live as the beasts of the field, rejoicing in the fleshly life. I favour the just and curse the rotten.'

The twelve don't know whether Mr Balliol is speaking to them or the man who is tied up or out to a higher being. But they are transfixed. There is no way out and nobody is looking for one.

He has chosen well.

'You.' Balliol points at a random mask. 'What do you want?'

'Er...'

'Want is it in life that you want more than anything else. Think. Tell me.'

'Money.'

'Be more specific.'

'I want billions,' he says with more confidence.

'Not good enough. You.' He points at somebody else. 'What do you want?'

'I want to run my own company.'

'Be more specific,' Balliol repeats.

'I want to own and run a Fortune 500 tech company.' He feels pleased with his answer.

'Better. But not good enough. You.'

It's Danny.

'What do you want?'

Danny wants to get this right. He has listened to the last two screw it up. Mr Balliol told them all that this was an interview where they would get the job. It doesn't seem like it from his response.

Danny wants a twelve-inch penis, and that is very specific, but he knows he has to aim higher. Balliol said that he can make these things happen.

'I want somebody to love me for who I am.'

Two of the men who haven't answered yet chuckle. Balliol gives them a look that suggests they have blown it.

'Finally, some honesty. And some specificity.'

Danny doesn't want to look at anyone else. Nobody would have been expecting that answer.

'That is the thing you want most in the world?' Balliol is clarifying. He, too, was not expecting such sincerity from a dick like Danny Elwes.

'I have everything else I need. I'm the managing director of the company. I own my house and my car. I have some respect. But I know what I am and I know that people don't like me. Women. Women don't like me. I want that.'

The woman he has been flirting with all night smiles beneath her mask.

'What would you do to get that?'

'Anything.'

'Anything?'

These alpha males and females have completely forgotten about the naked man tied up in front of them because they are so enthralled in this exchange. It's bizarre. It's a room filled with the worst that society has to offer.

And Mr Balliol.

He hands Danny a dagger. The handle is made out of bone. Light from the black candles is reflected off the blade.

'Would you push this through his heart?'

A gasp.

More fear in the eyes.

Still, some show excitement.

'How will that get me what I want?'

'I will ask the questions, Mr Elwes.' Balliol places a hand near Danny's lower back and guides him over to Sam Walker.

Sam's eyes plead. But not for mercy. He wants to be put out of his misery. He wants it to be quick.

'He is defenceless, Mr Elwes. You hold all the power in this situation. Will you extinguish his light to gain the things that you want?'

Danny has the knife in his hand. As far as he can tell, Mr Balliol is not armed in any way. He could spare this human altar and take out Balliol, save everyone, cut the head off the beast. But he freezes.

'What if I tell you that this man's light is not that bright, anyway. That he beats women and children. That he wasted his life. He enjoyed his sins but he was not a just man. Would that help you plunge the dagger into his chest?'

Danny grips the handle, trying to psych himself up for murder with witnesses present.

'It would be like stepping on an ant or throwing away rotten fruit. And you could get the thing your heart most desires,' Balliol whispers.

Danny pauses. He can't bring himself to do it. He has killed the prostitute in his hotel room but he doesn't even remember that. And he has certainly been physical with them in the past. Yet, he cannot extinguish somebody whose actions in life seem deplorable.

Perhaps Danny can only kill women; he has a particular quarrel with the gender he craves love from because they refuse to give it to him.

Maybe he doesn't want it enough.

Maybe he wouldn't do 'anything'.

Balliol sees Danny stalling. He turns to the audience, unblinking eyes behind theatrical masks. And he says, 'What if I say that I will inform the police of the dead prostitute's body in your bedroom if you do not take this man's life?'

Danny doesn't even think. He raises the knife above his head, grips it with both hands and brings it down hard into Sam Walker's heart.

One blow.

Sam Walker does not die quickly.

He does not see his life flash before his eyes. He sees his wife, on all fours, in their marital bed, being filled out like an application form by two strangers at the same time.

And it's only the beginning of his Hell.

RECEPTION

Keith blushes. Carol can see how much he is enjoying the way that Omar looks in his security uniform. She enjoys it, too. There's something so pure about the new guy. He doesn't seem damaged. Whatever baggage he has arrived with, he is keeping it suppressed.

They watch Omar make his way to the front doors.

'Damn, that is a fine-looking specimen.' Carol fixes her gaze on Omar's buttocks in those grey trousers and she nudges Keith with her elbow.

Twenty feet below Omar, Sam Walker is choking on his own blood.

'Carol, you are f-f-filthy,' Keith stutters. He's flustered. It doesn't usually happen to him.

'You keep an eye on him for me, I'm going to get Odie back to his mother.'

'Take as long as you need.' Keith sits down so that he can focus and give Omar his complete attention.

Carol pushes her hidden door and goes into her office. Odie is sitting at her desk with Jake's picture in his hands.

'What are you doing?' It's a reflex. Carol doesn't usually let anybody into her private space. It has to be separate from the rest of work.

'Who is this in the picture with you, Carol?' Odie responds to the question with one of his own. 'You look like you are in love.' It's so genuine, Carol can't be mad.

'That's my husband.'

'Your husband?'

'That's right.'

'I didn't know you were married.'

'Yes. His name is Jake.'

Children don't think in the same way as adults. They don't have as much to carry in the minds. So they don't ask the obvious questions.

'Does your husband pick you up when you finish work?' Odie asks.

Carol feels herself welling up. She has no idea where that question came from. Maybe Odie's mother had mentioned something about his father not picking her up or something. It is such an unworldly response. Naïve and beautiful.

'He hasn't picked me up for a long time, Odie. He's not around.'

An adult would understand what that means. That he left her or that he died. They would leave alone from there or offer some condolences. But not Odie.

'My dad isn't around anymore.' Odie looks down at his feet. 'Where did your husband go?'

Carol steps into her office. The door closes behind her.

'You know what, Odie? Right now, I'm not entirely sure where he is.' She leaves it ambivalent, like she doesn't know exactly where Jake is at this particular moment in time. She moves over to the desk and takes the picture out of the boy's hands. She places it back in its position. Straightens it. Kisses the tip of her finger and presses it lightly on Jake's image. 'But maybe it's time that I went to pick *him* up.'

BASEMENT

What Danny's actions say is that he will do anything for self-preservation but not to get the thing he, apparently, wants most in life. Which leads Balliol to believe that Danny is not telling the truth. He is still trying to play the game.

It isn't love that Danny wants. It's something else.

But Balliol bought the lie. And that makes him angry.

Danny Elwes is one of the most deplorable human beings to walk into Hotel Beresford. It would be easy to set the guy up for the murder of the woman in his room but he'd go to jail. Sure, there's a decent chance that he'd take a beating or a raping or be forced to open his mouth and take what he is given, but that's not enough.

Balliol wants eternal struggle for Danny Elwes.

He wants his soul.

That's what the conference experiment is all about. Hotel Beresford provides Balliol with a petri dish of society that he can examine and manipulate in the way he sees fit, sometimes merely for his own amusement. Everyone who works there has given their soul for somebody else, and the conference allows him to recruit the souls of the worst people, the ones who want something only for themselves, who deserve to suffer.

It's not the same as taking the soul of a Picasso or a Lennon or a Kennedy, where there is some worth, a difference to be made. It's personal. It's a cull. It's getting rid of the waste. Allowing the seven seconds of fame or power because it is a spit in the ocean compared to their damnation.

The soul of Danny Elwes is not as important as the joy of his punishment. His soul is worth as much as a reality-television contestant or a YouTube sensation or a Franzen.

The other eleven masked wannabes don't move. Sam Walker splutters as life leaves him, slowly. Balliol could save him but you can't fight every battle. Walker is a scumbag but he's collateral damage in the bid for Danny Elwes.

It is more than possible to live life to the full without harming others, without causing other people emotional distress, without being the bully in the boardroom. It's not that Danny doesn't understand that, it's that he doesn't care.

Danny could have this love he says he desires but it would not sustain him in the way that Carol's has. She came about hers honestly. She didn't ask for it, she didn't beg for it, she did not give away her essence to obtain it. To Carol it was real. She considers herself lucky. So, even though she is stuck in purgatory, a seemingly endless and repetitive loop, that genuine passion comforts and encourages her.

Danny doesn't have the same fortitude. His life is less real. One minute in Hell and he'll be crying like a baby. Because it will confirm that the love he had was fake. Forced. He made a deal for it. And it would eat him up.

That's what Balliol wants.

'It seems to me that your desires are not pure of heart, Mr Elwes.' Balliol hands the chalice to one of the crowd and instructs them to drink and pass it around. It eventually makes its way back to the woman standing between Balliol and Danny but she does not drink the dregs of wine. 'You appear to care more about saving yourself than you do about finding this true love.'

'I did what you asked. I stuck a knife into that guy's heart.'

'Because I threatened to expose your murderous ways.'

'You said—'

'I know exactly what I said. I make a point of being very specific. You have said that your greatest desire is to have somebody love you for who you are. Warts and all. Putting a knife into Mr Walker's chest shows me that you are the most important person in the world to you. It does not demonstrate that you crave to be loved.'

Danny listens, as do the other eleven onlookers, drowsy and confused. Drunk and immersed.

Reality and fiction have blurred.

Balliol takes a folded piece of paper from his inside jacket pocket and he tells Danny that it is a contract. In exchange for his soul, he will be honoured with the provision of somebody who will love him – despite the glaring flaws in his character and personality.

'All I had to do was sign a contract? So why make me kill somebody?' Danny is already signing the piece of paper. Without reading.

They always sign it without reading when it is something they have requested for themselves.

Why make Danny kill somebody?

Insurance.

Motivation.

Fun.

'It's a test, Mr Elwes. We need to understand how serious you are about your own success.'

'We?'

One of the eleven grabs their stomach and drops to their knees. In an almost choreographed wave, another nine begin to grab at their throats or fall to the ground or foam at the mouth.

Flinch. Gargle. Gasp.

Balliol, Elwes and the woman with the chalice in her hand watch as the masked idiots writhe and choke. They rip at their own faces before they eventually stop moving. The occasional twitch.

'Why are you still here?' Danny focusses on the woman he was desperate to fuck only half an hour ago.

'I'm not stupid enough to drink from a poisoned chalice,' she smiles.

'She works for you.' The realisation dawns.

'You're not as stupid as you look, Danny.' She tilts her head to the side, condescendingly.

'I should probably mention that she will not be the one who loves you.' Balliol seems smug.

Danny fights to not roll his eyes.

The conference is still an ongoing experiment to collect souls. It works differently to Hotel Beresford. And then there are the people who come of their own volition. Those people are generally in a state of pain or regret or suffering. It's easy. They are desperate.

Danny is not.

There is no real dissatisfaction to the way he leads his life.

He doesn't want to write the great novel of his time or lead any political party. He's not looking to achieve anything worthwhile or make a difference to the lives of others. Without this intervention, he would have continued to treat those around him as subordinates. He would have gone on to pay for sex with more women. He may have even gained a taste for killing those he deems to be worthless in society, oblivious to his own insignificance.

Danny Elwes does not need to sell his soul. Neither do the people lying on the floor of the great room beneath the building.

But people often do not know what their greatest desire is.

You want to hear a lie, ask a person what they want from life.

Danny didn't get to where he is today by being stupid. He didn't get discovered, go viral or get lucky. He buckled down and worked hard. But he is emotionally detached. So he doesn't really believe that the contract he signed holds any weight. Mr Balliol is a powerful man but he can't deliver a woman who loves Danny. That's ridiculous.

That's why Danny chose it.

Killing Sam was to save himself. Of course it was.

And he doesn't care about the nine people on the floor. He doesn't know if they are alive still. But he has no emotion either way. They're nothing to do with him.

Danny still has the dagger. Balliol looks at it. 'You know you can't keep that? I don't want you using my dagger on one of your prostitutes.'

'I didn't kill her. I woke up and she was dead.'

'Are you sure about that?' Balliol is the only one who knows what went on in that room because he has it all on video.

Danny wobbles on his feet and disappears into his mind for a second, conjuring an image of him choking the woman.

Clicks back into reality.

'I didn't do it.'

'Okay,' Balliol placates him, 'And you didn't kill all those people behind you either, I'm guessing.'

Danny turns around to see the other candidates on the floor. None of them moving. He screws his eyes up tight, hoping that when he opens them, nobody will be there. But they are. And he has a knife. And he has the thoughts.

'I didn't do that.'

'Are you sure?' Balliol teases again.

'Maybe I should just use this on you.'

Balliol stays calm. The woman beside him is equally unruffled.

Danny looks from one to the other. Is this another test? What is the fucking job at the end of this? Is he really the only candidate left?

He lunges at the woman because he is a coward. He thinks that she will be easier to take on. A split second and the knife is in her stomach. He lets go and looks at her. Once in the eyes, once at the knife. Once at Balliol.

'You fucking stabbed me.'

Danny just nods. He doesn't know what else to do. He just wants to get out.

She touches the knife.

'It kind of ... itches.' She scratches around the knife with her middle finger and smiles at Mr Balliol. Then she takes the handle and pulls it out.

No scream.

No blood.

As the tip emerges, she lets out a giggle as though it's tickling her.

'What the fuck is going on here? Who are you people?' The room spins. It doesn't feel real. The alcohol is kicking in, or the drugs.

Maybe they did something to him. 'You fucking psychos. You spiked me.'

'We did nothing of the sort, Mr Elwes.' Balliol's composure is frustrating.

'What the hell is going on here? What is this?' Danny wants out of there. But he's scared. These people are different. They say what they mean. They're calm. It's demonic. The blade had no effect on that woman. Danny reckons it would have had even less of an outcome on Mr Balliol.

Danny feels out of it. He curses, looks at the knife. There's blood everywhere. There was none a moment ago. He's hysterical. Frustrated at how the night has progressed. This is not what it was supposed to be.

He shouts. Curses again. There are bodies all over the floor and one on the altar that he knows he killed but he's even starting to question that. Danny turns around to the people who made him do it.

And they are gone.

'You fucking arseholes. How the hell am I supposed to get out of here? You won't pin this on me. You won't fucking pin this on me.'

Danny Elwes screams up to the heavens and drops backward onto the pile of dead bodies. He casts his gaze to the right and catches the eye of Sam Walker. The human altar.

His breathing slows.

His eyes are heavy.

And then there is nothing.

RECEPTION

Things eventually die down. There's always a rush on conference day. Carol handles the distractions, misdirection and subterfuge in her stride, now. She's done this so many times.

It runs like clockwork.

Arbi and her team of cleaners are disinfecting the room beneath Hotel Beresford. Mr Balliol grants them access through his private lift. They bag everything up to be burned in the furnace. Bodies and bedsheets. They bleach the stones. They melt the masks. And they don't ask any questions.

Omar mans the door with pride. Carol is gutted about Ollie but she can't let on the way that she feels. She has to move on. Stay professional. The detective says they'll check CCTV footage and see if they can pull up the plate of the car that hit and ran. They won't come up with anything. There's corruption everywhere. Apathy and languor.

Cops are lazy.

The health service is bankrupt.

There's no funding for the arts.

Not enough women in science.

Publishers are lazy and risk-averse.

Farming has turned into manufacturing.

How could this be any worse than Hell?

Danielle Ortega swoops down the corridor of Hotel Beresford like her feet aren't even touching the floor. People slowly turn their heads. They know there is something worth seeing without knowing the reason. Her movement is languid and liquid. Sensual but carefree.

She flows into the lobby to the sound of a Spanish nylon-string guitar. Carol spots her and holds her breath for a second. Such a waif, angular beauty. Danielle gives Carol a cool look before floating past Omar. He holds the door open. She thanks him and then disappears onto the street, lighting a cigarette as she moves towards another gig and avoids the drama of another night of conference antics. The sirens and car horns and street fights are Danielle's heartbeat.

Diana Walker tucks Odie into bed. She's earned good money today but her skin smells like alcohol and sweat. Her throat is slightly bruised. Her ego shaken. She kisses her son on the forehead with the same lips she wrapped around the detective's dick for free. She's a little more broken today. And it's only made worse by the fact that her boy refuses to be beaten down, he remains optimistic about life.

Odie doesn't belong here.

He's good.

All kids are.

Even the ones you think are bad.

Somewhere above the Walkers, I.P. Wayatt is halfway through a bottle of Johnnie Walker Blue but, more importantly, he's halfway through a new book. His difficult second novel. And he hasn't deleted a word.

In a month, it will be finished.

It will all be finished.

Jonesy has a smile on his face. There's a quietness to him. He walks softly. He moves silently. He's warm. And he is walking towards the reception desk.

'Good evening, Keith. Carol.'

'Everything okay with your room?' Keith asks.

'Perfect as always.' Bright, white porcelain teeth. Carol hears the words and it irks her. She remembers everyone. How did this guy slip through the net? And he claims that he has been here on more than one occasion. Something doesn't feel right.

She jumps in. 'Is there something we can help you with, Mr Jones?'

'Please. Just Jonesy. You have been nothing but hospitable. The hotel seems to be running smoothly. Full of such an array of characters. I believe you're hiding a famous writer.'

'One of Hotel Beresford's core values is the guests' right to discretion.'

'It's fine,' Jonesy laughs. 'He told me. He bought me a drink. Anyway, I believe I have seen quite enough for one visit. It has been a pleasure.'

He taps the counter with his knuckle quickly. Twice. Then walks off.

Carol and Keith look at one another.

'I'm sorry, are you checking out?' Carol calls after him. But Jonesy waves away her question with a couple of fingers as he continues to strut to the exit. She turns to Keith. 'He didn't even sleep here.'

Keith shrugs his shoulders.

'Well, Keith, he may not need it but I sure as Hell do. You okay to finish up?'

'Not a problem. The place is dying down.'

Carol pushes through to her office. Inside, she moves a wall to one side and there is a bed where she can rest her head for a while.

Keith continues with his tasks. He diligently wipes clean any trace of the people being bagged up in the basement and when he's finished, he puts a call in for room 731 to be turned over.

He goes to check Jonesy out of the room but when he looks it up on the computer, there is no record of him ever checking in.

ROOM 420

Bleach and patchouli. That's what Danny's room smells like. Bleach.

And patchouli.

When Danny Elwes opens his eyes, he's back in 420. Or maybe he never left. He's had bad trips before. He once did enough coke to stun a rhino and ended up over three hundred miles away with nothing but his wallet and a motorbike that had scratches down the left side.

First he smells the bleach. The room is immaculate. He hauls himself out of bed and into the bathroom. It's glistening white. Better than when he arrived. The tiles and grout look new. The mirror and shower screen are streak-free. He doesn't know when this could have happened. But if he was as out of it as he thinks, the maids could have been scrubbing and dusting around him.

He remembers the woman in the suitcase.

Fuck.

Danny runs back into the main room. And smells the patchouli. A candle has been placed in the centre of the dressing table. Not a speck of dust on any of the surfaces. And on the floor next to the door is the suitcase. It's filled with Danny's clothes, which appear to have been cleaned, ironed and folded.

No dead body.

Did it really happen? Did any of it really happen?

He rubs his face. That was a wild conference. Three women in three nights and some weird trip through Hell where he sold his soul to the Devil.

What soul? he thinks to himself and scoffs.

Most people would wake up from such an experience and panic. They'd wonder how they got back to their room. They would question their mental state. They would worry. Where are those other people? What happened to them? What did Danny do to them?

He looks at the clock. It's only half past nine. He couldn't have been asleep for that long, surely. Although he definitely lost some time with the sacrifice and the ritual and giving himself over to the lord of the underworld. Danny shakes his head.

A wild night.

He doesn't believe it. Doesn't want to. This type of thing has happened to him before. He thought something was real that wasn't. He thought somebody liked him who didn't. He killed a prostitute but didn't.

Then he looks at the clock again. To the right of the time is the date. He's lost a day. He's been asleep for over twenty-four hours. They must have cleaned up around him. They must have got rid of the body. If there ever was a body.

Now Danny panics.

Now he wonders.

Now he questions.

He should probably shower it off. But he feels clean. He smells bleach and patchouli and coconut on his skin. His teeth are smooth. His hair has been washed. Did he do all that and not remember? Did somebody do it to him?

Danny doesn't want to be at Hotel Beresford any longer. He goes to the door, where a suit and shirt are hanging up for him. He gets dressed, takes his suitcase and heads for the lift. When it reaches the ground floor, he steps out and crosses paths with Diana Walker. She must be returning from taking Odie to school.

She doesn't acknowledge him. It looks as though she doesn't even notice that he's there. Danny appreciates that. She's a professional.

He heads down the corridor towards the lobby with intent. He's checking out. He's getting out. He's had his fun, now it's back to work. Back to DoTrue. Back to his life.

His shitty, loveless life.

'I'd like to check out,' he tells Keith. No greeting. Classic, rude Danny Elwes.

'Of course, sir. Which room number?'

'420.'

Keith clicks his mouse, types something, scrolls, types something again.

'You said room 420, right?'

'That's right.'

'It's just that … er …' Keith makes another few clicks. 'That room has been empty for the past few days. Maybe you meant a different room.'

'I think I know what room I was in. I've been here for days. 420. Look, she knows me.' He points towards Carol. Keith calls her over.

'Is there something I can help with?'

'Yes, this gentleman is trying to check out of room 420.'

'Really?' Carol screws her eyes half closed. 'I didn't think anyone had been in there for a couple of days.' She walks around to Keith's console and starts to click parts of the screen. 'Nope. As I thought. I have a pretty good memory for these sorts of things. Do you maybe mean another room?'

Danny is frustrated.

'If you've got such a great brain for these things, then you will remember me. You haven't stopped knocking on my door.'

'I can assure you that I have done no such thing. I have never seen you before, sir. Now, if you would like to rent one of our rooms or apartments, we can help with that.'

'I don't want to stay here, I want to get out.' He is raising his voice now.

'Sir, anyone is allowed to leave Hotel Beresford whenever their heart desires,' Carol tells Danny.

'Everyone but the staff.' Keith tries to make light of the situation.

Danny isn't laughing.

'And, as you are not even checked into one of our rooms, you are welcome to exit through those doors, with or without the help of Omar over there.'

Omar tilts his head up to show that he has clocked the situation at the desk and he is ready should things escalate.

Danny leans into the desk and speaks with his best quiet menace.

'I know you're in on this. You and that fucking psycho upstairs. You remember me because I remember you. Before I'd even slept here, you were on that dating site. I'm not an idiot. Something is going on here.' He looks smug. Like he's cracked a fifty-year-old cold case. Whether Carol is who he thinks or is just a figment of some drug-and-booze-fuelled hallucination, Danny seems to have forgotten what a powerhouse she is.

Carol also leans in.

'What. Do you. Want?' It's not quite a snarl but it's cold.

'I want to check out.'

'I told you that you've never checked in. So what is it that you really want?'

Danny flashes back to the basement.

The candles. The wine. The bodies.

Crackle. Gulp. Spit.

'Oh, you're good. You're good. I know what you're doing.' He shakes his head like he's not buying what Carol is trying to sell.

'Whatever it is that you want, Mr...'

'Elwes. Danny Elwes. You know my fucking name.' He sees someone walking towards the reception desk who he believes was one of the twelve in the basement. He points. 'He knows me. Hey. Tell them you know me.' Danny reaches for him, wanting to pull him closer. 'Tell them you know me.'

The man backs away from Danny's hand. 'Keep your hands off me. I have no idea who you are.'

'Why are you lying? You were there.'

The man looks at Carol and shrugs his shoulders.

Danny peers over his shoulder and thinks he sees the woman from the basement. He turns back to Carol. Then back to the woman, who is no longer there. Then back to Carol. He's panicking.

'Mr Elwes, whatever it is that you want, I'm afraid it is not at Hotel Beresford. You're going to have to leave here to get it. Do you understand me?'

He's not really listening to her. But he should.

Carol repeats it. 'You have to leave to get what you want.'

'Oh, I'm leaving this shit-hole, you dried-up—'

Omar pulls Danny's arm up behind his back before he has the opportunity to insult Carol any more.

'You could've just left quietly. Now I have to escort you out.' Omar marches Danny through a door behind the reception desk. He doesn't want to drag him across the lobby and cause a scene.

Danny Elwes has never been to Hotel Beresford.

That's the story.

'Where are you taking me?'

'Calm down. I'm just dropping you out the back.' Omar pushes Danny forward and lets go of his arm. 'I'm giving you the opportunity to walk out of here yourself rather than with my help, so don't turn back around.'

Danny takes a few steps. But he is Danny, so he turns. Probably to spit more vitriol in Omar's direction, but the security guard doesn't give him the satisfaction. He slaps Danny Elwes around the face so hard that it knocks him to the floor. Omar could have punched him, but punching hurts the puncher, and a slap is so much more humiliating. He then wraps his hand around the back of Danny's shirt collar and pulls him down the rest of the corridor, kicking open the door that leads to the rear car park and dumps him on the concrete.

'I'll put your case out the front. You can walk around the outside to get it.'

Omar shuts the door and walks back. Carol asks him if everything went okay.

'That guy is a real piece of shit. I can see why He wants him.'

'I'm not quite sure who or what you are referring to, Omar. We are professionals here at Hotel Beresford. Discretion is key, okay.'

Omar suddenly looks small. Like his mother is chastising him.

'Of course. What I meant was that I've never seen that man before and I don't think we will be seeing him again.' He takes Danny's case to the front door and leaves it on the street outside.

Eventually, Danny gets himself to his feet. He doesn't care about the case. He just wants to get home. Back to normality.

He doesn't know how much time he has left, but what he does have, that he never had before, and that he certainly does not deserve, is a chance.

CONTRACTS

They don't read them. Of course. But the ten bodies that ended slumped on the altar room floor on conference night each wake up in their rooms. Sore head. Dry mouth. Clean skin and hair. The smell of bleach and patchouli. And they sign the contracts that have been left on their bedside tables.

This is by design.

This is honing the results of the conference experiment after the early months saw no signatures, no souls collected. This is Balliol watching people, examining the human condition, and understanding the competitive nature of these kinds of personalities.

How they don't necessarily buy what happened but they can't afford not to take the risk in case they could get something they desire. They don't want to miss out. That is why one of the twelve always has to be made the spectacle. The favourite.

This time it was Danny.

All of these things mean that the remaining candidates will have to take the risk, they will fill out the contract but they won't read it thoroughly.

They sign their lives away, not because they believe, but because they don't.

Some of them go big. They want to become a CEO, earn a million or two, fuck a supermodel, have a place to land their helicopter on the roof. They think it's ridiculous so they ask for the ridiculous. And, when they get it, they stupidly think it was worth selling their soul for.

At the other end, the disbelief is almost a joke, so they ask for a fast car or to never lose their hair or a night of passion with Tina from accounts. And it's not until it's too late that they realise they should have taken things more seriously, that they shit their own bed knowing they'd have to then sleep it in forever.

It doesn't matter to Balliol. He just wants them to sign.

CROSSROADS

A couple of weeks. Maybe a month.
That is terrifying.

You get told that you have a window of time when you are likely to die, the first thing you feel is fear. Then comes the regret. And, somehow, you manage to experience the loss before you've even gone.

Mr May went through all of this before his wife saved him. By damning herself.

It's been a year and somehow Mr May knows that tonight is his last. He can just feel it. He's been getting sicker but not letting on to Mrs May. And now he knows it is the end.

But he's not scared.

He has no regrets.

The loss is still there, though. You do not spend your life with a fearless and formidable woman like that and not know that you are about to lose the very thing that made your time on Earth so great. So meaningful. So full of devotion.

Mr May drank a large Scotch on his favourite chair while reading the newspaper. He had been trying to read a P.G. Wodehouse book that he will never get to finish, but life is too short.

In the newspaper, he scours through the property section with great scrutiny, eventually circling one of the properties. When he is finished, he folds the newspaper around his list. Every line has been crossed off but one.

He stares at Mrs May, drinking her evening sherry.

She did that.

She made it all happen.

All of those adventures with a line through them and he realises the most wonderful adventure of them all was being married to the great love of his life. He was a better person because of her. His life was richer with Mrs May in it.

And now it has to end.

They are in bed. Mr May's insides whisper to him that it is almost time. He turns to his wife to kiss her goodnight. Like he always does. Like he always has. But this time should be different.

How do you kiss someone when you know it is the last time that you will ever kiss them?

He leans in and places his lips on hers. He tells her that he loves her and holds her face in his hands. Mr May couldn't have asked for more. 'You're my one,' he tells her, and kisses her again.

It feels like goodbye.

Mrs May knows, too. It's been a year since that doctor so coldly delivered his verdict. She knows what that kiss was. But she can't let on.

'I love you, darling,' she tells him, trying to make it no different than the way she told him last night or the night before.

But it also feels like goodbye.

'Is it cold?' he asks her.

It's not cold. Mrs May shakes her head and shrugs.

'You feel a little cold, dear,' he tells her. 'Maybe lie down and I'll hug you until we fall asleep, eh? Keep you warm.'

Mrs May fights the tears. She knows what he is doing.

'That would be lovely. I think I am a little cold, actually.' She kisses him again and then turns her back so that he can sidle in behind her. A perfect tessellation. If only they could hold that pose forever. If only she could die in her sleep, too. It could all be perfectly preserved.

Mrs May wants him to hold her all night. She wants her calculations to be wrong. She wants him to wake up before her and make her a cup of black coffee, then not want to disturb her and let the coffee go cold. Then she can drink it and pretend it is perfectly fine. Just one more time.

But some time, in the middle of the night, Mr May will roll away in his sleep. Mrs May won't move until the morning, when she will wake up to no coffee, and a husband lying on his back having taken his last breath while the sky was still black.

And, for the first time in a year, Mrs May will not have to be strong.

EXPERIMENT THREE: THE BERESFORD

ACROSS TOWN

Carol has been throwing up all morning but she can't call in sick. It's conference day, again.

It doesn't feel like a month has passed since Danny Elwes was staying in room 420. Usually, Mr Balliol only sees one or two of the twelve candidates drop out or get marked down as collateral damage. Last month was lean. But Danny made it.

It had to be that way.

You have to make sure that the right people end up in Hell.

She flushes the toilet and washes her face.

'You look like shit,' Carol tells her pale reflection. Then she dutifully sprays a can of hairspray at her head and plasters make-up on her face. It's her mask.

She decides to walk in to work today. No reason other than a need for air. It's not fresh. The pollution from the city seems to blow a smog over this way in the morning like Victorian London. Even though the homeless area isn't nearby, there's still a smell that clings to every moist atom in the atmosphere. And the amount of stray animals seems to be getting out of control.

This town is home to so many. Even the ones without a home. But Carol has had enough of this place. She feels weak and heavy today. And she knows how it is going to go. Drinking and dancers and drugs and sacrifice.

The same old shit.

Nothing has been done about the Zhaos, it seems. The police are saying it's an obvious suicide. A lovers' pact, or something. Bloggers are getting together online and investigating things themselves. Carol can spot them a mile off when they come to check in. Pretending like they are staying in the area or visiting family when all they want to do is get on to the seventh floor and take a snoop around.

Even though there were no signs of forced entry, one person online said that the Zhaos were pushed and another hundred took that theory as fact. And it spread. Like all bad news does. Like any lie with the right marketing budget.

The police know who ran down Ollie. (Just thinking about him makes Carol feel as though she might throw up again.) The authorities have been hushed. It's obvious. Nothing will be done about it. None of his family care that he's gone, now that the military pension has kicked in.

The mist clears and Carol can see the red sign of Hotel Beresford in the distance. Students walk by with their faces glued to their phone screens. Tapping. Swiping. Clicking. Every few seconds their tiny brains lose focus and skip to something new that has been calculated in a fraction of the time by an algorithm specific to each person and their insecurities.

People who wish they were fitter see videos of 'influencers' with six packs doing pull-ups and lifting weights above their heads.

People who wish they were tougher are fed clips of fights where David beats Goliath.

People who want to live in a beautiful home get pumped full of carpentry hacks and adverts for one-coat paints.

All of these people who know what they want are being given the means and motivation to do it and it only makes them feel worse.

Carol checks her own phone but only for the time. There are no messages or notifications. She doesn't buy into all of that. She has to physically log in to the dating website to check for any matches.

Six minutes until she needs to be at work.

Men and women go by in the other direction. They have that city look about them. They're heading towards the station. Some have already picked up a cup of coffee for the journey. Others dive into a pastry breakfast.

A couple sits on the opposite side of the road, looking into each other's eyes, seemingly still in last night's clothing. Carol imagines that they met by chance and fell straight in love and have been walking all night, talking and learning. Young love. It makes her smile. Just the absolute dumb luck of it that they found each other, just the way that her and Jake did.

She reaches the door and Omar greets her with his trademark enthusiasm for a new day. He doesn't ask her whether she is tired or feeling under the weather, so Carol thinks that she has covered it up well enough.

Keith acts normally, too.

Carol goes straight to her office and makes herself a coffee. She sits at her desk and holds the picture of Jake in her hand.

She is sick. She is tired, but she is here. Today. On another conference day. It's going to be hard but it's the only reason she is here. For that short window when Mr Balliol is not watching and she can look through those files.

Carol knows that Jake is in there somewhere. She can feel it. They are forever connected.

It's the only reason she is here.

She's going to find him.

ROOM 803

Every conference day needs a distraction or two. Something to take the focus from the true motivations of proceedings.

I.P. Wayatt has been awake all night. He has long dispensed with the self-loathing and the deletion of his words. When he's this close to the end, everything flows. He knows what he is aiming towards. Now it is a race to get there.

Think. Type. Drink. Click.

All night, his ideas have travelled from his creative mind, through his fingertips and onto the screen. Then he drinks. Then he pulls the trigger in his mouth. Repeat ad infinitum.

The writer is not even tired. He has no idea how long he has been working. He doesn't care, he's just excited to be so close to finishing. But he wants to finish properly. With a large glass of whisky and his favourite song blaring.

Wayatt is wearing grey joggers and a yellow T-shirt with an image of the original Woodstock festival. Three days of peace, love and music. And a dressing gown. His facial hair is getting scraggly. He looks battered. And he loves it. Writing, to him, means baring his soul, airing his thoughts, constructing the words in a rhythm that will have the greatest impact on the reader.

He is buoyant but his bottle is empty.

There's no sense in getting changed. Things are flowing. Wayatt exits his apartment and heads for the lift, in his gown. He has to stay in the zone. One chapter left.

The lift comes from above. It stops on his floor. A smart, well-manicured and striking man is already in there. Mr Balliol.

'Good day, Mr Wayatt.'

The writer is jolted by the sound of his name. He steps into the lift. 'Good day.'

'Are you going to the ground floor?' Balliol asks.

'Second. The bar. Need a top-up.'

Balliol presses the button for him. 'How are the words?'

The doors shut. Wayatt knows that he is stuck in this space for the next thirty seconds and he has just been asked one of the most infuriating questions a writer can be asked. He doesn't want to talk about it. He wishes to remain anonymous. Of course, this flies in the face of the way he is acting, wandering around a prominent hotel in his nightwear, sleep deprived, surviving on a diet of Johnnie Walker Blue and air bullets.

'You know, the curse of the empty page.' He lifts his eyebrows. It's uncomfortable. Fake. He doesn't want to discuss his work. It is unfinished.

Another couple of platitudes are exchanged and, thankfully, the lift stops at the second floor. Wayatt opens the door.

'Good luck finishing the book,' Balliol adds. He's a fan. He loved the first novel. He's worried that the second won't live up to the hype. Maybe Wayatt's legacy would be maintained if there were no substandard works published. He would become a legend, a genius of literature if he just stopped now.

Wayatt ignores the comment. He doesn't ask how the man even knows who he is or that he is partway through a new novel. He just wants his drink.

He wants to keep going.

Balliol goes on to the ground floor. He sees Arbi and gives her a look. There isn't much time. Wayatt goes to the bar, collects his bottle of whisky and returns to 803.

He drinks. He types. He pulls the trigger.

He writes. He drinks. He pulls the trigger.

He finishes the book and pours a full glass of whisky and sits back in his chair. He looks at the last line. He loves it. This is a rare feeling. The pressure of exceeding the success of that first book was paralysing, at first. He plays 'The Weight' by The Band, and he plays it loud. Seventh-floor-of-Hotel-Beresford loud. He is jubilant in his accomplishment.

When the song finishes, I.P. Wayatt sits in silence, in reflection. He finishes the entire glass of whisky. It takes him half an hour. Then he hits save on his document, even though he has already done that twice and the computer is set to automatically back up.

He picks up his gun, smiles, puts it in his mouth and pulls the trigger. The bullet hits the bottom of his brain and blows a hole in the back of his head.

But this is not a conference-day distraction.

It is the preservation of his work.

THE PENTHOUSE

Johnnie Walker Blue is a smooth Scotch, but Balliol lifts a glass of twenty-four-year-old Macallan to toast the end of I.P. Wayatt's novel and, indeed, the end of I.P. Wayatt. It seems a worthy drink.

The writer looks so peaceful, his mouth agape, the blood spattered on the wall behind him. In due course, Arbi will report to Carol that she has found the body, and Carol will inform the authorities. And somebody there will inform the media. A picture will be leaked. News of a finished novel will surface. It will be edited. Some of the voice will be polished out but it will be published and unmistakably Wayatt.

And his legacy will be secure.

That's why Mr Balliol sent Arbi up to room 803 while Wayatt was collecting his final libation. She placed a bullet in the gun. Balliol has been watching Wayatt write for a year. He knows his routine, his psychology. He was not going to look at the gun closely, not after finishing his book. Balliol doesn't look at it like he has taken the life of I.P. Wayatt.

He saved it.

His writing can never be spoiled.

There will be no pieces written by I.P. Wayatt that will be considered his lesser work.

He will never have to sell out.

Balliol takes his drink into the living area where she is waiting. His right-hand woman. She will be part of the twelve selected for private drinks later. She is always there. For protection. For certainty. But now, she is his plaything.

Balliol has some time before he has to deal with the conference and, as always, this time will be used for pleasure.

CROSSROADS

Mrs May found the message from her husband. His list, wrapped up in the last newspaper he read.

One thing left.

Mr May knew that he was never going to be able to pay off the mortgage on their home and move close to the city. Not in a year. And not in a year when they were continually dipping into their savings in order to fund the variety of experiences they had planned.

But that last line was not for Mr May, it was something he wanted to leave for his wife. She should be the one to complete the dream.

Mrs May is not ready to change anything just yet. She is in a deep state of mourning. The chair where her husband last sat remains untouched. The entire area is as it was. She has not removed his glass from the side table and the newspaper remains on the arm. She can just see the blue paper of the list poking out.

It's not time just yet.

She doesn't know what to expect. Will Mr Balliol show up and take her away? Will he somehow remove her soul and leave her there to fester? Should she try to go on?

In the week since her husband died, Mrs May has already started to develop her own routine. Cold coffee in the morning. Eggs for breakfast. A prayer. A hot bath. A nap. Wine from lunchtime onwards. There's a lot of time to reflect on her life and their life together. She has been grieving for the last year, knowing it was coming. She feels guilty that she felt relief. But it was a huge burden to carry with her. Mrs May never previously had any secrets from her husband. But he died while she was holding on to one.

She wonders where he is now. Whether he has gone to a better place. What if he is looking down at her at this very moment and knows what she did. She can't bear the thought that he would be mad at her or disappointed.

God was lost to her a year ago. He didn't answer. He wouldn't help. It is not true that giving Mr May that disease was part of some grand, masterful plan. So she refuses to pray to that God to watch over her husband. She won't do it.

'It wasn't for me,' she says out loud, just in case Mr May can hear her. 'I did it all for you. Rest now. I've got it from here.'

She can't help but be strong.

Mrs May sits in her husband's old chair. The indentations in the seat and back rest make it feel like he is hugging her. He is there with her. She can feel his warmth. She rests her drink next to his empty glass, crosses one leg over the other, just as he used to, and opens the out-of-date newspaper.

He had folded it on the property section. She looks at the list they made and sees how it is unfinished. A third of the way down the newspaper page, on the right-hand side, an advert has been circled. The lease is up for sale on an old apartment building. It's just outside the city. It doesn't say which city; it could be any. Unfeasibly cheap for what you would be getting.

It seems too good to be true.

Somebody would have snapped it up by now, surely.

With nothing left to lose, Mrs May calls the number on the listing. She talks to the man at the other end of the line for fifteen minutes. Then she hangs up, takes the pen that Mr May had used to circle the ad for her and she crosses out the last line on their list.

THE CITY

It's corny as hell. Unimaginative. Unoriginal. A ring in the Champagne and then Danny drops to one knee in the middle of the restaurant and asks her to marry him.

But she says yes.

Because, for some reason, with his selfishness, losing personality, lack of sense of humour and his micro penis, she loves him for exactly who he is.

It has only been a month and she is ready to give up the rest of her life to be with the absolute travesty of a human being that is Danny Elwes.

There was no cute meeting, either. No accidental knocking of heads as they both bent down to pick up the same thing. She didn't spill coffee on his shirt. There wasn't a mix-up of luggage at the airport. She didn't accidentally have something that was delivered to Danny, or the other way around. Danny visited a supplier who was behind on fulfilling their orders to ball them out. He was there to shout at them.

He tried it out on her and she didn't take any of his crap.

Danny liked that.

She liked that he liked that.

They went out. They kept going out. And now he is on one knee in a restaurant asking her to be his wife and she is agreeing.

And Danny does not know what to believe.

Things are still hazy from that conference week. Part of him is choosing to believe he got in too deep with drink and drugs and that the whole dead hooker thing was something that happened in his head. He knows he slept with Diana Walker and he damn well knows that Carol was fucking with him at the end.

And the thing in the basement was so ludicrous. How has there been nothing in the news about ten missing people? Eleven if you count the guy on the altar. Mr Balliol is a powerful man but not even he could cover that up, surely. Too many people. Too many witnesses. Too many unanswered questions.

He thinks that the entire experience merely opened him up to the possibility that somebody could love him for who he is and, by putting it out there, into the universe, it somehow manifested. He let himself be vulnerable, perhaps.

That doesn't sound like Danny Elwes, though.

He doesn't feel like anything is missing, like he is no longer attached to his soul. But there is that nagging feeling, because how could a person like him find love? Is there really somebody out there for everyone?

Danny knows who he is. He doesn't shy away from it. He's not going to change, because he doesn't believe that he has to. Even more now that somebody has accepted him.

He doesn't ever want to go back to Hotel Beresford because he doesn't want to confront that possible reality. Maybe he could even learn to forget about it.

It doesn't matter.

Danny could turn 180 degrees and become kind and benevolent. He could volunteer at the local homeless shelter once a week and find God. He could devote his life to Christ and his community and the less fortunate.

It won't make a difference.

He made a deal.

He signed a contract.

Danny Elwes needs to embrace this love, he needs to live every moment like it can be taken away from him. Because, at some point, it will be taken away. And he will know that it was not a dream at Hotel Beresford. He will know that he did not hallucinate in that basement. He will know that he killed the woman who he paid to have sex with and that death is not the end. He won't rot in a box in the ground, being eaten by worms.

But he will rot.

And that is why there is a contract. For the certainty that people like Danny will end up in the right place.

RECEPTION

It doesn't make sense. Arbi knows that she is not to go into room 803 unless there is express permission from Mr Wayatt or instruction from Carol herself.

'I just went to check if he needed new towels. He usually answers me through the door, you know? Sometimes he is nice and sometimes he tells me to go away. But he said nothing.' She lies. Convincingly.

'So you went in there?'

'Well, I knew that he wasn't going to be outside. He never goes out.'

'He does go to the bar, Arbi. If he'd have come back while you were in his room...'

'He's not going anywhere. He's dead.'

Arbi's coldness doesn't sit well with Carol. But she is feeling too tender today to fight.

It's conference day. Something had to happen. Somebody had to go and fucking die. The place is getting a bad name. It's attracting worse and worse people. That's not supposed to be what it is about.

'Just go. I'll sort it from here. At least we know.'

Carol has seen more of Wayatt recently, and he has been behaving differently, but it didn't seem negative. If anything, it was the opposite of that. Zestful. Optimistic. Polite, too. Not like somebody who was on the verge of taking their own life.

What does a suicidal person look like? Are they supposed to have dark eyes and mope around beneath a black cloud? Can they not appear happy and grateful but be dying on the inside?

There won't be the same mystery that surrounds the Zhaos' death.

The scene looks cut and dried, and Carol knows how lazy the detectives are around here. The guy was a recluse. People will see him as a lonely freak. They're only half right.

The other reason that Carol doesn't want to get into anything with Arbi right now is because Mr Balliol is about to give his opening address to the conference attendees. This is her one opportunity each month to venture to the basement and go undetected. She gives herself ten minutes each time.

Arbi is dismissed and Carol mutters something in Keith's direction saying she needs to look into it.

All Carol has done is look for Jake's name on those files. She doesn't have time for anything else. And her nerves won't allow it. She has no idea if Jake is in there. She just has an intuition. A fear. She still feels a connection.

Carol disappears down the stairs as Mr Balliol begins to rouse the rabble. She runs this time. Those extra few seconds could mean all the difference.

She runs. Down the stairs around the corner and past the filing cabinets she has already sifted through. She runs, stopping somewhere past halfway and opens a drawer. Mathers, Woods, Hill.

No. No. No.

There's no order to the names at all.

Dafoe, Edwards, Driver.

Nothing. Nothing. Nothing.

The disappointment does not slow Carol down, though. She sifts through another eighty surnames that appear to have been thrown in the cabinet at random.

Then: Chambers, Jake.

Carol stops breathing. She wants to find him, she wanted to locate a file with his name on it, but a part of her also hoped he wouldn't be in there.

Same date of birth.

Same place of birth.

'Shit,' she says to herself.

She doesn't know what the files are but she has a pretty good idea.

There's still a few minutes left but Carol doesn't care. This is it. This is what she has been searching for. She slams the filing cabinet shut and runs again. This time in the opposite direction. Past the files that have taken her years to get through, around the corner, up the stairs and into her office.

Nobody will come in. If Mr Balliol does have a camera in there, she can make it look as though she is looking through some paperwork.

She catches her breath and places the folder beneath that morning's mail. It's killing her but she doesn't want anything to look suspicious.

She opens a letter about the hotel's internet provision. There are a couple of flyers for accountancy and fitted wardrobes. Then the file. She doesn't want it to be what she thinks it might be.

The first paragraph tells her enough.

Jake Chambers, residing at 50a Pheasant Street ('the Seller'), for and in consideration of the ***sum of one soul*** *does hereby sell, grant, and convey unto Mr Balliol, residing at Hotel Beresford ('the Buyer'), all the Seller's right, title, and interest in said* ***soul*** *in exchange for meeting his soulmate.*

It wasn't luck.

It wasn't fate.

Jake bought their love.

She can't understand it. It felt so real. But he knew. And he kept it from her. And that bastard is probably burning in Hell, right now.

Balliol knew. He knew it and he trapped Carol with it.

She throws up into the bin beneath her desk. It could be the shock or the heartbreak or the illness she has been struggling with for the past few days. But she no longer feels weak.

Carol has had enough.

She's going to burn this place to the ground.

BASEMENT

Twelve masks. Twelve souls. The same as always. The conference level is thriving with a sexuality that would make Bacchus blush. Keith is deleting their information and ensuring that any record of them staying at Hotel Beresford is expunged.

The police have gone but there are news vans parked in the street reporting on the suicide of I.P. Wayatt, with a sunny caveat that there will at least be one more book published by the personally haunted writer.

'I'm not feeling great, Keith. I think I have a little time before I'm needed, so I'm going to take a break in my office. Get some water. Take some pills.'

'Is there anything I can do, Carol?' There's genuine concern from the big man.

'Just man the fort. Anything that comes along, I don't want to know unless the building is on fire, okay?'

'Sure thing, boss. Take it easy.'

Carol enters her office. She feels fine. Focussed. Determined.

She takes a bottle of whisky, Jake's contract with the Devil and a lighter and descends her secret staircase to the basement.

It is vast down there. The files are nowhere near the room where Balliol conducts his monthly ritual. Carol gets close enough, though. She can hear a voice. Chanting. It has to be him, he loves to listen to himself pontificate. There's a wooden crate with some black robes draped over it. Carol takes a swig of the whisky, then she screws up the contract and pokes it down the neck of the bottle before setting fire to one end. She waits until the flame is large enough and travelling into the bottle and she throws it. It smashes on the floor and sets fire to the robes.

Then she runs.

And she doesn't look back.

Back in her office, she hopes the flames are spreading but she knows she has a little time.

She picks up her phone and hits *734.

Eventually, Diana Walker picks up.

'Who's this?' she answers.

'Diana, it's Carol at reception. I don't want you to say anything, I just want you to believe me and do as I say. Get Odie and get out of this building now. Don't use the lift. Take the stairs.'

'What are you talking about?'

'Just fucking do it. Get out of here. It's all gonna go to Hell.'

ROOM 734

Diana darts into her bedroom and grabs her bags of cash and her purse. That's it. Then she yanks Odie out of his bed by his arms and tells him to put some shoes on.

'Mama, you're scaring me.'

'I'm scaring me, too, Odie, but just do as I say, and we will be alright. Okay?'

He does as he is told.

He's a good kid.

Diana Walker does not let go of her son's hand. She doesn't know whether Carol was calling everyone in the building but she doesn't think so. She sounded genuinely panicked. She knows Carol doesn't care about her, she just wants to save the kid, and that's fine by her. It's a package deal.

She also knows that Danielle has always had Odie's best interests at heart. But she still hates that woman. Yet, for a split second, Diana thinks about knocking on Danielle's door to tell her to save herself. She doesn't know what she is saving herself from but maybe Diana should pay things forward.

But she walks on by.

Because she's not a good person. She's broken.

The Walkers run down the stairwell and push through a fire exit door, so they don't even need to go past the reception desk to get out.

They're safe. They're free. They see the news vans queueing up outside and human curiosity almost gets the better of Diana Walker but she sees the fear in Odie's eyes and keeps on going.

'What do you say we grab ourselves a hot chocolate and decide where we're going to live next?'

The boy smiles. His eyes are glazed but he fights the tears.

'Marshmallows on top?'

'Anything you want, baby boy.'

For many, Hotel Beresford is purgatory. They're stuck in a loop of nonsense and indecision. For Diana Walker, it was always a halfway house. A place to leave behind the life she hated. A chance to start anew.

Carol was hoping to get a glimpse of Odie as he left. Just one more look. To know that she had definitely saved him from the blaze, even if she had sent him away with that damned woman. But she doesn't.

A minute passes and there's a knock at her office door.

'Keith, I told you not to disturb me...'

He opens the door.

'Carol, the Goddamned building is on fire.'

THE PENTHOUSE

Mr Balliol had heard the bottle smash but he could not interrupt his ritual at that point. So, by the time he decided to leave everybody in that room and investigate, the flames were climbing the walls outside. He let them all burn. Including his right-hand woman.

He got into his lift and twisted the key to take him to the very top of Hotel Beresford.

And that is where he will stay.

Like a captain going down with his ship.

Balliol locates his bottle of 1945 Domaine de la Romanée-Conti Grand Cru. It feels like the right time to finally open some wine that cost him over half a million.

He takes a sip and moves it around his mouth.

Savoury.

He fills a glass, walks to his giant window and looks down on the streets. Guests are being ushered out from the lower levels. The fire brigade will get a shock when they open the doors on floor three. Balliol almost laughs.

The flames are lapping at the lobby and everyone is being led out of the fire doors by the stairwell. That side of the building is ruined. It'll take a long time to get to the top, or to damage the lower half enough that the higher levels become too heavy and the building collapses.

Yet, still, the cameras from the news vans seem to be pointing upward. But not at the penthouse, they can't see Balliol from down there. He moves to another window to see what they are looking at.

It's floor seven. Someone else seemingly willing to go down in flames.

ROOM 728

This is when Danielle Ortega is in perfect slumber.

The sirens are like whale song to her, so she sleeps through the first few minutes of the fire alarm as though a smooth reggae beat is playing in her dreams.

There is no panic. She's cool. Effortlessly cool. She moves like the fire that has taken over the basement of the hotel. Floating into the kitchen area, she grabs a bottle of mineral water from the fridge. It fizzes as it opens. Her cigarettes are on the coffee table. Her routine dictates that she straddles the windowsill and sparks up.

She's not leaving. This is her home. Her life. The way she is.

Thirty cameras point in her direction. There are crowds below. But there are always crowds. Every month. Danielle has noticed. A suicide. A murder. A hit and run. It's de rigueur for Hotel Beresford. And she is fine with that.

If there's a fire in the basement, so be it. She's up on the seventh floor. No way it's getting all the way up here with that many fire engines down there. Danielle is calm. She blows a plume of smoke out towards the city but the wind pushes it off downtown.

She sings out to her town.

'*Someday, when I'm awfully low. When the world is cold. I will feel a glow just thinking of you.*' She smokes. '*And the way you look ... tonight.*'

The cameras can see that she is singing but the microphones are not powerful enough to pick it up. She is broadcast live on local and national TV channels. This is the kind of thing that goes viral. This, stupid, innocent, laissez-faire attitude will make Danielle Ortega. The world will get to know her and hear her.

And they should.

She shouldn't have to sell herself to make it. She works hard and she has the talent.

'*Lovely. With your smile so warm, and your cheeks so soft. There is nothing for me but to love you. And the way you look ... tonight.*' She looks up, a cigarette hanging from her mouth in a way that would make James Dean look as cool as long division. And she waves. She sees Mr Balliol staring down at her with a glass of wine in one hand and a bottle in the other.

If they go down, they're going down together.

This is the image that Hotel Beresford will be remembered for. The silky-smooth jazz singer, made out of smoke, languishing in the open window of a burning building. Danielle Ortega was never interested in going viral, she was always content to work hard and work late. She wanted to sing to bigger crowds but it never meant that she gave any less to the smaller ones she was used to.

And now she is getting her fifteen seconds of fame.

Danielle Ortega doesn't care about that.

There's nothing that she doesn't have that she wants.

She's all soul.

RECEPTION

The blueprints do not even show that there is a basement level. It should never have got through building regulations. But rules were looser back when Hotel Beresford was built. Grease the right palm and things would go away, quickly.

The first and second floors will need to be entirely gutted. Reception is gone. Melted computer screens. Soot everywhere. The corridor that leads to the lift that takes people to the upper floors is wrecked. Fire danced across the walls and moved over the ceiling like liquid. It was a fight to get it out.

But the other side of the hotel remains largely intact. Neither Danielle nor Balliol were ever in danger.

Carol saved them.

She let the fire brigade know that they could get to the basement through her office. That nobody ever used it. Nobody went down there. She doesn't know how a fire could have possibly started. Most importantly, she tells the authorities that, as far as she knows, that's the only way to get to that level. The lift stops at the ground floor and the stairwell does, too.

She protects Mr Balliol.

She set fire to his building and then she kept him out of it.

Because she sold her soul for somebody else. And that means she did not rush into a decision. It was considered. She read that contract. There is nothing in there that says she cannot set fire to the building. But she does have to do her job. And she has to obey Mr Balliol. And she can't afford to break her contract otherwise she will never find what she is looking for.

This is her way out.

By sending the firefighters down with their hoses she not only made sure that the flames would not spread to the other side of the building, she let Mr Balliol know that it could only have been Carol that started the fire. And, in her mind, there's not a damn thing he can do about it without somehow implicating himself.

Because they found bodies down there. Destroyed by the excruciating heat of that altar room, they won't be easy to identify. She knows that Balliol has the power and influence to make it go away. It will come out that some kids were messing around with the occult. They'll find remnants of a Ouija board down there, or something. They'll say that it was a Satanic ritual that went wrong.

People will lap that up.

Religious extremism is trending.

And, somehow, the Devil manages to hide by blaming Himself.

THE PENTHOUSE

Half a million on a bottle of wine. The mind is a powerful place. Your brain tells you that there are only six hundred bottles of this wine in the world. It's rare and expensive for a reason. So, you taste it and convince yourself that it is nectar from the gods.

Balliol looks down on the street. The crowds have dispersed. The news trucks are driving away. The fire engines are ready to head back to their stations. The woman on seventh still looks out of her window, one bare leg hanging in the cold air.

Then he hears the lift.

Not the Hotel Beresford lift. The other one. The secret one that goes down to the basement. Many areas have been cordoned off for further examination. The photographers have already been down there.

Carol.

She has walked through the blackened ruin, a damp towel over her mouth so as not to breathe in the noxious air. She has called the secret lift and is heading up to the top floor. A place she has never been.

When she reaches the top, Carol steps out into what looks like a closed room. There are no doorways. She panics for a moment. She's made a mistake. Then one of the walls slides to the side and Mr Balliol is standing there with two empty glasses and a bottle of wine.

'Seems we have a long-overdue discussion.' He hands her a glass and fills it before pouring one for himself.

'You took Jake's soul.'

'Straight in. Okay. That is not how it works, Carol. It is a deal. A bargain made by both sides.'

'Bullshit. How difficult is it to offer everything to a person who is desperate enough to summon you?'

'Nobody summons *me*. I decide where I go and who I deal with.'

They both drink.

'My relationship wasn't real.' She's upset and angry. Balliol can tell.

'On the contrary. The way you felt about each other was absolutely genuine. He may have given away a part of himself in exchange for finding you, but you were still the one that he was meant to find. It could only have been you, Carol.'

This softens her a little. She hadn't thought of it in those terms. Jake and Carol *were* soulmates but they may have never found one another without the extreme intervention of Mr Balliol.

'You wouldn't let me save him.'

'I couldn't.'

'You can do anything you want.'

'I cannot exchange a soul for somebody who has already sold theirs. I could not tell you this at the time. It's in the small print.'

'It's a piece of paper.'

'It's a contract. It's important. We take it very seriously. Look at the world out there, Carol. It's a mess. All we have that means anything is our word.'

'You're a monster.'

'You of all people should know that I am not. I have taken care of you here, have I not?' He doesn't let her answer. 'You were desperate to save Jake that day. I could have easily tricked you and you would be where he is right now. Maybe you think that's what you want but it is not. I didn't want you there. You couldn't ask for something for yourself, it had to be for somebody else. That's the only way to get here.'

Tears fall from Carol's eyes but her expression does not change.

'And you repay me by trying to burn down my building. What am I supposed to do with you now, Carol?'

'Let me go.'

It's an audacious request. Carol is a formidable woman but Mr

Balliol could overpower her and throw her from the roof if he wanted. He could have already drugged her glass of wine. But he hasn't. And he won't. And he wouldn't.

Balliol has grown a little weary of his role. It seems that everybody wants love, now. There's just not enough of it left in the world. The 'Be Kind' slogans are not working. People are less motivated to do good. Evil is having a tough time keeping up.

But Mr Balliol is not evil. He is a businessman. A negotiator. A trader. He does not accept every request he receives. He begs people to be more specific with their requests. Fewer and fewer people listen. Even fewer read the contract.

'I need you for another six weeks. Eight weeks, maybe.' He doesn't say yes or no.

'The hotel can't go on in this way.'

'I have plans in place. Just stay for a few months. You shouldn't have started that fire, Carol. We did need a reshuffle, to be fair. This place has been many things over time, and it is time for another change.'

'Fine. Six weeks, then I'm gone.' Carol hands the glass back to Mr Balliol and turns to the main lift in order to see herself out.

Balliol does not confirm a thing.

Contracts are important to him and so is his word, which is why he remains silent.

No deal was made.

CROSSROADS

The Devil rarely comes. He's a little like God in that way. They're the same.

All of these desperate individuals who make their way to a fork in the road and call out his name because their God has stopped listening, what they don't realise is that the Devil isn't either.

He's too busy.

Enjoying himself.

He doesn't care who wants to be a pop star or beauty influencer or impressionist painter. He is just happy to receive the souls. He has grown weary of selfishness. But, without it, Hell would get lonely.

That doesn't mean he wants to hear about your cancer diagnosis or your financial struggles or how you became homeless after your divorce. He's very much like God in that way, too. Or any CEO of a profitable company. They have people for that. Buffers. Underlings.

Minions to take on the more menial tasks.

Just as it is in big business, where a worker may know who owns the company but has no comprehension of anyone above their line manager, the structure of the largest soul-trading industry is vast.

The commander-in-chief maintains his mystique by appearing under many guises and different names. Ibis, Azalea, Mammon, Apollyn, Old Nick, Old Scratch, Old Harry. None of these would ever appear at the crossroads, though. One is more likely to encounter a Belphegor or Lamia or Ashtoreth, if you believe in that kind of thing. And, if you are lucky enough, if you are passionate enough, you may encounter something in between. Somebody who once made a deal of their own, to experience a hellish life on Earth, only to have great power in the afterlife.

Wealth. Influence. Beauty.

Who goes by one name only.

Balliol.

And he is great at his job. He adapts to the changing times. He understands human psychology and societal variations. And this has given him a degree of autonomy over his role. He can decide which souls to take and he can decide where they go.

Ask for something for yourself and you end up in Hell.

Ask for somebody else, end up at The Beresford.

It's an eternity, still, but you can make it your own.

It is a purgatory with no chance of salvation.

But Balliol has been left to his own devices. He is in control of his corner of the universe. He has never gone back on a contract. He has never sent anyone to a better place. He, sometimes, does not accept a soul. But he is rarely checked on. His audits are infrequent. He needs to change the practice at Hotel Beresford and that could mean changing the staff.

Management is restructuring.

There are going to be some redundancies.

It's not personal.

Just business.

And Balliol is the boss.

Maybe the Devil didn't convince the world that He doesn't exist.

Maybe He just doesn't exist.

Stories require conflict. A protagonist and an antagonist. God had to create the Devil to perpetuate the struggle of faith. Good versus evil. Right versus wrong. And the Devil had to create his alter-egos in order to hide in plain sight.

It wasn't the Devil at the crossroads, it was one of his minions.

Ibis tuned the guitar, played a song, then handed it back.

Balliol runs Hotel Beresford.

The hierarchy is not important. Whether the Devil is real or hiding himself behind a thousand faces, whether he works against God or with Him, it doesn't matter. It only matters what people believe.

If we think there is a God, there is a God.

And, if that is true, there is always a home for His counterpart.

It may not be presented in the same way, but they both want your souls.

THE BERESFORD

It's finished.

Both ends of the old corridor have been bricked up. The Old Hotel Beresford is now a separate building from the new Beresford apartments. The red lights of the sign have been removed. This building still looms large above any of the structures around it and it is one of the first things you see when approaching on the train either to or from the city, but it doesn't announce itself like it once did.

But it is still there and the rooms are occupied and Keith continues to keep things ticking over but more like a site supervisor or management company. There's no reception desk. The third floor is now defunct. Balliol will have to come up with another way to fill the conference space and another way to keep that steady rate of sold souls each month.

Another experiment.

The former reception area and food court now house six large apartments. One will be the dwelling of the new owner and person who will run this side of the operation. And Mr Balliol wants to take Carol over there so that they can meet.

A handover.

She is waiting for him at the bottom of the lift.

'It feels odd that we can't just walk there through the corridor,' she tells him.

'Nope. We'll have to go around the outside.'

The front porch is unassuming. There's a driveway and path through the park beyond that leads guests in from the train station. But Carol looks in the front window and sees the large staircase that leads up to the old second floor. And there's a small library to the left as you walk in. The old staff car park out the back is now a garden with some spaces behind for housing development.

Balliol waits and Carol follows his lead.

A few moments later, an elderly lady emerges from the corner apartment. She seems sweet. Her feet shuffling as she walks.

'Ah. There you are. Carol, I would like you to meet Mrs May. Mrs May, this is Carol.'

'Pleased to meet you, young lady.'

Carol can't help but laugh. She has been introduced to one of the few people she has met who could legitimately refer to her in that way.

'The pleasure is all mine, Mrs May. This is a wonderful place you have here.'

'It sure is,' Mr Balliol chimes in, 'and I don't foresee any issues with it filling up and staying that way.'

Mrs May thinks about asking the younger woman if she would like a tour of the place but she can see by the look in her eyes that she doesn't want to be here any longer than she has to be.

'Carol took care of the Hotel Beresford for many years before the unfortunate fire,' Balliol explains. Mrs May nods along as though she is interested. 'So I guess that makes you the new Carol.' He fake-smiles and they fake-smile along with him.

'So what landed you here, Mrs May?'

'I'm sorry, dear?'

'What deal did you have to make to land this gig?'

Balliol is not amused.

'Carol, you know we don't discuss—'

'My husband. I kept him alive for longer than he was supposed to. You?'

'Mine is a long and complicated story.'

'Yes, and I'm afraid we don't have time for that now.' Balliol shoots Carol a look. She doesn't care anymore, she's getting out today. 'Now, Mrs May, you have everything you need and you understand everything we have discussed.'

She nods.

Carol can't wait to get out of there.

Balliol takes his ceremonial dagger from the back of his trousers, reaches around the top of her head, and slices through her throat. He lets go and she drops to the floor. Mrs May is wide-eyed.

'And so it begins. You have sixty seconds exactly before the first resident of The Beresford rings that doorbell. You'd better get cleaning up.'

He removes his tie, wipes the blade on it and drops the tie to the floor before walking out as casually as he entered.

Mrs May is old but she is not frail. She drops to her knees and knots each end of the tie around one of Carol's wrists, then she grabs it in the middle and drags her over to apartment number one. She picks up a tea towel from the kitchen counter and heads back to the communal area to wipe up the blood.

She has twenty seconds.

One towel is not enough, she runs back into her apartment and wets another one before finishing the job. She throws it through the doorway just as the bell rings. She assumes her character of the doddering old lady and shuffles to the door to begin a new Beresford chapter.

When Balliol returns to the penthouse, Carol is sitting there waiting for him.

'What the Hell was that?'

'Theatre?'

'You fucking slit my throat.'

'It was for effect.' He pulls a piece of paper from the inside pocket of his jacket. And sets it on fire.

'What are you doing?'

'It's your contract.'

'What?'

'The contract you signed when Jake wouldn't wake up.'

Carol doesn't know what to do.

'You remember what you wanted?'

Carol nods. She wanted to trade her soul to have Jake wake up and live. But Balliol would not allow it. He couldn't bend the rules. He asked her again what she wanted.

Be more specific.

She wanted to spend the rest of her days with her soulmate.

It's not specific enough. A lazier minion might have taken her up on that and let her live her days until Jake's plug was finally pulled and she would drop dead, too.

What a waste of a soul.

'What is a soulmate?' he asked her.

'The person I am supposed to love more than anyone in the world.'

'Wonderful. So you would like to be able to share the rest of your days with the person you love the most in the world?'

'Yes.'

'You would like that person to always know that they were loved by you more than anyone ever could.'

'Yes. Yes, of course. That's what I said.'

It wasn't. These were the words that Balliol put in her mouth. It had to be for the benefit of somebody else. And then he made her sign. And then he disappeared. And then Jake died. And then she came to Hotel Beresford and felt begrudged that the deal was so one-sided. And she tried to find Jake. And she did. And she burned down part of the building. And now Mr Balliol is burning her contract and setting her free.

She can leave.

'I could get in a lot of trouble for this.'

'Who is going to tell you off, sir?'

'There's always somebody higher, Carol.'

'You're not ... Him?'

Balliol ignores the question.

'The contract is null and void. You have served well. You won't have forever, now, Carol. Your time is limited. But you will have enough to ensure that the person you love the most in the world knows that you do. You'll meet them in about...' he places one of his hands on her stomach '...thirty-three weeks.'

She cries. Carol has been beating herself up about a stupid, lonely night with Omar a couple of weeks back. Part of her also wants to hug Mr Balliol.

'No. You have to go. The world thinks you are gone. So disappear. Don't come back here again.' He turns his back on her.

For a moment, Carol doesn't know what to do, what to say. She doesn't want to push it. She has somebody to protect now.

She walks towards the lift, catching a glimpse of Balliol's wall of screens on the way. She knows that things are not going to be that different here. There will be freak occurrences and there will be death and mystery. And there will be Mr Balliol, stuck in a Hell that he chose and configured. An endless purgatorial loop.

Carol has witnessed the worst that humanity has to offer, and for that she is grateful. Finally, she realises just how lucky she has been. God, she's lucky.

CROSSROADS

Anyone who thinks Hell is an awful place to be should try living here.

Balliol looks down from the top of his empire, waiting for Carol to emerge and cross the street. He remembers how easy it was to snuff out Ollie. A simple swipe of his finger and that car went through the security guard without even slowing down.

And that was only to cause a distraction.

This is to make a point.

He can't just let Carol go, even if a part of him wants to. Nobody knows about the souls that Balliol has saved. There's no story there. Nobody spreads the word about how they tried to sell their soul to the Devil and He said 'no'. But he can't have anybody think that he showed some weakness. If the word gets out that he let things slide with Carol, he's finished.

She has no ambitions to change the world, no talent that should be shared. She is good at what she does but good can be replaced.

Mrs May thinks Carol is dead but will wonder why her body is not there when she returns to her apartment. Balliol does not yet know that Mrs May will become the longest-running custodian of any Beresford incarnation. The Queen Elizabeth of purgatory.

She will never mention Carol again.

Balliol drinks his wine and waits.

He has everything he wants and will ever need. But even the women, the drinking and the wealth can start to feel like a routine, after a while. He breaks it up with some voyeurism or a sacrifice each month but it doesn't lead anywhere. There is no end.

Carol steps out of the building through the new entrance, separate to The Beresford. She has a bag over her shoulder. Balliol spots her bleached blonde hair from ten storeys above. A cab waits on the other side of the road and the two goons that ploughed Ollie down wait a little further away.

Balliol holds his finger up and waits until Carol gets halfway across the street. All it will take is a swipe to the left and she is finished.

He waits.

Carol looks both ways. She doesn't spot the car to her right.

She crosses.

When she gets part of the way across, Balliol, without hesitation, swipes his finger to the left.

Nothing happens.

The hoodlums don't even start their engines. Balliol runs this town, including their boss. They wouldn't go against his orders.

He swipes again.

Nothing.

Then a cough. A clearing of the throat.

Balliol turns around and, sitting in a chair behind him, with his hand held up as though stopping traffic, is Jonesy.

Old Harry.

'What are you doing here?' Balliol asks.

'Are you losing control?'

'No.'

'First she burns down the building, then you let her go.'

'I was fixing that. You stopped me.'

'You don't want to kill her off, you should have made her stay.'

'It wasn't going to work. She knew too much. She became a liability.'

Part of what Balliol is saying is true but he was also showing Carol some mercy. Sure, he was going to end her, but there was only one place she would go from there and that was straight back to Jake. It's the only way she would ever find him.

Balliol turns back to the window and sees Carol get in to the cab.

'So, I'm just supposed to let her go?'

'She doesn't have long left.'

Carol has a couple of decades in her but time seems to work differently at The Beresford. A month here is like a year out there. Things are concentrated. More happens. Twenty years is a quarter of somebody's lifetime but it's like a minute to Balliol and Jonesy.

'I don't like leaving any loose ends.'

'There's nothing to worry about.'

'Of course. It's all part of your big plan, right? Do we have any idea how that is going to play out?' Balliol is frustrated but says this through a half-smile.

'They can't handle the free will, it seems. But it's the greed and apathy that will kill them off. I'm sure you can tell. There's an imbalance. They want more and more and more.'

Balliol raises his glass.

The worst yet.

'What a team, eh?' He drinks his wine.

Good and evil. Heaven and Hell. God and the Devil. Opposing forces. But neither can exist without the other.

They have to work together.

It's the only way.

Jonesy shrugs.

'Who are we to decide?'

ACKNOWLEDGEMENTS

It's been another strange year. It seems that I come up with new ideas for The Beresford when times are a little weird. Of course, I have to thank my publisher, Karen Sullivan, for allowing me to flex my quirkiness. It's amazing to have such support and creative freedom to express the things that piss me off about the world. I've written a couple of challenging books recently but the Beresford books are pure fun for me. (For readers, too, I hope.)

After eight books together, West and I have developed a shorthand when it comes to the editing process. I'm not saying that I enjoy it, but it's certainly as painless as it can possibly be.

Thanks to the Orenda crew: Cole for creating the visuals that get people to notice my book, and for wearing the *Psychopaths Anonymous* T-shirt with such panache. I'm expecting a killer trailer for this one. Anne, for rounding up those unruly bloggers so that my book doesn't get lost among all the ghostwritten celebrity pulp. And Danielle, who is bursting with awesome new ideas. Loving your work.

To my new agent, David Headley – you didn't really have anything to do with this book but you've got me feeling buoyant about the future, which means you've already done more for me than most.

Thanks to my writer friends: Tom Wood, who gets excited by all my ideas and then frustrated when I turn them into something 'wanky'. To Sarah Pinborough, who tells me that my time is coming, and I'm trying to believe her, because she's always right about this kind of thing. To Steve Watson, who said that he should be in my acknowledgements because he's super supportive but basically bullied me into doing this. (Please also check out our podcast: *Let's Get Lit*.)

I'm happy for people to buy my books wherever they can find them but there are two independent bookshops that push my stuff brilliantly: Fourbears Books and Bert's Books. Please check them out and support them as much as they support me.

Phoebs and Co, you are the light and positivity in a dark world. The joy that a cynical bastard like me needs. Thanks for doing as you're told, too, it makes life easier. Siena, you're old enough to read my books now. Please don't. Zoe, who is also having a strange year, there's a strength in art. Dance. And Will, for whom today was better than yesterday and tomorrow will be better than today, don't change. Keep reminding people of this.

Lastly, Kel, who picked up this book and said, 'Has this one got God stuff in it?' I need you, woman. You've carried the weight for long enough. That thing we've been working towards, it's coming. I've got you. In this world where everyone else seems like such a fucking hero, you haven't stopped to notice who mine is.

I wrote the last Beresford book while locked down. The solidarity and sense of community that came from that time dissipated far too quickly. Things don't seem any better now. I don't know if the answer is activism or apathy, compassion or self-interest, escapism or critique, but we need to ask ourselves 'What do you want?'. Because we're not in Hell yet, but it does feel hotter.